COURTING FAVOUR

The countess, a fine-looking woman in her late fifties, was normally a cheerful character and good company, her young people very fond of her. It was seldom indeed that she seemed as grim as this day.

"George, you have two earldoms to oversee and rule, Dunbar covering much of Lothian, and the March, or Merse, which includes most of the eastern Borderland, down to Berwick and the Tweed, more than sufficient for any man. You will do it well, I judge." She turned from him to his brother. "And you, John – you too enter into responsibilities. For I choose, this day of decision, to change your life as the day has changed mine and George's. I am resigning the earldom of Moray. You are of full age. From this hour onwards you are John, Earl of Moray."

The younger brother, aged twenty-two, drew breath, gulped, and wagged his fair head. "Me! Why?" he got out. "Earl – *me*!"

'Fishing and hawking, porridge and game, the smell of peat and bitter cold Highland nights: a page from any of Nigel Tranter's Scottish historical novels evokes the lie of the land better than a library of history books . . . Tranter's research is impeccable and his historical notes at the end a fine complement to this extremely readable book.' *The Times*

Courting Favour

Nigel Tranter

CORONET BOOKS

Hodder & Stoughton

Copyright © 2000 by Nigel Tranter

This right of Nigel Tranter to be identified as the Author of
the Work has been asserted by him in accordance with the
Copyright, Designs and Patents Act 1988.

First published in Great Britain in 2000
by Hodder and Stoughton
First published in paperback in 2000
by Hodder and Stoughton
A division of Hodder Headline

A Coronet Paperback

10 9 8 7 6 5 4 3 2 1

British Library Cataloguing in Publication Data.
A catalogue record for this title is available
from the British Library.

ISBN 0 340 73926 6

Printed and bound in Great Britain by
Clays Ltd, St Ives plc

Hodder and Stoughton
A division of Hodder Headline
338 Euston Road
London NW1 3BH

Principal Characters in order of appearance

John Cospatrick: Second son of the 9th Earl of Dunbar and March.

George, Master of Dunbar: Elder brother of above.

Agnes, Countess of Dunbar and March: Mother of above, known as Black Agnes.

David the Second: King of Scots.

Queen Margaret Drummond: Wife of above.

Robert Stewart, Earl of Strathearn: High Steward of Scotland.

Sir William Keith: Great Marischal of Scotland.

Alexander Bur, or Barr: Bishop of Moray.

Sir William Comyn of Duffus: Important Moray vassal.

Duncan Murray: Keeper of Darnaway Castle.

William, Earl of Ross: Great northern noble.

Brodie of that Ilk: Thane, and Moray vassal.

The Mackintosh: Chief of Clan Chattan.

John MacDonald, Lord of the Isles: Magnate of the Highland West.

John, Earl of Carrick: Eldest son of the Steward (later named Robert).

Lady Marjory Stewart: Daughter of the High Steward.

Donald Macdonald: Eldest son of John of the Isles.

Lady Agnes Dunbar: Sister of the Earls of Dunbar and of Moray.

Sir James Douglas of Dalkeith: Important magnate.

William, Earl of Douglas: Great noble, Warden of the East March.

Thomas, Master of Moray: Young son of John and Marjory.

Annabella Drummond: Wife of John/Robert of Carrick, later queen.

John of Gaunt, Duke of Lancaster: Brother of the King of England.

Henry Plantagenet, Earl of Hereford: Son of above.

Christian Seton: Wife of the Earl of Dunbar and March.

John de Vienne: High Admiral of France.

James, Earl of Douglas: Successor to William.

Hotspur Percy, Earl of Northumberland: Great English noble.

Sir David Lindsay: Renowned warrior.

Archibald the Grim: Douglas Lord of Galloway.

Thomas Stewart, Archdeacon of St Andrews: Illegitimate son of Robert the Second

Howard, Earl of Nottingham: Earl Marshal of England.

FitzAlan, Archbishop of Canterbury: Primate of the English Church.

Alexander Stewart, Earl of Buchan: Brother of Robert the Third (the Wolf of Badenoch).

Mariota de Athyn: Mistress of above.

Robert, Earl of Sutherland: Northern noble.

George, Earl of Angus: Chief of the Red Douglases.

Part One

1

The two young men drew up their baited lines for the last time that day, George having felt a tug, John less fortunate. As they hoisted them inboard, the former splattered the other with droplets from a flapping, twisting flounder, hooked, and was made a face at by his brother as he detached the flatfish to add to his bag. Seven now, he counted, whereas John had nine, a fair morning's sport. It was time that they went back for their midday meal. Getting out an oar each, side by side on the bench, they pulled their boat landwards.

They had not far to row, for this bank of sandy shallows, favoured by the flounders, was just off the headland out from which soared the series of rock-stacks on which Dunbar Castle was based, five or six miles from where the Scotwater, or Firth of Forth estuary, opened into the Norse Sea. Quite soon, therefore, they were pulling under one of the short, lofty bridges that linked those pillars of rock, on top of which three of the towers of this extraordinary fortalice rose, these linked by the bridges. They went beneath the two easternmost stacks, George waving up to its watchman, to enter Dunbar harbour. *They* did not have to halt and await the lowered baskets, as the township's fishermen would have had to do in order to pay a tithe of their catch, this part of the earl's tolls for the use of his enclosed harbour, sheltered haven from the Norse Sea's storms.

They rowed in, to tie up their boat at the tail-end of the quayside, two fishermen, mending their nets there, hastening to aid them ashore with their fish-bags, and being waved aside, although in friendly fashion. Carrying their

3

catch of flatfish, they went over to climb the steep, zigzag track up to the postern gate of the landward main tower of the castle.

This double door, of iron bars and heavy wood, was opened for them before ever they reached it by the watchman who had answered their wave from the second tower bridge. He reached to take the bags.

"A fair catch, my lords," he greeted them. "The countess would see you forthwith. She has . . . tidings for you."

The brothers nodded in acknowledgment, and left him with the flounders, to climb stairs to the living quarters of this principal tower of the keep.

At first-floor level, in a withdrawing-room off the main hall, they found their mother and youngest sister, Elizabeth, awaiting them.

"I have news for you," the countess said, level-voiced. "Dire news – in one fashion. It will scarcely break your hearts, but it will . . . affect you notably. Your father is dead."

The brothers drew breaths, and looked from their mother to their sister and at each other. Neither spoke.

"Word has come from Northumberland, from Tyneside. He died there three days ago. In England – as was perhaps apt! Suddenly. The strange end of a strange life." The new widow did not sound desolated. "He was, of course, of eighty-four years. May a kind God rest his soul!"

George found voice. "Dead! Gone! And not in the Earlstoun of Ercildoune, but in England! With the Hepburns, no doubt? His . . . friends!"

"Yes. Where, I judge, he really belonged. Gone to his Maker. Leaving me . . . what?"

They did not try to answer that.

The countess shrugged. "So you, George, are now tenth Earl of Dunbar and March, with much to bear on your shoulders. I think that you will do it . . . better. And you, John – I have some word for you also. But – later."

Their sister spoke up. "Our father is to be brought home. For burial," she said.

4

"Yes. I want you to go, both of you, down to Northumberland, to fetch the body back. Here, not to Melrose. To be laid to rest beside his forebears. No pleasant task, for you. But necessary."

John nodded. "The Hepburns will not have buried him by then?" he asked.

"I think not. But if they have, you will have the body dug up and brought home. It is the least I can do for him, the less than loving wife whom he saw little of, these past years."

The situation and relationship between Patrick, ninth Earl of Dunbar and March, and Black Agnes, daughter of the late and esteemed Regent Moray, an arranged marriage never a love-match, had been a strange one. But then, the Cospatrick was a strange man, of wavering affections and loyalties, and she a spirited woman, a very disparate pair, despite the lofty royal blood which they had both inherited, although from different sources. Cospatrick, as he was known, like his ancestors not deigning to use a surname, was descended from the ancient Celtic royal line, the first of them the eldest son of Malcolm the Third, Canmore; although wrongfully, the king's sons by his second marriage, to Margaret the Saint, so called, succeeded to the throne, denying the right to their half-brothers – this a grievance with the said line ever since. And Agnes's father was the nephew of Robert the Bruce, who had eventually gained the crown, after Margaret's line died out, and won Scotland's freedom, an old story. But before being created Earls of Dunbar and March, the Cospatricks had been Earls of Northumbria, then part of Scotland, and had kept strong links therewith down the centuries.

The countess, a fine-looking woman in her late fifties, with a few strands of silver beginning to streak her plentiful dark hair – for which she was known as Black Agnes – was normally a cheerful character and good company, her young people very fond of her. It was seldom indeed that she seemed as grim as this day.

"As you know well," she went on, "I always saw our

duty, in holding high position in this realm, differently from your father, our support of the king and crown foremost, holders of earldoms in especial, since the earls are the direct successors of the *ri*, or lesser kings, of ancient Alba, who elected and supported the Ard Righ or High King. Patrick saw it otherwise, as lesser kings yes, but as such entitled to criticise and controvert, if they deemed the monarch in error, even to take up arms against him. He never forgot that the Cospatricks should have held the throne, as senior by birth to the Margaretsons. This affected his loyalties, so that he would support the English against his own king, on occasion. Especially as he still considered himself to be Earl of Northumbria, none other ever having been appointed to that position. I remind you of this, at this time, when you are entering into your greater responsibilities with his death. It is my simple duty.''

Her young people knew it all, of course, but heard her out heedfully, for they greatly admired their mother.

"George, you have two earldoms to oversee and rule, Dunbar covering much of Lothian, and the March, or Merse, which includes most of the eastern Borderland, down to Berwick and the Tweed, more than sufficient for any man. You will do it well, I judge.'' She turned from him to his brother. "And you, John — you too enter into responsibilities. For I choose, this day of decision, to change your life as the day has changed mine and George's. I am resigning the earldom of Moray. You are of full age. From this hour onwards you are John, Earl of Moray.''

The younger brother, aged twenty-two, drew breath, gulped, and wagged his fair head. "Me! Why?'' he got out. "Earl — *me*!''

"No less. As you know, I inherited the earldom of Moray when my brother, your Uncle John, third Randolph earl, fell in battle, unwed. King Robert Bruce made my father Earl of Moray, to be regent for his young son David. My two brothers succeeded, each without children. So I am Countess of Moray in my own right. Or was.

6

Because I now pass it on to you, Johnnie. This is the occasion so to do, I think. I am not so young as I was. And there are great lands and properties, with their folk, in the north, responsibilities which I fear I have neglected, failed to overrule, leaving it to stewards and bailiffs, with a sufficiency here to see to. I have been considering this for some time. This day is the time to change that. It means that we shall see less of you here – but so be it."

John could scarcely take it in. Himself suddenly an earl. As was his brother. And one with great lands and duties, far in the north, how much and how many he knew not. A younger son, he had never looked for this.

"It falls to be confirmed by King David, to be sure," Black Agnes went on. "But I have no doubts that he will agree. You are, after all, kin to him. In cousinship, since his father, the Bruce, was my father's uncle." She waved a hand. "But enough of this, meantime. First, you both have to go to Northumberland and bring back your father. And at once. Hoping that they have not already buried him."

George punched his brother on the shoulder. "My lord Earl!" he exclaimed. "And myself also! We have caught more than flounders this day, Johnnie!"

They did not delay more than a few hours on their unlooked-for and melancholy errand. Both were good horsemen, and they knew the route to Tyneside. Forty miles down through the Merse, to Coldstream on Tweed and the border, where they could pass the night in a monastery. Then on, skirting the Cheviot Hills to the east, by Wooler and Glanton and Rothbury to the Roman Wall and Corbridge, another sixty miles. They should be at the Hepburn seat of Newtonhall by late afternoon next day, all being well. Coming back with the body might be slower, admittedly, as well as not exactly doleful but embarrassing, uneasy. They would require pack-horses for that. Their mother suggested that it might be as well to take one of the Dunbar earldom's vassals with them, Patrick Hepburn of Hailes. The seventh Earl Cospatrick's daughter had married Adam Hepburn, from Northumberland, and the pair had been given Hailes Castle, on another Tyne, that of their own Lothian, only eight miles from Dunbar. Their grandson might well be helpful in dealing with his kinsfolk in England.

So, with two of their men, and the pack-horses, they rode off, due westwards first, for Hailes, and there had no difficulty in picking up Patrick, or Pate, Hepburn, short notice as it was, and them friendly, and then striking southwards through their sheep-strewn Lammermuir Hills, by Garvald to Cranshaws and then Duns and so into the Merse, the East March of the Borderland, all of which they knew like the backs of their hands. This March earldom, although secondary to Dunbar in date and status, was actually larger, encompassing a great area from the wild Berwickshire coast down to Tweed, and eastwards to Lauderdale, to flank the royal lands of Roxburgh and Kelso, some six hundred square miles of rolling grasslands and modest hills, fine cattle country and with fertile stretches, a worthy heritage of which George was now master.

Because of the pack-horses, they rode less fast than they could have done on their finer mounts, but even so they reached the Tweed at Coldstream by dusk, and rested themselves and their steeds for the night at a monastery and hospice for travellers, a branch from the major Priory of Coldinghame nearer to the coast, being well received by the monks.

Then on, half eastwards, next morning, across into England, to skirt the high Cheviots by the Till, Flodden Edge, Wooler and south by Rothbury, largely moorland country this, eventually to reach the Northumbrian Tyne by evening, a long day's riding.

The main seat of the Hepburns – the name was but a corruption of Haybarn – was at Newtonhall, east of Corbridge. Their arrival there was welcomed by Sir Thomas Hepburn, thankful to be quit of the corpse of the late earl, which they had not buried, nor exactly embalmed, but treated with resin and oil which had a preserving effect, and laid temporarily to rest in the local church, wrapped in grave-clothes. Sir Thomas and his sons knew young Hailes, and this was a help for the Cospatrick brothers.

That evening, well entertained, George was asked whether, as the new Earl of Dunbar and March, he also looked upon himself as the rightful Earl of Northumbria, as had done his sire, even though not officially adopting the style, which would have made him a peer of England now. George disclaimed any such ambition, declaring that he would have enough to see to with the two earldoms at home. John did not emphasise *his* new status as Earl of Moray.

In the morning there was the awkward and gruesome business of getting the dead body, wrapped in further coverings for the journey, out of the church and slung in a kind of hammock between the two pack-horses, all difficult as well as grisly.

The Scots party did not linger thereafter with their burden, and thanking their hosts, set off northwards. And now, with the swinging corpse to heed, and the two led horses less than at ease with their slung load, they had to proceed much more slowly than before, making not very carefree riding. In fact they got only as far as Wooler that day, where there was a hospice, with a chapel where they could deposit the body. The brothers could not feel that this was any suitable way to celebrate their elevation to earldoms, any more than to pay such respects as they could to their dead father. And it was a dull and gloomy experience to lay on Hepburn of Hailes; so in the morning, recognising that they would not reach Dunbar that day, they sent their vassal laird off on his own, for his home.

They only reached Duns for the second night, but here they were on their own March territory, and felt somehow less ill at ease. They ought to be home by noon next day.

They were, and found that, although they had been gone for only five days, however much more it seemed to them, meantime their effective mother had sent a messenger to

King David, at Edinburgh, acquainting him with the situation, and the accession of her sons to the earldoms; and she had received back the monarch's agreement thereto, with indeed his satisfaction that he now would have two more loyal supporters. They must visit him, to make their vows of fealty, before long, and receive his congratulations.

That afternoon Black Agnes and her sons conducted the dead husband and father to the collegiate church of Dunbar, which had actually been founded by the said earl in 1342, for a dean, a vice-dean and eight prebendaries, these to serve eight Lothian chapels; in those days, twenty-seven years back, he had been more sure of his directions and loyalties.

The service in the handsome cruciform church, conducted by the dean, all his subordinates present, also the prior of the Trinitarian monastery of Red Friars at Houston nearby, was solemn and dignified, however unworthy some there considered the central figure, the emphasis being on his founding of this place of worship, and his long line of distinguished ancestors. After consigning the late earl to God's good and kind keeping, and the benediction said, the body was duly lowered into the crypt below, actually its first occupant, where a lead coffin would be made to enclose it.

Relieved when it was all over, the family returned to the castle, that family including, for the occasion, the two daughters, Margaret wed to William, first Earl of Douglas, and Agnes, betrothed to another Douglas, Lord of Dalkeith, summoned by their mother – but not accompanied by their husbands, neither of whom approved of their father-in-law.

So ended a chapter in a long and dramatic story, a chapter most were glad to see finished.

2

The brothers were not long in answering the royal command to come and make their gestures of fealty, as new earls, to the monarch; and on this very special occasion their mother accompanied them, suitably, as a kinswoman of King David the Second.

They made for Edinburgh, thirty miles to the west. Bruce, when he had gained the throne, had seldom used Roxburgh Castle, where Tweed joined Teviot, as a base, unlike the Margaretsons and their descendants, preferring Stirling and Dumbarton Castles, more central for his kingdom, and Edinburgh on occasion. His son used the last more, but when there tended to occupy apartments in the great Abbey of the Holy Rood, as much more comfortable than the rather bleak quarters up in the rock-top fortress. Also the abbey was much more convenient for hunting in the royal parkland which surrounded the towering bulk of Arthur's Seat, and for hawking at Duddingston Loch on the far side of that lion-shaped hill.

In fact, the king was away hawking, a favourite sport, when the callers arrived at the abbey. So the brothers, who were fond of falconry themselves decided to ride the mile or two round to Duddingston, to join their liege-lord, although Black Agnes remained at the abbey with Queen Margaret Drummond, the monarch's second wife.

There were two other lochs in the royal territory surrounding the great hill, Dunsappie on the higher ground, and St Margaret's on the levels to the east, this last little more than a pond. But Duddingston was quite large, almost half a mile long and a quarter in width, its southern and eastern flanks dense with tall reeds, which made it a favoured haunt of wildfowl, and therefore providing excellent sport for hawking.

The brothers, circling the hill westwards, had no difficulty in locating the royal party, hovering and stooping hawks in the air guiding them to the south-eastern end of the loch, where they found the sportsmen and their hawkers and tranters sitting their horses on a slight mound, where they could obtain some prospect over the reed-beds and water.

They had met King David on two or three occasions in the past, but never thus, and they approached the group in carefully respectful fashion, halting their mounts a little way from the mound, to wait, not to seem to interrupt the sport. But David recognised them, even at that distance, and waved them forward.

"So – my two new earls come a-visiting!" he called. "I greet you, my friends. Come!"

David Bruce was a man in his forties, looking older than his years, possibly on account of the long spell he had spent as a captive in England after his defeat at the ill-judged Battle of Neville's Cross, and his troubles when Edward Balliol had assumed the throne, that son of John Balliol, the weakling whom Edward Plantagenet had chosen to hoist to the Scots throne when the last of the Margaretsons' line died without heir. David was a less strong character than had been his famous father, but amiable and making quite a worthy monarch, although no warrior.

The brothers rode up to him, doffing bonnets and bowing from the saddle.

"We come, Sire, to make our vows before Your Grace," George said. "We left our mother, the countess, at the abbey. We hope that you are having good sport?"

"Fair, fair," they were told. "I have known better. My falcon seems to prefer herons to ducks and geese!" He waved a leather-padded arm, this to protect it from the talons of the hawks when they were being carried, gesturing towards a heavily built man of approximately the same age as himself. "You know my nephew Robert, the High

Steward, Earl of Strathearn? These, Robert, are two freshly arisen earls to support the crown, the Earl of Dunbar and March, and John, to whom your own kins-woman, Black Agnes, has resigned her earldom of Moray.''

The High Steward nodded. "Let us hope that they help sustain you better than did their father!" he jerked. This was the son of Bruce's daughter, Marjorie, offspring of his first marriage to Isabel of Mar, arranged when he was but a youth and before he fell in love with and wed Elizabeth de Burgh, David's mother. So, in fact, these two were indeed close kin, uncle and nephew, the younger, David, the uncle. And, with the king having as yet no offspring, the nephew was heir-presumptive to the throne.

"The late Earl Cospatrick's judgment, I think, was . . . impaired! He had it that *he* should have been sitting on my throne!" David said. "The old tale of Malcolm Canmore and his sons. I hope that you, my lord George, have a less long memory!"

"Sire, I am your man, and will ever remain so. What happened three centuries ago is best forgotten!"

"So say I!" John added.

A tranter came up, on foot, a falcon on his arm, and dragging a long-legged dead heron, to present to the king. David snorted.

"One more of these!" he complained. "What is wrong with this hawk? Why cannot it stoop on useful fowl, not these creatures?"

"Because they are larger, Sire, I would think." The tranter's task was to go after the released hawks and bring them back after they had killed, tranter meaning walker.

The king bent in the saddle to take the falcon, and shook it in irritation. "I will try it once more. And if it does not do better, I will be done with it. Next time, choose another bird."

"You could try up in the Dunsappie Loch, Sire. Herons do not use that. No reeds nor deep mud."

"Few duck likewise! But, yes, I could try it." He turned to Robert Stewart, who was awaiting his own hawk's return. "I will leave you then," he said, "to try the high loch. These two will accompany me, and act tranters if I make a kill. Then back to the abbey." He fitted the little leather cap over the hawk's head and eyes, so that it would not take wing, and gestured to the Cospatrick brothers. "Up the hill, my friends. This Dunsappie lies high." And he pointed upwards, towards a kind of shelf of Arthur's Seat.

"We know it, Your Grace," John told him.

The trio rode off together, eastwards now, to round the loch-head and through the little village of Duddingston, thereafter to climb the steep slopes, dotted with gorse bushes and dwarf hawthorns. As they went, the monarch chatted to them companionably. He said no more about their father, but emphasised his respect and regard for their mother, saying how even in England her name was known, Black Agnes, for her renowned defence of Dunbar Castle those many years ago, when it was besieged by the English Earl of Salisbury. If her sons equalled their mother's dash and courage, he declared they would serve Scotland well.

When they reached the much smaller loch, quite surprisingly placed, high, they did see a couple of mallard take wing at sight of them. The king promptly unhooded his falcon, to free it. The bird launched itself off at once, to soar high, in spirals, and quickly spotted the circling ducks, and went after them, so much more swift a flier. Drawing rein, the men saw it positioning itself above the flapping fowl. They hoped that it would not stoop on these over the loch itself, in case the kill fell into the water and be lost to them, lacking a dog to retrieve it. But no, the hawk had its own wits; after all, it was a killer, but its instinct was to kill in order to eat the prey, and would no more want that to fall into the loch than would the sportsmen. So it hovered until the circling ducks were over grassy ground, and then dropped on one of them like a stone, to strike it with a force and weight that broke its neck, and quarry and slayer went down together to the dry land, a score of yards

14

from the loch edge. John was spurring his horse towards them even as they landed.

The falcon was tearing with its hooked beak at the duck's underside when the man jumped down to play the tranter. John was adept at the hawking himself, much pursued at Dunbar, and knew how to grasp the creature without being pecked at himself as he lifted it off the duck. But he had no leather gauntlet to protect his arm, and had to settle it on the doublet sleeve, and bear the tight grip of those talons through the cloth, holding the bird secure with the other hand. Then he had to bend to pick up the duck with that burdened hand and arm, and with the live and dead birds somehow climb up on to his horse's back, well recognising why the tranters were so called, to go after hawks and prey afoot. He rode back to the others, and was thankful to transfer the falcon to the king's protected arm, retaining the mallard duck.

"Well done, Earl of Moray!" David exclaimed. "We will make a tranter of you yet! But, in perhaps more onerous matters than hawking! I can think of affairs in the north of my realm that could do with your useful attentions!"

"Your servant, Sire."

They rode back, and down the north side of Arthur's Seat, to the abbey.

Later, witnessed by their mother and the queen, the brothers knelt before their liege-lord, to take his hand between both of their own, and swear the oath of fealty and allegiance, as earls, undertaking to support the crown in all things, even unto death itself. John wondered, as he did so, how his father, who had had to swear the same oath, although before a different sovereign, had reconciled his conscience to it all.

Afterwards they remained with the royal couple for a meal, in friendly converse, no courtiers present, nothing regal nor formal about it all. It said much about King David that he preferred this sort of behaviour, when possible, to the usual monarchial display, this emphasised by his choice of queen. He had been married early, in the normal arranged match for a king, to the Princess Joanna, sister of Edward the Third of England; but she had died, without offspring, and then he had become attracted to and married this young widow of no lofty degree, Margaret Drummond, daughter of Sir Malcolm Drummond, a mere knight, and who had been wed previously to Sir John Logie, another knight, executed for being party to a plot to replace Robert the Bruce, and had had a child by him. But, so far, she had not produced an heir for David. But they seemed reasonably happy together. Scotland had had not a few Queen Margarets, but never one of this sort.

The king, it seemed, was much concerned over the situation up in Moray, Buchan, Banff and the north generally, where, after the death of Agnes's brother John, third Randolph earl, there had been no resident overlord, and feuding and squabbling over lands and privileges by various factions up there developed, in especial the Comyns of Buchan and Badenoch, ever troublemakers, and William, Earl of Ross, and even the people of the old Earl of Mar. Something would have to be done about this, particularly with John, Lord of the Isles, son-in-law of the Steward, making inroads into the Highland mainland. These Highland clans were ever at feud; but the situation was getting worse, and there could be civil war up there, and the royal authority set at naught, more especially with Aberdeenshire becoming involved. He hoped that John of Moray would not be long in going up to his earldom and seeking to impose some order there, acting as his royal representative. He would give him full authority.

John was distinctly shaken over this unexpected elevation to become the king's lieutenant and arbiter up in those unruly parts, apparently, he who at the age of twenty-two had had no experience in such matters of rule and governance, especially over other and established earls, lords and chiefs. He looked doubtfully at his mother and brother, as David spoke. Black Agnes gave him a brief nod and smile, perceiving his unease, presumably intended to be comforting. It was, a little, for he had great faith in her.

They spent a comfortable night at the abbey, George, in their shared room, seeming much amused by his brother's new status and standing. He declared that, if necessary, he would come up to Moray hereafter and help to impose the royal will on the wild Hielantmen, with a contingent of his Dunbar man and Merse mosstroopers, this scarcely encouraging John, ere he slept.

Back to Dunbar next day, his mother telling him not to worry unduly. Those northern lords were all at odds, and could be played off one against another in the king's cause. They would never make a united front against the monarch's representative. Johnnie must use his wits, and he would not have to use his sword, she judged.

That was some slight relief, at least.

3

If John was in no hurry to assume his major and rather dreaded responsibilities in the north, his liege-lord was otherwise, and fairly urgent about it. So it was not long before the summons came to attend on the king for more detailed instructions. And, well understanding her son's lack of eagerness in the matter, Black Agnes announced that, for his first essay up to Moray, she would accompany him, where her reputation and standing as the late regent's daughter, as well as her knowledge of the land and its people, would be of positive help. Although he did not wish to be shepherded by his mother, John was in fact grateful for this.

But before they set out for Edinburgh again, and thereafter for the north, Agnes gave her son a fairly thorough description of the territory he was going to try to govern and control. Moray was a large earldom, as far as land was concerned, almost five hundred square miles of it, she revealed. It was one of the original seven Celtic mormaordoms of the *ri*, or lesser kings, and extended from the Moray Firth shores of Nairn and Forres and Banff to the edges of Aberdeenshire, even into that last in some small measure, a source of trouble; and westwards to Lochaber, even Glengarry and Mamore; and southwards to the borders of Atholl, including great Strathspey. Its capital was Elgin, but Inverness was almost more important, as principal port of the Highlands and key to the Great Glen, and Ross to the north. That was the original extent, but there had been some reductions since MacBeth's time – he had been Mormaor of Moray before becoming king – with the Comyn lordships of Lochaber and Badenoch, Buchan and Lochindorb hiving off. All this, far from enheartening John, made him the more doubtful, unfortunately.

When they saw the monarch again at the Abbey of Holy Rood, he was pleased that Black Agnes was going to accompany her son on this initial introduction to his earldom, where her influence would be valuable, he asserted. He gave them a survey of his principal concerns up there, emphasising John of the Isles' ever-growing attempts to grasp the areas of Lochaber and Glengarry, and his refusal to pay the dues and taxes levied upon his properties, acting the all but independent monarch, as had done his ancestor, Somerled. His behaviour was upsetting the clans Mackintosh, Grant, Shaw and Campbell. Also the Earl of Ross was increasing his dominance in the Inverness area; and there were troubles between the Grants of Strathspey and the Comyns of Badenoch, whose lands joined. David was concerned that these Comyns, and their allies the Comyns of Buchan, should not be unduly antagonised in the efforts to establish royal control and peace, for although in the past they had been great trouble-makers in the realm, he had managed to establish fairly good relations with them, and did not want this endangered. So John must seek to balance fair judgment and remedial measures with tact.

But the king's prime concern, at this stage, was with the royal lands and thaneage of Kintore, further south, in the earldom of Mar. The aged Earl Thomas was in his dotage, and in the care of two kinsmen of his divorced second wife, Erskines, who were misbehaving and causing upsets. They were seeking to oust the Keiths from lands in Kintore, especially Hallforest, this despite the fact that the Keiths were hereditary Great Marischals of Scotland, appointed so by Robert the Bruce. The Hallforest branch was not the main stem of the family, to be sure, which was at Dunnottar in Kincardineshire; but the Mar encroachments were worrying Keith the Marischal, and he was complaining and threatening to take strong action if the king did not intervene, since Hallforest was in a royal thaneage. So to give John the necessary authority, David was appointing him Thane of Kintore, as well as Earl of Moray, thus becoming royal representative with major powers. Thanes were of an ancient office, personal crown lieutenants, few of which still survived, Kintore one of them.

Not a little bemused by all this, John was scarcely grateful for the honour, although his mother said that it was a notable advancement, as well as adding to his powers.

David had one further honour to bestow. He there and then took a sword and knighted the younger man, in front of his mother. So he had suddenly become *Sir* John, Earl of Moray and Thane of Kintore. What would George say to that?

Mother and son did not commence the lengthy journey northwards from Edinburgh directly, but returned to Dunbar, to pursue it much more conveniently than on horseback, for some two hundred miles. The Earls of Dunbar and March had, in the past, established quite a trading empire with Norway, the Baltic states and the Low Countries, for which much shipping was required, for the wool, salted meats, timber, even hewn stone, basing their vessels on Dunbar harbour, Eyemouth and Berwick. So now they could travel north by sea, at least as far as the port of Stonehaven, near which rose the castle of Dunnottar, the Keiths' main seat, where they could obtain good horses for their onward progress to Kintore, and thereafter on to Elgin. There was a ship based at Dunbar named *Meg of Skateraw*, and it happened to be in harbour there at this time, although it was due to sail for the Baltic shortly. It could take the countess and her son up to Stonehaven in a couple of days, and come back in time to sail eastwards across the Norse Sea.

When George heard of all this, nothing would do but that he would accompany them as far as this Dunnottar, and then return with the *Meg*.

So two days later they set sail on John's initiation as earl and thane, a momentous occasion, George making a pretended fuss about his brother now a knight when he was not, senior as he was in age and status.

With a following south-west wind they made excellent time up the coasts of Fife and Angus to those of Kincardine, a comparatively small shire or sheriffdom, wedged between those of Angus and Aberdeen. They covered the distance, of just under one hundred miles, in a day and night. Just before turning in to the port of Stonehaven, they passed beneath the majestic castle of Dunnottar, built on top of what was all but a high rocky isle, linked to the shore by only a narrow and low strip of land, there seeming to be quite a cluster of separate buildings up there, not the usual towers within a curtain-walled courtyard, all but a small village indeed. There was no landing-place there, however, beneath the steep cliffs, so the *Meg* had to go on to Stonehaven itself, a quite large harbour and little town.

Landing there, the trio had no option but to walk and climb back the mile to Dunnottar, where, even when they gained the nearest landward approach, it was not at all clear how the castle was to be reached, so isolated was its steep hump of rock. Dunbar Castle made remarkable use of its own sea-girt stacks, but at least its gatehouse tower was based on land. Here there was nothing such.

They had to make their way down the steep, zigzagging path and on to the little neck of rock and grass, which acted as a sort of bridge over to the high isthmus, thereafter to start to climb up a still steeper track in a narrow defile, Black Agnes declaring that these Keiths must be very pleased with their own company to live in a place like this; and their horses remarkably nimble of hoof to pick their way up here, old droppings on the track showing that they did however.

Two-thirds of the way up they came to the first barrier, a high wall closing the defile, with a gatehouse over the arched entrance. Here they were hailed by guards, with the demand to know who came uninvited to Dunnottar? Probably few women, and on foot, ever arrived so.

John, making his first declaration of authority, shouted

back that here was the Earl of Moray, in the king's name, come to speak with the Knight Marischal.

That got the gate opened, and a man came down to inspect them somewhat askance. But apparently satisfied, he conducted them further up the steep track to another similar barrier and gatehouse, the heavy gate here open, however, and they passed through unchallenged. There was a third such obstacle to negotiate, where they were again inspected, before being admitted on to the top of the rock, Agnes by now somewhat breathless with all the climbing.

They found themselves on a level platform, of greater extent than appeared from below, perhaps four acres of it, dotted with individual buildings of different sorts, one actually seeming to be a church, extraordinary as this might be to find in such a place. There was a great square keep at the south-west edge of the rock, a line of stables, with living quarters above, storehouses, bakehouse, brewhouse, barracks, even a smith's forge. None of this was unusual perhaps in a large castle, save for the church, which was odd indeed, this no mere chapel.

The guard led them to the keep, where their arrival had been spotted, and a servitor waited to discover this small group's intentions. Black Agnes it was who announced that Sir William Keith, if he was here present, would be glad to see them, the Earl of Moray and his mother and brother of Dunbar and March. That had the enquirer ushering them into the vaulted basement entry, and hurrying off upstairs.

They had not long to wait before an elderly and a younger man came down, their interest and surprise evident. Sir William knew the countess, for he had married Barbara, of Seton of that Ilk, a senior Lothian vassal of the Cospatricks. He greeted them with a mixture of warmth and astonishment. Her sons he had not met. He introduced the younger man with him as his own eldest son, Robert.

The explained reasons behind this unexpected visit pleased the Keiths, needless to say, for they were much concerned over the Kintore and Hallforest situation, and the activities of the Mar kinsmen, and were glad that the king was thus demonstrating his concern.

They proved to be a congenial family, such of them as were there present, the Lady Barbara motherly and friendly, and three sons, Robert, Richard and Edward, easy also to get on with. There apparently was another son, Philip, a churchman, absent, and a daughter who was married to a Douglas. The visitors were well entertained.

George had to get back presently to Stonehaven and the ship, for the return voyage. He was lent a horse, and departed, wishing his brother well in all his activities in the north, and again promising help in the form of man-power, if required.

The Keiths had some affinity with the Cospatricks, for, like them, they were of ancient Celtic stock, not of Norman extraction like so much of the Scots nobility. They had come into prominence in the year 1010, and none so far from here, when, at a battle with invading Danes, an ancestor had greatly distinguished himself by turning the tide of the struggle and slaying the Viking leader, Camus, single-handed, this so pleasing King Malcolm the Second that he thereupon dipped the royal finger in the blood of the dead Dane, and drew three perpendicular strokes on Keith's shield, this symbol still being the heraldic device of the family, three columns of red on white, with a dagger dripping blood as crest. A successor had been created Hereditary Marshal, or Marischal, of Scotland. Sir William's father had commanded Scots cavalry at Bannockburn, and had been given lands in the royal thaneage of Kintore, Hallforest, by Bruce, and this had brought the Keiths up to these parts, for Keith itself, from which they took their name, was in Lothian, indeed bordering the Dunbar earldom lands.

John learned that a Keith cousin, in Hallforest, was being constantly troubled, his castle assailed, by the Erskine relations of the housebound and mind-wandering 13th Earl of Mar, these claiming that it was an intrusion on the earldom, and that not only Hallforest but the entire thaneage should belong to Mar and not be a royal possession. During King David's long captivity in England they had been nibbling away at it, and the Keiths' holdings had suffered sorely. So now John's first task was to act to right this situation. Sir William said that his eldest son, Robert, would be at the new Thane of Kintore's disposal, to assist in any way he could.

John and his mother remained two days at Dunnottar, quite enjoying their visit. They learned that Sir William had begun to build this castle some thirty years previously, on the remains of a Pictish fort, this whereon a Celtic Church missionary had established his diseart, or hermitage cell, to commune with his Maker, as was the custom of these Columban saints; and this, in time, had developed into a church when the Roman faith had taken over in Scotland, at the time of St Margaret – this however inconvenient its location must have been for the worshippers to reach. Keith had not sought to interfere with this odd situation in his castle-building, but the then Primate, Bishop of St Andrews, had been much incensed at what he called the desecration of holy ground, and had in fact excommunicated Sir William over it all. An appeal to the Vatican, however, had the then Pope reversing the excommunication, on condition that Keith built a new parish church in a more convenient position. This he had willingly done, and peace with Holy Church was restored.

John and his mother, with Robert Keith and half a dozen supporting men, left Dunnottar in due course, to head for Kintore.

They headed north-westwards a dozen miles through low hills, to reach the great River Dee at Banchory, there to swing northwards another twenty miles, by Dunecht, through Mar, to Kintore on the River Don, these two the greatest rivers of Aberdeenshire. They met with no problems on the way, whatever the unrest in the area. Kintore proved to have quite a large township, in pleasing country flanking the wide river, with its thane's castle nearby on the higher ground of Crichie, no very imposing fortalice, in the care of an aged keeper, who was much alarmed to find himself having to entertain and pay allegiance to a new thane in the person of the Earl of Moray and, more notably still, Black Agnes of Dunbar, whose reputation was nationwide. That effective lady promptly had the keeper's wife and daughters improving conditions, and making more comfortable quarters for the new arrivals.

John enquired as to the situation at Hallforest, apparently some three miles to the south, and was informed that the Mar people had made life so difficult for the Keith laird, stealing his cattle, burning his barns and wrecking his mill, that he had left the castle, and gone with his family to lodge in the priory of St Michael's of Kinkell, the most important ecclesiastical establishment of the area, its prior a prebendary of St Machar's Cathedral at Aberdeen. This religious community was only a mile or so north of Kintore's royal burgh, made so by William the Lion, despite its modest size, presumably because it was in the royal thanedom. John recognised that this conflict of authority within the earldom of Mar could be productive of trouble; but his duty was to establish King David's overall prerogative and peace locally, whatever the rights and wrongs of the matter.

It was decided to visit Hallforest first, then Kinkell, and possibly thereafter Kildrummy Castle, the main seat of the earldom of Mar, to learn the details and extent of the dispute, and seek to reconcile all in some fashion, without recourse to force if possible.

Hallforest lay amongst wooded slopes and shallow vales in what had been the royal hunting forest of the Bruce, formerly called Camus-stone, where a great stone monument had been erected to celebrate the victory of 1010, where the early Keith had distinguished himself. Well before they reached the small castle they saw signs of trouble, empty cot-houses with thatch roofs burned, wrecked barns and the like. They found the castle itself

25

deserted, but not damaged. Presumably the ravagers came from Kildrummy, some thirty-five miles to the west, although still on the Don, in which case they must have some more local base for their depredations. They did come across a man, leading a garron loaded with peats, who at sight of them bolted for a seemingly undamaged cottage, evidently assuming them to be more troublemakers. When they rode up to the door it was kept barred against them until Robert Keith shouted that he was a Keith, and had here with him the Earl of Moray, Thane of Kintore, on King David's business. That got the door unbarred for them, and the alarmed cottager, when asked, told them that the Mar raiders, when they came, based themselves at Fetternear, not far from Kemnay, to the west; but that they had not been in evidence for a couple of weeks.

Seeing no point in proceeding that far meantime, the enquirers turned back for Kinkell Priory, some four miles to the north, Keith guiding them.

He advised that they should visit the Camus Stone, erected by King Malcolm, this lying between Kintore and the thane's castle, and less than two miles from Kinkell Priory. Reaching it, they found a great circular stone, a vast object, bearing an incised wheel-cross of highly unusual design, elaborately carved. Keith, who naturally was very interested in this, since what had happened here had brought his family up to Mar, said that there had allegedly been a Celtic Church chapel beside the stone, but this had disappeared, only the remarkable wheel-cross remaining to mark the holy site.

Moving on, and over a ford, they found on the east bank of Don a fine and extensive monastic establishment and hospice, where the other John Keith and his family had taken refuge, the monks very helpful and sympathetic. But the prior was in a difficult situation, it seemed, for he did not want to antagonise the earldom of Mar by getting too involved in the Hallforest controversy, for he had six other dependent churches scattered around the area, five of them on Mar land.

"Yet you provide refuge and succour for the Keiths," John put to him. "Will that not offend these Mar raiders?"

"I hope not," he was told. "Keith of Hallforest is a good man, and has ever supported my priory. Bishop Alexander of Aberdeen deems him worthy. I would help him if I could."

John glanced at his mother, listening. He drew a deep breath. "And you *could*, Prior David, if so you wished," he said.

"How that, my lord? Other than sheltering him and his?"

"The threat of excommunication!" He heard his *mother's* deep breath, now.

"Excommunication! But, but . . ."

"It is a potent malison is it not? Sir William Keith, the Marischal, was excommunicated by the Bishop of St Andrews for what was named profaning holy ground, over the church on his rock of Dunnottar. These raiders are doing the like, are they not? We have seen the havoc they have wrought, and some none so far from the thane's castle. We have just visited the Camus Stone, with its great cross of Christ. And there was a chapel there once, we are told. Damage has been done thereabouts. The threat which your Bishop of Aberdeen could pronounce, of excommunication, if the raiding and damage does not cease? What of that?"

The prior eyed him, eyed them all, wonderingly.

"Here is a notion, indeed!" Black Agnes declared. "Would you do it?"

"It need only be the threat of it, I would judge," John added. "Excommunication is a dire matter. Not only, I understand, are the services of Holy Church denied, the eucharist, marriage, baptisms, burial, but being shunned by all the faithful, no rights of patronage, no dues payable from Church-used lands. More, you no doubt know of. The threat of it, see you."

"Bishop Alexander might well not agree to do it, my lord."

"Need he be approached, first? We will be going to the Mar seat, Kildrummy castle. Come with us, or send one to represent you, to declare that you will so urge the bishop if the assaults and raiding are not halted. This would greatly assist our efforts, and aid the king's cause."

"I . . . I will think on this," he was told.

When they were alone, Agnes informed her son that she was proud of him. She had told him, at the start of all this to use his wits in his new role; she had scarcely realised that those wits were thus sharp!

"It was the Marischal's account of his excommunication, which came to me," he said. "If one bishop could do it, over a church, so could another. And this Camus Stone and former chapel . . ."

"It is a notable proposal, my lord," Robert Keith said. "My father will deem this worthy, I say!"

The Hallforest Keith, when he heard of it all, expressed equal admiration, with the hopes that it would enable him and his to return to their home and see an end to their troubles.

They all passed a comfortable evening in the Kinkell hospice, learning that this priory was a very ancient and prestigious establishment, the very name of Kinkell meaning head church. It had always been dedicated to Michael the Archangel, reputed to be the chief adversary of Satan, and God's vice-regent. There was a celebrated Michael's Fair held here each year, to which clerics and others came from near and far. So its prebendary prior was one of the foremost churchmen of the diocese; thus, if he would do as urged, it would make the threat to the Mar people the more effective.

In the morning Prior David announced that he had considered and prayed over it, and decided that he should co-operate. He would not go with his visitors in person, but would send his sub-prior, Thomas, to make the pronouncement of the threat, hoping that this would be sufficient for their purpose, and not require him to go to the bishop requesting the fulmination. This well satisfied John and his mother.

They did not delay, and with a somewhat doubtful Sub-Prior Thomas, set off westwards to ride the thirty-five miles up Don, by Kemnay and Monymusk and Alford, fair country indeed, which had the visitors wondering why the Mar representatives were so ambitious to acquire the thaneage of Kintore when they had so much excellent land already.

Not riding very fast, with Agnes and the cleric to consider, it took them most of the day to reach their destination. They found Kildrummy to be a huge castle, used as they were to great houses, set on the rising ground west of the Don, on the edge of a ravine. It was curiously shaped, in the form of a shield, massive round towers linked by high curtain walls, these enclosing, amongst other buildings, a chapel – which might just have some relevance in their cause.

Even Black Agnes had never seen Kildrummy before, although it was a famous place, not only for being the seat of an ancient earldom, another like Moray, one of the seven original mormaordoms of Alba. Here it was that Elizabeth de Burgh, the Bruce's wife, and his brother Nigel, had been betrayed by the castle blacksmith, who had set fire to the castle while it was being besieged by the Earl of Pembroke for King Edward; Nigel had managed to smuggle the queen out, with her step-daughter Marjorie, in the darkness, with the Earl of Atholl to escort them, but he himself remained to fight. He was captured, and died horribly. The queen was again betrayed, by the Balliol supporter the then Earl of Ross, and captured at Tain. Here, again besieged by the usurping Balliol, Bruce's sister, married to Gartney of Mar, defended it successfully. Now, it seemed, Kildrummy was in sad decline, with Thomas, 13th earl and last of his line, without offspring, ill in mind as well as body; and some far-out kin, Comyns of the Buchan stem, taking over and misbehaving.

When John announced his identity, demanding, in the king's name, to see the Earl Thomas, the guard kept the visitors waiting for some time, before returning to the gatehouse with a youngish man, who announced himself to be John Comyn of Ardtannies, and who said that the Earl of Mar was sick, and could see no one. What brought the Earl of Moray to Kildrummy?

His Grace the king's business, he was told, and entrance required, in the royal name.

So, grudgingly, they were admitted, and in the principal tower met another and younger man, William Comyn of Dubston, no more welcoming, both these eyeing Black Agnes in especial warily. That woman, declaring that she had known Earl Thomas of old, demanded to be conducted into his presence, whatever his state. They were taken reluctantly upstairs to a chamber, which smelled unpleasantly, where they found a haggard old man lying on a great bed and staring up at the celling, muttering to himself. He paid no attention to the newcomers, even when Agnes went close and spoke to him.

Eyeing his mother and Sub-Prior Thomas, John addressed the two Comyna.

"Your depredations into the royal lands of Kintore, of which I am now thane, and in especial the Keith lands of Hallforest, have greatly angered the king," he said. "These must cease forthwith, and compensation be paid. Or you will suffer greatly for it."

"Kintore, my lord, is but a thaneage. Within the earldom of Mar," the older Comyn asserted. "It is not any lordship of itself, its thanes but holders meantime, not owners. As you, an earl, must know."

"The king's authority rules in the earldom of Mar, sir, as it does elsewhere in this his realm. I come, sent to see that it does."

"My lord Earl Thomas, here, is sick, and requires his rights to be upheld. And Hallforest, in especial, offends. Paying him no dues."

"Keith of Hallforest pays his dues to the crown, as is right. Your attitude as to his property offends His Grace."

The Comyn, tight-lipped, made no reply.

"So – you will cease your raiding?"

Still no response.

"Then, if not, you will pay. And pay dearly. As will the Earl Thomas, however poor his health. The king could order me to use armed force against you. But such might be . . . unsuitable against a sick man. So – there is another payment. More dire still." He gestured towards the bed. "Excommunication! How say you to that?"

The Comyns stared, lips no longer tight.

"It is the penalty for assailing Holy Church. And you know what excommunication results in! I think that I need not tell you." And John turned to the sub-prior.

That man took a breath, and spoke. "My Prebendary Prior David of Kinkell, under whose authority this comes, will petition the Bishop of St Andrews to pronounce excommunication upon yourselves and the Earl of Mar if this ill-doing does not cease, and if you do not vow that it does so. This I am to declare." That came out in something of a rush.

The Comyns eyed each other, lost for words.

"How say you?" John demanded. "For you, it would be sufficiently ill. But for an old and sick man . . . If he dies, no prayers for his soul , no last rites, no Christian burial. The chapel here barred off. And how think you his sister, wed to the Earl of Douglas, his heiress, would act?"

There was a long silence. It was Black Agnes who broke it.

"I know what *I* would do, if I was the Countess of Douglas and Mar. I would descend on your lands, wherever they are, and destroy them. And imprison you both, if not hang you! And receive the blessing of the Church for so doing!"

"We . . . we will have to think on this," the older Comyn got out.

"Think now!" John advised. "We are not here to wait on your decision. We return to Kinkell Priory." He pointed over to the bed, where Earl Thomas was still peering upwards, not at them, mumbling.

31

Comyn of Dubston gripped the other's arm, in agitation. Ardtannies nodded.

"Very well," he said. "It . . . it shall be so."

"You swear that all raiding shall cease? And satisfaction be paid? Swear here and now, before these witnesses?"

"Yes, I do."

"And I," Dubston said.

"So be it. See you to it. I shall not be far away. In Moray. And shall be told if you fail in this. And I will not fail to act!" John glanced over at his mother, and then towards the sick man on the bed. "We will leave you now."

It was a servitor, not the Comyns, who escorted the callers back to their horses in the courtyard, and then out under the gatehouse arch.

Mounted and away, Agnes told her son that he had the makings of a worthy Earl of Moray, if he could keep it up!

They halted for the night at one of the Kinkell hospices, at Monymusk, before returning to the priory, where a quite relieved incumbent was thankful to hear that he did not have to go to Aberdeen to try to persuade the bishop to pronounce the anathema.

Next day, it was north by west for them, for Elgin, Robert Keith insisting that his father would expect him to go with them.

4

It made long riding up to the capital of Moray, Elgin, fully
eighty miles – for this Mar interlude was a special assign-
ment of King David's, and not really part of John's Moray
responsibilities. They went by Inverugie, up that river by
Culsalmond, then into Strathbogie and up the Deveron to
Craigellachie, on the lower Spey, where there was a hospice and they spent the night, in Moray now. They
discussed the problems ahead as they rode. There were
three main sources of trouble: the Comyns, the Lord of the
Isles and the Earl of Ross. It was the Comyn situation that
was largely responsible for the state of affairs ahead. The
Comyn earldom of Buchan had been very strong up here,
especially allied to that of the lordship of Badenoch and
Lochaber. But Alexander of Buchan had died, leaving only
two daughters, the elder married to an Englishman, de
Beaumont, and the other to the son of William, Earl of
Ross. So the earldom was presently vacant, with conse-
quent disharmony, as the two daughters' husbands, and
lesser Comyns, squabbled over lands and seniority. Ross
was seeking to establish his son's claim and had invaded
Comyn land; and the Badenoch or Red Comyns, the senior
branch of the house, were taking the opportunity to extend
their power eastwards into the lower Strathspey, this
greatly upsetting Clan Grant, settled there. This Comyn
clash in Mar was bound to have some impact on it all.

But almost as important were the ambitious projects of
John, Lord of the Isles, the son of Angus Og of Islay,
Bruce's friend, to spread his dominions eastwards, his
allegiance to King David ever doubtful, acting the semi-
independent monarch, so far as to make his own pact with

Edward of England. And having obtained the wardship of the child Earl of Atholl, he had used this to extend his sway, this greatly alarming the Campbells of Argyll and Lorne. He now controlled Knoydart, Moidart, Arisaig, Morar and up the Great Glen as far as Glengarry, this upsetting the Macpherson and Mackintosh chiefs. And there was the complication that his son, Donald, was also son of Robert the High Steward's second wife, the Countess of Ross, by a previous marriage, that Steward now heir-presumptive to the throne.

So the challenge facing John was involved as it was grievous.

From Craigellachie, on the lower Spey, they went northwards a bare twenty miles, by Lhanbryde, to reach Elgin, the capital of Moray. This was quite a large town, walled, a city indeed, in that it had a famous cathedral, and was the seat of the powerful Bishops of Moray, these having tended to rule the area in the absence of an earl. Getting on with Alexander the bishop would be not the least of John's preoccupations.

They entered the city by the Panns Port, or gate, so named because here bread was dispensed to lepers, who must not enter the city, by the ancient Order of St Lazarus of Jerusalem, hence the corruption of the French word.

John was much impressed by the great cathedral, dedicated to the Holy Trinity, and erected by his predecessors in the earldom, his mother declaring that this had probably been paid for by death-bed repentances for sins committed in the past, and prayers to be said therein for the souls of the donors! There was a bishop's house nearby, archdeacons and dean's houses, and no fewer than twenty canons' manses, and the large house of the Order of St Lazarus. So ecclesiastical buildings dominated the east end of the city. It appeared that the earl's castle lay just outside the walls to the west.

Agnes pointed out other fine establishments as they rode through the quite wide streets: the Greyfriars monastery; the still larger Blackfriars one, which she said was the first

Dominican house to be established in all Scotland; the Bedehouse, or almshouse for the care of the needy; and the Muckle Kirk of St Giles, in the centre of the High Street. Bemused by all this religious and theological activity, John wondered why so much disharmony and ungodly behaviour went on in the area. Also what *he* could do to bring peace, where this holy authority could not?

Beyond the West Port, they found the slight ridge on which Elgin was based, within a great bend of the Lossie River, developed into a somewhat more prominent rise, called, Agnes said, the Hill of Our Lady, on which stood the earl's castle. John was a little disappointed in this, for although it was a fair enough fortalice, it was less impressive than all the ecclesiastical splendour nearby, and considerably smaller than Kildrummy, Dunnottar or their own Dunbar. Was this to be the base from which he would seek to control Moray? His mother told him that, in fact, it was not the main seat of the earldom, which was at Darnaway, a score of miles away, in the fertile Laigh of Moray; so it would be there, rather than here, that he would presumably station himself. This seemed strange, with Elgin allegedly capital of the earldom. Was it not, rather, just the capital of the bishopric?

Up at the castle, they found it, and its keeper, scarcely prepared for the coming of its new lord and his mother, and consequently in something of a state with nothing ready for the comfort and convenience of the new arrivals. So Agnes advised that they should go back and introduce themselves to Bishop Alexander, whom she did not know, and with whom it was clearly important to work.

They returned through the town, to the Bishop's House, but there learned that the prelate was not present, but was at his palace castle of Spynie, just over two miles to the north. Rather than deal with his subordinates at this stage, the dean and archdeacon, they decided to go on to Spynie, which Agnes knew of, this before going on to Darnaway, where her son would be making his base.

It was early evening when they reached Spynie, which

John felt was a little unfortunate, for it meant that they would presumably have to spend the night there, and if they did not get on well with this bishop, then it might become rather uncomfortable. But Agnes told him to remember who he now was, the Earl of Moray, in his own earldom, and all therein should be concerned to offer him hospitality, the bishop no less than others.

They found Spynie to be a most notable establishment, a lofty pile on rising ground in a very attractive and scenic setting, above what seemed at first sight to be a very large loch, but which proved to be an all but landlocked inlet of the sea, or at least the Moray Firth, with the tides surging in through a narrow channel cut in miles of sand-dunes, seven miles it seemed, called the Culbins, these apparently famous, or notorious, for shipwrecks. This channel was near the mouth of the Lossie, and had the effect of flooding all the low ground behind to form a sea loch of some three miles by two, this providing a sheltered and picturesque haven.

Spynie was more castle than palace, and perhaps said something about this bishopric. Its massive keep was six storeys high, within an extensive square courtyard, with towers at each angle, containing a range of residential buildings, all entered through a highly defensive gatehouse provided with arrow-slits and portcullis.

Bishop Alexander, when they reached him, was unlike any other senior prelate that even Black Agnes had ever met, a small, modest-seeming, smiling but urgent man of later middle years, clad in work-a-day clothing, only a cross on a silver chain around his neck indicating clerical status. Even his name, Alexander Bur, lacked the usual episcopal dignity, this perhaps a corruption of Burnet, a north-country family. He had been archdeacon of the diocese, having been one of the canons before that, when the previous bishop, John de Pilmuir, became a sick man, and for years had more or less managed the diocese for the ailing prelate; and when the incumbent eventually died had been elected to take his place, an unusual procedure but indicative of his effectiveness.

He greeted the callers agreeably even before he learned their identity, thereafter declaring himself proud to kiss the hand of the Countess Agnes of Dunbar, and thankful to hear that a new Earl of Moray had come to his troubled diocese – an encouraging start to their relationship. Without actually saying so, he indicated relief that his burden of trying to establish peace in his great area was now to be shared.

They remained at Spynie for two days, Agnes agreeing with her son that it was of priority to establish amity here and a good working association, especially as the bishop seemed so inclined to be co-operative. There was much comfortable accommodation in the castle, and the visitors were made very welcome in every way. They learned that there had been a Celtic Columban Church abbey here, and the first Catholic bishops had turned it into their cathedral; but this proving too modest in size, and too distant from the community of Elgin, they had transferred their shrine there and built the magnificent fane, the episcopal Pride of the North, as it was called.

Bishop Alexander told them that while the most immediate trouble in the earldom stemmed from the squabbling, land-hungry and presently leaderless Comyns, and the rivalry over the succession to the Buchan earldom, the major threat undoubtedly came from John of the Isles. His advances eastwards were continuing and greatly upsetting the clans of these parts, like those further west. If he was not stopped, there could be a risk of everything from Atholl and Mar becoming part of the Lordship of the Isles, ridiculous as this sounded, all but a separate kingdom, Scotland divided.

John declared that if the clans, the Comyns and the Earl of Ross would stop fighting each other and unite to repel the Islesmen, it would be better, make more sense. The bishop agreed, however much against battle and bloodshed he felt. It was most unfortunate that the three earldoms of Buchan, Atholl and Mar should all be either vacant or in the hands of a child or a dotard. But now, at least, Moray had a resident earl come to lead it.

Modestly John disclaimed leadership prowess, saying merely that he would do his best. He recounted the situation that they had left at Mar, with the Comyn usurpers threated with excommunication. Alexander was much interested in this, needless to say, wondering at it, and whether his opposite number at Aberdeen would indeed have agreed to pronounce the dire anathema. But acceding that even the threat of it could be effective. So far as he knew, no Church property had been deliberately desecrated in his diocese, but he would keep the matter in mind.

John asked who was the most senior or powerful of the Moray Comyns who were at odds over the grasping of lands, and was told that of Duffus, none so far off at the western end of the Loch of Spynie. He was the strongest and most aggressive.

When they left the castle in due course, the bishop assured John of fullest association and good wishes, with his authority to announce the fact to any and all who might usefully be told of it.

As they rode off westwards, John told his mother and Robert Keith of what occurred to him as being a possible course of action in this complicated situation that he had to tackle in the king's name. If he could get the Comyns to stop fighting each other and league with the Earl of Ross to gain his son the earldom of Buchan, then convince Ross to lead a united force of his own people and the local clans as well as the Comyns to halt John of the Isles, then the entire position might be greatly improved, some sort of settlement agreed. Black Agnes commended this line of thought, but emphasised that it would not be easy of attainment. These Highland clans were notoriously difficult to persuade to united action, feuding being all but their way of life. But he could try it . . .

They would start with this Comyn of Duffus, then, he asserted, since apparently they were going to pass nearby on their way to Darnaway.

38

Following the shore of the loch for some three miles, they saw Duffus Castle rising ahead on a mound, just where the loch ended, a quite impressive strength in a dominant position. They approached it, John pondering over his methods of dealing with its owner.

The problem was solved for him, that at least, when, well before they reached the castle hill, a party came riding to meet them, all lances and shields, led by a big, florid man of haughty manner.

"Who comes to my land lacking my permission?" he shouted, drawing up well ahead of them.

"Is it *your* land? Or mine?" John called back, but not aggressively. "I am John, Earl of Moray. Who are you?"

That had the big man silent for moments, before he got out, "I am Comyn of Duffus here." And then remembered to add, "My lord."

"So! I was told that Duffus was a Cheyne place? You have . . . gained it?"

"Through marriage, my lord."

"Not by force of arms, as, I learn, has become the shameful usage in much of my earldom, sir, and will have to stop. As superior of these lands, you are all my vassals. And the King's Grace is gravely concerned over this state of affairs."

The other did not answer.

"This is my mother, Agnes, Countess of Dunbar and March."

"The, the famous one! Lady, I greet you! I salute you!"

"Then if you do, sirrah, heed my son's and the king's commands."

The Comyn bowed from the saddle. "You, you will honour my house?"

"We ride for Darnaway. But yes, we can halt here for a little time. That you may know what is my will and duty."

They all turned and rode for the castle, and up the great gravel mound, which presumably had once been an island in the loch, and the site of a Pictish fort by the grassy ramparts.

The castle proved to be of the mote-and-bailey sort, built of timber, not stone, but plastered over with white-washed clay to make it fireproof against fire-arrows. With-in, given wine and oatcakes by a flustered wife, John pressed home his cause.

"I am glad that you should have inherited this Duffus, my friend – not gained it by the sword! As so many of your kind are presently doing, no? That must stop. The king's laws must reign, not cold steel. Or the royal sword will have to be drawn in Moray! You take me?"

Comyn inclined his head.

"You are one of the larger vassals here, I am told. Do you have sway with your fellow-Comyns? And others, hereabouts?"

"Some small reach, perhaps, my lord. But – not great."

"But you would have it greater, I think?"

The big man eyed John keenly.

"That could be possible. If you acted wisely and with some . . . zeal! In the king's cause. With your Comyns and the others. This is necessary, or you all will be at the mercy of the Lord of the Isles. You must know it. What is required is that all in Moray, and beyond Moray, act together to restrain the Macdonalds, the Islesmen. The Earl of Ross could greatly help in this. I will see him. But men are needed, many men, Comyns amongst them. Ross would have the earldom of Buchan for his son, as is just. For although his wife is the younger daughter of the late Comyn earl, the elder daughter is wed to an Englishman and dwells in Leicester, *her* son no suitable Scots earl. So, support Ross, if he will lead against John of the Isles. And have all that you can sway to do likewise."

"Ye-e-es."

John took a chance. This man was ambitious, he judged. "It will be greatly to your own benefit, I think, if you do this. I believe that I could persuade His Grace to create you a knight."

Comyn drew quick breath, glanced over at his wife, and found words.

"I, I will do what I can, my lord. Yes, I will."

"That is as well. I hope that you can move your Comyn folk to do their loyal duty. And this to their own best weal."

"I will so endeavour . . ."

The visitors left Duffus, encouraged, Agnes declaring this of the knighthood proposal to be brilliant, a spur to the man indeed. Why had her offspring been hiding his wits all these years?

They had a score of miles to ride, westwards, by Monaughty and Altyre and Rafford, to reach Darnaway, keeping well south of the township of Forres meantime. Altyre was a Comyn place, but John thought it wise to leave the Comyn persuasion to Duffus for the present, lest any sort of rivalry developed, hindering that man's efforts.

They were in higher country now, although this was part of the Laigh of Moray, not really hilly but with long slopes fairly heavily wooded, watered by many streams, and fairly populous. Agnes said that the Brodies were strong about here, she had heard, and it might well be worth while to visit Brodie Castle hereafter, to seek to win that ancient line to their cause.

They forded the great River Findhorn at the oddly named water-meadows of the Meads of St John, and began to climb through open forested braes to Darnaway, John eager to see this, the main seat of his earldom. It was long since his mother had been here, but she remembered it as a large and handsome hallhouse, stone-built, castellated in some measure but more palace than fortalice, where the semi-legendary Freskin de Moravia had established himself back in the Celtic days, although himself thought to have been a Fleming, and giving name to the area, Moray. His descendants, Murrays, were now wide-scattered over Scotland, north and south.

John was not disappointed. The castle, on the edge of a lesser stream, was all that Agnes had remembered, long, with wings stretching from a great and tall gabled hallhouse, and surrounded by lesser buildings. It might not survive a siege, against assault by battering-rams, mangonels and sows, such as Black Agnes had faced and repulsed at Dunbar – but presumably it had never had to withstand such. That it would accommodate large numbers was evident, and would serve as an excellent rallying-place, if necessary.

The old keeper whom his mother remembered was long dead, suitably Murray by name; but she had agreed to his son Duncan succeeding him. He had sent her reports as to the castle and its lands and the earldom in general, frequently, and she believed him to be an effective custodian.

This proved to be an accurate estimate. Duncan Murray, in his mid-forties, with a wife and four children, a good-looking man of muscular frame and obvious intelligence, dependable, welcomed them almost like royalty. He and his Catherine showed the newcomers round the premises with evident pride in it all, so much so that John almost felt that he was invading their home, rather than taking over his own. The great hall, with its magnificent arched and timbered ceiling, was such as he had never seen hitherto.

They were going to be comfortable and well looked after here, at any rate.

John was concerned to hear what manpower was available for him nearby, or at least none so far off in the earldom. Murray judged that a couple of hundred might be mustered from the Darnaway and Moyness lands; and of course the town of Forres, only four miles off, was very much under the earl's authority, being a royal burgh with a royal castle. Given a few days, a thousand men might be raised, he thought. And there were ample horses in the area to mount most of them.

This seemed eminently satisfactory to John, meaning that he could give a lead, in more than just his rank and the king's command.

So, after a fashion, the Earl of Moray had come home. They settled in.

5

Settling in did not mean that John did not go ahead with his tasks the while. There was no lack of contacts he could make, and friends to win over, from Darnaway: Brodie, at Brodie Castle, sprung from Freskin's line and actually called Thane of Brodie; Ogstoun of that Ilk, also a Freskin descendant; Burgie Castle, held of the Abbot of Kinlass and so, with Bishop Alexander's influence, likely to be friendly; and of course the town of Forres. There were also the Comyn houses of Altyre, Dallas and Blervie, none so far off; but these could be left for the time being. They would hear of their earl's activities, quite apart from Duffus's efforts.

John spent a week at this, aided by Robert Keith and Duncan Murray, while his mother took over at Darnaway.

They were reasonably successful at gaining approximate support and promises of aid, Brodie being especially helpful. And the good folk of Forres, not being land-hungry like so many of the lairdly ones, were fairly ready to play their part. They also learned of a large priory at Pluscarden, hitherto unheard of, which, with the bishop's goodwill, became an added asset, clergy support valuable.

Days of this and, with the information gained, John was ready to tackle his next major effort, the winning over of the Earl of Ross. In this he would be glad of his mother's help, dealing with a man of equal rank but senior in age and experience. William of Ross had vast lands to the north of the Great Glen, with many castles, but apparently was most frequently to be found at Edradour, at the head of the little Beauly Firth, within easy reach of Inverness, the so-called Capital of the North, which he tended to dominate. That city was, in theory, part of Moray, indeed had been MacBeth's base when he was Mormaor of Ross and Moray; but it had become a royal property as well as a royal burgh thereafter, and was no longer part of either of the earldoms of Moray or Ross. But with King David being a captive for long, and anyway based far in the south, Inverness's position had become somewhat vague, the keepership of the royal castle varying between Comyns and Rosses and the Captains of Clan Chattan, the Mackintoshes. Now, it was John's duty to bring it back into the hands of a direct royal nominee.

But first he must see William of Ross. So it was due west for them, through the sheriffdom of Nairn, by Auldearn and Geddes and Rait, to cross the River Nairn near Cawdor, and then on by Croy and Culloden Muir to Inverness, some thirty-five miles. Then still along the shore of the Beauly Firth, to cross that river into Ross at Kilmorack, and thereafter back down three miles to Edradour on the northern shore, another fifteen miles. So it was quite a lengthy ride, and, not wishing to arrive at Ross's house just in time for evening eating and bed, they would stop at the royal castle in Inverness overnight. That would give them time to call in at Cawdor Castle, *en route*, the seat of the hereditary thanes, who had been of the Dorward line but had called themselves Calder, and who, because of their status, ought to be helpful to the royal cause, despite their troublesome Comyn neighbours.

At the extraordinary Cawdor Castle, built round and incorporating in its stonework a tree, they found the thane actually glad to see them, and concerned over the lawless state of the area, prepared to assist John in any way that he could. Obviously, what had been needed here in Moray was leadership.

He told them the story of this castle. His father, who as thane was responsible for the keeping of Nairn Castle, was minded to build a private stronghold on his own land further south. He found one site that pleased him, but in a dream he was guided not to do so. He was to load a donkey with a coffer of gold, and let the animal go, he following. It would stop to graze under one hawthorn tree, rest under a second and lie down under a third. Where it did this, the thane was to build his castle, and his line would prosper there. He obeyed his dream so literally that he erected his keep round the tree, without felling it, and the visitors were shown the hawthorn, now dead but still upright, rising out of the earthen floor of the basement, and disappearing up through the stone vaulted ceiling, obviously built to receive it, unique confirmation of the tale.

Leaving Cawdor, they proceeded on down Nairn Water to Culloden and Inverness, this a large and attractive town where the short River Ness, flowing out of that great loch, reached the junction of the Beauly Firth with that of Moray. It was dominated by its castle on a spinal ridge lying parallel with the river.

Therein they found that word of their presence in the land had reached Inverness; and the present keeper, a Mackintosh, guessing that the earl would be coming, had prepared to receive them. In consequence, they were well entertained. Also informed as to conditions prevailing hereabouts. It seemed that the townsfolk, who had long been worried about the ambitions of the Earls of Ross to take over their burgh and its surroundings and commonage, were now much more anxious about the advance of John of the Isles, and indeed were looking to Ross to aid them against the dreaded Islesmen. Not that he had shown any signs of doing so, as yet. They all would be thankful for the arrival of the Earl of Moray, and him coming in the king's name.

Telling the Mackintosh keeper to inform the people that restraining the Lord of the Isles was the principal objective of their earl's coming, that and putting an end to the Comyn lawlessness, they passed a comfortable night at Inverness, glad to learn that William of Ross was understood to be presently at Edradour. They saw no reason why this Mackintosh should not be left as keeper of the castle.

In the morning it was along the shore westwards, by Bunchrew and Lentron Ness, to where the firth suddenly narrowed in to the mouth of the Beauly River, where was the township of Beauly itself. Kilmorack ford, not far off, enabled them to cross over into Ross. Actually they had been able to see Edradour Castle, on its height on the other side of the two-mile-wide firth, for some of their way.

They themselves were seen, in due course, approaching their destination, and a mounted group came out to meet them. This proved to be led by the Master of Ross himself, who declared that his father had heard of the Earl of Moray's arrival and had anticipated a meeting. The lady was no doubt the famous Countess Agnes?

This was a hopeful start, at any rate. The young man, about John's own age, seemed friendly enough.

Reaching this castle, they saw how difficult must have been its building on the erratically shaped mound-top of rock, which had required the walling to be aligned at odd angles.

The Earl William, a thin, cadaverous-faced man, greeted them more warily than had his son, eyeing Black Agnes more keenly than he did John. The latter was becoming used to this, but did not resent it, he being thankful for his mother's renown greatly aiding him in his entry to his earldom and tasks. But, for all that, he was determined that he himself should be seen as capable of taking his responsibilities effectively, and by no means appearing to be under the wing of a woman, however celebrated.

They were introduced to the Countess Isobel, daughter of the previous Earl of Strathearn, a lady as plump as her husband was lean; and mothers of families and offspring were discussed, there being apparently two Ross daughters, both married and away; John patiently listened to all this, while eager to get down to affairs and conditions as he was.

Ross himself was like-minded, it seemed, for presently he drew the younger man aside, to go to a window-embrasure which looked out over the firth.

"It is long since I saw an Earl of Moray," he said. "I served with your uncle, at the Siege of Perth, when he was earl. He died young."

Here was an unexpected opening for John. "It was then, my lord, that you slew Ranald of the Isles, I think? Brother of the present Lord John?"

"A traitor, he deserved his death!"

"No doubt. His brother, then, will not love you! He who seeks to take over much of your land, and mine."

Tight-lipped, Ross made no comment.

"It is to the advantage of us both, then, as well as to King David's cause, that John of the Isles be halted. Turned back. No?"

"That none so easy. Think you that I have not considered this?"

"Not easy, no, perhaps. But possible. For many fear his assaults and graspings. I have the royal authority to turn him back. And have been promised much support. Not least from Holy Church."

"The churchmen . . . !" That was scornful.

"They have considerable influence, my lord. And moneys to pay for men. The Bishop of Moray is on our side. I have spoken with many. Brodie, Ogstoun, Geddes, Rait and Duffus . . ."

"Duffus! These Comyns! They fight amongst themselves, not the enemy; a plague on them! My son's son should be Earl of Buchan. Earl Alexander Comyn died leaving only two daughters. One married to an Englishman and living in England. The other, Margaret, wed to my son William. So *their* child should now be earl."

"I know it. And would support your claim with the king. But not only with His Grace. I have spoken to Duffus on this. He is in favour of it. And he is seeking to have the other Comyns, or some of them, stop their bickering over lands, and united to halt the Islesmen. If they also support your grandson for the earldom of Buchan, then it should help to make it his."

The other stroked his long chin.

"I have, in the king's name, ordered the men of Forres and Nairn and Inverness burghs to rally in arms against John of the Isles, as well as the landed men. Join us then, my lord, with your strength, and we will halt the Islesmen. And serve your cause, and mine, and the king's. How say you?"

"If you can raise a sufficiency of men?"

"I am assured of well over one thousand already. Give me a week, and I think I will double that, at least. And these mounted. And you?"

"My earldom and lands can field a deal more than that. But they are far-scattered. It would take time to muster them hereabouts. More than any week."

John sought not to let his elation sound in his voice. Ross was coming round to agreement.

"You could raise some hundreds near at hand, I think? In a shorter time. From the Black Isle of Cromarty, Killearnan, this Beauly, Dingwall, Foulis. Five hundred?"

The older man snorted. "Five thousand, more like! Think you Ross, even Easter Ross, is some petty laird-ship!"

"No, no, my lord. It is but the time that I am considering. We must not delay overlong or the Islesmen will be up to Loch Ness."

"I know it. I am not a fool, Moray! One week from this day I can have three thousand and more here at Beauly. Can you say as much?"

John drew breath. "I can try," he jerked. "Keith the Marischal has promised aid. Whether he can get his people here by then, I know not. But his son, here, will be off to Dunnottar and Mar forthwith."

"Keith!" the other scoffed. "The Marischal he may be, in name, but is only a small baron. And Mar is a numb-skull. We need a large host. These Islesmen are fierce. I know — I have the like in my Wester Ross."

John did not argue with that. He had got what he wanted. He did not like this William of Ross, much preferring the son; but he could work with him, and must.

He changed the subject, asking after the son's wife and the child who was to be Earl of Buchan. He learned that they were not here at Edradour, but at his son's house of Cromarty.

They rejoined the ladies.

In the circumstances the visitors did not delay long at Edradour, with a sufficiency to see to elsewhere. Taking their leave, John declared that he would be back at Beauly in one week's time, hopefully with his thousands.

Agnes congratulated her son. She had been listening in the while.

It was a busy week indeed that followed, seeking to muster all the various and scattered manpower at Darnaway and at Inverness, Robert Keith off to Dunnottar for his father's contribution. Brodie of that Ilk proved helpful, as did Duncan Murray and Mackintosh at Inverness. Duffus had been fairly successful in converting his fellow-Comyns to cease their feuding, at least meantime, and co-operate against the Islesmen. And the Thane of Cawdor unexpectedly greatly assisted, as far as Nairn's people were concerned, for whom he had responsibilities. All in all, John was well pleased.

Some two thousand two hundred eventually mustered at Darnaway, amidst great to-do, indeed chaos, with some enmity shown amongst the arrivals, especially Comyns. Almost certainly never had Darnaway seen the like. They were all about to leave for Inverness, a less than orderly host, when Robert Keith put in an appearance from Dunnottar and Kintore with another three hundred. So they ought to reach the three thousand total.

Strung out in a fully mile-long column, many of the parties keeping their distance from others deliberately, they went by Cawdor and Croy and Culloden. At Inverness they did rather better than expected, picking up three hundred and fifty there, and with word that they would be joined by an unspecified number of Mackintoshes and

Shaws of Clan Chattan in the Moniack area, before they reached the Beauly crossing.

There were no fewer than four hundred Highlanders waiting for them at Moniack under the Mackintosh himself, these looked on askance in their kilts and plaids by some of the low-country levies. Much appreciative, John led all on over the ford into Ross. Probably never had an army in these parts had a woman riding at their head, but Black Agnes was not going to be left behind.

Beauly itself was seething with Rossmen, nearly five thousand, with more to come. So, in total, they made quite a major army, however uneasily the various contingents might view each other, William of Ross himself looking with scepticism at some of the new arrivals.

He was, at least, well informed as to the enemy, his people of Glen Urquhart and Balmacaan, much worried, sending him news. John of the Isles had indeed reached Loch Ness, and was already as far north as Invermoriston, alarming tidings. But there was word that might be encouraging. He was sending his Islesmen up both sides of the long loch. This meant, of course, that his numbers were divided meantime, and it was almost certain that the Lord of the Isles himself would be with the greater numbers on the west side, the most important and populous. So he would be the more vulnerable to attack, if that was the word where that man and his fierce Islesmen were concerned.

Ross, on his own ground and with the larger contingent of men, took it for granted that he was in command, John not offended at this, since he had had no real experience of warfare and battle, his mother actually more the warrior. Ross had planned his strategy. The west side of Loch Ness, almost thirty miles of it, could be dangerous for the attackers, for the hills came down fairly steeply to the waterside, leaving only a narrow strip of level ground, which meant that the enemy would be strung out along the shoreline. But there were incoming valleys from the north, down which assailants might descend upon them unexpectedly, and possibly divide them up into sections. Ross's plan was to send one group directly down the lochside, to seem to challenge the enemy head-on, which should preoccupy the Islesmen, while the main force would go down Strathglass, to the north, to Cannich and the head of Affric, there to split up, one section going down Glen Urquhart, to assail the foe in the Drumnadrochit area, the other proceeding on to Invermoriston, so getting behind the enemy, or at least dividing them. John of the Isles would almost certainly be with the leading files; so the Urquhart–Drumnadrochit section would be the most important for himself and Moray to lead.

These names did not mean a great deal to John, or even to his mother; but Ross clearly knew what he was at. It was his hope that the Islesmen's force would thus be split up into three, those on the south side of the mile-wide loch to be ignored, as unable to aid the others, who would be open to attack front and rear. It sounded good tactics.

Not all of their force was mounted, but nor would be any of the enemy probably, Highland warfare best carried out on foot generally. So the Mackintosh was put in charge of the foot, and sent on ahead up Strathglass, with instructions to have scouts out on the hillsides to discover the enemy whereabouts and send back word by running-gillies. The main force would head down Urquhart to the loch at Drumnadrochit.

Agnes approved of all this, so John agreed. There was no delay.

Up the River Beauly westwards they fairly quickly turned southwards down a side valley named Glen Convinth, themselves inevitably much strung out in the narrow valley floor. A few miles down this they came to the larger Glen Urquhart, into which they turned, hoping for news from Loch Ness-side, not far ahead now. They were not disappointed. The Mackintosh sent gillies back with the word that the Islesmen were indeed well up the lochside, sacking and burning the small communities as they went, extended over a couple of miles.

This information enabled the leadership to plan their tactics more in detail. The gillies were sent back to Mackintosh, telling him to attack forthwith down on Ness-side. This, it was hoped, would quickly be reported to the leadership up at the front, and cause them to halt and send back help to their assailed sections. Then, confronted by the main Ross and Moray force suddenly appearing ahead, there ought to be grave confusion created in the foe, and opportunity offered for successful attack.

As they neared Drumnadrochit, on Urquhart Bay, all began to prepare themselves for action, John sufficiently excited at the prospect. He hoped, however, that any great bloodshed might be avoided – for, after all, these Islesmen were their fellow-countrymen, however aggressive, and parley, terms, were much to be preferred to actual battle. At his suggestion, Robert Keith and his men were sent inland, further south, to remain on high ground until they saw the enemy passing below, wait a little longer and then charge down on them, this between the Mackintosh party and their main array.

Down at the lochside of Urquhart Bay, it was agreed to wait rather than go on to meet the enemy. Here there was more space than along the lochshore track, which would allow their cavalry force to spread out to make their assault rather than in narrow files, their numbers able to make greater impact on the inevitably strung-out Islesmen. For how long they would have to wait they could only guess. But Keith would send back warning.

In the event, the warning came quickly. The invaders were well ahead, at least their front ranks, scattered as they might be, this below the Bunloit area. They, the Keiths, were almost ready to descend on them.

Ross sent out a couple of scouts to watch. Bunloit, it seemed, was little more than a couple of miles from this bay.

As it transpired, they heard the enemy, or at least the conflict, before they saw it. There was a south-westerly breeze, carrying the sound of shouting and clash to them, this presumably the Keiths' assault. In a way this could invalidate their proposed tactics, if it turned the leading enemy ranks back to cope with the trouble behind, and so make this waiting on the more open ground ineffective.

This indeed was what developed. Their scouts returned to say that the enemy, many so far ahead, had turned back to aid their fellows. So wating at Urquhart was pointless, if the fighting was going to be nearer Bunloit, and still further south where the Mackintosh would be attacking. There was nothing for it but to ride on, down-loch, little more than three riding abreast as became necessary.

John was concerned about his mother. If it came to actual fighting, he did not want her up-front. Reluctantly she allowed herself to be positioned further back, but not all that far.

With Ross, his son, Brodie, Cawdor and others, John headed on, the sound of battle growing ever louder. This was all wrong, he thought, Keith bearing the brunt of it all, the main array not engaged. Planned tactics were all very well, but in actual war, so frequently, events made a nonsense of them.

The hillsides were coming very steeply down to the waterside now, narrowing the track still further. It was at the group of cot-houses of Auchnahannet that they actually saw the enemy, perhaps half a mile ahead – at least it was presumably the enemy, plus the Keiths, a mass of struggling men. Spurring their mounts, drawing swords and levelling lances, the Ross and Moray leaders waved on their long line of followers into a canter.

Preoccupied with the fighting as they were, the new assault was not evident to the Islesmen until it was fairly close, when those nearest began to turn in alarm to face the new threat. But they were hopelessly dispersed and dis-advantaged, on foot against horsemen, unable to make any sort of unified defence, assault front and rear, no room to spread out or to take avoiding action. The clash, when it came, was all in the attackers' favour.

John found himself slashing right and left in a sort of

figure-of-eight motion, driving into the tight mass of the enemy, himself pressed on by those behind, no heedful or selective fighting possible. The same would apply to all; wild and bloody, yelling confusion.

Carried on by the surge of the impact, suddenly John was brought to some sort of awareness of developments when he realised that a dirk-wielding man he was about to strike at was clad differently from these Islesmen, who dressed more like the Vikings of old, from whom they were part descended, in padded leather as armour, chain-mail only at the shoulders, and steel helmets of an ancient sort. This must be one of the Keiths. Shaking head in frustration, he stopped his slashing.

Raising his glance from the struggle going on around him, John became aware of something else that he had not noticed. Up on the beginnings of the slope to his right a small group of men stood surveying the scene, not fighting, these also Islesmen by their garb. One of them stood out, something about him authoritative, arrogantly grim. There was no need to question. This was the Lord of the Isles for certain, the descendant of the great Somerled who styled himself king, their prime target. And despite his haughty posture, he must be perceiving that his cause was lost, at least meantime.

John sought to pull his alarmed and nervous horse around, it rearing and curvetting, as he tried to signal to Ross, and point. But that man had already seen the watching party, indeed was gesturing towards them and turning his own mount in that direction. John, slashing again to clear a way for himself, drove half back to join Ross. There was no need for words. They were going to confront John of the Isles.

As, hindered by struggling men on foot, they forced passage through it all, Brodie and Cawdor joining them in this move, they reached the rising ground. Ahead of them the enemy leadership stood still, no backing off nor avoidance, no swords drawn, standing proud even in most evident defeat, this while the fighting went on below unheeding.

John and Ross rode up, to rein in a few yards from the waiting men, as the two groups stared at each other. Words were still unnecessary, indeed would not be heard in the din of yelling and screaming behind them. The position was sufficiently eloquent.

For long moments they remained thus, face to face. And, strangely, some recognition of the situation began to make itself apparent down amongst the combatants. Gradually the fighting lost its fury and urgency as the steel-wielders became aware of their leaders' position and attitudes. This was not so strange, in fact, men in battle fighting not only for their cause or duty but also for their own lives, could recognise that their individual release from threat and danger was becoming possible, that the battle was lost and won, their self-preservation now important. The assault and onset, the swiping and striking, lessened and became apparent to all.

Seeing it, something in John's mind rejoiced, and sheathing his sword, he reached instead for the hunting-horn which always hung at his side, and raising this to his lips, blew loud and long, this almost without thinking. But the effect of that clarion call was notable, telling as it was speedy. The last of the blows and battling died away, as men turned to gaze up at the two groups on the higher ground.

Oddly, it was John of the Isles whose voice rose first into the sudden comparative quiet, only comparative, for the moans and cries of the wounded still sounded.

"An end to this of slaying, I say!" he called, all but commanded. "Enough of it. I, John, mac Angus mac Alastair mac Angus mac Donald, say it!" That was surely the most lofty declaration of surrender anyone there had ever heard. "Who, then, are you?"

Ross all but choked. "I am Ross!" he got out. "William of Ross. Lord of this land which you despoil and defile so shamefully. You shall pay for it!"

"And I am the Earl of Moray," John added, in a different tone. "Come in King David's name and at his command."

"I greet you, then." That was to John; but turning to Ross, he said, "You it was who wickedly slew my brother, Ross! At Perth."

"As he deserved, man! A betrayer."

"A man can only betray one to whom he owes heed or service," the Islesman declared, dismissing the charge with a wave of the hand. "What now, Ross? And Moray?"

The two earls eyed each other. Here was a situation such as was seldom encountered, indeed.

"You and your robbers and rogues are now halted, and in our custody And will learn what it costs to harry Ross and his folk, Islesman!"

"Custody? How custody?"

"You shall discover!"

"As shall you. I have many more men than these. Many. None so far off. And you talk of custody! Watch your words, Ross."

"As have we, many . . ."

John saw this exchange as profitless. "My lord of the Isles," he put in, "this of taking over others' lands, and grievously breaking the king's peace, must stop, His Grace is much concerned. It is required that you bow to the royal authority, promise due submission and retire to your own lands and isles."

"Required, Moray? Who so requires it?"

"I do. In His Grace's royal name. This day we have shown you that we have the means to halt you, to force your submission. Better that you yield it, without more bloodshed."

"You speak foolishly, lordling. John of the Isles bows to no man."

"You bowed to Edward of England!" That was a different voice, a female one. Black Agnes had ridden up behind them. "And to Edward Balliol, Lord John. Now you would be wise, I think, to bow to David Bruce! Lest worse befall you."

"You are . . . ?"

"Agnes of Dunbar, sir. Who knows what she is saying.

56

Heed my son, here." Strangely this feminine intervention seemed to have more effect on the Islesman than had the others' challenges. He did not answer.

John tried again. "Face the facts, my lord," he urged. "Your people have been defeated. We have many more men to assail you than are here present. There are more behind you, also. And the clans are rallying to our banner and the royal cause. You have men across the loch, yes. But they cannot aid you swiftly."

"What do you want of me?" It was to the countess that was delivered.

"You are our prisoner," Ross declared. "You will learn what is required, never fear!"

"I am no man's prisoner! Nor will ever be. Try imprisoning the Lord of the Isles, and you will see! All the Isles, and much more, will show you so."

John at least saw that to try to take this man captive, and back to Beauly or Darnaway or elsewhere would be difficult, in the circumstances, and probably counter-productive. All the Hebrides, Inner and Outer, and most of the west coast of the Highlands would rise to seek to free him thereafter, and so well supplied with longships as they all were, could gravely damage the eastern coastal areas. It would amount to civil war, on quite a major scale. This would not help the king's cause. Peace was what was required, not war.

His mother saw the same, whether or not Ross did – and it was Ross's lands that would suffer worst. "Come into the king's peace, my lord," Agnes urged. "No more lands raiding. Return you to your own parts. An end to this killing and ravishment. Peace and amity in the realm. And you and your people will be the better for it."

Ross snorted. "Aye – and compensation paid for all damage done to my lands! Think you that I am to be treated so?"

"Your Wester Ross lies open!" came the warning. "Forget it not! As for paying taxes and dues, what benefit do I gain, or any of my people, from such charges?"

"All the realm's landholders have to pay them," John said. "That the king may defend it from our enemies, preserve our independence, and protect and cherish his people."

"*I* protect my own!"

"Perhaps, my lord. But if England took over our Scotland, as it ever seeks to do, could you hold out against them, alone?"

The other shrugged.

Agnes spoke again. "You and your forebears have accepted the King of Scots as Ard Righ, High King. Do you now deny it?"

"I do not. But I do not accept others, his minions, as of authority." That word minions was spoken with disdain, and the Islesman looked at Ross.

"Yet the earls here present, are the *ri*, or lesser kings, who support the Ard Righ, no?"

"*I* pay heed only to the Ard Righ, lady."

John took a chance. "If the Ard Righ David spoke with you, in person, would you heed then?"

"I would not go down, like any servant, to bow before him."

"But if he came north, to you?"

That produced a pause. "That would be . . . different."

"We could take you to the king, captive," Ross asserted.

"Try you that, sirrah!"

Frowning, John shook his head. That was not how to deal with the Islesman. "I will speak with His Grace on this. He sent me here as his lieutenant. You will meet him if he comes? And pay your due fealty as one of his great lords if we leave you free now?"

"On my own ground, yes. As is ever required of fealty-payers."

John looked at Ross almost challengingly. "The Lord of the Isles gives his word. *That* none may doubt; I say that we should leave him meantime. Free to return to his own isles. And inform the King's Grace of this word."

"*Leave* me to go? Think any to hold John of the Isles?"

Ross scowled, but said nothing. He required John's help hereafter with the king over having his grandson appointed Earl of Buchan.

"You invade here. You stand on Ross land, my lord. And your men across the loch are in Moray, my land," John pointed out. "We cannot leave you here thus. That you must see."

"I will go back some way. But only some way. Wait there. Arkaig, Clunes country is mine. Cameron is under my sway. His Arkaig and Morar. I will meet the Ard Righ at Bunarkaig and Clunes. That is my word."

John looked at his mother, who nodded. Then at Ross. "Very well. So be it. I will tell His Grace. You will hear, I think, in due course, wherever you are." To Ross he turned. "So, my lord of Ross, we can leave it so? Go our ways with our people, and let our friend go his! That is best. An end to invasion and bloodshed. The king's peace restored. You see it?"

His mother backed that. "It is wise and right," she said.

Ross shrugged, lips tight, and reined his horse round, sour of face.

John inclined his head to the other John, and gestured to Agnes to turn also, and to ride with him downhill, leaving the Islesman standing there. Thereafter little opportunity developed for debate or argument, while separating the two sides of the so recent battle – both of which were undoubtedly glad to be spared further fighting – and collecting the wounded and dead. Ross demonstrated his disapproval of the situation by riding off, leaving his son to bring on his people.

"You did that well," Black Agnes told her son. "It was the only way to gain our ends. William of Ross is stubborn. But the alternative was war. And Ross would have been the greatest sufferer. He will live to thank you! As, I judge, will David Bruce."

"I hope so. If the Isles come into his peace, that will be a great step forward for the crown. The rest will follow . . ."

At Beauly they took their leave of a disgruntled Ross and

his folk, and led their own contingent back to Inverness and eventually to Darnaway. There was dispersal, but with the word to be ready for remustering at short notice, if required.

John and his mother would be for the south in a day or two, to see the king. It was to be hoped that David would see it their way.

After their long journey, on horses borrowed from the Marischal, they found the monarch still at the Abbey of the Holy Rood in Edinburgh, in the company of Robert the High Steward, his kinsman. This time they were not out hawking, but in conference with an embassage from France, come seeking Scottish gestural threats against Edward of England, to inhibit the Plantagenet's occupation of Guienne, or Aquitaine. The king was reluctant to do anything such, anxious not to disturb the present uneasy peace with England; but the Auld Alliance was built upon the co-operation of the two realms against English aggression. So the interview was proving difficult, David and his advisers temporising, the Frenchmen urgent.

The arrival of John and his mother provided a welcome break in this, and indeed their report, both as regards the Mar and Kintore problem and the Moray and Islesmen situation, was heeded with something like relief, in more ways than one.

"John of the Isles would have me to go up to Inverness or thereabouts to receive his fealty? He is prepared to yield? To give it?" the king asked. "To end his invasions and revolts? Here is scarcely believable news!" And he looked at the Steward, who nodded.

"How much reliance can be placed on this?" Robert Stewart demanded. "That one is arrogant, and prides himself on his claims of independence. Like all his forebears. He is not the one to change. I know – he wed my daughter!"

"He gave his word," John said. "Before Ross and

ourselves and his own chiefs. And he is proud, yes – but proud as to his word, also. He will not break it, I think. He could withdraw it, but only before Your Grace. He said that he would receive you on his own ground, as is the custom for fealty-giving; but not come south here to do so, as at coronations. He will not go back on that, Sire, I judge.''

"My son worked your royal cause very well with the Islesman, Highness," Black Agnes said. "It was featly done. It did not please Ross. He is less skilful. He was for seeking to imprison John of the Isles. That would have provoked war, which surely is not your wish? This of freeing him to make his submission to your Grace, even on his own ground, was the wise course, far-sighted.''

"I see it, yes. It will bring the Isles under the crown, bring peace and accord. After so long."

"It is a long way to go to appease a prideful rebel and subject," the Steward said. "You, the king."

"But worth the journey, I would say."

"None so great a journey, Sire," John reminded. "We went, by ship, up to Stonehaven. You could go, in one of our Dunbar ships, right to Inverness. A day and a half's sailing. And in no great discomfort."

"That is well. I will do it, yes. See you, Robert, this also will give us some aid with these Frenchmen. Tell them that I have to forge peace with the Lord of the Isles. He who has supported England and Balliol. That will be in France's favour. We will let Edward Plantagenet hear of it! He will not like this. Charles of France will perceive it of value.''

"Perhaps . . ."

"When should this be? This meeting with the Islesman?" David asked.

"The sooner the better, Sire," John advised. "He may not wait at this place in the Great Glen overlong, but return to his Hebrides. More difficult, unsuitable for Your Grace to reach him, to go seeking him there. And it is now near to November. Winter storms could be coming. No time for sea-voyaging.''

"Aye – and it would get rid of these Frenchmen if I have to go at once! I think that this young man has served us well, Robert. And the Countess Agnes, to be sure. You will come with me?"

"If it is your wish . . ."

So it was arranged. The king and the Steward would come to Dunbar in a day or two, and John would have a ship ready. The entire mission ought not to take more than a week, if that.

The Cospatrick mother and son returned home, with many royal thanks.

At Dunbar, George was glad to assist in providing a vessel and making its cabins as comfortable as possible for its distinguished passengers. He congratulated his brother, wishing that he had been with him to witness it all. He had not realised that John had it in him!

Three days later the monarch and Robert Stewart arrived, with a few lords, including the lame Earl of Carrick, the Steward's eldest son. George announced that he also was going to accompany the royal party, one more earl perhaps being of some help. His mother declared however that she had played a sufficient part, and would remain at home, where she had plenty to see to.

It was the oldest ship in the Dunbar possession, the *Meg of Skateraw*, which had been chosen for this voyage, most others being necessary for the transport of Lammermuir wool, the main source of Dunbar wealth, to the Low Countries, and in consequence had but little of passenger accommodation, and smelling strongly of oily fleeces; but the *Meg* had been used in the past for carrying passengers, as well as goods, particularly to Norway and the Baltic, and so had more and better cabin space. So, prepared as it had been for a crossing to Flanders, it was unloaded and made as convenient as possible for the distinguished company, although the smell of wool still lingered. But only the one night, each way, was expected to be spent therein. The passengers expressed no complaints; after all, using the

Meg was much to be preferred to four long days of riding through mainly mountainous country, with doubtful over-night lodging.

David Bruce was an easy monarch to get on with, seldom distancing himself from his companions, and not greatly concerned with rank and status of his associates – as was indicated by the person of his present wife and queen, Margaret Drummond, no princess, and the daughter of no great lord, widow of an unimportant knight. He now showed a lively interest in the shipboard activities, questioning their skipper about all, to that man's embarrassment.

After passing the one night at Dunbar Castle, they set sail northwards, and with the prevailing south-westerly breeze made good progress, the seas not rough. As they passed the Isle of May, John told its dramatic story, which most of his hearers knew nothing of, and St Ethernan's lighthouse-beacon. Up the Fife coast they sailed, to cross the mouth of the Tay estuary, and on beyond along the Angus shoreline, past Arbroath, where the renowned Declaration of Independence had been drawn up and signed by the nobility, in the presence of David's father, Robert the Bruce. Strange as it might seem, none of the passengers, save John and his brother, had ever sailed up this way before, although the Steward had frequently taken ship along the west coast from his Clydeside lands. All were most interested.

They won as far as Montrose before the October darkness closed in; and with a long, rolling Norse Sea swell, most sought their bunks early, after being modest with their evening eating and drinking, the king wondering how the shipmen knew that they sailed a sure route by night, and being told of the compass, first invented by the Chinese allegedly, the use of the stars, and the tides' effects – and of course the need to keep well offshore, to avoid reefs and islands.

Daylight found them just reaching the great turn west-wards round the mighty headlands of Cairnbulg Point and

Kinnairds Head, of the long Aberdeenshire coast, to follow that of Buchan and Moray to the mouth of the wide Moray Firth. They had nearly ninety miles of this to cover, to the surprise of most of the passengers, before suddenly the firth narrowed in to little more than a mile, between Ardersier, after Nairn, and the Chanonry Point of the Black Isle of Cromarty, in Ross, Inverness only a dozen miles further.

They docked at that town as dusk was falling, and made their way, on foot necessarily, up to the royal castle. The king had never been here before, but assumed that his father had lodged in it on occasion. The keeper, Mackintosh, had been warned on the last visit that he would probably have a royal guest one of these days, and was duly prepared. So comfort was fair enough,

John asked what the word was about the Lord of the Isles, to be told that, as far as was known, he was still down in the Cameron country of Arkaig and Morar. There had been no more raiding. John told him to send a messenger to inform the Earl of Ross, at Beauly or Dingwall or wherever he was at present, of the king's coming.

David, it transpired, was quite prepared to ride down the Great Glen to this Arkaig to meet the Islesman; but John had come to the opinion, with the Steward's advising, that it would be much more suitable and fitting if that man came here to Inverness to make his fealty; after all, the monarch had come hundreds of miles thus far to meet him. *He* could make some small gesture. Let him bring a handful of earth from this Arkaig or wherever, to put into his boot when he paid his leal duty, as was the custom at coronations, when lords could say that they were standing on their own ground, as required, when making obeisance, so saving the monarch from having to travel the length and breadth of the land.

Recognising that this suggestion might call for some careful persuading, John decided to go himself to the Cameron country, if possible to do the persuading. George said that he would accompany his brother, and Carrick, the

Steward's son, offered to do likewise, so that three earls coming to make the suggestion might induce even the proud Lord of the Isles.

The king would meantime wait at Inverness for William of Ross, and visit some of the surroundings to meet prominent magnates such as Brodie, Cawdor, Ogstoun, the Mackintosh and Grant. Also to knight Comyn of Duffus.

The trio of earls, then, with a couple of Mackintosh guides, borrowed horses to ride down Loch Ness next day. They noted that there was already a dusting of snow on some of the mountain-tops. They had some forty-odd miles to go to Bunarkaig, it seemed, where they would be into territory over which the Islesman claimed superiority, whatever the Camerons might think of that, and where he had indicated that he would be based, for how long was unclear. It was good for John to be riding again in this area, peacefully and not, as before, prepared for battle. He was able to view much more of the land.

Once past Urquhart Bay he was into new territory for him, and dramatic and exciting terrain it was, great peaks and escarpments on either side, cataracts and waterfalls, herds of deer drifting over the hillside. John wondered whether they would see one of the fabulous monsters said to inhabit this Loch Ness, and which St Columba was alleged to have confronted all those centuries ago.

In this they were disappointed, however.

At the head of the long loch, at Bunoich, the mountains closed in still more sternly, as they followed the winding course of the River Oich, past the mouths of deep glens with plunging torrents, Fearna, Graidhe, Vigar, Garry, past Loch Oich itself to another of the Great Glen lochs, Lochy. Seven miles up the west side of this, rough going, was Clunes and the mouth of the Arkaig, Bunarkaig.

There was no sign of any large encampment here, only a few cot-houses and shacks, the inhabitants of which told them that the Lord of the Isles had gone up the short River

Arkaig to Achnacarry, Cameron of Lochiel's house, and was thought to be there still.

Another couple of miles, then, due westwards now, and they came to the Cameron chief's principal residence, a large hallhouse on the south side of the river near the foot of Loch Arkaig. Many men were camped in the vicinity, clearly Islesmen, which seemed to indicate that their lord was present.

An evening meal was being eaten when the new arrivals were conducted to the house, and, welcome or otherwise, Highland hospitality prevailed, and the trio were invited to partake by Lochiel, an elderly man of quiet dignity. The Lord of the Isles, sitting there with some of his chieftains, eyed them civilly but questioningly, as John introduced his brother. He did not need to introduce Robert of Carrick, for these two were brothers-in-law, however stiff in their relationship.

Seated at the long table, John was not long in informing all of the position, and what brought them there. "His Grace the King has graciously acceded to come to agreement with you, my lord, and receive your fealty," he declared "He has, indeed, travelled all the way up to Inverness for this purpose, a long journey. He hopes that you will come to Inverness there to meet him, and pay your due respects."

"Inverness?" the Islesman exclaimed. "My word was that I should meet him on my own ground, as is proper."

"That was understood. But His Grace has come these hundreds of miles to see you, a notable act for the King of Scots. You, my lord, can surely make the smaller move of riding up Ness-side, to enter his peace? You can take some handful of the earth from the ground here to put in your boot when you take the oath, as is done by us all at royal coronations, so that we stand on our own soil. That will preserve your right and custom."

The other looked at Cameron and his Isles supporters sitting there. "It is not what I offered," he said. "Is this Ross's work?"

"No. He does not know of it yet. It is mine. Ours." John glanced at his companions. "We are three of the earls, the *ri*, of the ancient realm, who support and advise the Ard Righ. We deem this right. You, as Lord of the Isles, are of a like standing, not an earl, but of high ranking."

"It is what *I* would do as holder of an earldom," George put in.

"And I, as a cousin of King David. And your kinsman," Carrick added.

"When, when would this be?" That at least sounded as though the thing was being considered.

"So soon as might be. We would escort you back to Inverness, assuring you of your free return, in the king's peace."

"I do not trust William of Ross. But, with your word, I will do it."

John tried not to give a sigh of relief. "That is well, my lord. Shall we ride in the morning?"

The other nodded.

So that was that. Thankfully John changed the subject, to ask their host, Lochiel, whether he and Clan Cameron had ever had trouble with Ross, whose lands came fairly close? If so, here might be opportunity to improve matters.

It was the Islesman who answered that. "Ross would be a fool to risk anything such, knowing well that I would protect the Camerons!" he barked.

Subjects of conversation would have to be carefully chosen here, it was clear. The visitors confined their remarks to cattle-rearing, milling, the snow in winter, deer-hunting and the like. Carrick helped by asking, however drily, after his sister Margaret and her family.

They made an early retirement that night, to quite comfortable quarters.

In the morning they discovered that they were to go in some style to Inverness, for John of the Isles appeared to be taking quite a proportion of his men with him, not only his chieftains, presumably to emphasise his declared princely status. These were not mounted, although he himself borrowed a garron from Lochiel. This had its drawbacks, for these Islesmen were not running-gillies and much too proud to hurry, although they walked well enough. It meant, with over forty miles to go, that they would take two days to do it. So the three earls had to ride slowly indeed, at first, until presently the Islesman declared that they should go without him. He did not require any escort. He would see them in Inverness on the morrow, towards evening. This was all but a command. The trio decided that it made sense. They had little doubt but that the other would complete the journey as agreed, but in his own time.

They spurred on.

At Inverness Castle they found all well. William of Ross had arrived, with his son and even his small grandson, who hopefully was to be Earl of Buchan, the king quite prepared to accede to this. The newly knighted Comyn of Duffus was there also, with some of his friends. The castle had not been so full ever before, probably.

The monarch was well pleased that the Lord of the Isles had agreed to come, and was on his way; the Steward even more so, for he had doubted whether his awkward son-in-law would do so.

Next day, not to seem to stay waiting for the Islesmen, the king's party rode the dozen miles south to Moy, the Mackintosh seat, amongst quite lofty mountains, where, on an island in a mile-long loch, rose the castle, out to which the royal company had to be ferried in currachs. A tiny islet was pointed out to them, the Eilean nan Clach, Isle of the Stone, on which, only a foot or so above the water, stood a gallows, where the chief could hang offenders, or, if they could not swim, allow them to be drowned by rising waters produced by heavy rains.

Well received, the visitors heard many tales of clan feuding and feats of daring, the Clan Chattan, of which the Mackintosh was head, being a redoubtable lot, its symbol being a wild cat, and the motto "Touch not the Cat but a Glove!", a warning to be heeded.

When all got back to Inverness they found John of the

Isles already at the castle there, his men surrounding its eminence, and being eyed askance by the citizenry. He actually greeted David Bruce as though *he* were the master of the house, almost like a fellow-monarch, the king bemused, the Steward most upset.

Right away the Islesman took the lead. "David, son of Robert, I, John mac Angus mac Alastair mac Angus mac Donald, come to hail you, and welcome you to these Highland parts. Your father and mine were good friends and comrades-in-arms. I now would reforge that link between my Isles and your realm, to the weal and satisfaction of both."

The king, blinking, cleared his throat. "I, I greet you also," he said.

"That is well. I learn that you hold certain requirements as to revenues and dues, for the support and maintenance of your throne and power. I will be pleased to grant that. Also that you, the redoubtable lord David, by the Grace of God, have been moved against my person over some such negligences in the past. This I can regret. I engage, therefore, that I and my vassals with me, all extend the hand of friendship." And he held out his hand, with something of a flourish.

David, glancing over at his supporting lords, found words. "It is well that you do, John of the Isles." He did not extend his own hand, however.

"This of what your people have called fealty," the other went on. "I have the earth in my boot, as it appears is the usage, from my lands, those under my sway. So that, on my own ground, I offer you this my hand. In token of goodwill, for here and hereafter." And again that hand was extended.

Ross raised voice, from behind the king. "Here is vaunting insolence!" he exclaimed. "I told Your Grace—"

"Quiet, you!" That was rapped out, and not by the monarch.

John Dunbar almost spoke in concern, but the High

Steward was before him. "Sire, the Lord of the Isles comes into Your Grace's peace. In his own fashion. That he does it thus is surely . . . sufficient. He is my good-son, and I know his measure."

The Islesman had lowered his hand again and looked around him, head high. "I come thus, on the Earl of Moray's counsel. Was I misled?"

"I see my lord's coming today as of due worth, Highness," John said then.

The king nodded. "So *I* see it. So be it." He held out his two hands, palms a little way apart. "I accept your homage, my lord John of the Isles," he said. "Your hand in mine."

The Islesman inclined his head, scarcely a bow, and extended his arm again so that his hand went within the king's two. "My fealty, my lord King!" he announced briefly.

"Accepted!" David said, equally so.

The three hands were parted. The thing was done. And all around them were murmurs, and Ross's snorts. But John was not the only one to let his breath out in relief.

There were long moments of inaction as men wondered what next. Then David smiled, and gestured.

"My lord, come you. We shall drink to this day's accord. Wine, my lords and friends all." And the monarch led the way over to the table, where the flagons of wine and the tankards were set, all following him.

But not all were so evidently pleased with this situation, there being more murmurs. The folk of Ross and Moray, Buchan and Strathspey had long had reason to fear the Islesmen, and some saw this as weakness on the royal part. Ross it was who gave voice to these doubts, and loudly.

"Are we to trust this arrogant man?" he demanded. "Fine words he uses – but mostly steel he wields! What certainty have we that his promises here will be kept? Some surety he must give." He did not actually address the king but looked at the High Steward.

Not a few clearly backed these sentiments.

71

David frowned, tapping finger on the table-top.

John spoke up. "The Lord of the Isles gives his liege-lord his word, here before all. That we can and must trust."

"*You* may, Moray! New come to the north. We here are less easily assured."

The Islesman turned to look at Ross with haughty disdain, not deigning to speak.

"Some token of good faith." The Master of Ross supported his father. "Is that so much to ask?"

"I trust the Lord John's word," the king said then.

"Your Grace is generous!" Ross declared. "But *we* here have to live with these Islesmen and their raidings."

Again there were supporting cries, all highly unsuitable in the monarch's presence.

The Steward raised a hand. "My lord King, your royal will is, and must be, paramount. But, to allay fears here, some warrant, some pledge of good faith, might be considered by my lord John. His wife is my own daughter. So I am concerned in it all. I would suggest that my grandson, Donald, might come down to my house on the Clyde, there to bide in my care meantime. Not as hostage, only token. This should serve, Sire?" But it was at the Islesman that he looked.

The king filled a tankard with wine, and raised it. "Here is to goodwill and the realm's betterment!" And he drank. After a moment or two, few there failed to follow suit.

David handed a filled tankard to John of the Isles, who accepted it with a combination of nod and shrug. He sipped, then put the pewter goblet down on the table again, bowed after a fashion, and then, turning, strode from the hall, his chieftains after him, without further speech. It had been a very silent fealty-giving.

Glancing at the king, the Steward went off after his son-in-law, no doubt to arrange the matter of this Donald's visit southwards.

In the talk and discussion that followed, Ross still looking disapproving, the monarch drew John aside.

"My lord, I thank you for this. You have served very well. I am grateful, and will not forget it. You shall be rewarded. And not only for this of the Isles. But for the Mar and Kintore matter also. Your brave mother has a worthy son." He turned to George who stood nearby. "*Sons*, I should say, since you assisted, my lord of Dunbar."

"I but accompanied my brother, Sire. He effected all. But I will seek to serve Your Grace well, in my own fashion. In the south." And grimacing, he added, "Better than our father!"

"Ah, yes. But that is past, done with. Your mother made up for it . . ."

Later there was feasting, but without the Lord of the Isles, who it seemed had departed forthwith, the Steward reporting that the son, Donald, would come south to him in due course. Ross did not shun the feast, but clearly had not changed his opinions.

In the morning, John conducted the monarch and his associates back to the ship at the docks for the return voyage, he being left with more expressions of gratitude and esteem, of which he felt scarcely deserving. George did not sail with the others, but remained with his brother, to visit Darnaway and see more of the lands of Moray.

John well realised that, with all this of his duties in the royal cause, he had neglected those of the earldom that he had inherited. There would be much of this to attend to, after years of no residential earl; but at least he would have the goodwill and assistance of the friends he had made in it all, Brodie, Cawdor, Ogstoun and Mackintosh. He recognised that the areas to the west, Strathspey, Cromdale, Rothes and Glenlivet, the Leslie and Grant country, he had yet to visit, to make his mark. Moray was a vast earldom, and it would take some time for him to get to it in any way fully, as he ought. But, that time he would make . . .

7

In the event, John was not given much time to explore his
territories and meet with his prominent vassals. A summons came to him from the king to attend a Privy Council
at Edinburgh, this just before Christmas, of all times. It
might be none so inconvenient for the lords and prelates
who lived in the south, but for those in the north with the
snow-covered Highlands to ride through, it was a trial
indeed.

John had not realised that he had become a member of
the Privy Council. It was not automatic for all earls to sit
thereon, although probably most did. Presumably it was at
the royal appointment, apart from the established officers
of state who sat by right.

So it was the long and difficult road for John, first to the
Spey, to follow that river up along the borders of Badenoch, separate Comyn country some sixty miles, past
Rothes and Craigellachie, Grantown-of-Cromdale, Dul-
nain and Nethy and the Alvies, More and Beg, to King-
ussie, amongst white, snow-covered mountains and passes
and ice-bound lochs all the way, no country for winter
travel. When the lengthy Spey at last turned due westwards, into the Monadh Liath or Grey Mountains of
Laggan, he and his small escort had to start real climbing,
due south, up past Dalwhinnie to the high Pass of Drumochter, one of the loftiest in the land, where their horses
faced their greatest test in feet-deep snow. John perceived
that, in future, he would have to seek to base some sort of
sea-going vessel at Inverness, to avoid this sort of winter
journeying.

They had picked up a local guide at Dalwhinnie, advisedly, where they had spent the night in a monkish hospice; without him they would have been hard put to it to win through that pass. When eventually they passed two great peaks called, apparently, the Boar of Badenoch and the Sow of Atholl, they were thankful to be able to see the land beginning to slope down ahead of them into the northern parts of the great earldom of Atholl, and their guide could leave them. Even so, going was not easy and distances covered only moderate. Fortunately these conditions were well understood by the churchmen, and their travellers' hospices set never far apart. The monks who kept these shelters must have to lead grim lives in winter.

Grateful when at last they won out of the mountains into the lower lands of the Tay, at Dunkeld and Scone and Perth, they had covered about two hundred miles and it had taken them six days; and they had another sixty to go. John could not remember ever having made so difficult a journey.

At Edinburgh, the brothers found the council meeting being held, not at Holyrood Abbey but up in the rock-top citadel, this on account of the large attendance and the more spacious accommodation in the great hall there. The fact that so many had come, despite the weather conditions and the interruption of Yuletide celebrations, was significant, for all the absence of some from the far north, these including the earls of Ross, Sutherland and Caithness. The importance of this gathering was the more emphasised.

John and George learned that the king was going to seek to make up for this awkwardly timed occasion by offering Christmas festivities thereafter for any and all who would care to attend, with their families where possible, rather than travel long distances homewards in the conditions, the celebrations to be held down at the abbey rather than in the grim fortress.

Although it turned out that they had another day to wait before the delayed start of the meeting, and found accommodation in the city below, the brothers were not long in learning of the reason for this evidently so important council. It was concerned with finance, and most urgently concerned, King David in a state of agitation. Something to do with Edward of England.

Next noonday, the delegates met, and proved to include not a few who were not actually members of the Privy Council: earls, lords, chiefs, bishops and mitred abbots. Although the Chancellor, as usual, presided, the monarch himself took charge from the start, his anxiety very evident.

He explained. His release from captivity in England, after the disaster of Neville's Cross in 1346, had been gained in 1357 only by agreement to pay a vast sum in ransom money, no less than one hundred thousand merks in silver, admittedly in instalments, but these of six thousand merks per year. That was twelve years ago. The payments had been made, at first, fairly regularly but in time had rather tailed off, with the Scots treasury empty. Edward the Third had not made overmuch fuss about this at the time. But now the Plantagenet himself appeared to have got into debt in a large way, this through extravagant living and his fondness for chivalrous activities, tournaments, international contests, grand entertainments and the like, but above all the building up of a large navy of fighting-ships. Now he was demanding full payment of the ransom total, which it seemed still amounted to almost eighty thousand merks, a dire total. And he was reinforcing his demands by reminding that the truce between the two nations, entered into at the time of David's release, was due to expire on the second day of February 1370, that is, in two months' time. Edward was not actually threatening war or invasion, but if the truce was not renewed various grievous conditions would come into force, short of battle but punishing enough. There could be attacks on Scots trading-ships sailing to the Low Countries and France by those English warships, ever a menace; customs duties for Scots goods going to England; more March raiding across the border; pressure on France to end the Auld Alliance; these and more. It all amounted to a most grave and wounding situation for the realm if the moneys were not paid within two months.

They all heard this with with dismay and apprehension. Pockets and purses and sporrans were going to be raided, and in a big way, most obviously.

The king waved to the High Chamberlain, who acted as keeper of the nation's treasury. That man looked grim. He declared that he had been assessing how the necessary moneys could be raised, to avoid national calamity. Various means must be devised, none of them going to be popular with great or small. Holy Church, holder of so much of the realm's wealth, would be besought to aid by increasing its contributions. Customs and excise duties, both on exports and imports, would have to be raised, but not so greatly as to damage trade seriously. The revenues on all crown lands granted since the death of King Robert the Bruce must be returned to the treasury, and these were large, owing to His present Grace's generosity. The nation's coinage would require to be reduced in silver content, although this would inevitably devalue the Scots merk against the English mark. But as well as all this, the assessments on all lands and estates, ecclesiastical and lay, would have to be raised; there had been no reassessment since the reign of King Alexander the Third; and certain lords, even earls, had failed to pay their dues of late, other than just John of the Isles!

This last, of course, had the meeting in all but turmoil, its members hit where it hurt most. The Chancellor had to bang on the table for quiet.

The Chamberlain went on, glancing at the monarch. Bishoprics and abbacies, sheriffdoms, royal burghs, earldoms, lordships and baronies, must all increase their contributions, and substantially, if the arrears were to be paid. He reckoned that to produce eighty thousand silver merks, this before the coinage could be devalued, would demand every penny they could raise. It probably would be necessary to pay a first major instalment by the beginning of February, with assurances that the rest would follow quickly thereafter.

There was more unfavourable comment, and discussion between individual members. Near where John and George sat, Campbell of Lochawe and the MacDougall of Lorne were debating closely. These two must have had a difficult journey also to be here, although they might well have come by ship to the Clyde.

The king held up a hand for silence. "I suggest a commission, to confer on this, with the Chamberlain and the High Steward," he said. "To decide on the necessary levies and amounts to be collected. And without delay. We have but two months. A small commission. Representative. Perhaps one earl, one lord, one baron, one bishop, one abbot and the provost of a royal burgh. This under my lord Chamberlain. To present their findings to another meeting of this council. Say in one week's time. And a parliament will be necessary, to pass all. Forty days is necessary to call a parliament, so we call it forthwith. That should enable us to collect at least a fair amount, sufficient for the first instalment. Is it agreed?"

There were noddings and murmurs, few enthusiastic.

One voice spoke up more loudly. "Sire, John MacDougall, Lord of Lorne, and myself, Campbell of Lochawe, have thought on this. We have decided that we double our present assessments on our lands. In the hope that others will do likewise."

There were many indrawn breaths at that. Double! The Campbell was Sir Gillespik, son of Bruce's friend Sir Neil of Lochawe; and this MacDougall of Lorne was another direct descendant of the great Somerled of the Isles, and reputedly no friend of his far-out kinsman, the present lord thereof.

"That is a notable gesture, Sir Gillespik," the king commended. "If others will do as well, we should raise our moneys without overmuch of difficulty. I say that *you* should be on this commission."

All there eyed each other. The Campbell, for whatever

reason, was not seeking popularity with most, however much he might gain with the monarch.

The Steward spoke. "Since it seems that I am to serve this commission, I would suggest for it the Primate of Holy Church, the Bishop of St Andrews; the Abbot of Melrose; the Earl of Dunbar and March; the Thane of Cawdor; and the provost of this city of Edinburgh. That, with Campbell of Lochawe, gives a fair nationwide delegation. Does Your Grace agree?"

"It sounds well to me," David acceded. "Are there any objections? Or other nominations?"

None was voiced aloud, whatever doubts and questions were unspoken. This doubling of contributions by the Campbell was simmering in men's minds.

"Very well," the Chamberlain said. "We can leave it thus, meantime. Another meeting in one week's time. If those mentioned for the commission will wait with me, we can plan our course."

"I thank all for attendance," the king added. "And commend Sir Gillespik Campbell's worthy offer. Hereafter, my lords and friends all, you are welcome down at the Abbey of the Holy Rood. With wives and families, such as may be in this city meantime, to partake of festivity and cheer. I hope to see many there." He rose, and all must stand also, the meeting over.

George Cospatrick, less than delighted at his nomination for this commission, had to stay behind with the Steward and Chamberlain to arrange their deliberations hereafter. So John went off with the Earl of Carrick. He was thankful that *he* had not been proposed for this duty. He was all but ignorant as to what were the present assessments payable by the earldom of Moray – he would have to ask his mother about that – but presumably they would have to be increased, like all the others. He saw the need, of course, and what could be the possible consequences of failure; he could not complain. Carrick was more vocal.

When George rejoined his brother, preparatory to making their way to the abbey, he proved to be more concerned over his wool trade than over the increasing of his two earldoms' assessments. The Lammermuir wool, exported to the Netherlands and elsewhere, was the principal source of his revenue, and if customs and excise duties were extended, it could have a serious effect on the trade, and therefore on the folk of Dunbar and Eyemouth in especial. On the other hand, if these ransom moneys were not paid, and on time, those English ships-of-war, pirates as he called them, already apt to be a danger, could become a still worse menace. He was a worried man – and not alone in that. The Scots lords were not used to financial worries.

In the early evening they repaired to Holyrood, and found great numbers assembled there, many women and young people amongst them. A splendid feast was produced, whether paid for by the monarch or the abbot they were not informed, although it struck John that, with all this worry over moneys, such bounty might not appear quite suitable. To be sure, Scotland was not really a poor country, save in actual money, silver; of real wealth, lands and goods, flocks and herds, manpower, there was no lack.

Before the repast, the king came to John to tell him that he had not forgotten his promise that his efforts in the matters of the Islesman, and of Mar and Kintore, would be rewarded. It was unfortunate that this sorry business of the ransom money had come up, with grievous charges laid upon all landholders, Moray included. But some gesture he could make. The customs of Elgin and Forres were quite substantial, and John would have a pension of one hundred and fifty merks from each, with another thirty from Inverness, this for his great help over John of the Isles. And one hundred and fifty from the customs of Aberdeen, over Mar. Also he was to have the baronies of Deskford and Findlater, in the sheriffdom of Banff, convenient for his Moray lands, these having fallen into the Crown through lack of heirs.

John was quite overwhelmed by this generosity, declaring that he had done no more than his simple duty, and no rewards were called for, but had his shoulder patted in reply.

After the meal, the hall was cleared for dancing, this although there was an insufficiency of females for all the men to partner, especially young and attractive ones, these, few in the circumstances, being eyed assessingly by lords that way inclined. John and his brother were nowise indifferent, being normal young men.

"Yonder, Johnnie," George said, not exactly pointing.

"The one with hair like ripe corn?"

"No, no – that is one of the Stewards daughters, Carrick's sister. I mean the one with the dark hair and much bosom. I think that she is with Lennox."

"You are welcome to her! That one will be huge when she is older!"

"All the warmer in bed! But, for dancing with, be not so . . ."

He got no further when a woman came over to them, and an unexpected and especial woman at that, Queen Margaret Drummond, no less.

"My royal husband says that I should dance with you, my lord of Moray," she said, smiling. "How say you?"

Surprised indeed, John bowed. "Your Grace, this is . . . most kind. An honour, indeed. I, I am no notable dancer . . ."

"But a notable young man, I am told. Son of a notable mother!" And she held out an arm to him. He bowed again, and took her hand to lead her on to the dance-floor. Margaret Drummond was a handsome woman, in her late thirties, tall and well built. She by no means held herself away from John, and after the first few steps he found himself enjoying the procedure. He was aware of the interested watchers as they progressed round the hall, not least that young flaxen-haired woman he had remarked on to his brother.

When the music stopped, the queen did not back away, but retained a gentle hold on John's arm.

81

"You are a good dancer, my lord," she declared. "We shall have another, no?"

"Your Grace is kind. That would be to my pleasure."

They waited there together, John feeling a target for all eyes, with most other couples parting. Would the king approve of this? He saw George grinning at him.

A second round went as well as the first. George was partnering the Steward's daughter this time. The king did not take to the floor.

When the musicians stopped again, the queen did step back, but ran a hand down his arm as she did so. "My lord," she said, "I will remember that. I see why David approves of you!"

George came over to him. "You seem to have a way with you, Johnnie. All will be noting it. That Marjory remarked on it."

"She did? Then I will seek her before she forgets." And he went across the floor to where Carrick and his sister stood.

"May I have the privilege? Lady Marjory it is, I understand?"

"If I am not too humble a partner after your last, my lord of Moray!" she said, eyebrows raised. She was striking in more than her hair, a slender but well-formed creature, lissome as she was lively of aspect.

"The queen but danced with me out of, of acknowledgment of some small services rendered to her husband," he asserted, making something of a labour of that.

"But she danced . . . approvingly, I noted."

The musicians struck up then, and inclining her lovely head, she came to him, all grace and with a sort of challenge. Taking her arm, he recognised that he would have to go warily with this one.

They did not speak for some time, and she held herself further from him than the queen had done, although her dancing was anything but stiff. For once, John was tongue-tied, unable to think of anything suitable to say.

"My brother Robert holds you as a man to watch!" she said, presently. "So I am warned!"

"To watch? Watch for what, lady?"

"He did not specify. But methinks he meant, shall we say . . . devious?"

"Me? Devious? That I am not. I am but finding my way. As a new earl, suddenly burdened with responsibilities for large lands, and the king's service. Unprepared for it all. I have had to pick my way, yes. Watch where I trod. But, devious . . . !"

"Yet you won over the Lord of the Isles to the king's will, Robert tells me. And he would take a deal of winning, I judge."

"I but sought to persuade him as to his own benefit. And the realm's. Little by little."

"Ah! Little by little! That is why you are to be watched, my lord?"

All this was said as they turned and side-stepped and swung to the music's rhythm, while avoiding collision with the other dancers, this involving some adjusting of persons and physical contacts, of which John was very much aware. He noted that George was again partnering the dark Lennox woman.

That gave him an opening to change the subject somewhat. "My brother is something of a ladies' man," he said. "Now *he* would be one to watch, perhaps! Although he is honest about it, frank, shall we say.

"Not devious! I see that he holds Margaret Lennox close!"

Was that a warning? Or an invitation? Scarcely the latter, with this one. "We are very different," he told her. "But close friends."

The instrumentalists halted their playing once more, and John was quite surprised when this partner also remained at his side, although she released his arm.

"Your mother," she said. "It must be quite strange to be reared by a mother whom all revere as a national heroine. And, and . . ."

He finished that for her. "And a father who was . . . otherwise! And but seldom with us."

83

"He was a disappointed man, my father says. Ever on his mind that *his* line should have been on the throne, not the Margaretsons."

"Yes. It preyed on him, my mother says. And he scorned *her* line, as up-jumped!"

"Like my own! The same line. We are far-out kin, after all. Your mother's father was Bruce's nephew. My father son of Bruce's daughter. Up-jumped, as you put it, also!"

"Without the Bruce we would all be under English sway now. If not dead!"

Then they were dancing again, John at least enjoying it the more. When he took Marjory back to Carrick's side, that one seeming to be no dancer, he thanked her for her company, and received in return a half curtsy, half mocking but half challenging also.

George and Margaret Lennox had disappeared from the hall. John thought it the right thing to do to choose one of the older ladies present to dance with, and selected a plump and genial person whom he did not know, but who proved to be the wife of the Thane of Glamis. She made pleasant company. He would have liked to have another turn with Marjory Stewart, but deemed it best to delay that a little while. However, after chatting with Lady Glamis, he perceived that Carrick and his sister had also disappeared. He was not long, after that, in himself departing.

It was late that night before brother George got back to their lodging in Edinburgh's Cowgate.

With his brother involved in the assessment commission's deliberations that week, John went back to Dunbar. It was good to be home, for he could not yet think of Darnaway Castle and Moray as that; and it was always a satisfaction to be in his mother's company. They had much to discuss together, and he questions to ask: for instance, this of the Moray assessments. She was interested not only in the Moray situation but in his relationship with the king – and the queen, too – and the royal recognition of services rendered, particularly the gaining of the baronies of Findlater and Deskford, which she saw as a worthy acquisition.

George arrived three days later, so they had two days together at Dunbar before they had to go back to Edinburgh Castle for the renewed council meeting. John solemnly asked how the other had got on with the Lady Margaret Lennox, and was told to mind his own business.

The council meeting was blessedly brief, for the work had been done by the commissioners, and it was only a case of hearing and accepting their findings, however unwelcome the details were to most present. There was very little actual dissent expressed, though many faces were pulled. It was thought that the parliament to follow in a few weeks' time would homologate all without overmuch debate or opposition.

In a talk with the monarch and the Steward thereafter, John made a point of it that while he would wish to be present at the parliament, it might well not be practicable. He had found no ship available at Dunbar to base itself at Inverness and there lie idle for any lengthy period; and the journey on horseback through the snow-covered Highlands might well be impossible. It had been bad enough coming here this time; but January and February were their worst months for snow, as the passes would be likely to be entirely blocked. So . . .

It was then that the Steward made his suggestion. Why not John come back now, with him, to his house of Renfrew, on the Clyde, and from there sail north in the longship that had brought young Donald of the Isles into his keeping, under the agreement at Inverness? Donald was kicking his heels at Renfrew, and would no doubt be glad enough to take John north, and see his father and family briefly before coming back south. And in three weeks' time sail north again, to collect John and any other Highland would-be attenders at the parliament, Ross for instance, who had not appeared at the council, thus doing something useful during his period of being a sort of hostage.

King David thought this an excellent notion, and John likewise. It did not fail to strike him that daughter Marjory would presumably be at home at this Renfrew, and some renewal of their association could ensue.

So next day he joined the Steward's party, to ride westwards for Glasgow and Renfrew, Marjory greeting him with upraised eyebrows and questioning smiles but no evident reserve, and asking after George. Indeed they rode side by side for much of the way.

They went by the Calders, East and West, and Livingston, to cross the empty moorlands that constituted the spine of this central belt of Lowland Scotland, and on by Airdrie to Glasgow, some forty-five miles. Thereafter they followed the south bank of Clyde for another six miles On the Steward's land now, to reach the burgh of Renfrew, where the Black Cart river joined Clyde, here beginning to become an estuary, this as dusk was falling. The castle stood on a mound above the main river where it was widening somewhat, opposite the Kilpatrick Hills, where Marjory said that St Patrick of Ireland had been born.

It was a very large house, all put palatial, as indeed it had needed to be, for Robert the Steward was of a productive and patriarchal character and had had ten children by his first wife and another six by his second, this as well as numerous bastards. His present wife, the Countess of Strathearn, was suitably large, a cheerful soul, who acted the born hostess with a warmth all could do with, for it had been a testing ride to get there, through wintry snow showers. Oddly enough, the lady was John's aunt by marriage, the widow of his uncle, John, third Earl of Moray and, still more strangely, sister of William, Earl of Ross. The Scottish earldoms were not numerous, and their holders tended to marry amongst their own kind, so this sort of situation was not uncommon. John had met Euphemia of Strathearn before once or twice, at court.

He was shown to a chamber in a flanking tower, where

warm water was brought for washing in, and wine there to refresh him.

Thereafter he met some of the family whom he did not know, such as were not married and away; also Donald, the young Islesman, a good-looking and friendly character of about John's own age, without the proud bearing of his father. When told of the suggestion that he should take the guest up to the north in his longship, he was delighted with the idea, and declared that he could get his vessel up the Firth of Lorne and Loch Linnhe right to the mouth of Loch Eil, in the Great Glen, whereafter John could borrow one of the Cameron garrons to ride the remaining forty or so miles to Inverness, this without difficulty, for the snow seldom lay to any depth in the valley floor.

At table that evening, John sat between this Donald and Carrick, with Marjory across from them, and able to converse. She was lively as ever however tired after the long day in the saddle. But still more lively, and less tired to be sure, was the young woman sitting next to her, not much more than a girl, one of her half-sisters, Margaret, or Meg as she was called, bubbling over with chatter and laughter, and evidently flirtatious as she was high-spirited. She told John that they must be cousins of a sort, since her mother had been married to John's uncle. Marjory eyed her amusedly, although Robert of Carrick shook his head over her.

They made an enjoyable meal of it, and although there was some music and singing afterwards, but no dancing – although Meg would probably have wished for it, the travellers were for bed fairly early, whatever the rest of the Stewart family chose.

The Lady Meg, who clearly had an eye for young men, announced that she would show John to his room, in case he had forgotten the way, he nowise discouraging. But as the goodnights were said to the host and hostess – the former had begun to nod as he sat before the great log-fire – John found Marjory at his other side from Meg, at the door.

"Just in case you require protection, my lord," she murmured.

He went, then, escorted by two females, along corridors and up turnpike stairways, to his tower, he making no complaint although he would have preferred only the one companion.

At his chamber, he was conducted within, to ensure that fresh hot water was steaming in a tub, that a fire blazed brightly, and that the bedpan was in place, Meg busily attentive, Marjory less so but watching. John went to sit on the bed, and had assistance in removing his long riding-boots. He was scolded for having a hole in the toe of one of his knitted hose. In the lamplight, he looked over the kneeling Meg's head at her half-sister, enquiringly, and received a nod accompanied by a single raised eyebrow and the flicker of a smile, which somehow he took as the most hopeful token yet between them.

When Meg could find nothing more that she could decently do for the bed-goer, he padded across to the door with them, with his thanks. There he was given a smacking goodnight kiss, with instructions to sleep well and have the right sort of dreams; this of course, when he turned to Marjory, leaving her with little option but to offer him her cheek to kiss, in turn, but only her cheek, although he did accompany it with a fairly comprehensive squeeze of her person.

So much for Stewart hospitality.

Whether the man's dreams that night were such as Meg would have approved of was doubtful.

In the morning, it seemed that there was to be no delay in his setting off for the north, Donald having already been down at the little anchorage having his oarsmen prepare the longship. After breakfast quite a party accompanied the travellers down to the vessel, with food and drink for the voyage, for the Steward reckoned that it would be all of two hundred and fifty miles by the time they reached Loch Eil; and although these longships were speedy, indeed known as the greyhounds of the sea, they would have to lie up in shelter overnight, and eighty miles per day would be as much as could be expected, so a three-day journey. Quite a lot of provender was required therefore, for there were a dozen oarsmen.

The send-off was quite rousing, with most of the family present, the Steward declaring that he would look to see his grandson back in under three weeks' time, with his passengers; and Donald to tell his father that he and the king wished him well – and would be glad to receive his due revenues to the crown at this time of national need. John got a hug and a kiss from Meg – but noted that Donald obtained a similar farewell – Marjory contenting herself with a pressing on the arm, this only moderately encouraging.

At the casting-off, however, amongst wavings and calls and blown kisses from Meg, her half-sister did make a similar gesture. It might have been intended, of course, for Donald, her nephew.

Although the weather conditions were less than ideal for voyaging, especially in an open longship, at least the snow showers had ceased and the wind was not fierce. Donald himself took the helm, and held a gong and stick, to beat the steady rhythm for the oarsmen, and this became the continued accompaniment for the journey, together with the grunts of the oarsmen and the creak of the long sweeps against their rowlock pivots. At this stage, with the breeze south-westerly, the single square sail was not raised; the time for that would come when they eventually reached and rounded the Mull of Kintyre. Meantime they had many miles to cover due westwards to where the Clyde estuary made its great bend southwards and became a firth.

John, wrapped in his riding-cloak against the chill, wondered whether he should offer to take a hand at the sweeps, the exercise of which might help to keep him warm. There were two men to each oar, but even so he doubted whether his contribution and lack of expertise would be welcomed. He was used to rowing small boats at

89

his Dunbar fishing; but these longships' sweeps demanded a very different pulling, obviously, not only because of their weight and length, but for the actual propulsion of the large and narrow vessel.

Along the Renfrewshire coast, they went the score of miles past Greenock and Gourock to the Clach Point, where they had to turn due southwards for their long, nearly seventy miles, pull down the Ayrshire, Cowal and Bute coasts, passing the small Cumbrae Isles and the great Isle of Arran, to turn back to the west again between that last and the towering and isolated rock-stack of Ailsa Craig, so like the Craig of Bass which John knew so well near Dunbar. And now the long peninsula of Kintyre was in sight on their right. Dusk was beginning to fall, and they were coming to the dangerous waters of the mull, having covered over eighty miles. Donald decided that they must draw in to some haven hereabouts for the night, and with the great Atlantic swell commencing to challenge the oarsmen, they found the fishing hamlet of Macharioch, where they could rest from labours. They did not go ashore, but after consuming some of their provisions, lay down under plaids in the boat, less than comfortable as their passenger found it. He slept, nevertheless.

At first light they were off again, due westwards now into the ocean for eight miles or so, their craft rearing and heaving as they passed between the little isle of Sanda and the fierce frowning Mull of Kintyre coast. And at last they were able to turn northwards, to the thankfulness of all, and the sail could be hoisted, the wind now behind them, and all but two of the sweeps shipped, these out in case of sudden need to avoid reefs, skerries and overfalls. They cruised on up the west Kintyre coast for fifty miles thus, Islay on their left, to thread the sound of Gigha and on past the mouth of Lochs Tarbert-West, Caolisport and Sween, now in the long Sound of Jura, with that island's dramatic peaks, the Paps, soaring to their left. There were tide-runs to cope with here, and also down-draughts from the mountains, but at least they were spared the Atlantic rollers.

With darkness coming and the hazardous narrow waters of the Sound of Luing, and the isles of Scarba, Luing itself and Seil ahead of them, they halted for the night at Crinan, having covered another eighty miles, and this time with little effort other than Donald's careful steering. Past the Campbell country and well into what he called his father's "kingdom" now, with great Mull none so far ahead and Eigg and Rhum beyond, they were well content. At Crinan they did go ashore to stretch their legs, and received welcome hospitality from the villagers of the fisher-haven, who were proud to entertain the son of the Lord of the Isles.

John was able to have some quite pleasant converse now with Donald, the pair getting on well together. He learned of some of the problems and challenges in the governance of an island principality stretching over hundreds of miles and literally thousands of islands, great and small, so different from those of the Dunbar and March earldoms, and even that of Moray; also of the clan feuding of the western Highlands. And as young men will, they got on to the subject of the other sex, the attractions and delights but also the pitfalls, frustrations and oddities presented by young women. Meg Stewart, of course, came in for comment and debate; and John learned that Donald was, in fact, much more interested in her half-sister, but not a Stewart one: Phemie as he called her, the Lady Euphemia, daughter of the second wife of the Steward, who was also called Euphemia, their recent hostess, this by an earlier husband and not the former Earl John of Moray but a still earlier one, son of Leslie of that Ilk – a much-married lady the Countess of Strathearn. But the daughter Phemie, whom John had presumably met but not identified amongst the crowd at Renfrew Castle, evidently appealed to Donald. How far they had got in their relationship was not actually divulged. John, for his part, indicated that he found Marjory Stewart to his taste, but that the tasting, so far, was at a very early stage. Donald, because of his liking for his Phemie, was by no means unhappy about his having to return to his stay at Renfrew, hostage of a sort as he might be.

In the morning, a dozen careful miles of navigating took them up past the notorious and noisy Gulf of Corryvreckan, between Jura and Scarba, and then through the Luing Sound and into the Firth of Lorne. From this they reached the mouth of wide Loch Linnhe. Here they were in sheltered waters at last. They passed the long isle of Lismore, famous from the days of saints Columba and Moluag, fertile enough to be named, in the Gaelic, the Great Garden. Sixty miles brought them to the head of Linnhe, where the River Lochy came in from the north and Loch Eil opened to the west. This, Corpach, was as far as the longship could sail. But Donald was not finished with his services yet. It being only mid-afternoon, he escorted John up Eil-side, on foot, to Achdalieu, where a son of the Cameron chief dwelled, there to collect a garron, one of the rough but hardy Highland ponies, to take John northwards up Ness-side. Despite being known as Cameron of Lochiel, the chief himself had his main seat at Achnacarry on Loch Arkaig, which John remembered.

So it was back to the longship, Donald riding pillion, where farewells were said, and arrangements made for them to meet here again in three weeks' time for the return to Renfrew.

Thereafter there was just the long ride up Lochy and Oich to Ness-side, with a halt for the night at the Bunoich hospice, Inverness and Darnaway ahead.

8

John spent a busy time, based on Darnaway but visiting all over his earldom, to make the revenue assessments for the crown levies, ably assisted by his friend the Brodie, and in some measure by the Mackintosh and Comyn of Duffus, little as these relished the moneys-providing. He sent word to William of Ross of the parliament, and the opportunity to attend it by travelling by longship. Also to inform the Earl of Sutherland. The customs collectors of Elgin and Forres were told of the king's wishes. And inspection of the baronies of Findlater and Deskford was made and approved. Altogether, John was well satisfied, save when his messenger returned from Ross with the information that that earl saw no point in going to a parliament for this unsuitable money-raising; and anyway would not demean himself by travelling in one of the rogue Islesman's boats.

In due course then, John set off westwards again, on the garron, this time escorted by a group of Mackintosh running-gillies, that chief considering it unseemly for the Earl of Moray to ride alone through the land. Again a halt was made at Bunoich, at the head of Loch Ness, the brethren there glad to act host to their young lord.

When they arrived at Corpach and Loch Eil, John found the longship already there, but Donald gone up to await him at Achdalieu. There he gave back the garron, thanked his gillies, and returned with Donald to Corpach.

He learned that John of the Isles was, however reluctantly, proposing to pay his dues – but not the long-outstanding sums, asserting that he had not agreed to anything of the sort, Donald deeming this fair enough.

So commenced their lengthy return voyage back to the

Clyde; and now, with the breeze remaining south-westerly, they faced reverse conditions, the wind in their faces all the way down to the Mull of Kintyre, the sail seldom hoisted, oar-work almost entirely. So they made less good time on this major stretch amongst the isles, but would gain the benefit when they entered the Firth of Clyde. They could not make the same night stops, to be sure, mileage very different.

On the whole, they had been fortunate with the weather, some rain but no storms, and nothing more than flurries of snow.

Eventually rounding Kintyre, the oarsmen could sit back and relax, those last eighty-odd miles undemanding.

It was good to see Renfrew Castle again soaring ahead of them, thoughts not all on bringing good tidings to the High Steward. Actually that man was not present, being with the king at Edinburgh; but his cheerful countess was, and much of her multitudinous family with her, including Marjory, Meg and Donald's Phemie, their arrival greeted with acclaim, variously expressed. John decided that Donald had good judgment in his choice, although not so good as his own. Meg, however, as before, made the running, to her various relations' head-shakings. Robert of Carrick was there still, as ever quietly undemonstrative.

Over the meal, the travellers entertained the others with accounts of their journeying, emphasising particularly the tide-races, the roaring of the whirlpools of the Gulf of Corryvreckan, the time that they had run their prow into a skerry just below the surface at the end of Lismore, and the extraordinary tirelessness of the Mackintosh running-gillies.

John managed to sit beside Marjory for much of the evening.

Of a winter night, with the dark and cold outside, the bed-going was the only opportunity for couples to be alone together, Meg well aware of this – but so was John. He beckoned to her, in that crowded chamber.

"Could you help me?" he asked. "I have some fish which

Donald and I brought from a haven we stopped at. But I have left it down at the doorway, at the porter's lodge. Could you see that it is taken to the kitchens? I would have taken it myself, but I know not where they are."

She looked doubtful. "I shall send a maid," she told him.

He was prepared for that also. At this stage of the evening, there were no servants in the family hall. So Meg would have to go to find one.

"I will be back," she said.

He nodded, and when she had gone, wasted no time. He looked over at Marjory. "Am I in the same bedchamber this night?" he wondered.

That one raised those eloquent eyebrows at him. "I would think so. None other has occupied it while you were gone. Have you forgotten the way?"

"So many passages and stairs . . ."

"Very well. I would not have judged you to be a forgetful man!" But she came to him as he rose.

He was already glancing towards the doorway out of which Meg had gone. Almost hurrying, he made for the other door, Marjory a pace or two behind.

Safely out, he waited for her. "It is good to be with you again," he said.

"Is it? Why is that, I wonder?"

"Because I like and admire you, Marjory. What is there to wonder at?"

"I thought that it was your brother who was the ladies' man!"

"Ladies, perhaps. Myself, I am more . . . selective!" And he took her arm.

"Ah! The Earl of great Moray can afford to be! And meantime, you select Marjory Stewart?"

"Not only meantime."

They had to climb a narrow turnpike stair, where it was scarcely possible to go side by side. So he had to release her arm, she going first. But at the landing above, she waited for him.

"You still need further guidance, my lord?"

"I still need *you*, lass! Can you not see it, hear it, feel it?"

"But . . . you scarcely know me, John."

"I would know more of you, yes. Know you better, wholly. But what I do know, I favour, esteem, cherish." And this time, walking along that corridor, he reached, not to take her arm but to put his round her waist as they went.

"I see that I shall have to watch my step with you!" she said. But she did not seek to free herself.

They went on in silence now.

At the second flight of stairs he had to fall back again, and found her not waiting this time but moving on towards the entrance to his flanking tower. He followed her, but did not hurry to catch up. Some instinct told him not to be over-pressing.

At the doorway to his chamber, she turned to him. "Safely there, then. Although I do not think that you could not have found your way alone!" And she opened the door for him.

"Perhaps I could. But, then, I would not have had your company."

"Is the need so great? For *my* company."

"Yes." That was brief but positive. And he took her arm again, to draw her within.

She held back now. "All will be in order here, I am sure," she said.

"Do you not wish to make certain?"

"Meg will be here any moment, I think."

"The more reason not to delay." And he held out his hand.

After a moment, she followed him inside.

He would have closed the door behind them, but she it was who did the touching now, holding his arm.

"Better to leave it open," she said.

"Do you fear, woman? Fear *me*?"

"Not fear, no, John. I would judge that no woman need fear you. It is, it is myself that I fear."

"Your*self*! How can you fear yourself?"

"I am a woman!" she told him simply. "With a woman's weaknesses."

"Weak! You! I would say that you are a woman of strength!" And his arm went round her again.

"There are more strengths than one, in a woman, John. As in a man. And weaknesses. Am I to need my strength? Here and now?" And within his arm, she turned to him.

"Lassie! Lassie!" he got out, and drew her close, to find her face upturned to his. His lips said the rest, but not in words. There had been over-many words already.

Her kissing, then, was as positive as the rest of her.

When, presently, she drew back a little, but only her head and face, she spoke. "You see? What I feared. In myself!"

It was John who was at a loss for words now.

"Was I wrong? In my judgment of you?" she asked.

"I do not know how you judged me, woman. All I know is that I would have you as mine. Mine!"

"Yours, yes. But for when? For how long? Now, I can see, feel. But I am not, I tell myself, that sort of woman. Strong or weak . . ."

"For always! For my life. For yours, my love. Can you not sense it in me? Love. For all time. Here and hereafter. The two of us. Together. Wed in mind and soul and body."

She buried her face on his chest, wordless.

Holding her, he took her over to the brightly blazing fire, and there put his hands beneath her chin, to raise it.

"Marjory, heart of my heart!" he said.

She nodded, slowly. "Heart of your heart. And of mine! Were my fears groundless? Or were they not?" she murmured.

He did not attempt to answer that, save by holding her the closer, as her arms went round him also.

It was thus that Meg found them, as she stood in the doorway, gazing.

With a stroking of his cheek, Marjory left him there, and

going to her half-sister, turned her round and, going out together, closed the door behind them.

John supposed that he ought to have travelled on to Edinburgh next day, to make his report to the king and the Steward. But developments here at Renfrew were such as to induce delay – and one more day would make little difference in national affairs, whereas it might just possibly do so in personal ones.

The morning proving reasonably congenial for the time of the year, he approached Marjory with the suggestion that a ride around the nearby countryside together would be pleasing, if this could be contrived, she co-operative. Unfortunately, when Donald heard of this, he declared that Phemie and himself should come also; and Meg, although eyeing both couples speculatively, was not to be left out. One or two others decided to join them, even Carrick. So quite a cavalcade set off up the Black Cart, westwards.

Where the White Cart joined it, nearly four miles up, they swung off northwards for the Barochan Moss, hunting country, where boar were to be seen, but not that day. And so round southwards again, by Houston and Fulton, to another moss, Linwood with its little loch, good for hawking, to reach the White Cart again and so back to Renfrew, a score of miles of interesting country which John had known nothing of.

Even though all this company was hardly his objective, he ensured that he rode at Marjory's side throughout, and in their newly established association this was very pleasant. They did manage to drift aside from the others on occasion, but never sufficiently or for long enough to do more than hold hands from the saddle. But the togetherness was itself a joy, and even the mutual frustration in not attaining aloneness held its own compensation.

Thereafter, impatiently, John awaited evening. Once or twice he was able to get his love alone, in a stairway or a corridor; but with a castle full of people as this one was, such endeavours were difficult, with it all too obvious.

At the evening meal they did sit together, with Donald and Phemie next to them, Meg, across the table, eyeing them all roguishly.

"I shall have a word with that one, presently," Marjory murmured, as the dining finished.

Whatever was said between the two young women, it was effective. When, Marjory, yawning elaborately, rose to depart, John waited only a minute or two and then, nodding to the others, himself made for the door. He saw Meg watching him, but she did not rise.

Hurrying, and glancing behind him once or twice, just in case, he made his way along and up and along. At his room he found the door closed. But entering, he was not disappointed. Marjory stood over by the fire, awaiting him.

"At last! At last!" he exclaimed. "Sakes, I near despaired of ever reaching this moment!" And he all but ran, to take her in his arms, indeed lifting her off her feet.

"Moment?" she gasped, when she could find breath. "More than one moment, or two, my dear, surely! You, myself, have had to be very patient. But now . . .!"

"Now, yes." He released her, and stood back, to eye her, consider her, in the firelight, telling himself not to rush it, not to spoil their attainment of satisfaction, their bliss – or *his*, and he hoped, in some measure, hers also.

She searched his face. "You look! You study. You calculate? Make judgment. What do you see?"

"I see loveliness. And kindness. And, and promise!"

"Promise, yes. But . . ." She left the rest unsaid.

He went to her, to pick her up bodily and carry her over to the bed. "Promise!" he repeated, setting her down, and sitting beside her thereon. "But – I need more. Some, some . . . fulfilment."

"I know it. Do not I, also? But we must be strong, my John. And you will help *me* to be so? Until, until . . . we may. In full." She gripped his hand and lifted it to her bosom.

He drew deep breath. "You, you test me!" he told her.

"I test myself also. Do I . . . mistake?"

"I know not. Only I know that you are all in all to me. And all of you is my joy. *All!*" That hand was busy, fondling, exploring. And the other hand not idle, either.

She turned to kiss, and be done with words for a while.

Fairly soon his busier hand found the opening of her bodice, and slipped therein, to reach warm, full, rounded flesh, and the firm projections therefrom. He groaned, lips against hers as they were, as he felt those breasts heaving. Marjory did not actually groan, but breathed the more deeply, while her fingers dug into the man's back.

They found themselves sinking back on the bed, from sitting to lying. He pushed aside the bodice urgently, yet not roughly, to bare the shoulders and the generous femininity below, to kiss and kiss, she stroking his head as he did so, and whispering.

When his hands began to move further downwards, she reached to halt this. "You were . . . to help me . . . to be strong!" she reminded. "This is . . . promise. Not, not . . . all! That should, *must* wait, no?"

John groaned again. But brought those hands up again to breasts and shoulders. She kissed his hair.

So they lay, close, but alongside, whatever his urge to be on top of her. He realised that this could not go on for very long without his succumbing to his masculine demands. She sensed it also, and perhaps her needs were not without their own pressures.

"I think, I think that we but torment ourselves, my heart," she said, at length. "Weak or strong, I know not. But we must spare each other, meantime. Until . . ."

"You probably . . . are right. Yes." He kissed those proud nipples lingeringly, and then raised himself up. "How long? The waiting will be . . . dire."

"So soon as it can be made possible, yes. Soon. Need there be delay? My father approves of you. And you are your own master. And to be mine, my lord of Moray."

"I will hasten it, never fear. But I will never be your *master*, lass – only your lover, for always."

They both stood, and arms about each other, moved to the door, Marjory not yet refastening her bodice. So, as he took his leave, his goodnight wishes were somewhat muffled by the availability of that inviting bosom for further appreciation, before, tapping his shoulder, she buttoned up to leave him. It would hardly do for him to see her to *her* bedroom, at this hour. Who knew whom they might meet?

Late as was the hour, that man did not sleep much that night, mind busy, joy, anticipation, but impatience also, competing in his so stimulated mind.

In the morning he forced himself to be off eastwards for Edinburgh, Marjory riding with him as far as Cardonald, to see him on his way.

9

The king was well pleased with John's account of his mission, but disappointed that Ross had refused the boat-journey southwards, and presumably would not be present at the parliament, and possibly further delaying payment of his dues. He declared that, by and large, the revenues were coming in fairly satisfactorily. But it would be the parliament that would make the difference.

John sought out the Steward, to announce, with a kind of embarrassment, that he sought his daughter's hand in marriage – and was told that the wonder was that he had taken so long about seeking it! He saw no reason not to grant it, nor why there should be any great delay about it. He was sure that the matter of the customary dowery and portion could be settled suitably for both parties. Once this parliament was over, all could be arranged.

There were still a few days before the parliament, which it seemed was now to be held at Perth, as more convenient for the many travelling from northern parts. But meanwhile the first instalment of the royal ransom money was despatched to Edward of England, with promise of more to follow fairly quickly.

With time to spare, John was able to head for Dunbar, where the word of his romance and betrothal, if that was the right word, was received by his mother with pleasure and congratulations, by George with amusement and the suggestion that his brother would be wise to keep that one under control, if he knew anything about women, and by sister Agnes with enquiries as to what it was about a woman that had men so eager? After all, John had met many personable females before this. What had Marjory

Stewart got that so appealed to him, and now, apparently to be in such a hurry about marriage?

The brothers were glad to be able to go to Perth in one of their ships, and offering to take Hepburn of Hailes, Lindsay of Luffness and Seton of that Ilk with them, saving long riding, this much appreciated. It was not likely to be an easy or brief parliament, with all this of moneys required, increased levies and customs, higher rates and trading contributions to be settled, finance never being a popular theme. Even the churchmen were unlikely to take it kindly.

The sail to the Tay estuary and up-river to Perth, some seventy miles, was comfortably completed in a day. St John's Town, as it was known, was conveniently well provided with accommodation, the city being fuller of monasteries, priories, friaries and religious houses than any other in the land; Carthusians, Dominicans, Carmelites, Franciscans, Trinitarians and the like, many of these establishments little less than palatial, hence its popularity for meetings of parliament. George and John went to lodge in the Carthusian monastery, or Charterhouse, in the attached chapel of which Edward the Third of England had stabbed his own brother, John, Earl of Cornwall, to death before the high altar, this for ravaging lands without the king's authority. Here, the brothers were left in no doubt about the clerics' feelings over increased contributions to the treasury, Holy Church already the greatest source of the nation's revenues.

In the event, next day, the parliament, held in the royal castle at the end of Skinner-gait, proved less dire than had been feared, the threat of English attack in the event of non-payment helping, especially in this city where Edward had so aggressively based himself thirty years before. Not that it was a happy session, objections, comparisons, excuses and special pleading being voiced throughout; but the general necessity not really being contested. The King's opening address was helpful, David making it clear that, since it was his ransom moneys, in major arrears, which made it all necessary, he accepted responsibility, and that he was taxing his own royal lands to the limit, and would continue to do so. The Church's spokesmen were less hostile than expected, possibly to the disapproval of some of their lesser representatives, this undoubtedly influenced by the fact that the Primate, Bishop William Landells of St Andrews, had actually led the mission which negotiated the release of the captive monarch, and agreed on the ransom sum. The royal burgh provosts were supportive, and with these examples of co-operation, the earls, lords, holders of baronies and landed men undoubtedly were less disgruntled than they might have been. The assessment commission's recommendations were accepted eventually, and passed.

The remainder of the general parliamentary business was more or less nodded through without much discussion, and the Privy Councillors were able to sigh with relief, whatever their personal commitments.

John had a word with the High Steward and Carrick afterwards, and it was agreed than an Easter-tide wedding would be suitable, that year the festival being in early April. The bridegroom-to-be told himself that he *could* wait that long, Carrick mentioning that Marjory had said to avoid the end of March.

The king announced that he would honour this occasion with his royal presence as a mark of appreciation of services rendered by both John of Moray and the bride's father. The wedding would be in Paisley Abbey, the greatest fane in the Stewartry.

So it was back to the ship and Dunbar, George declaring that his brother was really being thus favoured because, if rights were conceded, *he*, the Cospatrick, should be sitting on the Scots throne. Let John never forget it, and think too highly of himself!

For his part, John wondered what excuse he could invent to go over to Renfrew again, well before Easter. He ought to be going up to Moray, to see to his responsibilities there. There was, of course, the matter of dowery and portion for the bride to discuss, the first to be provided by the father, the second by the groom. It occurred to him that those two baronies of Findlater and Deskford, unexpectedly granted to him by the monarch, might suitably serve as portion for Marjory. He could hardly suggest that she should come up to Moray to inspect them, prior to the marriage, but she could send a representative, possibly her brother Robert of Carrick.

He consulted his mother on this, and she considered that this would be in order – but she had not realised that her second son had become quite such an impatient character. Or was it only where Marjory Stewart was concerned? Perhaps there was something to be said for George's attitude towards the other sex?

The snow would still be blocking the Highland passes. But instead of going by ship to Inverness, could he persuade Donald of the Isles to repeat that performance and take him up the west coast by longship? He possibly would be quite glad to do so, with his stay at Renfrew, doing nothing in particular, almost certainly becoming boring, apart from the dalliance with Phemia. He could be sent to bring back his father's contribution to the assessments, or some of them. It might all work out.

So back to court to see the Steward. But at Edinburgh he found that man had returned to Renfrew. Well and good. He would follow on. A man must use his wits, his mother had always insisted.

Alone, he made Renfrew in the one long day's riding, his unexpected arrival there welcomed, and not only by Marjory. In his undemonstrative way, Carrick was glad to see him; and Donald made no secret of it, Meg none the less friendly because of her half-sister's betrothal.

John's suggestion as to another voyage up to the Great Glen met with Donald's approval, Phemia less enthusiastic and Robert declaring that he would be happy to accompany them, to inspect the baronies on his father's behalf. His Carrick earldom was really only titular, the lands

105

thereof all belonging to his father and he having no actual responsibility there. So he was a man with time on his hands and no major preoccupations. The Steward said that he was well pleased to have those Isles oarsmen given something to do.

Marjory asked why she could not join in the voyaging, perhaps with Phemia as female companion? John had to point out that travel in a longship was no activity for women unfortunately, no privacy, no shelter, in view of the oarsmen all the time, and overnight halts equally uninviting. He was sorry indeed, but . . .

When it came to bedtime, no eyebrows were raised at the couple going off together. John said that this time he would escort Marjory to *her* room for a change, she doing the brow-raising at that, but not refusing him. They had not so far to go. Nor was there any denying him entrance to a very different chamber to his own, littered with women's clothing, the canopied bed smaller, chests, cabinets and mirrors much in evidence and wall-hangings varied and colourful.

Needless to say John was eager to demonstrate his appreciation. As hand in hand she led him over to the fireplace, he was ready to prove it. And he was not rebuffed, although Marjory somehow gave the impression of slight restraint, as he flung his arms around her and their lips met.

When words came, they were hers, and only faltering. "John, my heart, how, how sorely do we test ourselves this night?" she asked him.

A sort of urgency in her voice made him still his hands, and he paused to search her upturned face.

"Do we? Will we?" he demanded.

"Oh, I do not want to," she told him. "All that is me says . . . otherwise." And her arms around him all but shook him. "But, but . . ."

"Then need we? We are each other's. We know it. All know it now. Accept. We are promised, and in more than words, lass."

"Yes. I know it indeed. Yet . . . promise! *Promise!* Ought we not to hold that? The promise, to come. For the day, the night, to come. When, when the promise will be fulfilled. When we have been made one before God and man. Become one, indeed. Is such but custom? The word of the priests? Usage, in marriage?"

"And you would have it so?"

"I think so. Think, my love. *Think*, rather than feel! That it would be . . . best. Can you understand me?"

"I must!" he said then, almost grimly.

"Oh, John, my heart's desire! Am I foolish, in this? Unkind? Selfish? And yet, not selfish. For I too would give myself wholly. Take you wholly. *Now*. But that is my heart and body, not my head, my judgment . . ."

As he drew back a little, she went on, almost hurriedly now.

"But, see you, it does not have to be . . . all! We can still taste of the promise, John. No?" She reached to touch his cheek. Then, smiling, she opened the top of her hodice.

Drawing a deep breath, he took her hand, and led her over to her bed. But even as he did so, he knew a sense almost of shame, not in what he was about to do, but in her evident belief that she must satisfy his male needs thus.

Not that he let such questionings spoil the enjoyment of what followed, for he could scarcely be unaware that soon she was enjoying it also, even shrugging her white shoulders free of her clothing, and biting at his ear as he kissed and squeezed her breasts. It was not long before she was naked to the waist, and he knew a kind of satisfaction that she clearly trusted him not to go further, lower, even when he turned her over, bodily, to be able to kiss her back, and his fingers did move down somewhat to reach the beginning of a cleavage there, where he managed to restrain himself. Her own hand went behind her, only partly in a kind of warning and partly to run lingeringly over his person, fully clothed as it was still.

Turning over then, on her back again, she whispered, "I, I praise my John! You are good. Kind. And strong.

And I have needed your strength. Oh, my dear – I promise! And none so long . . ."

Lying alongside her now, he gazed up at the bed canopy in the flickering firelight. "You were right," he told her.

So they remained for some time, before he sat up. "I would stay all night, in this your room, my beloved, if you were to let me. But I dare not! We have sufficiently tested ourselves, I think. Why did the Creator make men thus?"

"And women also. We are none so different, see you. Or . . . some of us! But, yes – go you, dearest, despite me wishing to keep you here. Lest . . ."

He kissed her, briefly now, and left her. He did not ask to be guided back to his own chamber.

In the morning, Donald and Carrick and John were off in the longship, after Marjory assured the last that she would count the days and the nights, until the beginning of April.

The six weeks that followed were well enough spent, largely in travel, by sea, river and land, Carrick proving well satisfied, in his father's name, with the properties of Findlater and Deskford which were to be Marjory's portion, the customary arrangement of landed folk's marriages, so that if the woman was to be widowed and a male her successor to the estates, she would have somewhere to live and an income to keep her.

John wanted to inspect parts of the earldom that he had not yet visited, this the extreme south-western area, of the upper Spey valley between the mighty ranges of the Monadh Ruadh and the Monadh Liath, the Red and Grey Mountains, the peaks of the former the highest reputedly in the land of all Scotland, the latter as extensive but somewhat less lofty, Grant, Mackintosh and Macpherson country. The snow-covered hills did restrict access to some parts, and the rushing rivers making fording difficult. But they did see enough of a very challenging and scenically dramatic terrain to enable its new lord to appreciate why Moray was looked upon as one of the greatest earldoms of the nation, one of the seven mormaordoms of ancient Alba, more ancient and historically important than any south of Forth and Clyde, Dunbar and March included; and why Bruce had made his beloved nephew Thomas Randolph earl thereof. It all did have one handicap, or drawback, admittedly, and that here, in this south-western area, was the lengthy border with the most senior of the Comyn lordships, that of Badenoch and Lochaber, the Red Comyns; and these lords, like their fellows further north-east, could be aggressive and acquisitive. Their present chief was, apparently, not so inclined, but he was said to be elderly and there could be trouble with his successors, the Macpherson chiefs in especial so fearing.

John would have liked to return to Darnaway, due eastwards from the Alvie More and Alvie Beg area, this south of the Monadh Ruadh heights, even though that would have taken them through a corner of Mar; but the snows forbade it, and they had to go back by Spey again and on to the Findhorn and so north along that great river. Robert was much impressed with it all, saying that he had had no idea that Moray was so vast, even though not so populous as was the Stewartry.

Then it was time to return southwards to meet Donald again at Corpach, duties performed.

That young man showed them bagfuls of silver which his father had sent for the king – how adequate a payment was not specified.

They set off on their long journey, with a new set of oarsmen.

Back, eventually, at Renfrew, they found Phemia there and sundry of her kin, but not the Steward, his countess nor Marjory. And Phemia gave them extraordinary tidings. It seemed that the king had fallen out with his Queen Margaret. They had often squabbled, all knew, but this was different. He had more or less banished her from court, to the dower-palace of Linlithgow. And, more extraordinary still, David was now pursuing another lady, and this none other than John's own sister Agnes, at

Dunbar, scarcely believable as this was. Agnes was not yet twenty and the monarch old enough to be her father. The Steward, it seemed, had been greatly concerned, for if the king went so far as to seek a divorce sanction from the Vatican, and actually marry Agnes Dunbar, then his, the Steward's, position as heir-presumptive to the throne could be endangered. Margaret Drummond had provided no offspring for the king, although she had for her previous marriage to Sir John Logie; but this younger woman might do so. Hence this hurried departure for the court, to discover the full situation, the Countess Euphemia and Marjory to go to the queen at Linlithgow. It all might be somewhat exaggerated, less serious, than reported, but it must be investigated.

John was bewildered, to put it mildly, even his marriage for the time being rivalled at the forefront of his mind by this astonishing story. He very much doubted whether it could be true. The king had visited Dunbar, of course, and would have met Agnes, but there had been no least hint of any romantic repercussions. Surely he would have heard had there been anything of the sort. It all just did not make sense.

Robert and he were not long in setting off eastwards. They would go to Linlithgow, as on their way, in the first instance, to learn what they could there – and, of course, to see Marjory – and then proceed on to Edinburgh, or wherever the court was based meantime. John, no doubt, would be for Dunbar thereafter, to learn that side of the story.

Linlithgow, in the west of Lothian, was only about thirty-five miles from Renfrew, so they reached there next day by noon, to find much acrimony and mortification reigning. Queen Margaret may not have been of regal birth and status, but she had a very positive personality, more so indeed than had her husband, this possibly the source of not a little of the bickering that had gone on. Now, it seemed, she was not going to sit back and feel sorry for herself. She was about to set off on her own for Avignon, in a ship from the Forth, to try to convince Pope Gregory not only not to grant David's divorce petition, but if possible to place the realm of Scotland under interdict unless such marital separation was forthwith abandoned, this an all but unique measure. She was going to take her niece, Annabella Drummond, with her, another cheerfully positive young woman, who was strongly supporting her in this course. Apparently the king's present activities, as remarkable as they were unexpected, had not been exaggerated in the reports. He was said to be haunting Dunbar, and reputedly going so far as to settle a pension and portion on young Agnes there, and telling her that he was going to make her his queen.

John wondered indeed what his mother thought of all this. He intended to go and find out, at the soonest.

The Steward had gone on to Edinburgh, to the court, from which the monarch was doing his own curious courting, leaving his wife at Linlithgow.

All this, of course, could not but have some impact on Marjory and John, however glad they were to see each other. There was little opportunity for any sort of love-making in the circumstances, but they did manage to have a walk together round the loch below the palace, and a kiss or two, with talk of their wedding as well as this of the king, before John and Robert headed off for Edinburgh.

There, at the abbey, they found the Steward, but no monarch. Just where David had gone was uncertain. He had left the day before, but had not returned for the night. The Steward, looking sour, guessed that he might well be at Dunbar or thereabouts.

John had to go on there also, although in the circumstances he had no wish to meet his liege-lord, and be faced with problems of his own correct attitudes. He would wish to see his mother, brother and sister before he saw the king, to discover the situation. It was too late to ride on to Dunbar that night. Robert would probably go back to his stepmother and sister at Linlithgow next day.

So they put up at Holyrood for the night. The Steward

was interested to hear of the queen's intended journey to see the Pope, commending this. It was to be hoped that she would be successful in her efforts. He had urged the king to reconsider, in the nation's interests, but with no evident effect.

In the morning, then, it was for Dunbar, John wondering.

At that castle, he discovered upset indeed and disharmony, although at least the monarch was not present. It appeared that he was probably at the Trinitarian monastery of Houston, nearby, where he was apt to lodge on his visits to Dunbar. Black Agnes was much against this royal courtship of her daughter, deeming it most unsuitable, deplorable. The younger Agnes was in a state of uncertainty, flattered by the king's attentions, intrigued by the possibility of becoming a queen, but having no particular affection towards the monarch. George, for his part, saw advantage in having David as brother-in-law, the Cospatricks thereby moving that step nearer to the throne which should rightfully be theirs. If Agnes was indeed to have a child by the king, who was none so robust physically and might well not live to any great age, then the nephew or niece might need a regent, and who was more apt than the uncle, the Earl of Dunbar and March?

In this delicate situation, John was of course in something of a quandary. He got on well with David, had served him with some success, and, to be sure, had sworn loyal support to his liege-lord as an earl. Yet he tended to feel as his mother did. If his sister had been actually in love with the king it might have been different, however few royal marriages were love-matches. And his mother was even unsure that marriage was intended. According to her, a pension and portion had been offered to her daughter, but this, of sixty merks a year at once, with a possible larger sum to follow, might be a suitable amount for a mistress, but not for a queen. And she told John that Sir James Douglas of Dalkeith had recently been paying some attentions to Agnes, and she showing interest in his approaches, mildly encouraging – until this of the monarch.

What was to be done, then? Black Agnes urged her younger son to use any influence he had with the king to dissuade him from this misguided course; and hearing of Queen Margaret's mission to the Vatican and the possibility of its success, refusal of divorce sanction, made it the more essential that this courtship should be stopped. John agreed, but wondered what he could do to counter the monarch's infatuation, if that is what it was. David had said that he would attend the wedding at Paisley Abbey, in a week or two's time, a love-match. Was this the time to make objections to the other's romance, however unsuitable in a man of more than twice the age of the woman?

His mother said that there was one thing he could do, apart from seeking to dissuade the king: he could go and see Sir James Douglas at Dalkeith, tell him of the position, if he did not already know of it, and suggest that if he still felt amorous towards Agnes he should come and press his cause. If the king knew that someone, especially one of the powerful house of Douglas, was proposing marriage, he might be prepared to think again, the more so if his Margaret was proving successful with Pope Gregory.

In fact, John was quite glad to do this, for he distinctly dreaded a confrontation with the king meantime, who might arrive at Dunbar at any moment. He would be off to Dalkeith forthwith. They were on friendly terms with the Douglases, for his elder sister Margaret was married to William, Earl of Douglas, kin to Dalkeith.

Grinning, George told his brother not to be too urgent about it.

Dalkeith was slightly nearer to Dunbar than was Edinburgh, in the same general direction, a score of miles only, a modest town with a large castle nearby in a strong position on the lengthy peninsula where the Rivers North and South Esk joined, the fortalice crowning a rocky mound above the former. There John duly found Sir James Douglas, a handsome man of thirty years, fifth of his line, none so distant kin of the 1st Earl of Douglas, John's brother-in-law, and of the late Good Sir James, the Bruce's great friend and supporter who had sought to take that king's heart to the Holy Land and died so doing. This Sir James greeted his visitor in friendly fashion, surprised to see him, assuming him to be away in his far northern parts.

He proved to know something of the position regarding King David and his queen, and had heard rumours of the royal interest in the Lady Agnes Dunbar, but did not know how much credit to accord them. He announced that, set-faced.

"You, friend, have found my sister somewhat to your taste, I think?" John said then. "Or . . . was it but a passing fancy?"

"No-o-o." That was warily replied. "I deem her most . . . desirable."

"Ah. Then you will be unhappy over this of the king?"

"If it is all true, then I am, my lord. But . . . if Agnes could become queen . . ."

"There are, shall we say, doubts about that. Queen Margaret is seeking papal authority to prevent divorce. So King David may not be able to wed another. If such is his intention. We, my mother and myself, are less than pleased at it all. I get on well with the king, but . . . this is unfortunate." John paused. It was difficult to put this into words. "We think think that Agnes has some, some fondness for you, Sir James."

"I had thought it so, a little. Hoped for it."

"And you still feel for her?"

"I was not . . . light, in that, my lord."

"No. And John is my name. Forget the lord! You would wed her?"

"If I could."

"My mother thinks that if you sought her in marriage matters might well be . . . bettered. Give His Grace pause. To her benefit, the benefit of all. How say you?"

"Would she, Agnes, consider it? And the king?"

"We would hope so. When David hears of this of the Vatican, if the Pope accedes, as the queen believes that he may, then, yes, a proposal of marriage from you could better all. Agnes is not enamoured of David, only captivated by the notion of the monarch wanting her. Her head spinning at the notion of being queen. Her head, not her heart." John thought of Marjory's distinctions between head and heart. "And she is not yet of full age, he old enough to have sired her. How say you?"

"I would do it, yes. Seek her hand. Even if the king frowns on me."

"Do so then, James. You will have our mother's support."

"And your brother, the Earl George?"

"He is less . . . concerned. He sees benefits of closeness to the monarch. But he will also see further alliance with the Douglases as of value."

"Yes. Your other sister is Countess of Douglas. He, your older brother, will not forbid it? Marriage to myself. When she is not of age?"

"Not forbid, I judge. Not against our mother's will. *She* is the head of our family, still."

"Ah, yes – Black Agnes! How soon, then?"

"As soon as you can make it, James. Before the king goes further."

"I will be for Dunbar forthwith . . ."

Wishing the other well, and telling him of his own marriage plans, John left Dalkeith.

It was too late to ride the twenty miles back to Dunbar that night; but Edinburgh was only six miles, which he could manage in the dark. There he found the Steward still at the abbey, seeking to stir up other magnates to protest to the king. He was interested in this of the Douglas proposal, and commended it. Robert of Carrick, it seemed, had gone back to Linlithgow. John would have done the same, to be with Marjory, but recognised that he owed it to his mother, and possibly Agnes, to acquaint her with the Douglas's agreement.

In the morning it was back to Dunbar, to learn that he had just missed a visit by the king by only an hour or so the previous afternoon, sister Agnes being again excited by it but not committing herself against her mother's wishes. It was all a most complicated situation, with the king well aware of Black Agnes's opposition.

She was glad to hear of James Douglas's attitude; and in fact that man arrived at Dunbar not long after John did, to differing welcomes, warm from their mother, questioning from her daughter and cool from George. Black Agnes quite quickly manoeuvred things so that daughter and suitor were left together in one of the outer rock-stack towers.

When, after a period of rather tense waiting, Sir James came back to them, alone, he was not seemingly depressed, almost hopeful. He said that Agnes had not dismissed him, nor actually rejected his attentions, although not encouraging him, clearly in a state of divided mind, even thanking him haltingly for offering marriage, admitting that the king was honouring her with his company and favours, but not asserting her own preferences. So now he would formally ask for her hand in marriage, and offer a substantial portion, in lands, for consideration.

That was as far as matters could go at the moment; and as a midday meal was served, all undoubtedly wondering whether the king would arrive, and what would be the results if he did, a less than comfortable occasion followed, with Agnes very silent, George hearty while eyeing the others assessingly, and Black Agnes doing most of the talking.

John felt himself to be something of a coward when he announced fairly urgent business elsewhere connected with his own marriage arrangement – which was true enough, in a way, for he was eager to get back to Marjory. But he certainly did not want to be present here if his liege-lord turned up again, and have to demonstrate his opposition to this strange courtship. His mother would understand, whether the others did or not. He did not ask

116

whether Sir James intended to stay on, and if so, possibly have to confront the monarch with his proposal of marriage. Linlithgow for John of Moray.

It was nightfall before he reached the palace, there to find that Queen Margaret had already departed, from the port of Burghstoneness, or Bo'ness as it was called locally, taking with her Annabella Drummond, her niece. This, Marjory declared, to the disappointment of her brother Robert of Carrick, who it seemed was, in his own undemonstrative way, interesting himself in the said Annabella, an intriguing development, for, if all went as it ought to do, Robert himself should one day become King of Scots, and a wife the queen. This matter of possible queens was becoming something for guesswork.

Marjory also revealed that Queen Margaret had the guidance of John, Bishop of Dunkeld, an important prelate whose diocese included the Drummonds' estate of Stobhall, nine miles north of Perth. His advice to her regarding the Pope at Avignon, and the procedure to adopt regarding the divorce position, had been valuable, for he was close to the Vatican and believed that her stance would be successful.

There was nothing now to keep Countess Euphemia and her daughter at Linlithgow, and the court at Edinburgh being in some disarray because of the king's behaviour and frequent absence, there was no point in joining the Steward meantime. So it was to be back to Renfrew. With only a short time to pass before the wedding, John, needless to say, was for accompanying them.

The betrothed couple, as it transpired, found it less of a trial to keep their desires under control now than formerly – not because these were any less strong but, having waited thus long and with fulfilment only a brief period ahead, they were not going to undervalue their long restraint. Not that this prevented *all* their intimacies and manifestations of affection; but they did not seriously test themselves further.

John stayed at Renfrew for a few days. They went to see the Abbey and Abbot of Paisley, three miles to the south, where they would celebrate the wedding. They found Abbot Thomas most helpful; not surprising, for his abbey had been founded by the bride-to-be's ancestor, Walter the High Steward, son of Alan, the first of the line, in 1163, a Benedictine establishment dedicated to St James and also to St Mirren, of the earlier Celtic Church; and although the great building had been burned by the English in 1307, during Bruce's fight against invasion, the present Steward's father had partly rebuilt it. This was the burial-place of the family, and Marjory was able to point out the grave of her grandmother and namesake, Marjory Bruce, who had died when thrown from her horse on the Knock Hill nearby, this fifty-three years before, leaving the infant Robert.

They discussed all the nuptial arrangements, as far as they were able, with the abbot, to Marjory's satisfaction, John being less concerned, his priority merely to get the marriage over, and have his love finally his own. Abbot Thomas wondered whether in fact the king would be present, in view of the situation. That John was unable to tell him.

Much as he would have liked to linger at Renfrew, John felt that he had to get back to his mother and sister, in the circumstances, where his presence might be helpful; and, of course the attendance of the family at his wedding arranged. So it was farewell meantime, but not long to wait.

At Dunbar he learned that the king was much put about over the word of his wife's mission to the Pope, sufficiently so for him to be sending his own envoy to Avignon to seek to counteract her activities. So he had presently left this area and gone over to St Andrews in Fife, to confer with the Primate, Bishop Landells, on this. That at least was a relief.

Sister Agnes was still in a state of uncertainty, but her mother was fairly sure that she was coming round to see that her future lay probably with James Douglas rather than with David Bruce, and that her own affections and inclinations were a deal more important than any possible elevation to queenship.

John suggested that it might be a good move to invite the Douglas to the wedding at Paisley, where there could be opportunity for the pair to be in closer contact than here at Dunbar. Sister Margaret, Countess of Douglas, would be there, almost certainly, with her husband, and she might well help. If the king did appear, the circumstances would not be conducive for pressing his case before a gathering of otherwise-minded families.

John went to Dalkeith himself to invite James Douglas, and was thanked warmly for it.

Only a few days, and nights, to wait, now.

10

The cavalcade from Dunbar set out on the second day of April, with one hundred miles to go; so they would have to halt for the night, and chose the priory of Torphichen, conveniently placed. Since it was considered unsuitable for the bride and groom to see each other on the day of the wedding, the latter's party would go directly to Paisley, where the abbot had ample accommodation, and there were Cluniac and Black Friars establishments in the town for other guests. It was to be a great day, and not only for the happy couple, 4th April, 1370.

James Douglas joined the Dunbar travellers at Torphichen, and although there was little opportunity for male and female togetherness at the priory, he was able to sit beside Agnes at the evening meal in the large refectory, the latter not noticeably incommoded thereat.

Next day, skirting Glasgow to the south, to cross Clyde at Dalmarnock, they made Paisley by mid-afternoon, Douglas usually riding alongside Agnes and her mother and younger and unmarried sister Elizabeth. They found the eldest sister, Margaret, already installed, with her husband the Earl William, at the Blackfriars monastery quite near the abbey, they not having had so very far to come from Douglas Castle in Lanarkshire, a short day's ride to the south-east. Margaret did not require much bidding from her mother to advise her sister on the advantages of a Douglas marriage.

In the abbey guest-house that night there was a great gathering of the bridegroom's kin and guests, and some of the bride's also, practically all Lowland Scotland having some representation at the wedding of the High Steward's daughter to a Cospatrick and son of Black Agnes, Earl of Moray as he now was.

At bed-going, and sharing a room with his brother, John was given expert and detailed advice for the following night, which he could well have done without, however much the occasion occupied his mind. He did ask George when *he* was going to make an honest woman out of one of his females, and was told that there was no hurry at all, at all!

They were up betimes, with the ladies especially concerned over their dressing and appearance, hairstyle and the like, as though, George remarked, they were the centres of attraction. There was no sign of King David.

Left to himself John would have been at the church much too early, but sensible counsel prevailed, and they all went, on foot and more or less in procession, through the crowded streets. They were greeted at the abbey's west door by Abbot Thomas wearing his mitre. Mitred abbots were an especial ranking, usually in line for bishoprics.

Even so, they were a little early, and John and George were conducted up the central aisle to the chancel steps, nodding right and left to the already crowded lines of guests, to the chanting of choristers. Even though the abbey had been only partly rebuilt after the burning, it was still a large and splendid fane, larger indeed than Holyrood at Edinburgh or St Mungo's of Glasgow.

In the event they did not have long to wait there, despite the customary privilege of brides to be late, for Marjory was not like that, a very forthright young woman. The abbot waiting before the altar flanked by lesser clerics, she was led forward by the Steward, to enhanced singing, with musical accompaniment. She was looking lovely indeed, dressed with simple dignity and carrying herself with a sort of grave serenity. Her father looked neither right nor left.

John turned to greet her, not quite sure what the procedure was, and was rewarded with a warm smile, his brother bowing elaborately.

Abbot Thomas came forward to them, hands raised in

121

welcoming blessing. The singers and instrumentalists fell silent.

The service thereafter followed the usual course, John for one scarcely aware of it all, the introduction to all present, the address to the couple, the sacred nature of what they were about to solemnise, the binding ties of the marriage vows, and Christ's blessing on it all by his attendance of the wedding at Cana of Galilee, the groom's mind not exactly being elsewhere but possessed by a sort of impatience. Had he actually analysed his attitude it would have been to recognise that his perception of their joining together as man and wife had really taken place weeks before, when Marjory had admitted that she loved him and would give herself to him, as he would to her. This was, to him, their true marriage, this ceremony only a public recognition and confirmation of it and, as far as he was concerned, to be got over as quickly as possible. He wondered whether Marjory felt the same, although she gave no impression of anything such, she calmly attentive.

George in fact nudged him when it came to the stage of bride and groom coming closer, for the Steward to give his daughter away, and the ring to be handed over and fitted, with the necessary words, the pressure of her warm hand reaching the man effectively, and suddenly all becoming good, meaningful. Indeed John had to restrain himself once more, his impulse to grasp Marjory to him there and then.

The abbot gestured to them to kneel, to be declared one, man and wife, in the presence of Almighty God and these witnesses, to a well-timed outburst of praise from the choristers, and Marjory turning to him, eyes eloquent of love and joy and almost achievement; so it had been worth it all, he acknowledged, as he raised her up, *his* now undeniably, himself the most fortunate and blessed man on earth. But, oh – to get her alone!

A brief nuptial mass followed, then the general benediction, and the rousing and praiseful singing; they turned, and arm-in-arm proceeded down the aisle, acknowledging the smiles, gestures and words of congratulation and goodwill from all in the packed nave, Marjory at least doing full justice to the occasion.

Out at the great western doorway, first to be there, John could at least take his wife in his arms, words unnecessary, she, eyes closed, breast heaving, hands stroking his head and cheek; only moments but precious ones.

Then they were surrounded by well-wishers, and bliss postponed. But they were wed, wed!

John wondered whether all marriages were like this, seemingly endless celebrations, feasting, speeches and delay? Or was he the impatient one, more so than most? Marjory seemed to appreciate it all, although frequently she managed to catch his eye and nod. He was, to be sure, calculating, timing it all. For they had to get back to Renfrew, after the abbatial hospitality; there, after no doubt more and unnecessary refreshment, change into travelling clothes, and get away. He had planned that part of it all carefully, at least, and was concerned that nothing should unduly hold them up, for they had to travel some distance before nightfall. And there was to be no putting up in religious establishments or hospices, this night of all nights, where men and women were kept apart. He had arranged, with his new brother-in-law, Carrick, that suitable accommodation should be available for them in one of the Stewartry vassal's houses, this Elliotstoun Tower, where the Black Cart emerged from Loch Winnoch; but that was almost a dozen miles to the south-west; and the last thing he wanted was to have his bride worried about the time of day, riding in darkness and in any way anxious save for his husbandly attentions.

They reached Elliotstoun, a small, square tower-house, just as dusk was settling. The owners were Sempills, an old family, and had been duly prepared for these especial visitors' coming. They had a quite handsome repast ready, which was not really wanted, but had to be partaken of in appreciation, with other civilities required; so there was quite some time before it was decently possible to say their retirals, and be led upstairs to an attic chamber within the parapet-walk, where all was ready for them, a bright fire, steaming bathtub, and more wine on a small table by the wide bed. Expressing their thanks, they said their goodnights, and closed the door behind their hostess, waiting over, alone at last.

For some moments they stood, hands clasped, eyeing each other, John shaking his head but in anything but negative fashion, Marjory breathing deeply and indeed biting her lip. They did not speak; there was no need.

He led her over to the fire, and there she held out her arms, wide, for him.

"Yours, all yours!" she said. "And, and longing to be! Am I, am I . . .?" She got no further before her lips were sealed, but anything but closed.

Standing there they kissed, he all but shaking her as his pent-up feelings found the beginnings of release, although only the beginnings.

When he could master himself, and her, sufficiently, John found the words. "Mine, yes – mine, my beloved. But myself all yours. And you, dear one, you must, must not be, be forced! By my, my haste. And need. And man's demands. You must . . ."

"Think you that I fear anything such, foolish one?" she asked him, pressing herself even closer against him, turning her person this way and that. "I am no . . . delicate creature, no shrinking female, requiring to be spared and, and coaxed and heedfully readied. Have I not waited for this as long as have you, husband mine?"

"Yes. But you are woman, and so may be less urgent, less needful, less impatient?"

"John, John, have I not told you? Women are none so different. We incline to pretend that we are, but we are not, most of us. Look you, you have seen me as I am, kissed, fondled me, undressed me above my waist. But *I* have not done the like. Now I shall!" She drew back a little, and then reached out to start unbuttoning his doublet.

124

Promptly he began to assist her, but she pushed his hands aside. "No, this is my task, my privilege now," she asserted. "I will be none so feeble about it, you will see!'

Soon she was undoing his shirt, and even when he bent so that she could draw it off over his head, she told him to leave it to her. In time, she said, she would become practised at it.

Then it was his breeches, he at least being allowed to kick off his boots. Marjory had just a little difficulty here, on account of his significant masculinity, with herself gentle now, she even getting down on her knees to help free his legs and feet. She remained thus for a moment or two, and then rising, she stood back to eye him with frank and detailed appreciation.

"My lord of Moray!" she said.

John spread his hands. "Will I . . . serve?" he asked.

"We shall see, as to that, husband! Now – your turn!"

He required no such invitation, going to her, reaching for the bodice of her gown. He was somewhat less careful about it than she had been, less lingering, and the woman scarcely helping him by pressing against him and kissing various parts of him within her reach, while he drew down her clothing. However, when he encountered some entanglement with the skirts, over and under, also hose and footwear, grunting, he stooped to pick her up bodily, so that, waggling her long legs she freed all, in somewhat untidy fashion, with gurgling laughter, and she was naked in his arms, warm, rounded, anything but passive, stirring in more ways than one.

And thus he carried her over to the bed, all but tripping over the scatter of clothing on the floor.

She tugged at his ear. "The water?" she demanded. "To wash? To bathe ourselves."

"That can wait!" he jerked. "I can not!"

Nevertheless, when he laid her on the bed, he did wait, if only for a little, in order to gaze and scan and relish what he saw in the flickering firelight, all the rich and inviting feminine loveliness spread there before him, feasting his eyes and catching his breath, which was already in some commotion.

Then she held out her arms to him, and with a strangled cry he threw himself down upon her.

What followed was all too hasty, inevitably, Marjory's well-meant assistance in fact only speeding matters, causing his entrance to potential bliss to be the more precipitate, demanding, rather than blissful for either of them. She gasped and clutched him, all but shook him as she winced and bit her lip; but there was no stopping him now, from his jerking, vehement assertion, all but aggression. He took her, possessed her, mastered her, and with a cry of both climax and frustration, fulfilment and chiding, release and regret, he reared up and then collapsed on top of her.

"I, I am . . . sorry! Sorry!" he got out.

"Impatient one!" she told him. But she stroked his head as she said it, her voice catching.

"I will do better. Soon! Soon!"

"I will hold you to that. If, if I can!"

"Never fear. It was the waiting, my dear, the long waiting, so very long. Forgive, lass . . ."

They lay together then, side by side now, waiting.

"Can I help?" she asked, after a while.

"Just being *you* helps!" he told her. "And . . . I do not think that you will have to wait overlong."

She did not have to. The essential man in John rose to the challenge. Now he was all care and caring, while still being sufficiently masterly, he enjoying the caring to the full, the anxiety gone. Nor did he have to hold himself back for long, Marjory being, as she had said, all woman, her responses positive, her involvement far from passive. Her cry of satisfaction presently completed her partner's satisfaction and gratification, and he could let himself go without reserve.

Still holding hands thereafter, eyes closing, they both slept.

Not for all that night, to be sure, was sleeping called for, as 4th April became 5th April. But they did sleep late in the morning, their hosts not arousing them, although some arousement there was nevertheless.

They remained three days at Elliotstoun, happy to do so. They explored the countryside around. They climbed the Hill of the Stake, and Dunconnel; they visited the site of the Battle of Largs, of a century before, when it was the Norse invaders under King Hakon who were repulsed instead of the English; they got as far south as the Kennedy country, beyond the Steward's territory, new terrain even for Marjory.

Thereafter they took their leave, with sincere thanks to the Sempills, to head eastwards. They would go to Dunbar, to see John's family, and then he would take his wife up to Darnaway, to introduce her to what was to be her new home.

At Dunbar they learned that the king was not pursuing Agnes meantime, presumably awaiting word from Avignon; and that James Douglas was making the most of his opportunities, and with some success.

Well pleased over this, as with all else, the newly-weds waited until a ship was available to take them up to Inverness, Marjory being shown much of the dramatic coastal scenery of that seaboard, and discovering some of the secret valleys, gorges and waterfalls of the Lammermuir Hills, with their Pictish standing stones and circles, Agnes and Douglas accompanying them on two of the excursions.

Then it was Moray for its earl and countess.

11

The settling-in at Darnaway Castle kept Marjory busy, but rewardingly so, she having her own ideas as to domestic bliss, John glad to leave it to her, and far from disapproving of her decisions and arrangements. For himself, he found ample concerns and commitments awaiting him after his absence from his wide lands and responsibilities, with those Comyns still troublesome, clan feuding apt to get out of hand and impinge on neighbouring folk, and the port-keepers and harbour-masters having difficulties in collecting the increased import and export dues. But at least there was no raiding by the Islesmen, which was a major blessing, Donald's father being as good as his word. And William of Ross appeared to be preoccupied with the Sutherland situation in the north.

Word from elsewhere reached them mainly by information from the mendicant or wandering friars, those useful brothers who dealt with so much of the rural parish problems and were the greatest news-bearers of the land. Queen Margaret was back from France, and with the papal injunction against divorce, to her satisfaction. This would scarcely be the cause of it, but it seemed that King David had fallen ill, and was being nursed by the monks at Holyrood, just what his trouble was unspecified. So Agnes would be spared royal attentions for the time being. Pope Gregory was said to be considering leaving Avignon to return to Rome, so presumably the current problems of the papacy were being resolved, or some of them, the College of Cardinals allegedly gaining in power and influence. The crusading endeavours had recently been more or less suspended, because of Vatican problems, and it was now reported that David Bruce, thinking of his future, near and further, and not wishing to get on the wrong side of Holy Church, was saying that if Almighty God gave him back his health, he would himself lead a crusade to the Holy Land – this of course interesting John over the issue of his sister, but rather worrying Marjory, in case the monarch expected her husband to accompany him thereon.

John had one especial concern to see to at this time, the dealing with which did give opportunity to let his wife visit much of the earldom with him. It was the matter of forests, woodlands, timber. His brother George had sought his help in this, as had the Steward. The building of ships was becoming ever more important since parliament had so greatly increased the assessments and dues payable on the entire land, and trade overseas one of the greatest sources of revenue. The Cospatricks had been exporting Lammermuirs wool, hides, salted mutton and fish for long, to the Low Countries and the Baltic lands; this was to be greatly expanded and developed; and by other magnates and landholders also. So a major building of ships was required to carry the trade, demanding much of hardwood timber of high quality, oak and elm and beech in particular. And Moray was famous for its forests: Darnaway itself, but also those of the long Spey valley, Lochindorb, Longmorgan, Kilblain, and to a lesser degree those of Elgin and Spynie, Forres and Boyne of Banff. But there was a complication, and not only here. Traditionally forestry, the care of the trees and the cutting and selling of the timber, was in the hands of the churchmen, with the owners thereof, the lords and lairds, mainly concerned with the woodlands as hunting areas. The clerics, paying only small tokens for the privilege, had been building their churches, priories, monasteries and abbeys since time was, out of the wood, and making moneys out of it all also. So now John had to seek the co-operation of Holy Church for the use of his own forests. He went to see Bishop Alexander at Spynie, who had been so helpful to him before.

The bishop was understanding, indeed expecting this, for the Church, also having to increase its contributions to the treasury, had to exploit the timber situation. The clerics had their labour force of lay brothers, expert in the care and exploitation of the woodlands, the felling of trees and the sawing-up of the timber into beams and planking. It was accepted, of course, that the forests did not belong to them, their interest a matter of tradition and usage. So – a sort of partnership in this matter of such growing importance, to the benefit of both earldom and Church? That suited John.

There followed extensive tours of the various forests, in company with two of the bishop's forester monks, together with Duncan Murray, the Darnaway keeper, Marjory glad to go along frequently to see more of the land. The Spey valley, with its great forests of Rothiemurchus and Alvie and Glenfeshie, particularly captivated her, likewise Lochindorb with its castle-island, which they used as a base.

John found this of the forests and woodlands a fascinating exercise, locating the best areas for the trees they wanted, selecting and marking the ones to be felled, and arranging with local men to do the work. As well as all this, the sheer pleasure of threading the glades and shaws of the woods, seeing the deer, red and roe, hearing but seldom seeing the wolves, and watching out for dangerous boars. Marjory had never before seen capercailzie, the great turkey-like birds which burst out of bushes and thickets, good to eat. Indeed the keeper of Lochindorb and his wife fed them on these, as well as venison, and salmon from the loch, to their due enjoyment.

April over and passing into May and June, the snows disappeared from the mountains, and horse travel became no problem, save for the undrained marshland to be negotiated and rushing rivers crossed. Long days were spent in the saddle, with the results of the woodland surveys to be inspected and arrangements made for the felled and sawn-up timber to be dragged by teams of oxen and garrons to ports, where it could be towed off in the form of great rafts, behind sea-going ships.

Then, in early July, there was interruption. A messenger arrived from the king, summoning the Earl of Moray to Edinburgh forthwith, reasons not given. His wife said that it would be for this of the projected crusade, and wished that he need not go. But a royal command had to be obeyed.

Marjory went south with him. They would have sailed in one of the Inverness vessels, but these were being used to tow timber, and so much slowed down. So they took the long road on horseback, and this time had no difficulty in winning through the mountain passes.

At Holyrood Abbey they found a large assembly gathered, including Marjory's father and brother, and George of Dunbar. Heads were being shaken over the king's condition, and this nonsensical notion of a crusade, which the Steward declared was an indication that David Bruce judged that his last days were upon him, and this arranging for an expedition to the Holy Land to fight the infidel would help to act against the penalties for his sins and omissions of his earthly life. He, Walter Stewart, had endeavoured to dissuade him, without success; but he would do his best to delay the implementation of it all, in the hope that time would favour them. He did not actually say that the sooner the monarch died, the better, but that was implied.

When the king did put in an appearance, John was shocked to behold the change in the man from when last seen. His liege-lord was gaunt, haggard of feature, stooping and frail-looking. Whatever his ailment, it must be a dire one, and making him seem almost an old man. It could be seen why the Steward was urging delay.

David held the opposite view, needless to say. He declared that the crusade must start as soon as could be arranged. He himself would lead it, if that was possible; but if not, the High Steward would take his place. All lords who had shipping at their disposal, particularly the Earls of Dunbar and March, Moray and Fife, with the Steward himself, must assemble the greatest number of vessels that they could, to transport the force; and every earl, lord, baron and knight must muster their best fighting-men for the great venture, and this speedily. And there would have to be a regency council set up to rule in Scotland in the interim. He was heard in general silence.

Even this fairly brief deliverance had obviously taxed the king's strength and he was not long in retiring whence he had come, leaving a company concerned in more ways than one, for the king was well liked, even if this project was not.

John was no more eager than almost all there to go crusading, and to start assembling a contingent to take part in it; but the monarch was High King of Scots, and all had taken oaths to support him. There was much debate. Temporising was the favoured reaction, led by the Steward. Go through some of the motions of raising men, but delay. After all, it was verging on harvest-time when, by long tradition, manpower was not to be taken off the land until the essential crops were ingathered and stored. So they had excuse. Strangely, it was John's and George's brother-in-law, William, Earl of Douglas, who led the contrary view, seeming quite keen on the idea of crusading. He was a warrior-type of course, and descendant of a long line of fighters. Few backed his stance, however.

Some suggested that there should be a parliament called to consider this, the which, calling for forty days' notice, would help the delay; but even the Steward had to declare that this was hardly a matter for parliament, to debate the king's expressed wish. However, harvesting, especially in the north, could be and frequently was, put off until mid-September; and the mustering of an army, and the assembling of shipping, could well take them into October. Then they would see what was to be done. This was agreed.

John and Marjory went with George back to Dunbar. There their mother proved to be no more in favour of crusading at this present than they were. She said that if all could postpone the assembling of men and ships until the end of October, then they could claim that the shipmasters strongly advised against sailing until the winter was over, for the voyage of a great fleet all the way to the Holy Land would take weeks, and stormy seas make the entire project impracticable. That made sense.

George was pleased with the timber provision from Moray, but required more, much more. He had entered into an arrangement with a shipbuilder in Leith, the port of Edinburgh, to construct three large vessels which could be used for trading but also for carrying troops, and they were calling for more wood, oak in especial. Could John increase and speed up the supply? And the Steward was seeking more timber also, as was Kennedy of Dunure, and they would pay well for it.

Black Agnes said that perhaps they should slow down this shipbuilding as a further help in delaying the king's crusading, with insufficient vessels to convey the force.

So it was north again for John and Marjory, in some doubts as to priorities. But, in this of the timber, hardwoods had to be seasoned, after felling and sawing up, so his activities could go ahead whatever postponement might be contrived.

This of delay in the nation's affairs became even more urgent for John as August passed into September. Marjory announced that she was fairly sure that she was pregnant – and rejoicing as he did over this development in their togetherness, the thought of having to leave his dear one to go off crusading was anathema. As harvesting oats and barley for the time being superseded that of timber, he became ever more determined that he was not going to allow anything to take him away from Marjory before she gave birth. He would find some excuse.

Actually the word that the friars brought from the south was reassuring in this respect, however sad as regards King David. He was sinking steadily in his condition, and the physicians were doubting whether he would survive until the turn of the year. In the circumstances, although the dying monarch still wished his crusade to go ahead without him, his royal urgings were becoming less vehement and questioning. It looked as though the winter storms warning would be successful in halting any long voyages until spring, by which time the matter might well be of little import. The nation, however concerned for its liege-lord, was beginning to sigh with relief.

The harvest in and the barns filled, it was back to the forestry in Moray, Marjory still insisting on frequently accompanying her husband on his inspections, declaring that at her present stage horse-riding would not hurt her pregnancy. She calculated that it would be January before she had to restrict her activities somewhat, and late February before she was delivered. This distinctly worried John, whose attitude now was to treat her as an invalid, more or less, to be watched and cossetted – for the which he was chided as foolish.

At any rate, all went well, and in due course Yuletide came and went, the king still alive, Marjory showing her condition and proud of it. She was going to bear a son, the Master of Moray, she was sure.

And she did. On the second-last day of February she was brought to bed, and after a fairly supportable labour produced a boy, healthy and lively, especially as to the lungs. He was to be named Thomas, after his great-grandsire, Thomas Randolph, first Earl of Moray, the Bruce's nephew. There was relief and rejoicing, John prouder of himself than over anything else in his life as yet, marching about the castle and showing off the infant to one and all.

And then, four days later, a mendicant brother on his travels told them that King David had passed on to a better kingdom, on the same day as young Thomas had been born, and leaving no direct heir. Scotland, for the present, was without a monarch.

12

It was not long before a summons came to Darnaway for John to repair to Edinburgh for a council meeting to confirm the succession. Little as he desired to leave the new mother at this stage, making excellent recovery as she was, he felt that he could hardly refuse her father's call even though it was not a royal command, however nearly so, the Steward having long been heir-presumptive to the throne, indeed had acted as regent during David's captivity in England. Marjory assured him that all was well with her and the child, and that he deserved a break from husbandly and fatherly preoccupations for a spell.

He sailed south in one of the Inverness ships with a tow of timber behind, to head for Leith, snow again closing the passes.

The council was held at Holyrood, and even before it began John learned that there was trouble ahead. George was there and told him that their own brother-in-law, the Earl of Douglas, was the cause of it. He was claiming that he had as much right to the throne as had the Steward, and contesting that man's right to succeed. This astonished the brothers, who could see no substance behind such assertion.

At the meeting they learned more, the Douglas not being present. He was saying that he was descended, in the female line, from both King John Balliol and the Red Comyn, former Guardian of Scotland. Balliol may have been a poor monarch, he was accepting, but he was senior by birth to Bruce, and the Comyn Bruce's rival. Moreover, he held that the Douglases were the most powerful family in the realm, and better able to maintain the authority of the crown than any other.

None gathered round that table was for accepting this claim, even Douglas's stepfather, Sir Robert Erskine the Chamberlain, all supporting Robert Stewart – at least, none voiced other opinion.

The council passed a resolution that the Steward should be crowned King of Scots, and at the earliest possible date. But meanwhile every effort should be made to have the Earl of Douglas withdraw his extraordinary claim, to avoid any unsuitable dispute with that warlike house and its supporters. Douglas was reputed to be at Linlithgow, just why, at the queen's dower-house, was not known. Was he trying to enlist the late monarch's widow on his side? The Steward proposed that the three kinsfolk of the Earl William, his stepfather and two brothers-in-law, the Earls of Dunbar and March and of Moray, should go to Linlithgow forthwith, and seek to have this unfortunate matter put right, offering notable inducements, and report back. The trio were quite prepared to attempt this.

They rode off, with little delay, the eighteen miles to Linlithgow, halfway to Stirling. Sir Robert Erskine was a large man of middle years, who had married the widow of Archibald the Grim, brother of the Bruce's friend the Good Sir James Douglas of great renown. He, the Chamberlain, said that he was on good terms with his stepson, but had heard nothing of this claim to the crown. He thought it more a case of personal enmity towards the Steward than any real ambition to be king.

At Linlithgow they found Earl William and his son the Master of Douglas, James, with quite a large company of his people, being entertained by Queen Margaret. No explanation was offered for his presence there. He was a handsome man, oddly enough a year or two older than his stepfather, and greeted the newcomers in friendly fashion, although he probably guessed the reason for their visit.

His stepfather led off. "We have been sent by the council, Will," he announced. "It has unanimously declared in favour of Robert the High Steward becoming king. *Your* presence was missed. And there were whispers

136

that you might be putting forward some claim to the throne yourself? We scarcely believed this, but have been sent to enlist your support for the council's decision."

"You have? And why should the Douglas support the claim to the Scots throne by a FitzAlan? Tell me that. Stewart is but a style, an office. Their line is English!"

There was, of course, some truth in this. David the First, on his return from his years as a hostage in England to become king, in his late brothers' stead, had brought with him many Anglo-Norman friends whom he had made there, including Walter FitzAlan, whom he had appointed High Steward. The present Robert was seventh in line. So, although he took the name of Stewart, in fact the family name was otherwise.

"Robert Stewart is the Bruce's grandson," George put in. "Do we not owe the hero-king's memory some honour?"

"Robert FitzAlan will do no honour to the Bruce's name, no hero he! Douglas, now, meant something to Bruce."

"No doubt. But . . ."

"And I can claim descent from King John Balliol, Toom Tabard as he was! And also from the Red Comyn, who also had a claim to the throne, and was Bruce's rival Guardian for a time."

"If all folk of royal descent were to seek the throne, they would be legion! What of myself? I am Cospatrick. *My* ancestor should have worn the crown rather than his younger half-brothers, the Margaretsons."

John thought to join in, to bring a different approach. He might be wrong, but he gained the impression that his brother-in-law was not really concerned to gain the throne, but to consolidate Douglas power and have his house recognised as the most prestigious and powerful in the land. John sought to ring that bell now.

"The High Steward recognises the importance of Douglas support," he said. "He would show his goodwill over the aid you could give. On ascending the throne, he would

137

appoint you Justiciar South of Forth, and Warden of the East March. He would offer your son the hand of his daughter Isabella, my own wife's sister, in marriage. How say you to that, good-brother?"

The other eyed him, brows raised. "You say so?" He looked at the others. "Is this so? A price being paid?"

"It is an acknowledgment of Douglas worth. For the realm's weal, I would say."

"You will have the power in the land without the weight of the crown on your head, Will," Erskine added.

Douglas turned to his son. "How say you to wedding a princess, James?" he asked lightly.

"I would seek to see her first!" the young man declared, grinning.

"*I* have seen Isabella," John added. "She is lively, and sufficiently fair for any man."

"This of the offices offered," the father went on. "Justiciar South of Forth is well enough. But Warden of the East March?" He looked at George. "That is *your* March. Do you agree to this?"

"The Steward sought my word on it, yes. I would be glad to have you as Warden, Will. Better than one of those Homes! And you would be more at Tantallon, and I would see more of my sister Elizabeth."

"I could keep the English raiders in their place, yes. As to Justiciar, I have no great desire for making judgments, but . . ." He left the rest unsaid. It was obvious that he was accepting the situation, and was not going to oppose the Steward's succession – if he really ever had intended so to do.

All saw it, and they left the matter there.

The visitors stayed the night at Linlithgow Palace, with Queen Margaret as hostess, no reason for Douglas and his son and company there being explained. In the morning it was back to Edinburgh, mission accomplished.

At Holyrood their report was welcomed and their services acknowledged. They learned that the coronation of the new monarch, at Scone, was being planned for one month hence. There would have to be a parliament held first, to confirm the council's decision, but that would be largely a formality, and could be held the day before, at Perth. John would have only another three weeks at Darnaway before he had once again to make the voyage south. There were some disadvantages in being Earl of Moray.

Marjory would have liked to attend the coronation of her father, needless to say, but with a baby to nurture and feed she recognised that this was out of the question. She sent John off with instructions to come back to her just as soon as possible. She was going to be a princess hereafter, remember, and her wishes to be the more respected!

This time, the ship, loaded with timber and not towing it in rafts, to avoid the delay, was able to sail into the Tay estuary and right up to Perth, there to drop John and proceed on to Leith, dispose of its cargo and return in four or five days' time to collect and take him back to Inverness, all very convenient.

At Perth John found George at the Blackfriars monastery again, and there learned that his brother was at last contemplating matrimony, the lady, fortunate or otherwise, being Christian Seton, daughter of Sir William of that Ilk, the Dunbar earldom's most senior vassal. The brothers had known Christian for long, a calmly assured creature such as her spouse-to-be probably needed.

Perth town was full to overflowing with the great ones from far and near, even William of Ross and his foe the Earl of Sutherland being present, these also having come by ship. The coronation was to be two days hence, with the parliament the previous day. It was a long time since there had been a coronation in Scotland, for David had been crowned as a child of five, forty-two years before. Most present therefore had never attended one, and there was much interest and involvement.

The parliament was held next day, there in Perth. In fact, it was not truly a parliament at all, although proclaimed as such, there being no king, nor regent, at present. To be a true parliament, in Scotland, the king had to be present, otherwise it was a Convention. But since parliamentary sanction was required to confirm the council's decision as to the monarchy, this was of necessity *called* a parliament, the Steward presiding, with the Chancellor conducting the business; after all Robert had been regent those years ago. And there was a great turnout, much larger attendance than at most parliaments, because of the next day's vital affair.

The proceedings were brief, however necessary, there being no opposition voiced as to the Steward's succession, Douglas being present but not speaking. Any fears as to dispute proved to be groundless. So all could go ahead next day, as planned.

Scone Abbey itself, some four miles away, and across Tay, had accommodation for only a small number of the assemblage, with the many senior clerics based there. So Perth town had to house much of the important folk of Scotland that night.

The great day dawned wet and windy, but nothing was allowed to dampen the proceedings in other respects. A mile-long procession of notables, not to mention much of the town's population, set off to cross the river and head on to where allegedly the fresh water from Loch Tay overcame the salt water of the firth, this why Scone, from earliest times, indeed the pagan sun-worship days of the Picts, was considered to be a vital and precious spot, fertile, bountiful, almost holy; and why, when St Columba's Iona was overrun by the Viking hordes, the Stone of Destiny had been brought here, and the abbey built to house it, crowning-seat of kings.

The abbey itself was not large enough to hold all those attending, even of the important folk; so the ceremony at the Moot Hill nearby, after the religious service and anointing, would be the main event of the day, when the actual crowning would take place, and the loyal oath-giving would follow.

The Lord Lyon King of Arms, who this day took the

older style of High Sennachie, was very much in charge of all the arrangements, and concerned that everything should be done according to long tradition, with dignity, precedence in rank and status very much in evidence, with high officers-of-state foremost: Chancellor, Chamberlain, Constable, Marischal – John was glad to see Sir William Keith again – Justiciars and Wardens of the Marches. And on this occasion there was an unusual presence there, although not unique, a woman, Isabella, Countess of Fife in her own right, to act Coroner, or Crowner. The lady was elderly, but she had served as Coroner before when she was Countess of Buchan, and crowned Robert the Bruce, her brother, the Earl of Fife whose role it was, being under age. *He* had been able to crown David, but, dying without offspring, Isabella had become countess in her own right, and now had this role to play.

The other earls were well represented, save for Mar and two juveniles. Some were officers-of-state, to be sure. Then there were the lords, the barons, the chiefs and knights and lairds, also the provosts of royal burghs. Holy Church was well represented, of course, with Bishop Landells of St Andrews, the Primate, to conduct the service, with the aid of the Abbot of Scone. Oddly, John found himself sitting, in the abbey, between Ross and Atholl, senior to his brother, Moray being one of the original seven mormaordoms of ancient Alba, Dunbar and March not.

The anointing and religious part of the proceedings over, the monarch-to-be was led by the Lord Lyon, the Primate and the Countess-Coroner out to the Moot Hill close by, so called from the Gaelic *Tom-a-Mhoid* meaning the Hill of Justice, a quite tall flat-topped mound, up which these four had to climb, the Steward courteously assisting the lady. He then seated himself on the throne placed thereon, this having to serve instead of the ancient and renowned Stone of Destiny, which was now somewhere in the Hebrides, having been handed over to the then Lord of the Isles, Angus Og, by Bruce on his death-bed, to ensure that it did not fall into the grasping hands of

English invaders "until a worthy successor sits on my throne". The Islesmen still retained it, hidden securely; this a source of discord and controversy ever since.

The area around the hill was packed with cheering people, through which the royal procession had had to find its way. Fortunately the rain had stopped, although the wind was blustery.

Once the Steward was seated, the great officers-of-state climbed the distinctly slippery slope to take their places behind the throne. Then, after a great flourish of trumpets, the Primate announced that, in the sight of God and of all men, the ancient realm of Scotland this day would crown its monarch, already named, anointed and blessed before Christ's altar. He called upon the High Sennachie to remind them all of the royal precursors and succession.

Lyon had a lengthy peroration to make. This he read from a roll of parchment, containing the names of the previous monarchs of allegedly the most ancient line in all Christendom, back from pre-Christian times, some of which he had difficulty in pronouncing until he came to such as Aidan and Nechtan and Brude and Fergus and Angus and Kenneth and Duncan and MacBeth and Lulach, down to the Malcolms, the Margaretsons, William, the Alexanders, John Balliol, Bruce and David. This over, he bowed to the Countess of Fife, and she took the crown from a cushion carried by the Chamberlain, held it out to be blessed by the Primate, and then, after holding it high, and bowing, stepped over to place the golden circlet on the Steward's head, exclaiming, "Hail, Robert, High King of Scots!"

Loud and long the cry was taken up by all present. "Hail the king! Hail the king! Hail the king!" Robert Stewart remained sitting, the only one so doing in all that great assembly.

Then it was the oath-giving of allegiance, the officers-of-state the first to kneel before the new monarch, each taking a handful of earth from pockets or pouches to scatter before the throne so that the new king could place a foot upon it while he received the kneeling subject's oath, this the time-honoured custom representing the fact that allegiance should be sworn and received on the land of the swearer, this because in theory all the land was the monarch's, and to save him having to travel to every corner of his kingdom to receive it; so soil had to be brought by every landholder for the royal foot to stand on, a quaint artifice. It was claimed that this Moot Hill was ever growing in height because of all the earth brought to these coronations, although that was probably a myth.

The order of precedence for the oath-taking and giving was strictly regulated, as was all else; but on this occasion, Robert had given instructions that, as a gesture of expedient goodwill, William, Earl of Douglas, although not one of the ancient *ri* or mormaors, should be the first of the earls to climb the hill and kneel, taking the king's right hand between both his palms, after depositing his earth, and swearing to honour and support the monarch, to the best of his ability, all the days of his life.

All the while, choirs were chanting, music being played, and drums being beaten rhythmically.

When it was John's turn to mount the hillock to his father-in-law's throne, he did so wishing that Marjory could have been there to witness it all. He had duly brought some Darnaway soil. The oath given, Robert gestured to him to remain on the hill-top behind the throne, as a sign of favour and kinship.

So John was there to witness George's allegiance-giving, and got a face made at him in consequence as his brother had to descend to the levels again.

It took a long time for all the magnates and landowners present to make their vows. But eventually it was over, the heap of soil now quite substantial, and at last King Robert, the second of that name, could rise, hold a hand high, and, led down by the Lyon, go to join his people.

The House of Stewart had commenced its tenure of the throne.

13

John did not get back to Darnaway quite so quickly as he had expected and wished. For the new monarch was eager to show that he intended to rule effectively, as well as reign, and to improve on the late David's recent behaviour. So, recognising that the parliament of the day before had not been really adequate, little more than a formality, his first act as king was to call a true parliament while all the attenders were there present and so to avoid the forty days' notice, this again at Perth, in three days' time.

So almost all of those at the coronation had to remain in the vicinity meantime, and St John's Town of Perth had to support and entertain them as they waited, the many religious houses filled, much hospitality and patience demanded of them, the Blackfriars monastery included.

John and George, like many another, filled in the time by exploring the countryside around, eastwards into the great vale of Strathmore between the Sidlaw Hills and the Highland Line as far as Coupar Angus; north to the forested lands of Dunkeld, the seat of the former Keledei, the Celtic Church Friends of God; and west up Strathearn almost to Crieff, fair country indeed.

The parliament that followed, very much King Robert's entrance into rule, although chaired, as ever, by the Chancellor, was really the new monarch's own. He was not an assertive or forceful character, indeed all but modest in his manner, but he had firm views as to national priorities, and now made that clear. He was concerned, although by no means a warlike man, to strengthen further Scotland's position, especially in relation to the ever-present English problem. David's truce with that kingdom did not expire until 1384, thirteen years yet; but truces had been broken before this, and Edward the Third was typically Plantagenet and aggressive. So the first resolution he put to parliament was the prompt payment of another of the great ransom moneys which had gained his predecessor release from captivity, and of which thirty thousand merks remained to be paid, despite all David's increased assessments and taxes. He declared that the treasury could just afford to send four thousand merks forthwith, and promise to pay the remainder without lengthy delay, this without the need to demand further increases from the lieges. At the general relief over this last assurance, the item was passed without opposition.

More actual enthusiasm was shown for the next matter, the official renewal of the Franco-Scottish alliance, so important as a means of keeping the English aware of possible threats from south and north, which suited both signatories. An embassage was to be sent from the new monarch to King Charles of France.

Then there was the formal appointment of Robert, Earl of Carrick as heir to the throne. This was not quite as straightforward as it might have seemed. The former Steward's marital affairs had been somewhat complicated. His first marriage to Elizabeth Mure of Rowallan had been a somewhat rash one, in that the pair were within Holy Church's forbidden degree of consanguinity, and the two young partners had omitted to gain papal dispensation. Indeed, the first-born child, John – his name being changed to Robert after the failures of King John Balliol – was ten years old before the Vatican's legitimacy was sought for and pronounced. So purists in Church and state could possibly declare that Carrick was in fact born out of lawful wedlock and therefore ineligible to succeed to the throne. It was conceivable that one of his half-brothers, fruit of the second marriage to Euphemia of Ross, might one day think to challenge the succession. So parliament was asked to decide on Robert of Carrick as undoubted heir, with instructions that the envoys to the King of France should

145

also go on to Avignon and seek a papal declaration of his legitimacy.

George, sitting beside his brother, nudged him, to remind him that their potent new monarch was alleged to have as many as twenty-one offspring, how many legitimate or otherwise uncertain. What about Marjory? It was John's turn to make a face.

Parliament then confirmed sundry new appointments, including the style of Earl Palatine of Strathearn for David, eldest son of the second marriage, the Steward's own old earldom, this of palatine to emphasise princely status, before adjourning.

John's ship was waiting for him at the town's quays, and he was not long in boarding it and heading for the open sea.

Marjory was much interested in all that he had to report, glad to hear that all had gone reasonably smoothly, and wondering whether being a king's daughter would make any difference to her life here in Moray. Amused too, over the legitimacy query regarding her brother, Carrick – which applied to herself also. When John mentioned the allegation that there were twenty more of her royal father's offspring, she admitted that she was never quite sure who they all were.

She was interested also to hear of George's forthcoming marriage, and declared that that one needed a wife, and a strong one, like another member of the family! When would they be going south for the wedding? And what of young Agnes and James Douglas? John had to admit that he had quite forgotten to enquire.

Young Thomas, Master of Moray, was thriving, lung power even increasing.

The timber extraction and conveying was proceeding apace, and John's inspection and decision was required for a hopeful forestry project which Duncan Murray had been told of in the upper Spey area beyond Glen Feshie and Rothiemurchus – only there was some doubt as to the Moray boundary there, he thought, verging on Atholl, the marches being unmarked. He did not want to get into dispute with that earldom, Stewart-held as it was – not that wood-felling appeared to be of any concern there, as yet.

So it was to horse soon for John, and heading for fairly near to the snowline.

He enjoyed this sort of task much more than his recent affairs in the south, and wondered whether he was really the man to be Earl of Moray, an earl at all. Perhaps his mother should not have given him the earldom. But then, would he have been in a position to meet and wed Marjory?

Duncan led him, once they had covered the thirty miles to the Spey at Cromdale, up that great river to the Rothiemurchus area where the mighty Monadh Ruadhs loomed above them in white majesty, this large forest already producing its measure of timber, although most of its trees were ancient gnarled pines, not broad-leafed oak and elm, which made John wonder whether they were indeed likely to find what they wanted up at this level where they were now heading, eastwards. But he was assured that the monks said that there were large groves of oak at Rynettin, however lengthy a distance it would be to get the felled timber to shipping. But unskilled labour could be used for that, to be sure, and the time taken not so important as the supply. This wood trade was proving to be of great value to the earldom's revenues, something hitherto little exploited.

They picked up a monkish guide at the hospice at Inverdruie and then rode up the course of the Druie and on past Loch Morlich, a large sheet of water very close to the mountains now, John the more doubtful as to the practicality of it all. Their guide turned them northwards up the course of a stream he called the Allt Feithe Duibhe for four more miles. Then over a little pass where there were still patches of snow lying, and down another burn flowing in the opposite direction and past a lonely forester's house he named Ryvoan. And there, ahead of them on lower ground, stretched a great area of forest: Rynettin. John was impressed by the apparent extent of it, but shook his head nevertheless. So remote. And where was the Atholl border? The monk declared that it was not Atholl ahead but Mar, the very north-western tip of that earldom. This at least had the effect of encouraging the doubter somewhat, Mar, in present circumstances, not likely to cause any trouble if its bounds were slightly encroached upon.

But there was further encouragement when in another mile the stream they were following down suddenly joined a quite major river, hidden from view up till then by all the trees. This was the Nethy, the monk informed. And it would be possible to float down cut timber the seven miles to Abernethy where that river joined great Spey. This, to be sure, made all the difference to the entire project. Now, where were these oak trees? All they had seen so far had been pines and a few rowans, mountain-ash.

They were led another mile or so north-eastwards by pine-needle-strewn paths, roe-deer, squirrels and capercailzie abounding, until they came to a wide open space containing a marshy pond, too small to be called a lochan. And beyond this could be seen tall, dark, heavy-branched trees, different from the evergreen pines, broad-leafed, although not yet more than in bud.

Inspection proved these to be oak and elm indeed, and evidently extending for a considerable distance. How these had planted themselves here amongst the pine woods was a mystery, but there they were, well worth selective felling and extraction. Much cheered, the visitors explored the vicinity, made guesses as to where the boundary was with Mar, before turning back.

At the Nethy, John and Duncan left their guide to make his way whence they had come, back to Inverdruie, they themselves deciding to follow the Nethy down to Spey, a much shorter route home. It would also enable them to see the river's prospects as a waterway for the timber.

The seven miles or so, despite loops and bends, produced no falls or cataracts or other obstacles for rafting the wood; and once Spey was reached the river was clear for passage all the way to the Moray Firth.

Well satisfied, the pair returned to Darnaway after a potentially profitable excursion. Was this sort of activity to be John's fulfilment in life, other than in happy marriage and rearing a family? And would the realm's affairs allow it?

That spring and early summer John was in fact left in peace to follow these favoured pursuits, with Marjory also well content, and soon able to ride abroad with him, often with young Thomas wrapped in a plaid and seemingly enjoying it, when not lulled to sleep by the trotting motions of his mother's horse.

They heard at intervals the news from the south. Robert was proving to be a quietly effective king – after all, he had had long experience as a regent, and his Steward's duties had prepared him for those monarchial. The ambassadors to King Charles and the Pope had returned, reporting success in renewing the Auld Alliance, and in gaining Vatican confirmation of Robert of Carrick's legitimacy. Presumably this applied to his sister also, so John could no longer tease her with possible bastardy. Carrick was to be married to Annabella Drummond, Queen Margaret's niece, in the autumn, and major attendance at the wedding was required, since one day this lady would herself be queen. Still no word came as to the marriage of George, nor of his sister Agnes. Edward of England was not exactly lying low, said to be threatening an invasion of France, but meantime concerning himself with Welsh affairs, ever a preoccupation of the Plantagenets. So Scotland could relax in that respect for the time being.

With the harvest in and autumn upon them, the expected summons to the royal wedding duly arrived. Thomas was now old enough to be left in the care of Duncan Murray's wife, Catherine, a reliable soul. The nuptials would be celebrated at Scone Abbey, as suitable and in Drummond country; so once again it was possible to sail south by ship, saving long riding although the snows were gone. Voyaging was becoming part of John's life; to some

149

extent it always had been so, reared at Dunbar, but then for shorter sailing. Majory was a good sailor, not suffering from sea-sickness.

Arriving at Perth, they were interested to learn that there were to be two weddings, not conducted jointly but one the day after the other. The second one was to be that of Donald of the Isles and his Phemia, now also a princess, whereafter Donald was to be allowed to return to his Hebridean homeland, his father's behaviour now considered to be acceptable. John of the Isles, however, was not expected to grace the marriage with his presence.

George was already there at Perth, and announced that he too was arranging a joint wedding; but this would be different, held on the same day, brother and sister, Agnes at last marrying James Douglas, this to be held one week hence, so that not a few attending the royal one could come on to Dunbar thereafter, a convenient arrangement. So John and Marjory would not have to make another journey southwards.

The first two weddings were suitably fine, with Donald's and Phemia's actually the more interesting from the congregation's point of view, this because they were a lively pair and so obviously themselves enjoying it all, where Carrick's was much more solemn, however important, and Annabella seemingly somewhat overawed by all the dignified ceremonial. In fact, it might almost be said that this latter pair probably enjoyed the second one more than their own, for they stayed on till the next day to attend, before setting off on their own for the Isle of Arran – at least this was Marjory's assessment. There was much banqueting, of course, with dancing and entertainment afterwards, the second night's jollifications more hearty than the first. The couple from Moray found it all a notable interlude, enjoying themselves.

After three days of this, they sailed for Dunbar with a shipload of other guests, George doing the same in his own vessel.

As it transpired, the second weddings, again of sister and

brother, were remarkably different. For one thing, they were held in the large local parish church, not any splendid abbey, and the townsfolk of Dunbar were very much in evidence, especially after the nuptials when George had laid on an open-air feasting in the market-square, on a grand scale, for all who cared to partake, lofty and humble alike, this going on for hours, the Douglases and the Setons and their guests finding it all as entertaining as it was unusual. George declared that this was the *real* celebration, he not especially religiously minded, and he wanted all his people involved, this saying something for his popularity.

The merriment went on in the castle thereafter almost until dawn, Black Agnes entering into all as much as the rest, and getting on well with the mature Earl of Douglas. And that did not finish it, for next day, after a late start, there was a procession through the town and down to the harbour, for the important guests to be taken aboard two ships and sailed down the exciting coast to the south as far as beetling St Ebba's Head and Eyemouth; then turning back, up again to round the mighty Craig of Bass, amongst the whirling clouds of screaming gannets and the plunging seals, again an unusual wedding procedure, this before returning for more feasting. John was interested, at the harbour, to see stacks of his timber seasoning, and a vessel of some fifty feet in length in process of being built. Then another night's revelry at nearby Tantallon Castle, hosted by the Douglases and a third at Seton Place, some fifteen miles to the west, where Christian's father had a very fine house near to his fishing-haven of Cockenzie, Sir William anxious to prove himself as bountiful a host as the earls.

John and Marjory sailed back to Inverness thereafter all but exhausted, but happily so, and feeling that they would not be able to look at any substantial meal again for days.

14

That late autumn and winter was a hard one for Scotland, weather-wise, the spring also, storms of rain, sleet and snow continuing, the rivers all rising in flood, the lower ground awash, sweeping away barns and their contents as well as some cottages and mills, and this preventing spring ploughing. None could remember so bad and lengthy a period of these shocking conditions, and gloom was everywhere expressed as to its results in food production, not only in grain but in beef and mutton and even poultry meats, livestock being drowned in large numbers. There would be famine in the land, almost certainly.

Moray, as it happened, escaped the worst of it all, although problems there were bad enough in all conscience, the local opinion being that the great mountain barriers of the Monadh Ruadh and Liath ranges directed the storms south-eastwards. The great herds of deer came low on the hills, making the provision of venison at least relatively easy; and fish became all but a staple diet in these parts.

There was less word from the south than usual, inevitably, even the mendicant friars inhibited in their perambulations; but such as was heard was grievous, and likely to get worse as stocks of food ran out. This first year of King Robert's reign was going to be remembered for famine. Some of the superstitious declared that God was angry with Scotland on account of its new monarch's marital indiscretions.

At least no demands came for John's appearance at court.

In the spring, fertility of a different sort was in evidence, Marjory announcing that she was pregnant again, John hoping that a diet of fish and venison would not produce oddities in their offspring!

They had an unexpected visit from George in June, coming by ship, the winds having sunk although the rain continued. He came to urge that timber-sending should be resumed, it having fallen away during all the storms and floods. He at least could get on with the shipbuilding at Dunbar but he was short of wood.

He announced that Christian had had a baby in March, somewhat soon after the wedding admittedly, although he did not claim that it was premature A daughter unfortunately, but he hoped soon to rectify that and provide the necessary son to become the next Earl of Dunbar and March.

The food shortage, famine indeed, he reported, was requiring grain to be imported from Ireland and even from England, humiliating as it was to have to go to the auld enemy for the like, and them charging highly for it; they seemed to have escaped the worst of the weather. The king was greatly concerned. This importing was demanding the use of much shipping, and affecting the Dunbar trade with the Low Countries and the Baltic in that their vessels were required for use nearer home, especially Ireland. So shipbuilding was the more important. Hence his visit.

George had another point to make. Douglas, the earl, was taking responsibilities as new Warden of the East March seriously indeed, almost too seriously. The English still occupied the castles of Berwick-upon-Tweed, Roxburgh and Lochmaben, and with the latter much of Annandale, this as it were left over from their last invasion. Annandale was Bruce country, not Douglas, but, enemy-held, it was a grievous inconvenience in relation to the Douglas lands in Galloway, Threave and Urr in particular. These invaders ought to be ejected, however strong the fortresses they occupied. But the new monarch was reluctant to order this for fear of seeming to break the truce, and possibly cause major warlike reaction. Douglas, a warlike character himself, scoffed at this feebleness. As Warden of the East March, and at the Steward's appointment, he declared that it was his simple duty to get rid of the invaders. Admittedly Roxburgh and Lochmaben were in the Middle and West Marches respectively; but if they made a start at Berwick and the lower Tweed, they might as well go and free the others also. He had convinced the Kerr Warden of the Middle March that this was necessary, and that man had promised to raise men for the attempt. And now he was calling on Dunbar and March to assist, to raise the Merse, in especial the Homes, Swintons, Haigs and Maitlands, to add to the host. In a way George agreed with him, but not against the king's wishes And if there *was* major English reaction, the Merse would almost certainly be the greatest sufferer. How did his brother feel about this?

John saw both sides and points of view. The English should not be allowed to remain thus on Scottish soil. But if Edward chose to judge this ejection a breaking of the truce provisions, which he was quite likely to do, and full-scale war resulted, then the price to be paid was too high. This might be an unheroic attitude, but . . .

George admitted that it might well seem so. But Douglas was going to use all persuasion to try to change Robert Stewart's view on it, and to be prepared to call the nation to arms if the Plantagenet reacted violently to it. The king might quite possibly be anxious not to be made to look weak compared with the former proclaimed contender for the crown, and so might yield in this. So there just could be a national rallying-call, and they would all have to muster their fullest strength. How would Moray answer that?

John, scarcely a warrior type, indicated no enthusiasm for the project. But he supposed that, if it came to that, he could probably assemble a quite large force from the earldom's lands. The Highland clans always were inclined to draw the sword, and might well supply into thousands, competing with each other. The low-country folk would be less keen, almost certainly, although those Comyns were an aggressive lot. So, if required to, he could probably produce, say, a couple of thousand. But he prayed that it would not come to that.

What about a lesser contribution, if Douglas gained permission to go ahead with his Marches endeavour? Would John help there?

No. That was definite. Unless by royal command. There was no way that he felt that he could embroil his northerners in such an affray. He had his responsibilities to his people here.

His brother had to accept that.

George was taken on one of the woodland inspections, despite the weather, before he returned to his ship with the promise of increased supplies of timber.

For a few weeks thereafter John waited, somewhat apprehensively, for a royal call-to-arms. But nothing such came, so presumably the Douglas was being restrained. The only word from the south was of ever more havoc caused by famine.

Then fairly local news reached Darnaway. William, Earl of Ross, died suddenly, leaving something of a gap in northern affairs, for his son, the Master, had died the year before, and now a daughter, another Euphemia, herself a widow, succeeded to the earldom. This was fairly quickly followed by reports of King Robert's shrewd strengthening of the Stewart position throughout the realm. He had promptly had the lady married to his second son, the one *baptised* Robert, whom he created Earl of Buchan, which title was in abeyance, and who thus became also Earl of Ross in his wife's right. And this proved to be only the first of the promotions. It so happened that some of the other earldoms and great lordships had fallen to heiresses, or were in dispute as to succession; the king quietly took the opportunity to instal Stewart kinsfolk into some of these. Carrick was already an earl, as was David of Strathearn, the Earl Palatine, but he was now made Earl of Caithness also. His brothers were created Earls of Fife,

Menteith and Atholl. These all automatically having seats on the council, the royal dominance thereof was much enhanced. Out of the sixteen earldoms seven were in Stewart hands; and like Moray, others were held by the husbands of daughters of the king. Never before had such a situation existed. The new royal line was to be pre-eminent indeed.

The inevitable delayed meeting of the new council was called in October, and John had to attend. Ostensibly it was to deal with finances, but almost certainly it would be more concerned with all this of the royal appointments, and the consequences; and, of course, the problems of the famine also. It was to be held at Edinburgh, so the journey could be made by ship to Leith once more. Marjory, with raised eyebrows, told her husband to convey her felicities to all the new earls, her brothers.

The council, when it met at Holyrood, was indeed dominated by Stewarts – or FitzAlans, as Douglas murmured to John and George – all seven of them being present, and the king presiding, creating the largest attendance for long. The Chancellor, the Bishop of Brechin, welcomed all, straight-faced, and declared that the king had much business to attend to. They would start with the important matter of the realm's treasury. He called upon the Chamberlain, Sir John Lyon, who was in charge of national finances, to render account.

Lyon, a solemn, youngish man, was able to declare that the treasury was in fact in good state, an unusual situation for Scotland. He had satisfaction in informing them that there was a surplus of no less then three thousand pounds, a very large sum, this despite the moneys necessarily spent on buying grain and foodstuffs to help counter the famine. It was thanks to careful handling – he did not actually say his own – and the success of the increased customs duties and landed assessments. Also trading developments which many landholders were beginning to take part in, exporting hides and leather goods, weaponry and other ironware, split slate for tiling and roofing, oaken furnishings, and the like, as well as the long-standing trade in wool and salted products. This improvement in income for the treasury should continue, especially once the food shortage was over. However, some of the landholders were in arrears with their contributions, even certain sheriffs, and the council's strictures on such were required.

This was agreed to, the Chancellor thanking Lyon, and turning to the monarch.

Robert declared that they were all grateful to Sir John for his good handling of these matters, and, to express his personal thanks, he was hereby making him Thane of Glamis, and ordering a pension to be paid from the treasury, in retiring him from the rigorous responsibilities which he had borne for so long. In his place, as Chamberlain, he proposed that the council should appoint Robert, Earl of Fife and Menteith, here present. What Lyon thought of this ejection from office and of his new status as Thane of Glamis was not very evident, his set features being fairly expressionless anyway; but he did not make protest. The taking over by Fife and Menteith was accepted without discussion.

That was just the first of the new appointments, other Stewarts being given offices-of-state and keeperships of royal castles, with one or two coming tactfully to the Douglases, Sir James of Dalkeith being made Deputy Warden of the East March. Sir James Lindsay of Crawford, the king's nephew, was made Justiciar North of the Forth.

So it went on. Never before had so many of the nation's leading positions been held by kinsfolk of the monarch. John was just a little doubtful about this, although, on the face of it, it did strengthen the crown's authority. But what if one of these many Stewart earls and officials at some future date decided to dispute the succession to the throne of, say, Robert of Carrick, on the old story of possible illegitimacy, and sought the crown in his place? Such could then possibly call on the backing of many others of his highly placed kin. Had the king thought of that?

Routine business followed, with little debate. Seldom had a council meeting been so devoid of controversy. Was this a good omen for Robert's reign, or merely the result of his careful manipulation of proceedings?

It was noticeable, at least to John and his brother, that Douglas did not raise the subject of expelling the English occupants of the borderline castles. He was still talking about it, privately, to George, but he perhaps judged that to bring it up before all these Stewart supporters could result in a specific injunction against any such attempt by the council. He probably preferred to keep his hands untied, especially now that he had Dalkeith appointed his Deputy Warden.

A final and lengthy announcement by the king related to the situation in England. Matters were in a grievous state there, he announced – which, to be sure, had its advantages for Scotland, in that fears of another invasion could probably be dismissed meantime. But turmoil and upset in any realm, especially one sharing the same island, could have its dangers for others. King Edward now was reported to have not only grown infirm but all but in his dotage. His son and heir, the Black Prince, had fallen gravely ill on return from warfare in Gascony, and was not expected to recover, and he had only a five-year-old son, Richard, to succeed him. John of Gaunt, Duke of Lancaster, the king's brother, was in fact ruling the land, but not very effectively, for he was being countered not only by his half-brothers, the Earls of Kent and Huntingdon, but by, of all people, Edward's mistress, Alice Ferrers, wife of some London merchant, who was all but controlling the king. So England was in no happy state, and many of its magnates were becoming out of hand and not paying their dues and taxes, according to reports.

Most there present, hearing all this, were nowise worried about it; but the longer-sighted saw that there could be possible side-issues for Scotland also in an upset England. Nothing tended to unite a squabbling nation more effectively than a call to arms, warfare; and John of Gaunt, realising this, might possibly see an attack on Scotland as advantageous, the English being ever aggressively inclined.

The king went on that it had occurred to him that, with this treasury surplus, they might use some of it to send an additional payment of the ransom moneys, and even indicate that more might follow this, as it were buying off any possible threat of invasion for quite some time. If the English exchequer was in a poor state, this might well be to good purpose.

Sir John Lyon was against this, seeing the results of his careful savings going to fill English coffers; but he was no longer Chamberlain now, and his successor would not seek to counter his father's wishes at so early a stage.

Two thousand merks was agreed to be sent to John of Gaunt.

After the meeting broke up, John was drawn aside by his father-in-law. He had an errand for him. He thought much of John's abilities as an envoy and negotiator, proved over the matter of the Lord of the Isles and the late Ross. He would wish him to go to London with this additional sum of money, and seek to win over John of Gaunt to friendship, or at least non-enmity, with Scotland. Also to seek to get him to withdraw the English garrisons in those border castles. And while there, in the process, learn an accurate assessment of conditions in England, where danger lay, and what was likely to happen if both Edward and his son, the Black Prince, were to die, as seemed not unlikely. In present conditions there, almost anything might happen, and it would be much to Scotland's benefit to be prepared. Would John do this?

Needless to say, his son-in-law was not eager for anything of the sort, especially with Marjory expecting another child. But when the king added that, with his so useful ship-owning, he could sail down to the Thames in much shorter time than going by land, and be spared having to negotiate the required safe-passage agreement to ride through England, he saw that he could scarcely refuse. Calculating timing, he reckoned that if he was to go fairly shortly, say in ten days' time, he could hope to be back in another two weeks. Home by early November then, and Marjory not expecting until Yuletide.

He intimated acceptance, and supposed that he ought to feel flattered by this royal faith in his competence. Better than leading armed men to fight for the realm, at least, he told himself, as he made his way back to Leith and his vessel.

15

Marjory was less than delighted at her father's method of showing his appreciation of his son-in-law's abilities. But she recognised that it was a compliment indeed, for he could of course have sent one or more of his sons on the task. So in this of diplomacy and negotiation, he must rate John the higher. But let her love be as speedy about it all as was possible. And she hoped that it would not be the forerunner of other such missions.

So, with strict instructions to his wife to take the utmost care of herself, it was the sea again, on a longer voyage this time, John wondering what his reception would be at London. At least the money, in silver coins, two thousand of them, ought to gain him some sort of welcome from whoever he could hand it over to, the Duke of Lancaster rather than the enfeebled King Edward, presumably, not to get it into the hands of this strange mistress of his. John was not sure just how to deal with the silver, when he picked it up at Leith. It would be a weighty load, no problem while on the ship. But when he landed at London?

He found the money awaiting him at Holyrood, in the care of the abbot, King Robert presently gone to Renfrew. In great leather bags, four of them, it was carried down in a horse-drawn wagon, by monks, to Leith and taken aboard the vessel; and the awkward heavy handling of those bags left him in no doubt but that it would all have to remain on the vessel, at London, until he had introduced himself and his mission, and got transport arranged.

That voyage was a chilly one, with a north-easterly wind, but this helped to make it speedier than with the normal prevailing south-westerlies. Four days and three nights, never out of sight of the coastline, and they entered the Thames estuary, busy with other shipping.

It was further up to the main London docks than John had realised, even after the firth had narrowed into merely a wide river. And they had to pass lesser ports and havens at Gravesend, Tilbury and Woolwich before they came to what amounted to well over a mile of quays and docks. Where to berth, in all this? The shipmaster was, in this matter, out of his depth, but John at least knew what to look for: the mighty Tower of London, the fortress-prison, notorious as it was, which stood near the riverside and which should stand out. It did, lofty, massive, unmistakeable.

There were no vacant spaces for them to draw in for some distance after this, and John was wondering whether they should turn back when they saw ahead of them a group of buildings over which flew the well-known banner of the Blackfriars; and there were gaps at the quayside here. This would serve, John always having a respect for the Blackfriars. They moved in and tied up. No one arrived to ask them their business.

John was not long in landing, a stranger in a strange land – but at least where they spoke the same language, if with a different accent. When he asked a man unloading wine-casks from a cart as to where was the Palace of Westminster, he was eyed strangely, dressed in his best as he was and with his Scots voice, but directed helpfully enough, and westwards some distance, he was told, past the great river-bend near Aldwych and then on another half-mile.

There was no point in going back to the vessel and moving it again, so he had quite a walk ahead of him, but was glad to stretch his legs after all the time on shipboard. He was interested in all that he saw. London was unlike any other city he knew, Edinburgh, Glasgow, Perth, Dundee or Aberdeen, quite apart from its great size, lacking the larger hills he was used to, its streets comparatively straight, but narrow and crowded, its buildings and houses tall, the upper storeys tending to project out over the street and denying sunlight, built mainly of timber, some of brick but practically none of stone. And the air therein was still, lacking the winds that prevailed in Scottish cities, and the smells throat-catching in consequence. The people appeared to chatter more than at home, but were seemingly friendly and easy-going. Street-pedlars were everywhere, shouting their wares, dogs barked, church-bells rang and carts rumbled and chattered. It all made a lively impact.

Following directions, and still parallel with the river nearby, John was presently aware of some alteration in the scene. The buildings were changing in style, growing larger, finer, set wider apart, some even with garden-ground of a sort. Clearly this was where the rich and lofty lived. Horse-drawn carriages were to be seen.

He found Westminster Palace at last, on a kind of meadow near the river, a long, rambling building close to what was obviously the mighty abbey. It was said to have been built by Edward the Confessor just before the Norman conquest, and enlarged by Henry the Third. It had more and larger windows than were the rule in Scotland. Uniformed guards stood at the entrances.

When he approached one of these, John was eyed with suspicion. He asked whether His Grace the King was in residence.

That earned him a blank stare.

He repeated his question, adding that he was the Earl of Moray, sent by the King of Scots to speak with His Grace, or with the Duke of Lancaster.

The guard told him, still doubtfully, that he should see the chamberlain, and led him within. In Scotland, the Chamberlain was one of the great officers of state, but the way this had been announced gave the impression that here it was otherwise.

In a corridor of the palace John was handed over to a servitor who was told to take him to the chamberlain. More corridors, and up a staircase, to a chamber where a group of men sat drinking. To one of these he was handed over.

"I am from Scotland, come from the King of Scots on important matters," he declared. "Is His Grace the King here?"

"His Majesty is at Windsor," he was told. "Who are you?"

"I am the Earl of Moray. And you?"

"I am chamberlain here, my lord. Rivers by name."

"And the Duke of Lancaster? Is he also at Windsor?"

"No. He is here. In the palace meantime. Do you seek his presence?"

"I have come a long way so to do."

"Wait you then, my lord. I will see whether the duke may give you audience. Have wine while you wait."

"Tell Lancaster that I come regarding the ransom moneys. He will know what that refers to."

John went to sit and sip wine, considered sidelong by the other men there.

It was some time before the man Rivers returned. "His Grace will see you, my lord," he announced. "Follow me." Grace referred to the monarch in Scotland; here differently, it appeared.

They went by more passages and stairs, the former being hung with tapestries now, to enter a handsome panelled chamber where a fire smouldered and a tall, stooping man stood before it, cadaverous of feature, stern of expression. He did not advance to greet the visitor.

"You are from Scotland, I understand, wishing speech with me?" he jerked. "On matters of moneys, I am told."

"I am the Earl of Moray, sent by King Robert, my lord Duke. Either to King Edward or to yourself. On the matter of our late king's ransom."

"What of it? Payment is in arrears, long has been so. What brings you, Earl of Moray? Further failure to pay?"

"Not so. Otherwise! I bring silver. Much silver. As token of goodwill. And, if our meeting goes well, more to come before long."

"Ha! You have *brought* moneys?" The change in attitude was very evident.

"Yes. Two thousand silver merks, my lord Duke."

"Mmm. That, that is well. But . . . what is behind this, my lord? Somewhat . . . unexpected!"

"Goodwill, as I say, between the realms. Peace and harmony. The extension of the existing truce. And the prospects and promise of the withdrawal of the English occupiers of royal castles in Scotland: Berwick, Roxburgh and Lochmaben in Annandale. Their withdrawal to English soil."

John of Gaunt smoothed his chin. "You seek to *buy* our goodwill?"

"I would not put it so. It is a token of the new reign in Scotland's desire for friendship. Recognition that both kingdoms have much to gain by acting together, rather than an age-old feud. We believe that you will see it that way also. So I am sent with this token."

"And more promised?"

"Yes. And shortly. On *your* token, of withdrawing your invaders from those Borderland castles."

A pause. "I will have to consider this. My brother, the king, is . . . poorly."

"I understand."

"You have this silver with you?"

"At my ship. Docked at the Blackfriars monastery. A weighty load."

"To be sure. See you, while I think on this matter, you can go to fetch it?"

"Then you judge that, in accepting it, you will agree to what is here proposed?"

"Possibly, yes."

"It is not my aim to have you over-hurried in your decisions, my lord Duke. But if I hand over the moneys . . .?" he left the rest unsaid.

"The moneys are owed to England, I would remind you, sir!"

"Perhaps. But until I hand it over, it is still Scotland's siller! In a Scottish vessel."

The other took a pace or two to and fro before the fireplace. "Look you, we should not chaffer over this, like merchants! I have to consult one or two of my friends, councillors. You wait here, my lord. I will have refreshment brought for you. Then, if we agree, I will have you sent in a carriage to your ship, to fetch the moneys."

"Very well."

The duke left him there. Presently servitors brought more wine and edibles.

John did not have very long to wait and wonder. When John of Gaunt returned he brought with him two others, a cleric whom he introduced as the Archdeacon of Canterbury, and a younger man, his son the Lord Henry of Hereford. These, he declared, would accompany their guest to the Blackfriars, and bring him back with the silver. Presumably that meant acceptance of the terms, these two, as it were, guarantors. John did not press for further confirmation.

Leaving Lancaster, he was conducted by the archdeacon and Hereford down to a rear courtyard of the palace, where a carriage was already awaiting them, with two armed men beside the driver. They set off back eastwards whence John had come. The cleric was civil, the young man silent.

Boarding the vessel at the dockside, under the supervision of the shipmaster, crewmen carried the four precious bags of coin to the carriage, and the return journey was made, John telling the skipper that he did not know just when the return voyage to Scotland would start, but he did not anticipate remaining more than a day or two in London.

It occurred to him, as they drove back to Westminster, how obsessed was mankind over moneys, silver and gold, just metal after all, dug out of the ground and yet dominant in the minds of all, or almost all. The ownership of land might carry status and power, but that metal could *buy* the land. So it ruled. This was a disturbing thought. Was he himself guilty in this respect also?

Back at Westminster, he was left in the care of Archdeacon William, who did look after him adequately well, John of Gaunt and his son presumably having more important matters to see to than entertaining a mere Scots envoy – now that they had the money. But from the cleric John gained much that he wanted to know regarding the present state of England, this to take back to King Robert.

He learned that there was great division in the land, and significantly so between the royal house and parliament, and, for that matter, amongst the royal family itself. With King Edward, now aged sixty-five and wandering in his mind, his various brothers, half-brothers and sons, including the Earls of Kent, Gloucester and Huntingdon, were squabbling and competing for power. Parliament had largely got into the hands of favourites, and was inimical towards many of these kinsmen of Edward, going so far as to imprison two of them. The death of the Black Prince, heir to the throne, leaving only the child Richard, had been a dire blow. John of Gaunt, seeking to rule the nation as a sort of regent, was not supported by parliament which refused to recognise him as such. So he had adjourned parliament, and in theory no parliament sat, however many meetings of members were held. It was near-chaos, with the churchmen seeking to hold the balance, but not very successfully.

At any rate, it looked as though Scotland did not need to fear any serious trouble with England for quite some time to come.

John returned to his ship next morning, on foot again, without seeing John of Gaunt, and set sail for home.

16

Having delivered his report to King Robert, who received it with satisfaction, it was back to Darnaway without delay, John praying that Marjory had not had any real problems, in especial a premature childbirth. There, thankfully, he found all well and his wife in good spirits. She saw no reason to worry about her delivery, which she reckoned would be in about three weeks. She was, as ever, much interested to hear of her husband's doings in England, and relieved to hear that there was not likely to be any warfare in the foreseeable future.

So it was back to acting lord of a great earldom, endeavouring to settle disputes between vassals and tenants, fostering forestry and trade generally, and visiting the as yet remoter parts of Moray which he had not been able to explore hitherto – but nothing to take him away from Darnaway for more than a single night.

In less than a score of days, just before Yuletide started, Marjory was brought to bed, and after an easier labour than the previous one, produced a cherubic little sister for Thomas, to be named Mabella, to great rejoicing.

John concluded that life was good; and to celebrate the fact, decided to found a new church at Dyke, none so far away on the Findhorn, which his friend Bishop Bur of Elgin considered was required.

News from the south was scanty, undramatic, with nothing disturbing nor ominous, save that there was no sign of John of Gaunt fulfilling the agreement to withdraw the English occupants of those three Border strongholds. This would be upsetting not only for the king and his council but for brother George, who would be especially concerned over Berwick and Roxburgh, these both verging on his March territory. And the Earl of Douglas would be becoming itchy as regarding that sword of his.

When the nation's affairs did require John to travel southwards again, it was to attend another parliament, this again to be held at Scone, which the king saw as a helpful location for attracting more attenders from the northern parts of the realm than were Edinburgh or Stirling, however inconvenient for the Galloway and West March folk. Also it could be reached readily by ship, up Tay, and ships were becoming ever more important in the kingdom, as witnessed by the ever-increasing demand for timber. This, of course, suited John, who could make the voyage to Perth in two days and one night.

When he got there it was to discover that, of all things, this parliament was to decide on ecclesiastical matters. Holy Church was in great trouble, and not only in Scotland, something that the itinerant friars had not reported on. The Pope, Gregory the Eleventh, had, for whatever reason, decided to transfer the seat of the Vatican back from Avignon to Rome, this apparently against the wishes of some of his cardinals. And no sooner had he got there, than he had died. There had followed major upheaval amongst those who supported this move and those who did not. After much unseemly bickering, the small majority of cardinals elected a new Pontiff, who took the style of Urban the Sixth. And his unsuitable behaviour, indeed tyranny, soon had the opposing cardinals electing a replacement, who was called Clement the Seventh. Urban, however, did not accept deposition. So now there were two Popes, and Holy Church in complete disarray. It was back to Avignon with Clement, with Urban remaining at Rome. Something being called the Great Schism had commenced.

France, it seemed, was supporting Clement, Avignon being in that country. And suddenly, in the midst of this upheaval, Edward Plantagenet died, and his ten-year-old grandson became Richard the Second, this against the wishes of some of his royal uncles.

So Christendom was in all but chaos. Scotland must select its course therein.

Needless to say, the clerics were very vocal in this parliament, and were backing Clement at Avignon. This suited most of the assembly well enough, because of the Auld Alliance with France, most laymen not being otherwise knowledgeable nor concerned. What did concern them was the English attitude. Normally it would probably be anti-French and therefore pro-Urban; but in the present state of dispute and contention south of the border, decisions were doubtful indeed, and anything might happen. Scotland did not want a holy war to add to its problems.

It was decided to send Bishop Wardlaw of Glasgow to interview the Archbishop of Canterbury and to consult and debate the issue; then to go over to Avignon and seek Pope Clement's guidance. There happened to be a new Emperor, Wentzel by name. If he decided to back Urban, as seemed likely, and by armed force, widespread war might result, in which Scotland did not want to become involved. It was all folly on a major scale, but could be dangerous, grievously so. And all, allegedly, in the cause of the God of love.

William of Douglas raised the question of what to do about the continued English occupation of those three castles, and advocated military action, in which he was supported by George Cospatrick and not a few others. This had the king turning to John, who found himself in the strange position of opposing his brother and brother-in-law, advocating patience. He declared that John of Gaunt had accepted the withdrawal of the invaders as part of the price for receiving the ransom moneys, and almost certainly intended to fulfil it. But conditions of rule in England were at present so difficult and confused, with rival factions all but at war with each other, that Lancaster, as regent, was probably too preoccupied to concern himself with this, to him, comparatively unimportant matter. John suggested that Bishop Wardlaw should ask the Archbishop of Canterbury, when they met, to remind the duke of this, and the growing feelings in Scotland over it, and request prompt action. This was agreed, although Douglas declared that, as Warden of the Marches, it was his simple duty to have these invaders ejected, and if it was not done by orders from London very soon, he would be constrained to act, George nodding and others backing him, John being frowned at.

Apart from this matter, the parliament was concerned only with routine issues, appointments, taxation, trade and the like.

The session adjourned, the brothers and Douglas had something of an altercation, John holding that these three English garrisons were being content to remain in occupation of the fortalices without being otherwise aggressive or terrorising the various areas; and that it was not worth risking outright war with England by taking such action against them at this stage. Give Lancaster time. The others took the opposite view; but without royal and parliamentary approval had to restrict themselves to objections.

Unhappy to be at odds with his brother, John decided to visit Dunbar and their mother before returning to Moray. So the two ships sailed off, side by side, down Tay next day.

Black Agnes, although the reverse of being a peace-at-any-price female, proved to be in favour of John's attitude on this contentious issue, saying that unnecessary bloodshed should be avoided and time given. But she did suggest that representations should be made to the Berwick, Roxburgh and Lochmaben English leaders to inform that the Duke of Lancaster had agreed to their withdrawal, and that if they did not move out soon they would be ejected by force. She also reminded George, as one who had herself resisted siege here at Dunbar, that overcoming resistance by strong castles was apt to demand the use of heavy siege-machinery, bombards, battering-rams and the like, also much time and patience.

Abandoning disputes meantime, George took his brother to see the use being made of the timber sent down from Moray. At the harbour, two ships were being built, one almost finished. George was now adding to local prosperity, and his own coffers, by constructing vessels for sale to churchmen, great merchants and less enterprising magnates. The English had long been more ship-conscious than the Scots, strange as this was, with the enormous Scottish coastline, the dependence of the West Highlands and Isles on their longships and birlinns, and fishing so important, with salt-cured fish a major export. But things were changing now, the churchmen leading, as ever, and the landed gentry beginning to perceive the opportunities for profit.

The larger of the ships being built, George revealed, was for the transport of coal, and destined for the Prior of Culross, a community on the Fife shore some fifty miles up-firth, a famous place, for here in the sixth century St Serf had founded a monastery of the Celtic Church, and at it had been born Kentigern, the grandson of King Loth of the Southern Picts, son of Princess Thanea, who became known later as St Mungo, the founder of Glasgow. This Celtic establishment had in time become a Cistercian priory, and the monks there had discovered and developed seams of outcropping coal, which they hewed and mined and were now exporting, not only around their own country but to the Netherlands and the Baltic, especially Hamburg and the Hansa merchants, and to Sweden. And in return, from that last, they were importing iron, large sheets of beaten iron, for Sweden was as good as built on iron-ore; and this the monks used, not only to make implements, chain-mail, weapons and pots and pans, but to create great salt-pans, which could be heated by their coal, to evaporate the seawater infinitely more quickly and effectively than by the normal sun-heated pans elsewhere; so that now they were also exporting salt itself in a big way. Salt and coal, then, was turning Culross into one of the wealthiest communities in the land; and more and more ships were required, hence more timber. George had ongoing orders for vessels; but Dunbar harbour unfortunately allowed only two to be built at one time, John should himself start constructing ships at Inverness or Burghead or some other of the Moray ports, with all his timber available.

While they were examining the ship-construction, John noticed a smaller manufacture going on nearby, three or four men working at a yard, with more but less-heavy timber. Asking about this, he was told that it was the fashioning of trons. George had discovered that, with increased trading, foreign and otherwise, the weighing of heavy products such as coal, salt, meats, grain, wool and even timber itself, was necessary, to decide on value and price. And these trons, weighing-machines, were required by the Culross monks who urged their construction. So he had started this as a subsidiary industry, using lesser timbers than were needed for the ships. Trons consisted of a tall mast-like pole, on top of which, balanced on an iron pivot, swung a long cross-beam, at each end of which hung a chain to hold an iron pan of some size, one pan for holding the goods to be weighed, the other to bear the necessary weights, until one balanced the other. These had to be strongly built and accurate, needless to say. There seemed to be an ever-growing market for them.

John was much interested, and said that he would wish to visit this Culross, and learn more. His brother agreed to take him there and to introduce him to the Prior Dominic and the industrious and prosperous monks.

Next day, then, they set sail westwards, up-firth, accompanied for the occasion by his countess, Christian Seton, and their baby son, another George. They would spend the night at the priory.

After a pleasant sail up the picturesque Fife coastline, they found Culross spread along a narrow shelf of land backed by rising slopes, its priory and church dominant, with sheds and warehouses lining the sandy shore, this dotted with black heaps of hewn coal. Three ships were already berthed within the sheltered anchorage, formed by a natural line of rocks and a man-made breakwater, these all flying foreign flags, the beach bearing a number of fishing-boats.

Landing, and progressing into three parallel streets, named apparently the Low, Mid and High Causeways, John had pointed out to him, on the first, a prominently placed tron, its pole bedded firmly in a stone platform. They were received by the busy brethren pleasantly, Prior Dominic amiable, and interested to meet the Earl of Moray from whom came the timber for the ships he wanted. He introduced them to monks in charge of various groups of lay brothers, coal-hewers, hammermen or iron-workers, potters who also made clay tiles, salt-workers and other tradesmen, even the weighman in charge of the tron, an important individual on whose calculations much depended.

John asked many questions and learned a lot, sufficient, together with what he got from George, to convince him that shipbuilding and even tron-making, could be well worth introducing into Moray. He knew of no coal in his earldom, to fuel salt-pans, but there might well be fire-clay for pottery and tiles.

They spent a comfortable night in the refectory after an excellent repast, although Christian had to be parted from her husband for the night. In the morning they were shown the site of St Serf's monastery, and other features of interest. Then, John assuring the prior that he would send increased quantities of wood to his brother, and turn Moray hands to ship-construction, it was return to Dunbar.

Next day it was northwards again for Inverness, the brothers having made up their disagreement over those English-occupied castles meantime. John had a lot to tell his Marjory, to be sure.

Part Two

17

Thereafter followed an untroubled, happy and very rewarding period of John's and Marjory's life, with King Robert's reign being the most peaceful and prosperous for long years, and comparatively few demands made on his lords, other than financial ones, which the general prosperity made the less onerous. The situation with England, to be sure, greatly helped in this the troublous reign of young Richard the Second, John of Gaunt's failure to control his royal kin – he even had to take refuge in Scotland for a spell – Wat Tyler's rebellion, and other reverses there freeing Scotland from the age-old menace. The only warfare, if such it could be called, was what became known as the Wardens' Raid, when those occupied castles still were not evacuated, and George Cospatrick and William Douglas did take matters into their own hands, and succeeded in ousting the English from Roxburgh and Lochmaben, although not from Berwick-upon-Tweed, which proved too strong for them; and in this John fortunately was not involved.

John of the Isles died, and being succeeded by Donald, a new and peaceable relationship was established there, even between the Islesmen and the Campbells.

Scotland gained its first cardinal, Bishop Wardlaw of Glasgow being so promoted by Pope Clement; the Primate, Bishop of Aberdeen, may have been somewhat questioning about this, but he did not announce it.

John, having only to attend occasional meetings of council or parliament in the south, was very busy, and successfully so, the timber-harvesting ever increasing – his lands, fortunately, very rich in great woodlands – the shipbuilding at Inverness and Burghead prospering, with ever new demands for vessels. He did have a few trons constructed, but that was a minor matter, and soon the need dwindled.

With Marjory he was blissfully happy, especially when she presented him with a second son, whom they named Alexander, and who even rivalled Thomas in lung power. So there were five of them, a close and lively family.

There were sundry other deaths than that of John of the Isles, including that of William of Douglas, soon after the Wardens' Raid; and his son James, John's nephew, became second Earl of Douglas, and gave indications of being almost as warlike as his father. He too was created Warden of the East March.

The king's first major call upon John's services came at of all times the least convenient, in the early December of 1381, and was connected with the English situation, details not given. He was able to go south by sea, to Leith, and at Edinburgh's Holyrood learned what was required. John of Gaunt, still styling himself regent for young Richard, but said to be in failing health, was being largely superseded by his brother Thomas of Gloucester. And between them, these two had decided, in the circumstances prevailing, that friendship with France, rather than enmity, was advisable for England. They had managed to convince the French that this would be advantageous for both realms, and a treaty was being prepared. But reports indicated no mention of Scotland in this proposed treaty. So John was to go down to England and seek to have this country included in the compact. Also, if possible, to get Berwick-upon-Tweed returned to Scottish possession.

John was prepared to attempt this, despite the time of year and Yuletide approaching; but unfortunately, owing to present animosities south of the border, and London being more or less in the hands of the anti-Lancaster and Gloucester faction – indeed John of Gaunt's palace there put to the torch – the regency, if such it could still be called, was now being based at Oxford. This meant that it was no longer possible to go by sea, so a lengthy winter horseback journey was indicated. The king had obtained a safe-conduct agreement for John and fifty attendants to travel through England – as many as fifty apparently to indicate the necessary authority, however much these numbers might add to the problems of overnight accommodation. John had not brought any of his own men with him from Moray, so he had to sail on to Dunbar and there "borrow" the required company and horses from his brother, George co-operating but declaring that he was thankful that *he* was not considered to be a worthy royal envoy and given such tasks.

So it was that three hundred and fifty miles riding to Oxford in middle England, in harsh December weather, although at least there were no snow-filled passes to negotiate, with halts at large enough religious houses to cope with fifty troopers, this complicating routes and timing, although the safe-conduct did gain them the necessary hospitality at their various stops. It took them five days and four nights to reach their destination.

John found Lancaster and his brother Gloucester at the latter's castle, built by the Norman conquerors to block the River Cherwell, if necessary. John of Gaunt looked his age, but was less frail than John had been led to believe.

The visitor's welcome was reserved but not hostile. On the issue of the French treaty, there was no great difficulty in convincing the two Plantagenets that Scotland should be included, John's argument that it would be to the benefit of all, Scotland being in alliance with France, and the truce with England still having some years to run, this not contested. He declared that the French certainly would not disagree – this without stating that he did not quite understand why the French had conceded to this treaty-making in the first place.

But the matter of Berwick was otherwise, nothing that he could say about it being clearly in Berwickshire and therefore obviously part of Scotland carrying any weight with his hearers. The Tweed was half English, they claimed, and the mouth thereof important both as a port and for its sea-fishings, with Berwick Castle commanding it. The town in Scots hands would leave much of northern Northumberland open to border raiding and endanger the bases of Norham and Wark and many other communities. No, Berwick must remain in English hands.

Disappointed but not really surprised, John had to leave it at that.

Had his long and difficult journey been worth it all? Perhaps King Robert would deem it so. A gesture had been made, and Scotland shown to be demanding its rights.

In the event, back at Edinburgh in five more days, the monarch expressed himself as reasonably satisfied. Over Berwick he shook his head.

John reached Darnaway on Christmas Eve.

18

The next call to travel southwards was not until early summer, and not from the king this time but from brother George. Their mother, now an old lady, had had a heart attack, and there were fears that she might not survive another. She still was in command of her wits, as well as much else, but she believed that her time in this world might be short, although she was quite looking forward to the next. But she wished to see her other son and grandchildren.

Much concerned, John found no difficulty in persuading Marjory to accompany him, by ship, forthwith, with the three children. His wife was a great admirer of Black Agnes.

In fine June weather the voyage was speedy and pleasant. Young Thomas enjoyed it immensely, scoffing at his sister for at first being unable to keep her feet on the heaving deck, himself having to be restrained from becoming too adventurous.

At Dunbar, although it was not so long since he had seen his mother, John was distressed at the change in her physically, but certainly not mentally nor in spirit, her eyes still bright, her speech clear and positive although a little breathless. She was obviously delighted with her grandchildren, who eyed her wonderingly, but soon were on excellent terms with her. She had presents for them stored up, jewellery, a crucifix and little heirlooms of the family, their great-grandfather Thomas Randolph and of Robert the Bruce, which one day they would surely treasure.

John, of course, was much moved by it all, as indeed was Marjory, admiration and affection even heightened, the thought that this would be the last time that they were likely to see her in this life, wherever the next, very much on their minds.

While here, George wanted his brother to accompany him on a visit down the coast to the Tweed and Berwick, for an inspection of the town and its fortalice, as far as this could be possible. He declared that, since the English would not give it up voluntarily, they must be made to by force of arms, truce or no truce. After all, the town itself, and its castle, were on this northern side of Tweed, the part over on the other side, called the Spittal because of the monkish hospice there, being only an extension, to which the English were welcome. The new Earl James of Douglas, who was eager to make the attempt to win it all back, was collecting heavy siege-machinery and weapons, George himself having his tron-makers constructing battering-rams and mangonels to aid in a possible assault. Berwick was, or should be, *his* property, part of the Merse or March earldom; and if the port was in his hands, it would greatly enhance his trading ventures, to the benefit not only of himself but of the realm.

John was distinctly doubtful about this proposed attack, but agreed to go with his brother to view the situation and the challenge it presented, this without committing himself to taking part in any armed venture, as suggested, by using his Moray ships to assail the port by sea.

With only a small escort, since they did not want their inspection to be conspicuous, and dressed in work-a-day clothing, they rode off southwards, by Coldbrandspath, St Ebba's Head, Coldinghame, Eyemouth and Burnmouth, some thirty miles, where they turned inland some way in order to approach their goal down Tweed itself, as the less likely to reveal them as surveying the scene; for this way, after the communities of Foulden and Paxton, English and Flemish travellers by land, merchants and traders, were apt to travel, after crossing the great river at the Norham or Horncliffe fords.

They rode only as far as the St Leonards nunnery for

lepers, where, dismounting, with only two of their men, they left the others, to proceed on foot. It was now early evening, but the June light would last late; and this was probably the best time for their inconspicuous inspection.

They approached the town first, well aware that the castle's guards would be patrolling the walls before dusk fell, and might spot even casual individuals hanging about.

They did not actually enter the walled town, for the gates were shut for the night; and although they could have won within by one of the posterns, these would be manned by members of the town guard, and reasons for their late arrival have to be given. But they could, and did, circle the high walls at a discreet distance, north and then east, round again for the Tweed-mouth, noting approaches and possible weaknesses, and where a force might best strike. Until they came eventually to the river again, there was quite a wide area of grassy links, grazed by the town's cattle, and this could be useful as an approach for an armed force to assail the castle, which rose on higher ground just north-west of the town.

This stronghold, of course, was their principal concern, for if it was taken, the town and port would be a much lesser problem for any large force. Set on a lofty platform with steep sides, save for one narrow access, it would not be easy to attack with siege-weaponry, for there was very little room before the high walls on which to base this, save at the actual gatehouse, which of course would be strongly protected with ditch, drawbridge and portcullis. Scanning it all in the fading light, and from some distance off, they well realised that this was going to be very hard to take. They had always known of this, to be sure, but inspection in detail showed it to be worse than anticipated. And any prolonged siege was out of the question, with the town so close at the besiegers' backs, and enemy rescue so readily summonable from comparatively near at hand.

Less than heartened by what they saw, the viewers returned to their men and horses, and rode off northwards into the night. They would get as far Lamberton, four miles, where there was a small hospice.

George was very silent on that ride.

Back at Dunbar, John and his family stayed for another two days before sadly making their farewells – although faring well was scarcely a possibility for Black Agnes. They did not suggest, of course, that this would probably be the last time that they would see each other while in this mortal state, but the recognition was very much there, with the adults at least, the old lady the most cheerful of them, declaring that love and life were both eternal, and the best part of their journey onwards was yet to come.

Kissed, and clutching their treasures, the children led the way to their ship.

19

That summer and autumn the news reaching Moray was reasonably good in national affairs, although as regards England it was otherwise, troubles there proliferating, King Richard's minority reign dire indeed.

Then in late October came the word that Black Agnes had slipped away peacefully, assured of bliss to come, however much those left behind might doubt it. And not long afterwards another message from George announced that the projected assault on Berwick was to be mounted, with harvest now in, cattle brought down from higher summer pastures, and men available for the attempt. John, with his ships, plus the Dunbar ones, was asked to lead the sea attack, George and the Douglases heading a large force, all but an army. King Robert, it was added, was giving the enterprise his backing.

Taking this as in the nature of a royal command, John felt that he could hardly refuse, however unenthusiastic; and Marjory, needless to say was still less so.

With four ships, and with urgent instructions to take the greatest care, making no risky moves, and to come back safely and soon, he sailed from Inverness, with Brodie and Ogstoun, even some Comyns, and almost three hundred men, a reluctant warrior.

At Dunbar they found five more ships awaiting them, under Sir James Douglas of Dalkeith. George was already gone, with his mounted men, to join the main assembly at Duns, where the Mersemen and the Douglases were mustering. Instructions were for the ships to put to sea forthwith, but to heave to off St Ebba's Head until they saw beacons and smoke-signals thereon, intimating that the

185

land force was moving on to Berwick, when the little fleet was to proceed and coincide its assault on the port and town at the same time as the main land attack.

It was only a short distance, however, to St Ebba's Head, and there they all duly lay off, with no smoke signals rising to urge them on. Rolling and swaying uncomfortably in the tides, there they waited.

And they had a long wait. For two days and nights they lingered there, less than happy with this part they were having to play, when they could have been biding in comfort only a score of miles north at Dunbar. Presumably there was some hold-up at Duns, the rallying-place for the others. Idling was never good for men's morale.

At last, on the morning of the third day, they saw two smoke columns arising fron the headland. Sails could be hoisted. It was less than another twenty miles to Berwick.

When they reached the wide mouth of Tweed there was no sign of any armed force, nor of any alarm when they rounded the northern headland and were able to approach the docks outside the walls of the town. John, for one, found this very strange warfare. What were they expected to do now? Wait again? He did not see it as any part of his duty to attack shipping moored there, largely foreign merchant-vessels almost certainly. What would the folk ashore think of nine strange vessels suddenly appearing, and not trying to dock? He was beginning to judge his brother's wits less bright than he had thought.

They could not see reactions in the town, of course, because of those high walls, whether the townsfolk were in a stir or not. He supposed that they would not necessarily be seen as enemy ships – although surely it would be unusual for as many as nine large craft to arrive together and then lie off?

Fishing-boats did pass by them, the occupants eyeing them curiously. And one larger vessel came out from its wharf, to head for the sea, flying the Hansa flag, its crew also no doubt wondering at them.

For hours they lay there, feeling distinctly foolish. They

could see the castle up on the high ground to the north, a mile away, but all seemed quiet there.

It was late afternoon before there was any change in the scene. Horsemen began to appear below the castle-mound, many horsemen. More and more came in sight. But these did not seem to be mounting any attack on the stronghold, no sign of warlike activity on either side.

Then, to his surprise, part of that armed force up near the castle began to move on down towards the town, how many it was hard to judge, but possibly a thousand at least. What now? Was his sea contingent expected to do something in concert? Land men at the dockside? Make some gesture? It was all a very odd action, this. Presumably this horsed force *was* part of the Dunbar-Douglas host? It was too far off to see banners and identify them. Could they possibly be English? Part of an enemy force arrived first on the scene?

Unfortunately, because of that high walling and the tall buildings of Berwick town itself, the ship-borne folk could not see the approaching horsemen as they got closer. So inevitably they remained in ignorance as to what was happening. They could still see the remainder of the host up near the castle, and there seemed to be total inaction, no sign of any siegery commencing.

There was nothing that the ships could be concerned in, as yet. They could move in closer to the dockside. Should they land their men? If those were English, not Scots troops arriving, then that would be folly.

Sir James Douglas, John's brother-in-law, came close, to transfer to the Moray ship for discussion, as perplexed as was he. They came to the conclusion that there was nothing they could usefully do meantime, but to go on waiting for guidance.

It was fully another hour before they got anything such. Then a small group of horsemen appeared, issuing from a gateway in the walling which opened on to the dockside. These came down to the wharfs, to wave over to the ships. And close behind one of them was one bearing a banner

187

that was well known to John, for it was the Cospatrick standard. So that must be George, in front.

Astonished, John ordered his shipmaster to move his vessel in, to fill the gap at the dockside which the Hansa craft had left vacant.

And there was George waiting for them when he and Douglas disembarked. And, considering the circumstances, looking cheerful, hailing his brother and grinning. Whatever had happened, or had not happened, he seemed to be well enough satisfied.

Dismounting, George came to explain. The castle had surrendered to them without a fight. It made an extraordinary story. It seemed that the Percy Earl of Northumberland, known as Hotspur for his dashing behaviour, English Warden of this East March, had a day or two before summoned the governor of Berwick Castle, Sir Thomas Musgrave, to Alnwick, his seat some thirty miles away, leaving the deputy governor, Crozier by name apparently, in charge. And Crozier had somehow learned that a Scottish force was approaching from the north. And he, Crozier, had his own bones to pick. It seemed that he was at odds with Percy of Northumberland, who had deprived him of certain lands in Tynedale unjustly, and accused him of partiality towards the Scots, this because he owned certain properties in the Ladykirk area on the north side of Tweed, in the Merse, which he had inherited from his mother who had been a Home. Musgrave, the governor, had backed Northumberland, and the pair were not on the best of terms. So, when this situation arose, Musgrave had gone to Alnwick and the Scots force approaching, Crozier had decided to change sides, throw in his lot with his mother's people, the Homes, linked by blood with the Cospatricks, and so become a Scot of sorts, his England being in a chronic state of disorder anyway. He had surrendered Berwick Castle to the new arrivals without a blow struck, the garrison presumably quite glad to escape conflict and possible slaughter. He had indeed quite willingly come down with George and Earl James Douglas to the town, to order the mayor and aldermen to yield up all without dispute. This seemingly they had done, with little argument, those ships lying off a further menace, and a Scots army waiting outside the walls. Many of the folk, of course, were of Berwickshire origin and there was a large influx of Flemings and Netherlanders settled there as traders, who wanted no involvement in warfare.

So Berwick and its castle were at last in Scots hands, to great rejoicing, and not a drop of blood shed.

Astonished, John could only wag his head in wonder, thankfulness also of course. This was almost beyond belief, and all caused out of bitterness between two Northumbrians.

What was to happen now, he asked.

George said that full arrangements had not been decided on as yet. But he thought that two garrisons of Scots would have to be left, a strong one for the castle and a smaller one to hold the town. And, while their main force returned northwards, they must be ready to come back again, should there be any major English attempt to retake Berwick. And he would see that this Crozier was amply rewarded for his notable services with lands in the Merse. A turncoat he might be, but a very useful one. That night the Scots leadership spent in a Greyfriars hospice in the Trongate, in comfort, no animosity shown. John met Thomas Crozier, a very silent individual, obviously with much on his mind. He did admit, however, that he would probably change his name to Home of Ramrig, near to Ladykirk.

Decisions were made. Archibald Douglas, an illegitimate half-brother of the Earl James, would be left in charge here, with a mixed company of Dunbar and Douglas men, these to be replaced by others in due course. All the Merse would be readied to rally to their support should the English seek to regain Berwick. John did not offer to contribute Moray men to this garrisoning, and it was not demanded.

So that was that, the oddest Cospatrick or Douglas campaign on record.

In the morning John did not linger, and set sail again northwards for Inverness via Dunbar.

20

That peculiar Berwick affair, all but a fiasco, may have been extraordinary, easy and trouble-free; but the victors, whatever the English reactions might be, were scarcely prepared for what followed in conseqeunce, on both the national and international fronts, John certainly not. The first development, admittedly, was not unexpected, although hardly the size of it, when the Earls of North-umberland and Nottingham arrived before Berwick with no fewer than eight thousand men. However worthy a defence Archibald Douglas put up, he could not withstand such weight of numbers, supported by siege-engines, and Berwick fell once more into English hands, this before any Scots force could be raised to help the defence.

But that was only the beginning. John of Gaunt, declar-ing that the Scots had blatantly broken the truce, marched north to protest, demanding a meeting with Scots repre-sentatives, in the form of a March wardens' assembly, but bringing two thousand men with him to reinforce his demands, coming as far over the border as Aytoun in the Merse, this before the Earl of Douglas and George were able to reach there. Possibly he saw this as an opportunity to help unite the squabbling English factions, since nothing was so effective in healing breaches in a national front, at least temporarily, than military action against a common foe. It had been a stormy meeting, with Douglas demanding vengeance and retribution for the murder, by Hotspur Percy, of his half-brother who, after yielding Berwick Castle, had been shamefully butchered, hanged, drawn and quartered. Had it not been for those two thousand men watching and waiting, there would undoubtedly have been more violent exchanges than in mere words. But John of Gaunt, having made his protest, and declaring that Berwick hereafter must remain in English hands, under threat of outright full-scale war, turned back over the border – no doubt remembering his taking refuge in this Scotland none so long before, and receiving a fair reception.

It did not end there, however, although the further repercussions took longer to eventuate. The French king, young Charles the Sixth, taking the rule, evidently decided that the treaty with England was unprofitable, with the Plantagenets still claiming Guienne and Aquitaine as theirs, and declared that this march into Scotland by Lancaster and Northumberland was in breach of the joint accord, renounced the said treaty, and demonstrated his renunciation by sending word that the Auld Alliance was still very much in force, this by sending a company of thirty French knights to Scotland, these coming by sea, and landing at Montrose just south of Aberdeen; why there, rather than at Leith, was not clear. At any rate, the Earl of Moray was ordered by King Robert to greet them, as a suitable representative, and to conduct them south to Edinburgh.

So John had this unlooked-for duty of welcoming the Frenchmen. He found them ensconced in Keith the Marischal's castle of Dunnottar, he uncertain as to why they had come and what to say to them.

The visitors proved to be a splendid and haughty group, very finely clad and armoured, and gave the impression of looking down proud noses at the less lofty-seeming Scots, even though one was an earl and the other Knight Marischal. John had come by ship to Montrose, where the French vessel still lay, so Keith lent them all horses to ride there, and the two ships could sail together for Leith.

John, whose French was not of the best – and the newcomers did not deign to speak English – did learn that these fine knights were only the forerunners of a greater French demonstration of pro-Scots and anti-English attitudes. Just what this was to be he did not find out there and then. He did not suggest that he should sail south with them in *their* vessel.

At Holyrood he was thankful to hand over the visitors to his father-in-law, whose French it seemed was better than his own, with Cardinal Wardlaw to help. Before returning to Inverness, he did learn that King Charles of France was determined to get rid of English claims to parts of his realm once and for all, and saw the Auld Alliance as a means of achieving this. He was going to send further aid to Scotland, to leave the English in no doubt that they would be wise to renounce all such claims, and to realise also that permanent peace with Scotland was advisable.

John returned home wondering at the fact that the Berwick interlude, and their brief hold of that castle, could have sparked off this involvement between three kingdoms.

Marjory told him to be sure never to get mixed up in the like again.

Such advice was all very well, but her father thought otherwise, and his was the royal command, not to be rejected. John was summoned south to a council meeting only one month thereafter.

The council, at Holyrood, was to consider the Franco-Scottish situation, and what to do with these thirty French knights. It seemed that King Charles was going to send, and very shortly, a greater demonstration of support than had been realised, and that this could be arriving any day, a support that King Robert was not greatly wanting. If it was just to be a gesture, that was none so ill; but by the way these knights talked, it was military action that was being contemplated. What was to be done about this? Did Scotland desire outright war with England?

There was no question but that the majority of the councillors was against anything such, even though the Earl of Douglas led one or two who seemed to relish the prospect. Even George Dunbar thought otherwise; after all, his Merse lands would be the first to suffer if warfare went against them.

They were still debating this matter when one of George's people arrived hot-foot from Dunbar, to announce that a great French fleet had appeared there and was lying off, the harbour far too small to accept them, the leadership having come ashore and now being entertained in the castle by the Countess Christian.

Much concerned over this, George and John were sent off forthwith to deal with the situation there, and to bring those in charge back to Edinburgh.

It was evening before the brothers could reach Dunbar, to see no fewer than eleven large ships at anchor off the harbour. In the castle they found half a dozen lordly Frenchmen, Christian thankful indeed to see her husband back.

The newcomers proved to be led by no less than the Lord High Admiral of France, John de Vienne, an authoritative individual, who seemed to be bemused by this extraordinary fortalice on its rock-stacks, and demanding whether this was typical of Scottish castles, and if so, how were horsed forces to operate therefrom? He had brought fifteen hundred men from France, and of course, no horses. His English, fortunately, was fair although heavily accented.

George told him that, given time, he could provide horses for a fair proportion of the Frenchmen. But – what were these numbers intended for?

For an invasion of England, he was informed. To aid the Scots army. And he had brought more than men. In his ships there were eighty suits of the best armour, sent by King Charles in case some of the Scottish lords lacked such. Also fifty thousand gold francs.

All but dizzy with this information, especially that last, in *gold*, a sum all but unheard of in Scotland, the brothers stared at each other. What was to be done about all this? What would the king and council do? Small wonder that Christian was in something of a whirl.

When they had had time to sit quietly and think on it all, they could decide only on temporary measures. George would give orders for horses to be collected from Lothian and the Merse; the Frenchmen would have to be brought ashore from their ships, even though they would in fact almost outnumber the inhabitants of Dunbar and be scarcely welcomed; and meantime this de Vienne and his senior lieutenants, counts, chevaliers and the like, plus the armour, and of course the gold, must be taken to Edinburgh, for the monarch and his advisers to decide what was to be done about it all.

At least Dunbar Castle's hospitality did not have to be apologised for, even though Christian's resources were strained. The whisky proved to be especially appreciated, and a distinctly noisy evening resulted.

John, for one, was thankful to get to bed late that night.

In the morning a sufficiency of horses, fine mounts for the lofty ones and pack-animals to transport all the weighty gold, was mustered, orders given as to the rest, and poor Christian left to deal with another fifty knights and the leaders of the men-at-arms who were to be landed at the township. A start was made for Edinburgh, thirty-five miles.

The French at least were impressed with the scenery, exclaiming over the vast Craig of Bass rising out of the sea with its halo of screaming fowl, the lofty green cone of North Berwick Law, the red-stone might of Tantallon Castle, the long, heathery ranges of the Lammermuir Hills, and, far ahead, the upthrusting, couched-lion-shaped bulk of Arthur's Seat, which drew them on to Edinburgh. They did not ride very fast, because of those laden pack-horses.

At Holyrood, the vistors were more taken with the soaring hill so close by, which they called a mountain, than with the abbey itself. The brothers were thankful to hand over their charges to Robert, his son Carrick, and the other councillors. What these would make of the situation was questionable indeed. Wardlaw would be a help, a linguist, knowledgeable as to Frenchmen and a prince of the Church.

The remainder of the evening was somewhat chaotic, with nobody very sure about procedure or policy or how to deal with this French invasion – nor indeed the gold, although that was not far from most minds. John and his brother were concerned as to what they were to do with all the shiploads of Frenchmen back at Dunbar.

King Robert himself was in a state of uncertainty. Nothing in his experience had prepared him for a situation such as this, these visitors spoiling for war against England, himself and his people the reverse. And all these men and armour and monies being produced. A council would be held on the morrow when, it was hoped, some sort of decision would be reached.

Held it was, however wise and worthy the conclusions, that gold talking loudly. Some sort of gesture must be made to support the Auld Alliance, even though it was unlikely to satisfy the Frenchmen. The obvious place to make this was against the English East March where Hotspur Percy and Nottingham had wrought so much havoc in the Merse. They would not engage in siege of Berwick Castle and town, which would give time for large English forces to come up and do battle; but some assault along the south bank of Tweed would possibly serve their turn.

So, of course, it was the Earl of Dunbar and March and his brother, together with the Earl of Douglas, Warden of that March, who must cope with it, aided by token contributions from other lords. The French force was already at Dunbar, and horses were being collected for them. And to help in all this, a suitable share of the gold would be made available. Douglas, who could and would supply most men, to get seven thousand five hundred francs; George four thousand; and even John, who scarcely saw why he should be awarded any since he was producing no Moray men, got one thousand. That left thirty-seven thousand five hundred to be distributed elsewhere, with the national treasury getting most, undoubtedly.

The following day was spent showing the visitors round

Edinburgh and its fortress, the hunting and hawking facilities of Arthur's Seat and its surroundings – up to near the top of which de Vienne and his friends climbed, on horseback, amidst cries of astonishment – this with feasting and entertainment. Douglas left to assemble men from his nearer properties, although his great Galloway lands and manpower were too far away to be of practical help on this occasion. He would meet the Dunbar and Merse contingent at Edenmouth on the Tweed, east of Kelso, in three days' time.

Next day, then, it was back to Dunbar, with the admiral, for a marshalling of forces, to the relief of Christian and the townsfolk. A large number of horses had been gathered, and all was readied for the venture southwards. John had wondered whether the ships could play any part, but it seemed not. The Tweed, inland from Berwick, was not deep enough for other than small boats; and Berwick was not the target on this occasion. So he would just ride with George, wearing one of the handsome French suits of armour – in which he felt somewhat fraudulent.

The subsequent ride down through the Lammermuirs into the Merse drew exclamations from the visitors, the sheep-strewn heathery hills with their hidden ravines, their lochans and torrents, much interesting them; which seemed strange, for they must have many hills in France, mountains indeed to the south, but presumably not such as these.

At Duns they picked up a further company of Mersemen under a Home laird; and thereafter they were in Home country most of the way until they reached the Swinton territory. The great Borders clan of Home was descended from the Cospatricks, a son of one of the early lords having married a Home heiress and taken that name. When, presently, they passed near Home Castle, rising tall on its isolated ridge amidst fertile green pastures, the new-comers were further impressed, especially when it was explained to them that these Borderland strongholds, on their heights, had beacons that could be lit, producing glowing balefires, as they were called, by night, and smoke columns by day, and so able to signal over great mileages of any English invasion anywhere along the line. Within an hour of anything such, all the Borderland would know of it and be prepared.

They reached Tweed at Edenmouth, where they found Douglas awaiting them with two thousand mounted men. So now their force amounted to over six thousand, a sufficiency for the gesture they were to make, however inadequate the Frenchmen may have thought it.

The three earls, consulting, decided that their first target should be Wark. Norham was more important, but it was very defensible and, because of its situation, had a good and long view of its ford over Tweed, and so was able to prepare for any attack. Wark was less well placed in this respect, with its township between it and the river; also not so strong. They wanted no prolonged siegery, needless to say.

Six miles down Tweed they came to the ford where they were to cross. Wark Castle was near but not actually in sight because of its village. Considerable to-do was made of this crossing, alarming to the French at first owing to the depth of water up to their horses' bellies, until it was explained to them that there was an under-water causeway of stone, which allowed safe passage in all but the highest spates and floods; but also because, once halfway over, they were in England, with everything suddenly changed.

That crossing, and the approach thereafter to the village, could not have gone unobserved, and almost certainly word would have been sent up to the castle. So they wasted no time at the first houses. But, as feared, at the stronghold they found the gates shut and barred, the drawbridge up and the portcullis down, guards on the watch. There was nothing for it but challenge in words.

Douglas, at the moat-edge, shouted, "In the name of Robert, King of Scots, I, Earl of Douglas, with the High Admiral of France and the Earls of Dunbar and March and of Moray, would have speech with the keeper of this hold. Have him to speak with us, I say."

The answer came back promptly enough. "I, Sir John Lisburn, hold Wark Castle, in the name of my lord of Northumberland. What seek you here, with this host of men?"

"We seek the surrender of this hold to King Robert, because your Northumberland has taken our castle and town of Berwick unlawfully, after we repossessed it, part of our sheriffdom of Berwick. We demand the exchange!"

There were a few moments of silence. Then came the answer.

"I refuse any such betrayal of my duty, my lords. If you want Wark, you must take it!" And a hackbut was discharged in their direction by way of confirmation. Presumably the defenders had seen that the would-be attackers had no siege-engines with them.

"Take it we shall, sirrah!" Douglas cried. "You will regret this defiance. We shall not leave here, I promise you!"

This situation, of course, was not unexpected by the attackers. But what would be unexpected, by the defenders, was this sudden assault. Therefore, the probability of them having supplies to withstand a siege of any length was highly unlikely. No costly attempts to scale the walls or to set the place afire with fire-arrows ought to be necessary. There was a sufficiency of men to surround the castle and ensure that no help arrived. All this had been thought of previously.

So Wark township was raided for food for the besiegers. Most of the inhabitants had prudently fled to the surrounding woodlands and hillocky country with their cattle. The invaders took over the village, but left the castle enclosed in a great circle, isolated.

A conference of the leaders decided that the likelihood of the defenders being able to hold out for more than four or five days was improbable. So, leave perhaps one-third of their force to besiege, while the remainder went off to find other targets none so far off. All Northumberland lay open to their attentions, after all.

De Vienne and his friends were all for this course, although George and John were cautious about how far and for how long they should remain across the border and allow time for a defending army to assemble and contest the issue, Douglas rather pooh-poohing this.

They passed a reasonably comfortable night in occupied quarters.

In the morning, James of Dalkeith left in charge of the siege with two thousand men which ought to be sufficient, the remainder set off south-eastwards for Ford, some ten miles off, where there was a smaller castle belonging to the Heron family who were apt to make nuisances of themselves in cross-border raiding. They could be doing with a lesson.

By Learmouth and Branxton and Flodden they came to the large River Till, the principal ford of which gave name to the Heron tower-house and township. Presumably word of the assault on Wark, although comparatively near at hand, had not reached Ford yet – they could have done with a beacon-warning system this side of the border – for the invaders found all unprepared here, and they were able to ride up to the castle, gates open, and the owner absent, his wife and young family in consternation over this dire arrival. Not wishing to make war on women and children, Lady Heron was told to betake herself off wherever she might wish to go, and to tell her husband in due course that the visitors would be glad to have words with him whenever possible. Then the leadership took over the castle, entertained themselves therein, and then set it on fire, while the men-at-arms acted similarly towards the township.

It was all very satisfactory, although the Frenchmen saw it as tame.

What to do next? There was another small castle further down Till a few miles, called Etal, which they could assail. Or further south there was the castle of Coupland, six or seven miles, worthy of attention. But Douglas, with his concern over what Percy of Northumberland had done to his half-brother, was for heading east for the Percy seat of Alnwick, near the coast. George and John thought that this was stretching matters too far, for Alnwick was considerably further south, about forty miles, and would take them some time to reach, especially with other places on the way which they could hardly leave unmolested, such as Doddington and Chatton, Ellingham, Craster and perhaps Longhaughton. And all this time the Wark situation would be uncertain.

They persuaded Douglas to head back towards Wark after they had dealt with Etal, at least part of the way.

Etal had a reputation, like Ford, for its owners harrying over into the Merse, and the more so in that their name, Carr, was significant. Presumably they were originally part of the great Scots line of Kerrs and Kers, of the Middle March of Scotland, for that is how this name was pronounced, stemming from the Norse Kjerr, although these spelled it differently. That such should harry their far-out kin and fellow-countrymen across the border was to be deplored. So the Scots now approached Etal the more grimly.

But, in the event, they were denied any real satisfaction there, for the news of their assault on Wark and the sacking of Ford had reached this area, part-way between the two, and the Carrs had decided that discretion was wiser than valour, in the face of these thousands, and had departed, taking with them what they could in the way of stock and valuables. There was no large community here, so the invaders had to be content with wrecking, so far as they could without undue delay, Etal Castle, before moving on. Again the Frenchmen were disappointed at the lack of opportunity to display their martial prowess.

It was almost ten miles back to Wark, so Douglas suggested that they need not all waste precious time by returning there to see how the siege progressed. He requested that John and a small party should go and discover the situation. Meanwhile their force could assail Cornhill, where there was another castle on the English side of Tweed not far from Scots Coldstream, which would repay a visit, before they headed on eastwards for Alnwick.

John was prepared to do this, and rode off westwards with a mere score of men, indeed quite glad to be spared further sackings and burnings meantime, which he did not enjoy.

Arriving back at Wark, he was in time to take part in a development there, this pleasing the besiegers, who were getting very bored with sitting around the castle and doing nothing. The owner's son, another John Lisburn, had come out from the hold under a white flag, to say that his father, family and retainers would be prepared to yield up the castle, under terms, and without bloodshed – obviously hunger was dictating this proposal. The conditions offered were that they should be allowed to depart unmolested, with what they desired to take, that the township should not be further ravaged, the castle occupied if desired but not sacked.

James Douglas of Dalkeith was considering this when John appeared. He was less aggressively inclined than his namesake Earl James, and in the circumstances was prepared to agree these terms, which would allow him and most of his men to leave Wark and rejoin the main force, objective achieved, leaving only a strong garrison to hold the place.

This much commended itself to John, who would also have accepted these conditions. So young Lisburn was sent back to his father, and a garrisoning party was chosen, under Home of Blackadder. The rest of the besiegers were well content to pack up and prepare to leave.

After quite a wait, Sir John Lisburn and his family and people emerged from the hold, under that white flag, and exchanging distant salutations with their foes, moved off, part mounted, part on foot, with laden pack-horses, all very orderly and sensible, the kind of hostilities John could accept.

By this time it was evening, so the Scots leaders spent the night in a house they had been threatening, and found it all to their taste save for a lack of provisioning, a rewarding outcome.

Next morning some sixteen hundred of them rode eastwards along the south bank of Tweed; and before they had gone a couple of miles saw pale smoke-clouds rising ahead of them. This proved to be Cornhill Castle, no very strong place, with its castleton, set on fire, a few bodies lying about indicating that there had been some resistance – but no other sign of the attackers, save for many more horse-droppings.

John and his brother-in-law led the way on south-eastwards, in the wake of their main force, presumably now heading for Alnwick. They reckoned that they were probably the best part of a day behind. Those smokes had been thin and dying.

They crossed Till again, but lower than previously, and presently found Duddo also in smouldering ruin. How close they were behind the busy main body was hard to calculate.

The signs led them almost due east thereafter, which indicated a change in the former intended direction, as making not for Doddington and the other more southerly targets, but for the coast, possibly in the Fenwick area. John guessed that this was Earl Douglas taking some heed of George's worries about timing and the probability of powerful English reactions. So no unavoidable delays in reaching Alnwick, the coastal route faster, although moving well clear of the great fortresses of Bamburgh and Dunstanburgh.

An army thousands strong cannot cover its route without leaving ample traces behind, and the Wark force had no difficulty in following. And so doing they saw no more devastation. Douglas was evidently recognising the need for haste.

It was evening before they reached Alnwick, five miles from the coast, the sight of many glowing camp-fires beckoning them on.

They found their colleagues and the Frenchmen settled around Alnwick Castle on the outskirts of a small town. But the fortalice itself was anything but small, an extensive, almost palatial establishment, but powerful also, within its great lengths of walling, occupying a low rise above a bend in the Aln Water, scarcely a ridge, but a good defensive position. It had been first built by the Norman de Vescys, and only coming to the Percys seventy-odd years before, from nearby Warkworth. Here Malcolm the Third of Scotland, Canmore, had met his end; and William Wallace had besieged it. This would be a hard nut to crack, all perceived.

They discovered Douglas and George, even de Vienne, well aware of this, and debating their further activity. They assumed that Hotspur Percy was not in residence, for, if he had been, surely he would have made some gesture towards the invaders, even though he might not have had a sufficiency of men actually to assail them. Since nothing such had occurred, George feared that he might well be away assembling a host, possibly at Newcastle, his "capital", with his friend Nottingham, to counter the Scots-French assault. The question was, whether to wait here, threatening his castle, head on towards Newcastle or wherever, or return to Scotland?

John backed George in favour of that last, possibly assailing some more holds on the way; but the Douglas was anxious to get to grips with Hotspur; and de Vienne and his lieutenants were itching for the clash of arms. If Percy, informed of the invasion, was indeed mustering a host sufficiently large to confront them, and he had the means to do so, then almost certainly it would be based on Newcastle, the largest city north of Durham, and some thirty-five miles to the south.

The argument was quite strong, George and John, backed by Dalkeith, very much against heading all that way further, Douglas in two minds, but the admiral loud in his urgency to advance. He and his had not come all this way just to turn back without striking a real blow.

What did the Scots lords think that gold had been sent for?

That last did have its effect on his hearers' pride. A move on towards Newcastle, then – but to be prepared for withdrawal promptly if the need arose.

The combined host made an early start of it, with the dawn, riding due southwards now, with scouts ahead, over moorland, many miles of this, to cross the River Coquet at Felton, then on through fairly empty upland country to reach Morpeth on the Wansbeck, a quite large town with a castle and an abbey, this being deliberately bypassed, halfway to Newcastle. At Stannington they had to ford another river, the Blyth, and more moorland beyond, this leading to the lower lands of the great vale of Tyne. The Scots had not realised quite how much of low hills and fells and moor made up Northumberland, fair enough cattle and sheep country. They had tended to think of the more populous coastal plain as typical. Then crossing the ancient Roman Wall, they knew that they were nearing Newcastle.

It was at Gosforth that they learned much, including the unwisdom of proceeding further, and this by a strange chance. A small force of riders, coming down Tynedale from the west, approached them openly, and were dumbfounded to learn, too late, that this was not, like themselves, a contribution to the great array being assembled on Newcastle Green. They had come from the Haltwhistle and Hawdon area on the summons, not of Percy but of none other than the Duke of Lancaster, John of Gaunt, who was apparently in Yorkshire and marching north to meet the Scots, this a quite separate reaction, it seemed, from Hotspur's mustering.

The news, of course, quite altered the entire situation. It seemed that their Scots force was likely to be facing two different armies, whether acting in co-operation or not was not known, a dire prospect. Even de Vienne was alarmed. They were all surprised that news of their border crossing had so quickly reached the south, for they had been only nine days in England; but presumably long enough for the challenge to be known and acted upon. Now, at all costs they must not be caught between two powerful enemy forces. It must be turn around and back to Scotland.

What to do about these unwilling informants from upper Tynedale? They could scarcely slaughter them, as it were, in cold blood. Douglas decided that they should take them north with them as captives, in the nature of hostages; they just might be useful as such. There were only about one hundred of them, so not in any position to menace their captors.

De Vienne, although acknowledging this dangerous position, was against retiring directly to Scotland in seeming fear and humiliation. Why not change direction in their assault on the English? Turn westwards, out of this Northumberland. Attack Cumberland, where they would not be looked for. Wreak havoc there. Seek to destroy Carlisle, instead of Newcastle – this before the two enemy armies could join up and act in concert.

The Scots were against such tactics. The English would see this as an opportunity to invade across the border in their great numbers, more or less unopposed, and conquer the undefended land, or at least the southern half of it. Their first duty now was the defence of the realm, not further raiding and sacking. Cumberland could wait. It was back across Tweed for them.

Much disapproving, the Frenchmen, concerned not to seem as though fleeing in the face of the foe, could not dissuade their allies and had to accept prompt retiral. The unhappy and bewildered Tyneside men had no option but to go along.

With some forty-five miles to cover, to pick up the garrison left at Wark Castle – they could not leave them to be the victims of the punitive English – they rode as fast as they might; but thousands cannot travel at the speed of smaller parties of good horsemen, and still retain any sort of formation. They got only as far as Rothbury that July night, camping for only a few hours by Coquet-side.

sent off to hide with their families and stock and belong-
ings, their acceptance of this strategy taken for granted;
after all, the alternative to them going would be slaying,
ravishing and burning by the advancing foe, far worse a
fate.

They got as far as Duns, in the Merse, when their
forward scouts sent back the awaited tidings. A large
English army, reckoned to be of at least one hundred
thousand, was advancing into Scotland, presumably under
King Richard and Lancaster, but not coming by the direct
route, Berwick and the east coast, nor yet the central
Merse, but by the west, up Liddesdale and over into
Teviotdale, this unexpected indeed. Had they got word
of the Douglas and French sally, by some means?

This surprising news meant a major change in direction
for the laying-waste programme, although at least it spared
George's lands from devastation meantime. So they turned
south-westwards. They would start their sad activities
west of Jedburgh, but perhaps have to work their way
backwards thereafter, coming nearer to their own terrain.

John had never taken part in this sort of activity which
was now facing them, and he hated the thought of it. They
would have to clear the folk from quite a wide swathe of
country in the path of the oncoming foe, telling them to
flee into hiding with their flocks and herds and such
possessions as they especially treasured, into the hills
and hidden valleys and forested ground where they would
be safe. Then the stocks of grain and hay and foods of any
sort would have to be destroyed, barns, sheds, mills, and
cot-houses burned, so that the oncoming host would find
nothing to sustain men and beasts – and a great army
cannot advance effectively without supplies. It would send
out patrols right and left, of course, to seek food and
fodder, but to feed many thousands and their mounts it
would be very difficult to find any sort of sufficiency, and
must much delay the advance.

It was the small lairds' tower-houses John found the
most difficult to deal with, the owners reluctant indeed to

abandon them, loth to become refugees in wild places, and having to be persuaded that otherwise it would be disaster for them, death, rape, utter destruction, even though their stone towers, unlike the common folks' timber and thatched buildings, would not burn easily, although their contents would.

The people of Kelso, Roxburgh and Jedburgh had to be warned first, amidst consternation; and then the devastators had to divide into two, to proceed with their sorry task up both Tweed and Teviot. John found himself allotted the former to deal with, this the less likely route, for coming from Liddesdale, the Teviot would be the enemy's quickest and easiest road. This knowledge did allow John and his people to be less thorough in their oustings and burnings. He had never had a duty he found so distasteful and distressing.

He got as far as Mertoun, up Tweed, when a messenger from George, in Teviotdale, came to tell him to turn back. Scouts ahead informed that Denholm and Hawick were going up in smoke, enemy work this. So it would not be long before their outriders reached this far. Leaving his own legacy of smoke behind, John led his weary ejectors and fire-raisers eastwards again, his only consolation that there was no lack of good, wild escape-country in these southern uplands, ravines, scattered woodlands and empty valleys, where the temporarily dispossessed ought to be safe.

He found his brother worried about his own Merse territory. The probability was that this English host, coming from the West March, would not include Hotspur's force from the Newcastle area. If that also decided to invade, it would be apt to do so well to the east, in fact into the Merse. This thought troubled him sufficiently to leave his colleagues Seton, the Kerrs and Homes, to continue their work here, while he headed back eastwards with John, Andrew Kerr of Kersheugh much upset at having to herd his neighbours of Jedburgh out of their town. The Homes might have to be sent for to help defend the Merse. Everything was very much in doubt.

The brothers wondered whether they would have to waste and burn their own lands. No point in doing that until they were sure that the Percy was coming their way, for this was well out of the line northwards for the main English army. But once Hotspur did cross lower Tweed, it would not take him long to move up to the edges of Lothian. So all must be readied in time to halt, or at least delay him, if possible.

George, then, would head for Dunbar, to prepare fullest alert and mustering for immediate action. John should go on south-eastwards, this decided at Duns, to a vantage-point, probably the hill known as the Witches' Knowe, near Mordington, where he would be able to spot any invading force coming from Berwick or a nearby Tweed crossing, and send hasty warning back to Dunbar.

They parted, then, John retaining only a few men.

They rode by the Whiteadder for about a dozen miles, to reach the coastal plain in the Foulden area, all seeming peaceful so far, John well aware that much of this land might well have to be scorched hereafter. He felt almost guilty as he surveyed it all. What an evil was war, and yet the nations had a dire aptitude for it.

He knew the Witches' Knowe of old, the highest view-point for miles around, from which they could see right down to the mouth of Tweed. They climbed it, nothing to effect being seen as yet. The Percy might not come. Or he might be with Lancaster and King Richard. Or taking a different route altogether. The situation could not have been more questionable. But then warfare was apt to be like that.

Dismounted, they waited.

For how long should they wait, if nothing dire appeared? After all, with the main English army driving north, all the Merse and Lothian manpower would be required elsewhere if no assault here developed.

John had ample time to wonder about it all. What was happening at Edinburgh? Was a suitably great Scots army now assembled, as would certainly be needed? How far

211

north had the English got by now? Was George being successful in his efforts – and would he be allowed to keep his men hereabouts to repel Percy or if necessary waste the lands? Might he not be summoned to join the main array at Edinburgh? And was Brodie gathering a sufficiency of Moraymen to bring south? All this while *he* was skied up on a ridge doing nothing but watching!

By the fall of dusk no enemy had appeared. It was unlikely that any large force would attempt to advance in darkness. So the watchers would take it in turn to sleep, two always awake. Fortunately the late July night was warm for sleeping outdoors.

Daylight still showed no sign of invaders. John sent a messenger to inform his brother of the fact. Then, in early afternoon, his messenger came back, and with tidings that changed all. The Scots assembly at Edinburgh had reached about thirty thousand; but the word was that King Richard's great host was even larger than hitherto estimated, reported now to be perhaps two hundred thousand strong, this probably including Percy's force. Such certainly could not be challenged by King Robert's muster, and the decision had been taken to retire northwards to the Stirling area where, as Wallace and Bruce had proved, a smaller array could hold up a much larger one at the narrow crossing of Forth, the wide estuary to one side and the great marshy Flanders Moss on the other, as was done at the Stirling Bridge and Bannockburn battles. So all possible contingents were ordered to proceed there forthwith, including that of Dunbar and March. So John was to come and join them without delay. John of Gaunt and his nephew were said to be more than halfway up Lauderdale, nearing the Lothian border, and had burned the abbeys of Jedburgh, Kelso, Dryburgh and Melrose, as well as countless other communities and fortalices.

Scotland had not been so endangered since Edward the First's onslaughts. And Edinburgh, the capital, was to be abandoned to their ancient foe.

John rode north in haste.

At Dunbar he found George impatiently waiting, concerned at having to leave his lands unprotected. He would send Christian for safety over to a small Lammermuir house, deep in the hills, with the children. He was also worried over the question as to whether he and his people could get past Edinburgh before the English arrived there, as they must do to reach Stirling. He had managed to raise four thousand men, no less, so although the leadership could go by ship up Forth, the force could not, by any means – and it was the force that was needed. Seton had arrived from his waste-laying task in lower Lauderdale, but the Kerrs and Homes were gone to try to protect their own lands.

A start was made for Edinburgh, amidst considerable anxiety, Seton calling in at his fine house on the way for a brief word and advice for his family, again as to safety.

Nearing the capital they could see a distant haze of smoke to the south where the Pentland and Morthwaite Hills joined, near the pass into Lauderdale, a score of miles away. It looked as though they were in time to win past Edinburgh.

They were, and as they skirted the city they passed hundreds of fleeing citizens making for any hiding-place they could find, not a few hurrying down to Leith to seek for vessels and fishing-boats to carry them over to Fife.

The Dunbar contingent got as far as the Seton's western Lothian castle of Niddry that night, safe from enemy attention meantime. They ought to reach Stirling by noon next day.

Were the English in Edinburgh by now? And would its fortress-castle remain secure? On its great rock-top it would be a hard place to take, numbers of men no advantage. Only prolonged siege, it was judged, would force it to yield. And its keepers would have had time to stock up with supplies.

At Stirling, with its so similar lofty citadel, they found King Robert and his lords waiting, their army encamped down around Cambuskenneth Abbey, where the English had surrendered after Bannockburn. The anxious Robert was glad to see the Cospatrick brothers and Dalkeith, and wondered whether they had any news of Earl Douglas and de Vienne? They had not. John found Brodie there with five hundred Moraymen.

It seemed that plans were made for a defensive campaign here, following the same tactics Wallace had so successfully used at Stirling Bridge almost ninety years before, massing on the north side of the only practical crossing of Forth for any host, the narrow bridge itself and equally constricted causeway beyond constraining any attackers to little more than three abreast. Consider two hundred thousand trying to win across that, with defenders awaiting them in solid array. John of Gaunt at least would know of this all but insuperable hurdle. Would he consider it worth risking the attempt?

So it was waiting again, but this time feeling more secure, and the leadership at least in comfortable quarters, in the fortress, in the town or in the abbey. They had patrols out, of course, almost back to the outskirts of Edinburgh, thirty-five miles, to warn as to the situation. These sent reports that the city was occupied, and a fair amount of smoke arose therefrom, but the citadel itself was thought to be holding out. No word of any movement northwards was sent, save for small enemy patrols scouting around.

It was a full week into August before firm tidings were received. The English were retiring southwards, presumably seeing no point in lingering in ravaged Edinburgh, and with a desolated countryside to pass through on the way to their border. Had they left behind any garrisoning force? it was wondered. Scouts were ordered to try to discover this before any move from Stirling was made.

Another three days were spent waiting. Then messengers arrived to declare, no: the English had left havoc and ruin and death behind them, but no occupying forces. So a move could be made back to the ravaged capital. There was no reason for all the levies of the northern lords going to

214

the capital; they could remain at Stirling until the king and his advisers discovered whether the invaders had continued on to cross into England. Edinburgh would be in no state to welcome large numbers of troops. If the foe was indeed all gone from the land, these could return home, but be prepared for any urgent recall.

John would have liked to return north with his men from Moray, but felt some sort of duty to accompany the monarch, his father-in-law, to the capital, and thereafter, hopefully, George to Dunbar.

Edinburgh, when they arrived, was a sad sight indeed. The fires had died out by this time but devastation was everywhere – save up at the castle. Most of the major buildings had been sacked, and practically all the churches including the greatest one, St Giles. But, strangely, Holyrood Abbey had been spared, this by the special orders of John of Gaunt himself, who had those years before taken refuge therein and been well treated, this the abbot told them. He added that the excuse for sacking all the churches was that, in the present Great Schism of Holy Church, England was supporting the alternative Pope from Scotland and France, and so their Scots clergy were as good as damned.

The city's fled inhabitants were returning; but Edinburgh was no place for an army to remain in meantime. So the king returned to Stirling with his sons and close associates; and most lords and their contingents were for home, but ready for recall, these including George and John. The word was that Earl Douglas and the Frenchmen were still in Galloway, after ravaging Cumberland and making a gesture at taking Carlisle, the fortress of which was too strong for them. So throughout most of this period of stress and strife they had been sitting comfortably in that all but detached province of the south-west, with Archibald the Grim, an extraordinary situation for these so warrior-like knights-errant, which aroused not a little anger and accusation from most Scots.

Back at Dunbar, they found all in order, and George's

family back from the Lammermuirs, with no sign of invaders. So obviously Percy had been with the main English army, all thankful indeed. And John found a vessel to take him back to Inverness, at last.

21

It was good to get back to Darnaway, to Marjory and the little family, after so long and less than enjoyable absence. The longer he lived, the more John recognised that he was a home-loving and family man, with no real ambition to be anything else, save perhaps an able and effective keeper of lands and dependants. The fact that he seemed to be considered good at acting the envoy and ambassador by his liege-lords and others in authority was of no particular satisfaction to him.

He and Marjory had much to relate to each other, he interested and pleased to hear that she had found time, and inclination, despite having the youngsters and a large establishment to look after, to act her husband's deputy in the matter of the timber and forestry concerns, the extraction and even export. In her domestic circumstances, of course, she could not be away from home for long, and so had to restrain herself and restrict her visits to comparatively near-at-hand areas of their great lands. She had quite enjoyed this activity, admittedly being greatly assisted by Duncan Murray, his Catherine good with the children.

All had not been trouble-free in Moray however during its lord's absence. The late elderly William, Earl of Ross, had been no comfortable neighbour; but his succession by a daughter, after his son's premature death, she a widow marrying a Leslie of Rothes, south of Elgin, producing a rather feeble son, Alexander, who became in her right Earl of Ross. This young man had proved to be no aggressive character, like his grandfather, but productive of troubles nevertheless, this by lack of interest and activity. And as could so often happen with a weak lord, advantage was taken by underlings. He was much more concerned with Rothes, where he had been reared, than with his Ross earldom, seldom visiting Dingwall and Cromarty, and utterly ignoring the vast western Highland parts of his inherited territory. There the clans, ever disposed to feuding anyway, the Macleods, Mackinnons, Macleans, Macdonalds, Camerons and the rest, feeling themselves free to raid and grasp at will. Nor were they interested in observing boundaries such as those of earldoms, and with Ross and Moray sharing lengthy borders, inevitably trouble spilled over into the latter, the Mackintoshes, and to a lesser extent the Macphersons and Grants, becoming involved. John's friend, the Mackintosh chief, was asking for help.

The last thing that John wanted was to have to get himself involved in more military-style ventures there in his own territory; but he could not ignore the Mackintosh's appeal. So, since Brodie and his three hundred were still more or less on stand-by alert, he summoned a proportion of them to ride southwards with him on what he hoped would amount to no more than a sort of showing-the-flag mission. Marjory was apologetic about landing this on him. She had been wondering what to do about it.

Two days after returning, then, he led his party up Findhorn for some twenty-five miles to reach Moy, the Mackintosh chief's seat on its island in the loch. There they learned that there was constant raiding from across the Great Glen, by Mackays and Mackenzies in especial, and these clans had more or less taken over upper Strathnairn. The Nairn, the River of Alders, was long, rising amidst the mountains near the head of Loch Ness, and running for about forty miles to reach salt water at the town of that name, none so far from Darnaway. Its upper reaches were all in Mackintosh country, including the lands of Farr and Dores, Duntelchaig, Dunmaglass and Conaglen, and much of this wide area was being ravaged, and even occupied, by these Ross clans.

John was concerned about this, of course, but especially as the Strathnairn forest was one of his farthest-away sources of timber, only recently developed, and useful in that the cut wood could be floated down those forty miles of river to ships at Nairn port. He agreed to seek to demonstrate his authority in some suitable fashion, but hoped that there would be no call for armed conflict.

Passing the night at Moy with the Mackintosh, they headed, in the morning, across the quite high hills due westwards, empty country of deer-haunted heather slopes and ridges, rushing streams, lochans and peat-bogs, this for some six or seven miles, necessarily round-about, until they saw lower ground ahead, perhaps a couple of miles of this, but with hills again beyond. This was Strathnairn, the present stretch of it heavily forested. Passing the scattered black houses of Farr, where stacked timber was in evidence, they moved on. It was not so much hereabouts, Mackintosh said, that the raiders and troublemakers were invading, but still further west beyond more rocky hills. And there, flanking the side of great Loch Ness, was something of a plain, perhaps fifteen miles long by four wide, dotted with quite large lochs, fair country for cattle and sheep, some tillage and hay ground, heavily wooded again along the shores of Ness. This was where the Ross clansmen were taking over, dispossessing the local Mackintoshes, MacGillivrays and Shaws, especially around the quite large Loch Duntelchaig and the smaller Ruthven and Ashie.

Moving down, and crossing the Nairn through fine woodland alive with roe-deer, blue hares and capercailzie, near Loch Farr, seeing people here, and these friendly, they had to cover that narrow, second belt of hills, this through quite steep passes, before they reached the troubled area, and found themselves looking across a wide vista now, first of levellish ground with scattered lochs of various sizes, then the great Ness itself with endless blue mountains behind.

They rode down to the largest of the plain's lochs,

Duntelchaig, and there were not long in seeing signs of trouble, burned and broken-down cot-houses and sheds, abandoned sheep-stells and the like, all so reminiscent, for John, but on nothing like the scale of which he had recently been deploring in the south. But all was not abandoned, for at the clachan of Dunlichity at the head of the loch blue peat-smoke was to be seen rising from the chimney-holes in the thatched roofing of cot-houses, and men were visible, and some small black cattle. Mackintosh, pointing, nodded and said that he had heard that Dunlichity had been taken over.

The coming of over one hundred horsemen, of course, had not gone unobserved, and riding thither they saw men hurrying away from the houses and hutments, the arrival of mounted men seen as unwelcome and, in these numbers, dangerous.

John sent men cantering after some of the tartan-clad would-be escapers. Three or four were caught and brought back, far from gently, to face authority.

There, interrogated sternly, these admitted that they were Mackays from the north, from Abriachan and Clunes, but offered no admission of guilt nor regrets. John, announcing his identity, declared that this raiding and taking over of other folk's land was to stop, and forthwith, or he would have to take retaliatory action against their Ross lands, which would much displease their earl. He could hang them, here and now, but would not on this occasion; but they were to tell their fellows that he would not hesitate so to do hereafter, unless they were all gone from these Moray lands promptly. And to emphasise his point, he had these offenders bound hand and foot with cords and tied securely to the doorposts of three of the black-houses, as an indication to their fellow-clansmen, when they returned in due course, that the Earl of Moray was supporting the chief of Clan Chattan, the Mackintosh, and would be back to see that his orders were obeyed.

Then, leaving them thus, they rode on southwards down the lochside.

In a mile or so they approached another clachan of cottages, which Mackintosh called Letterchullin, and here again there was a hurried departure by the present occupants. Riders were sent after them again, but here nearby woodland hid the fleeing men before the horsemen were able to reach them, and they could hide amongst trees and bushes, so that their pursuers were able to bring back only one captive. But while the others watched this, a woman appeared from one of the houses and, brought to John, she announced that she was the wife of a Mackintosh, her husband slain and herself raped and maltreated. Others of her neighbours had got away, fleeing into the hills.

Again they bound and tied the captured man, a Mackenzie this time, giving him the same warnings and instructions. They took the woman away with them behind one of the riders, not quite sure what to do with her.

Proceeding, near the foot of the loch, they came to one more group of black-houses, this at the waterside. But here they were unable to capture any of the invaders, for these saw that their best way to escape the horsemen was to pile into small fishing-boats drawn up on the shore, and row out into mid-loch. They might have been warned by other escapers.

This, of possible warnings being circulated, decided John that more of their present action might well not be effective, or perhaps necessary. The word would get around the district and the incomers, almost certainly, and it was to be hoped that this would have them perceive that their situation was untenable and that they had best return to their own places across Loch Ness. Meantime he and the mounted force could return home also.

The Mackintosh accepted this, and so it was back northwards for them. They dropped off the unfortunate widowed woman at Farr, where she would be safe and looked after. Mackintosh left orders that he was to be kept informed as to the situation in these parts.

John hoped that his bloodless sally would be a sufficient flourish to see an end to this trouble.

* * *

Whether or not it was his action that put matters to rights he could not be very certain, for shortly thereafter a new development altered all – and this by none other than Donald of the Isles. The tidings reached Darnaway that he was presently in the Great Glen area, visiting Ross clans, with a sizeable company of his Islesmen. John was wondering at this when, with only two or three companions, Donald himself arrived at the castle, to the surprise of all.

He came in goodwill, to announce a major move on his part. He, like his forebears, had more or less controlled the western side of highland Ross, and the clans thereof, for generations. Since the death of William of Ross, conditions there and elsewhere in the earldom had become chaotic, as John knew so well. Now he, Donald, had decided to lay claim to the earldom of Ross himself, for the future, and for the peace and security of Wester Ross, this in the right of his wife, Phemia. Her mother, the queen, much married, had been a daughter of the earlier Earl of Ross, the late William being her brother. Now *his* grandson, this Alexander, so feeble, had a daughter as only child, and she was announcing that she was going "to take the veil" and become a nun. So she could not succeed, if she did this, as Countess of Ross. Phemie's mother, then, could claim the earldom, and in consequence thereafter Phemie herself, an involved but undeniable situation. He now had a son and daughter by Phemie, so their boy, another Alexander, would one day be Earl of Ross as well as Lord of the Isles. He himself, Donald, would only claim the style of earl for the future, to ensure that his son gained it. But meantime he could use the claim to bring peace and security to Ross, Easter as well as Wester. He had come to an agreement with the western clans, Macleods, Macleans, Mackinnons, Mackenzies and the rest, over this, so the future wellbeing and concord in the earldom could be firmly established. How thought the Earl of Moray over this?

John was well pleased with this prospect and said so. He would use any influence he had with his father-in-law the king to support Donald's claim. It could bring peace and discipline to a vast area of northern Scotland, and in so doing much advantage Moray.

Donald wanted to add the support of the Mackintosh and Clan Chattan in this, for parts of that widespread federation extended into Ross, Macphails, Cattanachs, MacQueens, MacPhies and the rest. John promised to speak with the chief on this.

Marjory, who liked Donald of the Isles, pressed him to stay for a day or two.

John was always thankful when word from the south was scanty, or unimportant as far as he was concerned. The only such brought by the wandering friars was that the French paladins had gone back to their own country but, strangely, not de Vienne, the admiral, who was remaining meantime, not exactly as a hostage but to await satisfactory assurances from King Charles that the Auld Alliance was still holding fast and in force. For apparently there were rumours that an agreement had been reached with the Plantagenets, or some of that quarrelsome lot, over the disputed French duchies. And this new association had been given some credence by the fact that a French fleet, which de Vienne had arranged to come and support his and his company's efforts for Scotland against England, had not done so, to the High Admiral's wrath. So now he, and only two or three others, remained in Scotland, waiting for just what was uncertain.

John was thankful to see all this as no great concern of his.

What did interest him more was word that Hotspur Percy had fallen out with his friend the Earl of Nottingham and the Nevilles, and actually come to blows over conflicting influence in south Northumberland, Durham and northern Yorkshire. This at least ought to prevent Percy incursions into the Merse, and the borderline generally, for the present, and any military involvement for John on his brother's behalf, this to Marjory's thankfulness. She was expecting another child fairly soon, and did not want an absent or endangered husband. This would be early in the year 1386. Yuletide ought to be trouble-free.

22

John did not find himself a proud father again, as it transpired, for after a very difficult labour Marjory produced a stillborn infant, to much concern and grief. Her husband declared that this must be the end of family-producing for them; he was not going to go on hazarding his beloved. Three children was sufficient. His wife agreed.

Later in the spring, with Marjory happily quite recovered, they learned that the Earl James of Douglas, with Archibald the Grim and one of the king's sons whom he had created Earl of Fife, had made a quite major raid into Cumberland, this to give warning to the aggressive Percy that, after gaining victory over the Nevilles, and seeking to extend his sway westwards into that county, seemingly seeing himself as suitable master over all the north of England, he should watch his step. Whether this activity on the part of the Scots would in fact inhibit Hotspur remained to be seen; but at least John had not had to become involved.

However, perhaps that man was congratulating himself too soon, for not long thereafter Hotspur of Northumberland, possibly in retaliation, made a major incursion over the border, not in the west but into the Merse, laying waste much of the land north of Berwick, in the Aytoun and Eyemouth area, to George's anger, for Eyemouth was second only to Dunbar itself as port for the export of Lammermuir wool, hides, salted mutton and the rest. For his part, John feared the worst.

When the call came, as he knew it must, it was for action on a larger scale than he had anticipated. It seemed that

Douglas, Fife and sundry of his royal brothers had convinced the king that now was the time and opportunity to take overdue vengeance for the invasion of King Richard and John of Gaunt a year before, which had reached as far north as Edinburgh. Percy's depredations and his move into Cumberland made an excuse. It was known that the usually uncomplaining Earl of Westmoreland had protested about this to his monarch, and no doubt other Cumberland magnates had done likewise; so a great rally against Hotspur would not greatly offend London, might even be welcomed. There had been a further great upheaval in England. What was being known as the Merciless Parliament had made itself felt, and a powerful group calling itself the Lords Appellant was now running the land in the name of Richard, some of its members Planagenets. These might well be glad to have the Percy dealt with.

Now was the time, then, to try to get rid of Hotspur once and for all, this without seeming to break the odd truce between the two realms. A large army to strike over the border, the largest seen for many a day. This could not be, as it were, official, because of that nominal truce. But King Robert had nodded over it. There was to be a muster in the Middle March, not in the East, for some reason. John was expected to contribute as many Moraymen as he could raise, this by the beginning of August when, after a good summer, the harvest should be safely in.

Despite his lack of enthusiasm, John told Marjory that if, in fact, they could indeed dispose of the Percy for good, for very good, then they all might well be spared further cross-border warfare for some considerable time, she doubtful.

So it was word to all the Moray lords, lairds and chieftains. Muster at Darnaway on the Day of Transfiguration, 6th August. And in fullest numbers.

On that day, John was far from disappointed at the turnout. It had to be limited to mounted men, with the long journey to the rallying-place in the Borderland, this preventing the Highland clans from producing a great many, for these did not go in for horseback warfare. But some there were, on their short-legged but sturdy garrons, the Mackintosh producing fully one hundred, some from over in Ross. Brodies, Ogstouns, Cawdors, Comyns, Murrays, Duffs and Fordyces all did well, so that John had seventeen hundred to lead southwards, a worthy contribution. His children were greatly excited about all these gathering at Darnaway, and Marjory put on a brave face as they rode off.

It took them five days to reach Edinburgh, by Strathspey, Drumochter, Atholl, Strathtay, Perth and Stirling, good going for so large a company, the weather helpful; and another long day to get to Southdean, between Jedburgh and the borderline at Carter Bar, the assembly-point, over the last miles of which they were riding in company with other contingents from near and far.

They found Southdean, pronounced Sudden, to be a great hollow amongst the Cheviot Hills; and huge as it was, overflowing with men and horses, knightly pavilions erected, lordly banners flapping everywhere. Brother George was already there, with no fewer than five thousand men, Setons, Hepburns, Lindsays from Lothian, and Homes, Kerrs, Swintons and Turnbulls from the Merse. Dalkeith had fully one thousand; and his kinsman, the Earl James, with Archibald the Grim, Lord of Galloway, the greatest host of all, thought to number at least ten thousand. Oddly enough, the other earls present, royal ones, had produced the fewest men, although Fife and Menteith had raised some fifteen hundred – but then, these were newly-made earls, and not yet settled into wide lands.

The leaders were in deep debate over strategy. In theory, Robert of Fife and Menteith, the king's second son – the other Robert, really John, of Carrick, was not present – was in overall command; but in fact the Douglas, a seasoned warrior, was the real leader, the entire campaign having been of his devising. His proposal was that this vast host, totalling at least fifty thousand, should split into two, one to strike westwards into Cumberland, the other due south down Redesdale to the Kielder and Rothbury area. It was not known just where Hotspur was at this juncture, whether in his home country around Alnwick and Newcastle, or assailing Cumberland and Westmoreland. But almost certainly he would have learned of so great a concourse as this being assembled across the border, and would be anticipating invasion. So Douglas thought not to attack his eastern base at first, but to make for somewhere in the middle of the land, where he could turn east or west as required; and if east, be able to link up with the Cumberland force without too much difficulty.

This seemed good tactics to John but not to all there, especially some of the princes, who thought that this huge army should not be divided thus, but remain a whole, and unbeatable. But Douglas told them that if Percy saw it as such, unbeatable, he would almost certainly flee south. Their objective was to trap, catch and take him; so their two forces were better than just one, and the division be unexpected. The hidden meeting-place here at Southdean, in these jumbled green braes, would not get known to their enemy as would have done an assembly at Jedburgh, for instance. Just where it was would be uncertain. So, depending where Percy might be at this present, two separate advances, and secret ones at first, could be bait to trap him, east or west or in the middle.

This was eventually accepted, somewhat doubtfully, and the division of forces agreed upon. Actually the greater number would go westwards, under Archibald the Grim and the princes, for these had not only the greater area to cover but could well see the most fighting, the West March English being well organised and probably prepared for *Percy's* attacks, and so able to switch to fighting the Scots. Also Douglas wanted the faster, harder-riding force, and chose his own people, the Border mosstroopers, and much of George's Mersemen. John found himself attached to this company, with Keith the Marischal and only about one-half of his Moray contingent, Douglas knowing exactly whom and what he wanted. John appointed Brodie in charge of these going with the western array.

No camp-fires were permitted that night, so as not to draw possible attention to this hidden assembly-point.

In the morning, early, the two forces separated and went their different ways, arranging to keep in touch by means of mosstrooping Borderers who knew the country intimately.

Douglas's force headed due eastwards at first, making for Carter Bar, on the actual borderline, where the meetings of the Scots and English March Wardens traditionally took place, a high summit area with extensive views both northwards and southwards; and from there turned right-handed, to ride down Redesdale into England, sending Home of Hutton well ahead with his party of scouts, to whom this area was known like the palms of their hands.

John, riding between his brother and brother-in-law Dalkeith, knew a certain exhilaration, however unwarlike he might be, at this proceeding into England in search of Hotspur Percy. Douglas undoubtedly knew what he was doing, even though George was a little doubtful as to the strategy. He would have preferred a larger force than this. Why could not the entire army have come thus, midway between east and west, and then turn right and left when they discovered where the Percy was, Dalkeith tending to agree with this. But John had faith in Earl James Douglas's judgment, as had Keith the Marischal.

Passing the long loch of Catleugh in the Rede Water's pass-like valley, after some fifteen miles, they came to Otterburn, where the Cheviots began to draw apart, this under Fawdon Hill, with its peel-tower. This last the force surrounded, and Douglas demanded its surrender, with the shouted promise that its occupiers would be spared hurt if they did so and agreed not to send warnings of the Scots advance thereafter. Faced by thousands, the squire thereof, a Ridley, was not long in agreeing to these terms, a wise man, and Fawdon and Otterburn passed into Scots hands without bloodshed. A small garrison was left there to see that the terms were carried out, but not before Ridley was persuaded to tell them that the Earl of Northumberland was presently at Berwick-upon-Tweed, presumably expecting retaliation for his recent Merse raid on Aytoun and Eyemouth. So he would have a sizeable force with him there.

This news, of course, was vitally important, if true. The western army must be informed. But not suggested, Douglas judged, that it should promptly turn east and rejoin them. From previous experience they knew how hard a nut Berwick Castle was to crack, and with a large array also holding the town, Berwick itself, that would not be good tactics to assail. Best for their own force in the west to continue on into Cumberland and Westmoreland, but kept informed, ready to turn east. Meanwhile he, Douglas, would head directly on southwards, to seem to threaten Alnwick, Newcastle and possibly even Durham. Hotspur would undoubtedly get to hear of these moves before long, and almost certainly leave Berwick to meet this dual challenge in some fashion. Get him away from there, that was the priority.

So it was onwards, east now to Rothbury, a fair-sized community on the River Coquet, its inhabitants fleeing before them, and some of the township put to the flames. They were none so far west of Alnwick here, and almost certainly the smoke-clouds would warn the Percy seat's folk there of danger, and hopefully draw its lord southwards from Berwick.

They spent the night at Rothbury, where they found ample provision, and in the morning moved on southwards for the Tyne, Douglas sending mosstroopers to keep Archibald the Grim in the picture. They crossed Hadrian's Roman Wall after fording the North Tyne at Chollerford, then burning Sandhoe, Douglas determined that the word of it should get back to Berwick. Then on to the main Tyne, in its long dale, at Corbridge, where they halted for the night again. It had been a very bloodless advance, despite all the burning, no organised resistance encountered.

They were debating whether to assail the larger town of Hexham, a few miles to the west, next morning, before turning east for Newcastle itself, when Pate Home's busy scouts sent word that a large force was on its way south from Berwick by the coastal route. Almost certainly this would be Percy, coming to save his threatened heartland. Would he stop at Alnwick or proceed on to his great walled city of Newcastle?

The Scots waited at Corbridge for information as to this.

By midday they had the answer. Hotspur was heading for Newcastle.

So now Douglas had to make the great decision. Send word westward to have the larger force come hastening to join them here, to assail Newcastle in strength? Or to proceed thither themselves? The former would give time for the Percy to summon reinforcements from the south, to strengthen position. Better probably an immediate challenge. Newcastle, within its walls, would probably consider itself safe to withstand siege from no very large force, while Hotspur waited for assistance. According to Home's scouts he had many men with him, but probably not all his Berwick host, presumably leaving some portion of it to hold that border stronghold. Or possibly to constitute a threat behind the Scots? Weighing it all up, Douglas decided that it was Newcastle for them, with scouts vigilant behind them.

John recognised that it could be actual warfare ahead of them very soon now.

They had almost a score of miles to ride down Tyne to their goal. Or was it their fate? With a force of almost ten thousand it was all too easy to feel secure, all but dominant. But facing another large force, and a fortified city, this could be an illusion indeed. The thought of Newcastle's walls and gates was not to be taken lightly. And at this Corbridge, they had learned that the Lord Ralph Percy, Hotspur's brother, was none so far away to the south-west, in the Neville country, with the Prince-Bishop of Durham. If he was summoned . . .?

They rode by Prudhoe and Blaydon to near Newcastle. Douglas himself, who knew the city and its surroundings, went ahead with scouts to prospect, while the main force held back, this only about three miles from the town. When he came back, it was to declare that he had been able to see a possible course of action. To the north-west of the city was some higher ground covered with scrub trees and bushes. Below this was what was called the Leazes and the Town Moor, where the citizens' cattle grazed. Their array ought to be able to wait there, hidden amongst the cover. There was a small stream running down from this to the Tyne, in a quite deep little winding valley, scarcely a ravine but sufficiently enclosed to hide a party which could ride down to near the northern walling of the city. There were a number of gates in this. The principal North Gate would be strongly defended, but the lesser ones, for the folk to reach their common lands, would not be so well guarded. The small party moving down this valley could reach one of these, hopefully unseen until almost upon it. They could assail the gate and probably gain entrance. Then, need for secrecy over, another larger group could go to round up some of the cattle and drive them down and into that gateway, this to cause confusion within, some of the beasts to be hamstrung to litter the streets, while the first attacking party pushed round inside the walls to take the strong main gate by surprise, from within, the full Scots force meantime descending in strength, and preoccupying the defenders with this open approach. In this way the attackers ought to gain access to the city. And however many of Percy's men were therein, in the narrow crowded streets it would be difficult for them to act in any organised and coherent way. Maximum confusion ought to result, and, although this was bound to apply to some extent to the Scots themselves, *they* would be prepared for it and ought to remain in fair command of the situation.

His hearers digested all this as best they could, with-holding their questions.

Douglas himself would lead the party down the little valley to storm the lesser gate; the Marischal would take a group to round up and drive the cattle; and George, John and Dalkeith would command the main force, to advance on the strong North Gate when they saw the cattle getting into the city.

It was onwards, then, for Newcastle, few there as see-mingly confident as the Earl of Douglas.

Soon they saw the higher ground ahead of them, quite extensive and with sufficient cover to keep their force hidden from the city. To reach it they had to cross the little valley described.

From their viewpoint, the leaders could see down across the sloping Leazes and Town Moor, with its scattered cattle, to the great sprawling walled city with its towering castle, the tall spires of St Nicholas and other churches, some perception of all the streets and market-places and wynds, all overhung with the thin smoke of countless household fires, and, of course, those gates and gatehouses in the high parapeted walling. It all made a challenging sight.

Douglas, with his final instructions, left them, with a salute, to lead his party of some three hundred into and down the little valley, the Marischal preparing his people to be ready to marshal cattle instead of fighting-men, John with his brother and Dalkeith doing the marshalling of men, and watching the situation below, at the city walls, keenly.

It seemed some time before there was anything to see. Then, suddenly, the Douglas group emerged from hiding and spurred urgently for the minor gateway, which even at this distance could be seen to be open, indeed with a horse-drawn sled for hay being led out of it. Whether any attempt was made to shut and bar it before the horsemen reached it was not obvious; but at any rate, if so it was unsuccessful, for Douglas and his mosstroopers poured in through the narrow gap, strung out now inevitably, and appeared to be winning within.

Promptly Keith and his company rode forward and out of their woodland, down over the open slopes facing the city, to round up a sufficiency of the cattle which dotted the grassland. There were many grazing there, but only a score or so were required. It did not take more than a few minutes to herd such, and to drive them, in panic, down towards the walling; by which time the last of the Douglas riders had disappeared through that narrow gateway and would be heading, within, for the large and defended gatehouse arch which even from this distance could be seen to be shut.

Herding those plunging bullocks, cows and calves towards and into the restricted open entrance-way was not easy, obviously, and waiting impatiently, John and the others fretted. But at last they saw signs of the chaos at the postern, blocking the gap by hamstrung and fallen beasts. These would prove as difficult an impediment for the main Scots force to get past to enter the city as they had been to herd there – but at least they would prevent the gates being shut and barred.

George blew a long loud blast on his horn, as signal, and the waiting host kicked mounts into action at last, and surged forward, out of cover, to thunder openly down towards the city, cheering.

They did not hurtle in one mass, however, but split into three, George in the centre with the larger group, Dalkeith to the left with another, seeking other possible entrances, and John to the right, making for that cattle-blocked gateway, his task to get in over the slain beasts and inside to seek to aid Douglas, while his brother rode directly to challenge the main closed North Gate, hoping that Dalkeith was finding other access.

John well recognised that his task of getting a large number of horsemen in through that choked and anyway restricted entrance would be anything but easy, the horses themselves bound to be reluctant to clamber over fallen bodies, some still kicking and jerking. Leading the way, when he got close, he jumped off his mount, gripping the reins, and urged his beast forward, he seeking to pick his way over and amongst the heaps of dead and wounded animals as best he could. Some behind him did the same, others sought to drive their steeds over it all without dismounting. It was complete confusion, disarray and din, as warfare so often is. A few men, still in the saddle, got over and past John, but most were held up by those struggling in front.

But at length he was through the press and into the street beyond. He had to wait for most of his men to make it over the obstructions to join him. Then he turned them to ride northwards, through the empty streets, making for that main gate.

At least they had no difficulty in finding this, and in joining Douglas, who was demanding surrender from its guards, and appearing to be getting heeded by the men in the gatehouse. Small wonder, with brother George's host now doing the same on the other side of the walling. Douglas' men were indeed unbarring the great doors, having disposed of the couple of guards there. John and his group were not needed, as the gatehouse people yielded.

The gates were thrown open, and George led the way inside.

It seemed very strange, to John at least, that all this had been allowed to happen without any evidence of defenders in the city itself, Percy or others. He said so to Douglas, who informed that there was, in fact, a second defensive walling further in, this an earlier barrier closer around the ancient part of the city and its castle. Douglas guessed that this was where they would meet with the opposition. Hotspur might well be waiting for his brother to arrive from the south with reinforcements.

It was no simple matter for their host to proceed in any sort of order through the narrow, devious network of streets and wynds, where the men could ride only a very few abreast. Leaving others to attempt this, the earls pushed ahead.

Soon they came to the second line of walling, and they could see that this was very fully manned, indeed they were met by a shower of arrows from bowmen up on the parapet-walk thereon. Now they were faced with reality, inside Newcastle town as they were.

Douglas was prepared for this. He produced a white flag, and raising this high, flanked by George, John and Dalkeith, rode forward towards a gatehouse, hoping that those archers would respect the flag of truce. Fortunately they did, and halting not far off, Douglas raised a hand.

"I am Douglas, the earl!" he called. "With me are the Earls of Dunbar and Moray and my lord of Dalkeith. We seek Hotspur Percy, Earl of Northumberland."

"What seek you with him, Douglas?" came back to them. "You, with a host of men."

"Speech! Give him my greetings, and tell him that we have come to his town to put matters to rights between us."

"Rights! Who are you to speak of rights, Scotchman, you burning and slaying in this our land."

"As has done the Percy in ours. So the rights are to be settled! Tell him so, fellow."

"I who speak am no fellow, Douglas. I am Ralph Percy, brother to Hotspur."

"Ha! Then you have arrived! He has been awaiting you, I think, my lord Ralph. Wisely, perhaps! Fetch him, will you, if you please."

"No need," came another voice. "I, Northumberland, am here, Douglas. But I have nothing to say to you. Save to leave my city and land, and at the soonest."

"So-o-o! That is Hotspur Percy! Hiding behind a wall of stones! I have come far to speak with you. And do not intend to go without satisfaction."

"But you will. I will see to that. Take your white flag and be gone."

"You fear to give me satisfaction, Percy?"

"Why should I fear in my own town? *You* have the reason to fear."

Douglas looked at his companions. "He plays for time, I judge," he said, in a different voice. "His brother is here, yet there has been no attack, no attack on us. So – Durham? The Prince-Bishop, who was said to be coming to join him and his Ralph. *He* may be near, then."

"What can we do then?" George demanded. "We do not want to be caught in this trap of a town between two hosts, spread as we are. I say that we should retire. Out through the walls again. Muster once more on the high ground yonder. And await any joint attack there."

"I came here for Hotspur Percy, who slew my half-brother shamefully. We may have to do as you say. But first, I will challenge this proud Englishman." He raised voice.

"Percy, you have a name for prowess. Knightly prowess. Yet you slew my Douglas kinsman in unknightly fashion. *I* am another knight. Let us settle this matter as knights should. In combat."

There was no reply to that.

Again Douglas shouted. "Combat, here and now. With swords and lances. Or battle-axes or maces. Mounted or afoot. Between your folk and mine. How say you?"

"I say that this is folly. Why should I risk my men's blood to appease your foolish and vain pride, Douglas?"

"So? You fear for them? Then . . . yourself, Percy! You have the name of being a fighter. Just the two of us, then. Myself and you. Horsed or on foot. Yours the choice. I, Douglas, challenge you. A tourney. You call yourself Hotspur. Prove it!"

There was silence from the wall-top for a little. That challenge did put the Percy in a difficult position, there before all, his people and the Scots. Something of a renowned paladin, to refuse single combat could be much damaging to his reputation. And tourneys were a recognised knightly pastime. At length came the reply.

"Very well, Douglas. Since you seek it. You shall learn

your lesson! You may come in here, to this market-place within these walls. But only you and a few of your people. I will not have your armed host gaining entry by such ruses. If more than a small number seek to come, my bowmen will halt them, white flag or none."

"As you will. But how do we know that you will not use this, your own ruse, to hold me and my friends? Hold captive?"

"No. You have my word on it. Is that not good enough for you?"

Douglas nodded. He turned to Keith, and told him to remain with the host, which had now come up behind them, and was filling the streets around, he to retain the white flag. And to be ready to advance or retire as occasion demanded. Then, signing to John, George and Dalkeith, he moved over to that gateway. It was opened for them.

Within, they found Hotspur awaiting them, a tall, handsome man in his thirties, arrogant-seeming but keen-eyed, his brother standing beside him a little younger but equally proud of bearing. They all viewed each other assessingly.

"Come you," Hotspur ordered, and turning, strode back towards the towering castle and the open space before it. Dismounting, the Scots followed him.

"Horsed or on foot?" Douglas called after him.

"Mounted, to be sure," was thrown back at them.

What transpired thereafter took some time, inevitably. The Percy had to have a horse brought out for him, and a lance and certain armour other than what he was already wearing. Douglas waited, in that market-place, with what patience he could muster, watched but by no means joined by the English magnates. All around the square the citizenry could be seen, silent.

At length Hotspur accepted the horse, and mounting without a word to Douglas, took the long lance. He already had a sword at his side. Still scarcely acknowledging Douglas's presence, he rode to the far western side of the market-place.

Douglas frowned, not at the arrogance but at the direction taken. It was now late afternoon and the sun was beginning to sink towards the west, which meant, of course, that the Percy had chosen to take his stance with the sun's glare behind him, and therefore in his opponent's face, a dazzlement and grave disadvantage. So much for chivalry. He could have faced north or south, after all, equalising the situation.

Some two hundred yards apart, the contestants mounted. George and Ralph Percy paced out into the centre of the market-place, bowed stiffly to each other, agreed to second lances being available should one break, and that either side should bear off the champion unopposed if the other should fall. Then a long blast on the horn was sounded.

Back at their bases the duellists shut down the visors of their helmets, couched their lances, and dug in their spurs. Forward their mounts dashed, the sinking sun, in Douglas's eyes, gleaming on their armour. At full tilt they charged.

Then, at only a few yards apart, Douglas savagely jerked his mount's head to the right, the horse all but falling over at this sudden change of direction. Right-handed as he was, his lance became useless for the moment, an extraordinary gesture as they plunged on past each other. Hotspur's lance was able to thrust at his foe, after a fashion, but distinctly askew, and Douglas took the thrust on his shield, from which it slid off harmlessly. They hurtled on.

There were howls and shouts from all around at this less than effective display by the Douglas, even John being astonished. But in only yards he was violently reining in his unfortunate mount, the creature's forelegs pawing the air, as he forced it right round, and then drove it cantering back after Percy.

That earl, with the restricted vision caused by the visored helmet, was moments before he could know what was happening behind him, and began to turn his steed. By which time Douglas was almost upon him. And now, of course, the slanting sunlight was in *his* eyes. Hopelessly disadvantaged, before he could get his horse into the required fast forward movement again, Douglas's lance struck home. The other managed to take the blow on his shield, but his mount still only trotting against the other's charging rush, the impact was violent, irresistible. Hotspur was jerked backwards, shield and all, and the horse, in fright, plunging sideways, its rider was flung right out of the saddle, to fall heavily to the ground – and that ground was not turf or soil but the market-place's cobblestones. With a crash, and actual sparks flying, the iron-clad earl landed, and as Douglas went cantering past, lay still, stunned.

His challenger, slowing his mount, glanced backwards to see what was the situation, and then trotted on, almost nonchalantly, to his own base and friends, to wild shouting from all around.

He was being excitedly congratulated by George when he raised his visor, but did not dismount.

"Wait, you!" he panted. "He may rise. It may not be finished."

But the Percy lay motionless. The Lord Ralph and other supporters ran out to the armour-clad figure lying still, others going to capture the riderless horse. That Hotspur was unconscious was obvious. He was half dragged, half carried away, to continued angry yelling.

Douglas shrugged. "It will serve, I think. Scarcely my finest hour, but he sought it! It will serve our present needs." Then, looking back again, he pointed. "See, they have overlooked something in their haste. Hotspur's lance and guidon lying there still. Get it, Jamie." This to Dalkeith.

That man ran out to pick up the trophy of victory, and they all returned with it to their own ranks of cheering men.

But they did not cheer for long. A messenger-scout was pushing through to Douglas. "My lord," this man panted. "The Bishop. Durham. He and his thousands are none so far off. At Rainton we saw them. They will be much nearer by now. An army."

"Ha! Durham! So be it. We must be off, then. Three forces against us. We must not be caught in this town. Out with us. Waste no time with these folk here. Out, and north with us. To where we may face them all on good ground." He turned to Dalkeith again. "Jamie, go tell Ralph Percy that his brother will be welcome to come and try to regain his guidon, his pennant! Then, after us. We ride, I say."

None disputed the wisdom of this. Without any further exchanges with their foes, the Scots turned to head for that North Gate, a sudden end indeed to the journey. But they bore Hotspur's lance and pennon.

Safely out of the city and up on the height above the Town Moor again, they halted to look back. There was no indication of any move to follow them. Where was the bishop's large force? Nothing was to be seen of any approach, as might have been visible from this viewpoint.

Douglas was concerned. Could it be possible that the Durham army might seek to get *behind* them? Between them and the border? So that, with Percy's people, they could be trapped front and rear? It was possible. Better, then, to move on northwards, while they could, to get to some defensible area where, if battle was to be joined, they could choose the ground, to make the land fight for them, even English land.

So, in fair order now, the entire array set off.

Darkness overtook them just south of Ponteland, with their scouts reporting no sign of the enemy following from Newcastle. But they did disclose that the Durham army had halted for the night at Birtley, still four miles south of the city. Relieved in one way, yet almost disappointed in another that the Percy was apparently not going to seek to regain his pennon and redeem his knightly renown, Douglas judged that they could spend the hours of darkness here at the hamlet by the River Pont, a minor stream, but ready for action the while.

It had been a long and challenging day. With relays of guards on the watch, they slept, undisturbed.

In the morning, with still no reports of enemy pursuit, the leaders wondered. With the numbers that Hotspur and his allies could now command, surely they were unlikely just to let matters lie? John suggested that they might see the Cumberland invasion, to the west, as the more dangerous, and would head in that direction. Douglas admitted that it was a possibility, but it did not seem probable to him. Why should Percy, or the Prince-Bishop, be so concerned over what was all but rival territory?

George, for his part, with some anxiety, thought that their enemies might instead elect to wreak havoc again on *his* lands of the Merse, these more or less unprotected meantime, and then swing round to assail this force in flank. That also, it was agreed, was a possibility, indeed more likely than the Cumberland one. Douglas was prepared to take measures to counter this, if it seemed necessary. They would proceed slowly northwards this day, still looking for good sites for battle if Hotspur did follow them. And if not, to make a line back whence they had come, to pick up that little garrison left at Otterburn, then up Redesdale to Carter Bar, and back down to Jed and Tweed, making directly for the Merse, in case George's fears were well grounded. That was accepted.

All that day, in no haste, north by west, by Belsay and Capheaton and Kirkharle, they moved on. They saw sundry areas, amongst lowish hills and woods, where they could make a stand, or even ambush. But the scouts behind still sent no word of the enemy. It began to look as though they were not to be pursued. Were George's fears to be substantiated?

By evening they had got as far as Fawdon Tower at Otterburn, on the Rede, where they collected their men left there. They would camp here, and in the morning make a swift move up-river for their border, and then north-east for the Merse.

What was Hotspur doing? Or failing to do?

Laying aside their armour, and wrapped in plaids, in time most of them slept. John wondered whether, after all, they were going to he spared battle and bloodshed.

When it was, during that night, that he was rudely awakened by being shaken by the shoulder, he knew not. Gathering his wits, he found that all around him others were being urgently roused, amidst much confusion inevitably. The enemy were almost upon them, it was being shouted. Hotspur, come in darkness! Attack by night!

Horns were being blown, to summon all to arms, some armour was being buckled on, men anything but prepared for disciplined warfare in the darkness; needless to say they had not slept in their armour.

The leadership sought to organise and control. Douglas, even as his breastplate was being buckled at the back over his shirt-of-mail by his armour-bearer, Bickerton of Luffness, was jerking out his orders. The sentries had announced that the enemy was choosing to assail them by the riverside, in flank. The Rede, here, was bordered by marshland, soft, reedy ground, into which horses' hooves would sink. So the attackers would not be mounted. Easier to fight on foot in the dark, anyway. The Scots would best remain thus, also.

There was no time to be lost, or Percy would be upon them. With lance and stabbing-spear, battle-axe and mace and sword, but many, like John himself, without helmets on, they sought to form up into groups and lines, Douglas in front, leading, with John at his side, George sent to command on the far right and pose a threat from there, also to ensure that no enemy, who might be on the other bank of the river, could cross and get behind the Scots camp.

Douglas shouted his orders to the lords and lairds nearby. If he fell, Moray to take command until Dunbar could be brought to do so. If Moray fell, Lindsay of Crawford to replace him. Keith to go and take to horse, with some five score mounted men, and ride round to the left, to halt any English cavalry that might seek to outflank them on that side. Scott of Buccleuch to be ready to go and aid him.

Then, pacing forward in some sort of order, they headed for the riverside. There was a faint half moon, somewhat clouded over, but offering little light. However, that would apply to the foe also.

There sounded clash and shouting to the right, where presumably that wing had reached the enemy, this din ever growing. Douglas swung his advance somewhat in that direction.

They went tripping and stumbling over uneven ground, tussocks and stones. A messenger came after them, on horseback, to announce that Keith and Buccleuch were under strong horsed attack on the lower slopes of Fawdon Hill, needing reinforcement. Swiftly reacting, Douglas sent Maxwell back, with quite a large party, to the horses, to aid.

Then the Scots front saw the main English mass before them, indistinctly in the gloom, this not helped by a scatter of bushes and dwarf thorn trees. The ground was beginning to feel soft beneath their feet now. They were evidently getting near to the river.

At that sight of the foe, Douglas raised his mace high, and shouted, "A Douglas! A Douglas!", that ancient and dreaded war-cry; and, all around, it was taken up. "A Douglas! A Douglas!" And they began, not exactly to charge, because of the ground, but to break into something of a trot. Many, finding their long lances a handicap in this, cast them aside, to draw swords and dirks for close hand-to-hand fighting. Unfortunately, the discarded lances could trip up some of those behind.

John, sword in one hand, dagger in the other, and his shield left behind, saw men only yards ahead of him. These seemed to be stationary, waiting. He raised his sword, to swing down not to thrust. Nearby, Douglas was swinging that mace.

They crashed into the enemy ranks, smiting. And thereafter all was utter turmoil, yelling, screaming confusion.

Hand-to-hand fighting in darkness could not be otherwise. The Scots, in their stumbling charge, had some advantage over the stationary English, who presumably were taken by surprise at the onslaught.

Slashing and stabbing wildly, John was really aware of little save chaos. Someone cannoned into him, whether friend or foe he knew not, all but knocking him over. The press behind carried him forward. Then he nearly fell over a body on the ground. Staggering on, he came to realise that where there had been men, many men, in front of him, now there were none – save fallen ones.

It took moments for him to perceive the situation, Douglas, nearby, shouting something and pointing forward. These opponents had been only a forward group of the enemy, not the main force. They were still to advance therefore.

Douglas broke into a trot again, and they all had to do the same, unsure of what lay in front of them now, the rest of the foe not readily discernible,

Their first real sight of the Percy's principal force revealed that, in the midst of a long line of men, on foot, was a schiltrom, that is a tight mass of men, stationary, in the form of a sort of armed and armoured hedgehog, kneeling and standing, with bristling spears and lances out before them all round, a highly defensive grouping which even cavalry would find hard to ride down, this in the centre of the line. If Hotspur was within that, and banners flew above it, he would be secure, however defensive, although hardly knightly and leader-like.

Seeing it, Douglas scornfully, angrily, shouted, "Percy! Percy! Hotspur! Here is Douglas! Percy – to me! And die!"

Whether his challenge reached his target in the uproar was not to be known – even whether Percy was there; but no change nor movement in the schiltrom was evident, whatever the effect on the English ranks on either side and behind it.

Still pressing forward, there did occur a sudden change in the situation, and direst change. Douglas, leading still, abruptly staggered, and not just through tripping over some obstacle. His mail-clad person convulsed in violent spasms, and his shouting choked into a loud groaning, as the mace fell from his apparently nerveless fingers. He all but sank to his knees, the man Bickerton behind him seeking to hold him up.

The earl, tottering, was obviously trying to gain some control of his swaying person.

John stared, appalled, and went to his nephew's side, to help.

"My back!" Douglas gasped. "In . . . in my back!"

Behind him Bickerton let go his hold, and turning, flung himself away, through the press, as the others close by faltered, to gaze bewildered.

"Hold . . . hold me up!" Douglas got out thickly. "Hold . . . Lead me . . . forward!"

At one side, John, discarding his sword, reached to grasp and support his nephew, Lindsay doing the same at the other side, more, behind, seeking to aid the clearly injured earl. Yet there had been no flight of arrows. What had happened?

"What, what is to do?" John panted.

"My, my back!"

What that meant was not evident, save that Douglas was clearly in a grievous state and in pain. His back . . .?

"On! On!" that man gasped. Hold me. Forward! I . . . I am a dead man!"

Lindsay shouted, "Lay him down. He is wounded. Somehow."

"No!" The Douglas was still the leader. "No. Forward with me! Hold me up! On! On!" However weak and thick his voice, the iron will was there. "A, a Douglas! Cry it!"

They all tried to do as he ordered, bearing him up and forward, however dragging were his legs and feet. Bewilderment.

"I am . . . Douglas," he got out. "A dead man! Old . . . prophesy! Our line. A dead man . . . shall gain . . . a field!"

Astonished, but seeking to do as ordered, the others close to the earl lurched on with him.

"Raise it! A Douglas!" That was a command, thick but urgent.

They did obey, shouting the slogan, and all behind and on the flanks took up the cry. "A Douglas! A Douglas!"

"Keep . . . on," they were ordered. "I die, I die! But . . . as did my forefathers . . . praise God! On a field . . . not in . . . my bed!" That got out, the voice became a mere whisper. But John heard it. "Conceal my death. Forward . . . with me. We shall win . . . the day! Win, yet! My last command . . . to you all. Shout, I say . . ." He collapsed and would have fallen had not John and the others held him up. But he spoke no more.

"A Douglas! A Douglas!" the cry continued. What was left of the leadership lurched onwards, Dalkeith beside John now.

Mind in a whirl, John was wondering what they would do when they reached that schiltrom of spears and lances. He had only his dirk now, in one hand, Lindsay also without his sword. And holding up this body, they could not assail that hedgehog formation anyway. They would have to avoid it somehow, go round it, leave it to all those at their backs. Seek to fight a way through the flanking files . . .

Then he became aware of something else. Above and beyond the Douglas shouting, there sounded a din, half right, half forward, loud yelling and the clash of steel. That must be, could only be, George and his force, the right wing. It had worked its difficult way up the riverside, attacking the left of the English array. Here was hope. If *they* got behind the schiltrom . . .

The enemy in front of John evidently perceived the situation and their danger also. For now there was movement, disintegration, as the stationary close-knit body of men, unclearly seen in the gloom, began to stream away, their flanking supporters also swinging around. Suddenly again all was changed on this strange field of battle. The enemy were concerned not to be caught between two forces. Bravo, George!

There was a further development quickly thereafter. Keith and his horsed party came down on the left, not charging on the soft ground but making their advent very evident, with shouting and cheers, "Douglas!" shouting also, if further off. Assailed now on three sides, Percy's force was all but surrounded – and the river prevented any escape to the west, a barrier.

John, recognising that his leadership, such as it was, would no longer be needed meantime, signed to Lindsay and Dalkeith, and they lowered their burden, as men streamed past them on either side. Douglas was indeed a dead man. And there, at his back just below the neck, a dagger-hilt projected between the start of the chain-mail shirt and the plate-armour of chest and back. That armour had not been fully buckled up. And the only man who could have known of the fact was the armour-bearer, John Bickerton of Luffness.

"The dastard!" Dalkeith exclaimed. "Bickerton! The evil dastard! He has slain his master! Stabbed him in the back!"

It could have been none other. Why? Why?

The cry went up: find Bickerton! But there was no sign of him to be discovered in all that confusion and darkness. Presumably he had fled the field after his murdering.

Preoccupied with all this, wondering at it, and guarding Douglas's dead body, John took no further part in the fighting going on ahead. Shocked, not knowing what part he could play now, he heard a well-known voice close by.

"We have him! We have him! Hotspur Percy. He is ours! Captured. He has yielded. But – Douglas? Where is the Douglas?" It was brother George.

John pointed downwards. "Slain. Murdered. Stabbed in the back by the man Bickerton, his armour-bearer. Why, God knows! Dead!"

Staring, George sank to his knees beside the corpse. "Dead! Douglas dead! God in heaven – the Douglas!"

Incoherently John began to recount. But Keith coming up, and likewise shattered, bewildered, brought George to his senses again, to perceive immediate duties. *He* was now in command of the Scots army, Douglas's named successor in this. Now was no time for talk, explanations, discussion. He with Keith, Lindsay, Maxwell and Dalkeith, hurried off to take charge of the situation, so far as they could. John was left with his nephew's body.

It took some time, that night, to restore some sort of order, although only desultory fighting was still going on amongst small groups, the mass of the enemy having fled southwards. But Ralph Percy was not captured, like his brother. Where he was, and the remainder of English, could not be known in the darkness; but he might well attempt a rescue of Hotspur, well guarded as that man now was, and not deigning to speak to the victors. But some of the other captives, roughly questioned, admitted that the Durham force had not as yet joined them for this night-attack. Just where it was, how far off, was not known.

George, in hasty consultation with the others, decided that the situation called for discretion, not just rejoicings at partial victory. The Scots could still be greatly outnumbered, if Ralph Percy and the Prince-Bishop joined up and collected the scattered remains of Hotspur's people. This had been Douglas's little war, and now, his objective attained and himself gone, it should be the border for them forthwith, up Rede, and into their own country, with their prisoners, where, if they were followed and attacked, they could draw on large manpower. None argued otherwise.

So it was back to the horses, the dead earl being carried deferentially by relays of sorrowful men.

What sort of a victory was it, that night, at Otterburn?

They left a strong rearguard behind them when they packed up the abandoned camp and set off for the north.

John wondered what they would do with Hotspur Percy. After all, the feud had been between him and the dead Douglas, not really with the others, although there was repayment due for the raiding into the Merse. The new Earl of Douglas would be Archibald the Grim, Lord of Galloway, all knew, this by special entail, the late James having no heir; and Archibald might well not be greatly concerned with the Percy situation, there in Galloway.

With time to reflect, as they rode up Rede, they realised that their losses in men had been remarkably light, they reckoned not more than one hundred dead; how many English, they had not counted. They had captured a number of English knights, as well as Hotspur, including the Seneschal of York, Sir Thomas Walsingham, a famous character. Bickerton, of course, although searched for, was nowhere to be found. Where he was now, who could tell? And why had he done it? None could hazard a guess. What would happen to Hotspur? Presumably he would be held for ransom, a great ransom no doubt. And the other knights.

They wondered how the western force, under Archibald the Grim and the princes, was faring. There had been no couriers to indicate progress or intentions. There was no point in seeking a link now, no enthusiasm for prolonging this expedition. Not only the Mersemen, mosstroopers and other Borderers found home beckoning, John of Moray likewise. Their campaign had seemed, all along, somehow irrelevant, save to the anti-Percy ones. Had it much importance nationally?

They reached Carter Bar in due course, their rearguard sending no word of any close pursuit. Perhaps their western people had turned east and were now threatening the Northumbrian and Durham allies?

John was no fonder of warfare, out of all this, than he had been before. Marjory would agree with him.

23

It was a joy, as ever, to be back at Darnaway with wife and family, and life, hopefully, to return to normal. John learned that while he had been gone, Donald of the Isles had paid another visit, and Marjory had apparently enjoyed entertaining him. He had been consolidating his compact with the clansmen on both sides of the Great Glen, and seeking to establish peace between them all, thus strengthening his hold over a vast area of the western Highlands, as well as his own seaboard and Hebrides. In fact, Donald was now all but ruler over something like a quarter of Scotland. His ancestor, the great Somerled, had styled himself *King* of the Isles, as well as Lord; now Donald might almost lay claim to that title, with some justification, and could make a good monarch over parts which the Kings of Scots had never been able, or particularly wanted, to control. Marjory was eloquent about all this, and John said that he would have to be watching his wife lest she got too pleased with this Donald.

There was no lack of other matters to claim the attention of Moray's lord, decisions to make, after quite a lengthy absence, other than just the three children's development. There was the usual controversy between neighbouring vassals and lairds; Inverness complaining that Nairn and Burghead were taking trade away from it; forestry and timber extraction; fire had burned a large area in Rothiemurchus forest on Speyside, even cut and felled timber destroyed. There had been no trouble with the clans, thanks to Donald; but there had been upset over fishing rights in the inner Moray Firth between fishermen in the Black Isle of Ross and his own folk of Milton of Culloden,

Allanfearn, Ardersier and Delnies, which required authoritative decision. John was quite prepared to deal with all this as part of his responsibilities, and this much to be preferred to the challenges of military leadership, Black Agnes's son though he was.

So he had a busy late autumn and early winter before, in February, the next summons from the south came for him, this to attend a council and parliament at Edinburgh, important apparently although details were not sent with the messenger.

Since he would have to go by ship, snow dictating it, Marjory declared that she would like to accompany him, for a change, to see kin and friends. She enjoyed being Countess of Moray, but did not want to get out of touch with her father, whose health was reported to be failing, and her many brothers and sisters and their offspring. This well suited John; the youngsters would be well looked after by the Murrays.

A somewhat stormy voyage brought them to Leith. And at Holyrood they found King Robert, very much looking his age of seventy-three years, and Carrick himself seeming not so much younger than his father, unlike his brother Robert, Earl of Fife and Strathearn, who was his usual vehement and forceful self, Marjory however admitting that she liked him the least of all her brothers. Other princes were present also; indeed the Privy Council, these days, seemed to be largely made up of the king's progeny, legitimate and otherwise.

They learned that the said council hardly needed to meet, since the decisions had already been taken by the royal family, to put before the parliament. King Robert was not exactly abdicating, but was going to retire from national and public affairs to his castle of Dundonald, in the Stewartry part of North Ayrshire, to devote himself to study, history and matters of religion. Always these had interested him, and now he felt that he had earned time to pursue these, and rest from his royal labours, although he would still advise his eldest son, Carrick, on matters of state, the better, perhaps, for these studies. Meanwhile, although John/Robert of Carrick was heir to the throne, because of his physical handicap, constant pain in his leg kicked by that Douglas horse so long ago, as well as his retiring temperament, parliament should appoint his next brother, the christened Robert, of Fife and Menteith, to be governor of the realm, hardly regent but acting for father and brother in the rule of the realm. He ought to be an effective and strong royal representative.

John could not deny that this would probably be so, even though he agreed with his wife that Fife was not the most likeable of the family. But was that important? He was determined, energetic and a leader, and the kingdom needed such.

John had a word with the new Earl of Douglas later, and learned about the western sally into Cumberland and Westmoreland, which Fife and his brothers had joined. They had, it seemed, made a successful campaign of it, winning skirmishes with Neville of Raby and the Earl of Westmoreland, and penetrating as far south as Penrith, level with Durham, without involving themselves in any siege of Carlisle Castle, this before messengers came from Douglas to inform them of the Durham bishop's aid coming to Percy. They had then turned eastwards to help counter that. When they learned that a battle had been fought at Otterburn, that earl dead and their allies returned to Scotland, they had gone back westwards without encountering the enemy, and enriched themselves with much booty and spoil from Cumbria before coming home.

At Holyrood, John also heard that Sir Ralph Percy, wounded, had indeed been captured by a detachment of Keith's force, and brought north, like his brother; and the pair of them had been ransomed for a very great sum of silver, this shared between Archibald the Grim, Dalkeith, and George of Dunbar, none having come John's way, although admittedly he had scarcely earned it. The Percy brothers were now back in Northumberland.

The council, next day, made a pretence of meeting, but

all to the point had been already decided. Whether the parliament, two days hence, would agree with it all remained to be seen.

Marjory was concerned about her father, his state of health worse than she had realised. She feared that he was not very long for this world and kingdom. But, to be sure, he had had a full and long life, rewarding; and he deserved this final period of retirement. What sort of monarch her brother Carrick might make was questionable; but meantime Robert of Fife would act the king, and possibly well enough, for *he* did not lack strength.

George, attending also, reported that before letting Hotspur go, he had obtained a promise from him that there would be no more raiding into the Merse and Middle March, which was satisfactory. He did not suggest that John should share in the ransom money.

They spent the next day with the Setons, no great distance to the east, and pleasantly.

The parliament, possibly the last that King Robert would attend, went well enough, with Fife, already Lord Chamberlain, playing the dominant role, the Chancellor, Bishop Peebles of Dunkeld, in some doubts about deferring to him or to the monarch. If some present were less than happy over the projected governorship – none carefully named it a regency – they did not voice it save by questions and hinting; and some murmuring when it was put to all that an annual payment of one thousand silver merks should be remitted to Fife for his necessary expenses. That man took it for granted that he was now in charge of the realm, and spent little time in remarking on it. What he did emphasise was the importance, at least in his eyes, of the invasion of Cumberland and Westmoreland, giving the impression that he himself had led it rather than Archibald of Galloway, and touching but little on the eastern campaign and the death of the Earl of Douglas. He did indicate that Percy of Northumberland had learned his lesson, and was unlikely to trouble them further. His contention was that his western inroads into England, winning so far south, and isolating Carlisle, had demonstrated to the Auld Enemy that the Scots were now in the ascendant and a power to be reckoned with, especially with England in its still divided state and this King Richard's reign so feeble. So this situation must be built upon forthwith and the position established. The Scots were now strong enough to assert their power and authority, finish with truces with England and enter into a permanent treaty relationship, a very different status, which, together with the French alliance, ought to ensure an end to hostilities between the two realms for the foreseeable future.

That, needless to say, went down well with the parliament, and boosted Fife's standing.

That man went on to declare that, to this end, he proposed that an embassage should be sent to London, and soon, not so much offering terms as proclaiming strength, and the dominance over the north of England, and so *requiring* peace and harmony, implying threat if this was not forthcoming from these Lords Appellant. The present situation was in their favour and it would be folly not to make the best use of it.

However much John, George and others might question the superiority and value of that western wing of the recent campaign, all saw the proposed change in relationship with England to be supported and attempted. King Robert and Carrick nodded approval.

So ambassadors to go to London, to act not only as envoys but as guarantors of the intended treaty. The king spoke up, however thin his voice, and John found himself become involved personally. For the monarch declared that he and his predecessor on the throne, David the Second, had found John, Earl of Moray, to be a most able and worthy representative, who had greatly aided Scotland's cause. He urged that Moray should be one of the guarantors sent.

A little embarrassed, John rose and bowed to the throne, and sat down again. Up in the gallery – for the parliament

was being held in the great hall of Edinburgh Castle –
Marjory was watching and listening. Would she be
pleased, or the reverse, at her father's contribution?

It was accepted, at any rate, by Fife and all. That man
then proposed his illegitimate half-brother Thomas Stewart, Archdeacon of St Andrews, Holy Church always
having to be represented on such occasions. Some of the
other senior clerics looked doubtful over this, but none
actually challenged it. Douglas of Dalkeith put forward the
name of the new Earl Archibald of Douglas, and this was
agreed. Then George of Dunbar proposed Dalkeith himself, which John seconded.

Fife frowned, and declared that that was sufficient, four
guarantors, the Earls of Moray and Douglas, the Lord of
Dalkeith and the Archdeacon of St Andrews. Their embassage would not be long delayed.

Parliament went on to consider other matters, Fife
continuing to lead the way. Cross-border raiding and
feuding must cease in the new situation envisaged, and
the Wardens of the Marches should be given greater
powers to enforce this. To aid them, a senior Warden
should be appointed, above those of the East, Middle and
West, and none would be more suitable than the Earl of
Dunbar and March, whose lands flanked the borderline
extensively. He could be styled Lieutenant of the Border,
and his would be the responsibility for peaceful conditions
from Tweed's mouth to Solway Firth.

Black Agnes's sons were being made very prominent at
this parliament – no doubt to ensure their support for
Fife's new regime. But George did not look too happy at
this access of responsibility, for keeping peace along all
that borderline would be an all but impossible task, especially on the West March where raiding and reiving, cross-
border robbery and blackmail, kidnapping and extortion,
were part of life, and had been from time immemorial,
with little heed actually given for the boundary between
the two realms, Armstrongs and Elliots, Nixons and John-
stones, Grahams and Forsters being found on both sides.

If he was to be held answerable for law-abiding there, over one hundred miles of very wild territory, he was going to be kept busy indeed, and blamed for failure. John sympathised.

The next business was exceptional indeed, almost unique, in that parliament was being urged to censure its own president, the Chancellor himself, the Bishop of Dunkeld – this undoubtedly all Fife's arranging, although he himself left it to his brother, the Earl of Strathearn, to bring up. It concerned the great Forest of Ettrick, in the shire of Selkirk, which Archibald the Grim was now taking possession of as his own. It had been part of the late Earl of Douglas's vast lands, but was now being claimed by Sir Malcolm Drummond of Strathord, brother-in-law of the dead earl and also brother of Carrick's wife, Annabella Drummond, who would be the next queen. The Chancellor had found in favour of Archibald, presiding over a small Privy Council committee, and issued a written judgment to that effect. So here was the royal family, or part of it, versus the Douglases, and possibly seeking to bring down the Chancellor in the process, no doubt to be replaced by one of their own choosing.

It made a tricky situation indeed for the assembly to decide upon, sides to be taken. Whatever the rights and wrongs of it, on the one hand there was the royal family not to be offended, especially with one of them now to rule the realm as governor. But the great house of Douglas was in fact the most powerful in the land, not to be crossed with impunity. And also there was Holy Church, with its representative, the Bishop-Chancellor, being censured for what might well be a viable judgment. Here was a testing of loyalties, priorities and judgment itself. Had a Chancellor ever before been censured by a parliament over which he was presiding?

The actual challenge was made by Sir James Sandilands of Calder, another brother-in-law of Drummond and married to one more of the Stewart princesses, who announced that he too could claim some share of the disputed

Ettrick, a huge area of the Southern Uplands. When he sat down, there was a highly unusual consequence, a prolonged silence, as men stared at each other, and considered.

The late Cardinal-Bishop of Glasgow's successor, Matthew, was the first to speak. "Censure is not the correct line to take in this matter," he declared. "Whether the judgment come to was the correct one or otherwise it was taken heedfully and after due study. If it can be proved to have been mistaken, then it can be rejected and rectified. But to censure a Chancellor and prelate of Holy Church thus is not to be considered."

All the churchmen present, bishops and mitred abbots, agreed with that, needless to say.

Archibald the Grim rose. "Ettrick has been Douglas land for long. It shall remain so." That was brief and grim enough, in all conscience. Church and Douglas were at one in this, as was not always the case.

As men weighed the position, oddly enough it was the usually silent and retiring heir to the throne who finalised the issue.

"My wife, the Princess Annabella, has no wish to seek any possession of these lands," he said. "Let it stand."

After that, stand it must. Fife had sustained his first reverse, and from his own brother – and, it was to be presumed, from King Robert himself without whose agreement Carrick would probably not have spoken.

There were sighs of relief from the majority present.

To help ease the situation and prevent further dispute, lest any sought to have the matter put to the vote, John took a breath and rose, to change the subject.

"Donald, Lord of the Isles, is proving to be a good and effective ruler over a quite large part of this realm," he said. "He has established his sway over many of the feuding clans of the north-west, those lands flanking my earldom of Moray. And brought peace to much of Ross. As my brother, George of Dunbar and March is being charged with keeping the borderline folk in order, Donald has done as much in *his* area. I move that the Lord Donald be invited to attend future parliaments, in recognition. He has never done so, hitherto."

George rose, to second that.

Few there, save perhaps the Campbells of Argyll, had any interest in the Western Highlands, or knowledge of what went on there. The motion was nodded through without a vote.

Fife probably saw that here was a good opportunity to end the session before any further possible issues were raised that might be contrary to his interests or tend to limit his powers.

"I move, my lord Chancellor, that this parliament should now adjourn," he announced.

His brothers Strathearn and Buchan stood to second. None contested and the assembly broke up.

Marjory came down from the gallery, to congratulate her husband on this of Donald of the Isles, although she did not mention the embassage to London. She went with her father down to Holyrood, promising to visit him at Dundonald before long.

Thereafter the couple paid a brief visit to Dunbar, by ship; and then it was re-embarking for the north again, with mixed feelings. That parliament of 1389 would be long remembered.

24

It took longer for the London visit to be arranged, thanks to the difficulties in the rule in England and the squabblings amongst the Lords Appellant, than was anticipated, John in no way complaining about that. It was, in fact, midsummer before the word came from Fife that safe-conducts had been obtained for the journey through England; and a start would be made on the Eve of the Visitation of the Blessed Virgin, from Edinburgh.

John would have preferred to go by ship to the Thames; but there was Archibald the Grim to consider, from Galloway, and the Archdeacon Thomas who, although nominally based on St Andrews, appeared to live at Renfrew. So by road it would have to be, and this would give opportunity for Marjory to be escorted as far as Dundonald, to see her father there. John would pick up Archibald at Dumfries and cross the border near Carlisle.

At this time of the year it made undemanding and quite pleasant riding through the mountains and down to the Lowlands, by Perth, Stirling and Linlithgow to Edinburgh, where John received his instructions from Robert of Fife, before proceeding on westwards, by Glasgow, for Renfrew on the Clyde estuary, Marjory's old home, where they saw Carrick and his Annabella, and collected one more of her numerous kinsmen, the half-brother whom she hardly knew, Archdeacon Thomas, whose mother had been some good-looking serving-lass who had caught the High Steward's very roving eye. He was a proud character nevertheless, with quite a presence to him, and seemingly close to Fife.

They rode on for Dundonald next day, almost a score of

miles further south, near Irvine in North Ayrshire. Marjory knew it, of course, although John did not, for it had always been a favourite seat of her father's, in the green, rolling country of the River Irvine, backed by the modest Claven Hills, these excellent for sport – not that the king would now be indulging in such activity. The castle was to be seen for miles around, prominent on an isolated, steep, rounded hillock, a massive fortalice of thick walling rising to fully seventy feet, within the usual courtyard and angle towers, the base of the hillock being encircled by a water-filled moat, the gateway, reached after a zigzagging climb, decorated with Stewart armorial bearings. Margaret related that it had got its name and early fame, according to legend, when, two centuries before, it had been built entirely of wood, plastered over with clay to resist fire-arrows "with never a wooden pin, by worthy Donald Din", a beggar who had himself discovered a pot of gold, in a dream, and used it to erect this and became a great man. The High Stewards had rebuilt it in stone.

They found the king in his small withdrawing-room off the huge great hall, surrounded by papers and books, a man well content to end his time here thus, saying that his realm would be well enough served by Robert of Fife whom he wished had been his eldest son rather than John of Carrick, and so would have succeeded to the throne. Carrick would need him, undoubtedly, and, he believed, would not resent his dominance in affairs of state. In the course of conversation, he pointed out that Fife would have the support of a great many brothers and half-brothers and sisters' husbands – this without naming them all. Later the archdeacon did inform John that he had nine illegitimate half-brothers as well as the six earls born out of the two wedlocks, and no fewer than ten lawful half-sisters, with how many bastard women he knew not. Surely seldom had there been a more fertile monarch!

Regretfully John had to leave the castle next morning, with the archdeacon, for the quite lengthy ride to Dumfries, ninety miles no less, which he could scarcely expect the cleric to cover in one day, although *he* might just have achieved it at this time of the year. They went by Ayr and inland through the Glenkens Hills to St John's Town of Dalry, where they passed the night in the hospice. Thomas Stewart proved to be a quiet but not difficult companion.

They reached Dumfries by noon the following day, to find the Douglases, Archibald the Grim and Dalkeith, already there, in the Greyfriars monastery. They wasted no time in setting off eastwards for the border crossing at Gretna, with a small escort of Douglas men-at-arms. They made a somewhat odd assortment of ambassadors, the famous warrior of Galloway, now elderly but as vigorous as he was curtly forceful, the amiable Dalkeith, the illegitimate cleric sired by a king, and the reluctant if successful envoy John. There was no question, however, as to who would take charge.

With safe-conducts from London there was no need to avoid Carlisle; and anyway, those Douglas banners bearing Bruce's heart beneath three stars, so well known and feared in the north of England, ensured undisputed passage. They got as far as Penrith for the night, where Archibald had made his presence felt none so long before, vanquishing the Earl of Westmoreland's force.

They then headed south-eastwards into the Yorkshire dales country, by Appleby and Brough and Richmond in Swaledale, never once having to display their safe-conducts as passes, the lullaby of that heedful mother of years before serving instead:

> Hush ye, hush ye, do not fret ye,
>   The Black Douglas will not get ye!

Archibald was the illegitimate son of the feared Good Sir James the Black, Bruce's friend.

It took them four more days to reach London by way of Nottingham, Leicester, Bedford, Luton and St Albans. Bypassing Nottingham, Archibald told them how, on a previous venture, he had challenged Howard, Earl of

Nottingham, to a tourney-duel, and had been refused by him, although he claimed knightly prowess and was in fact Earl Marshal of England, a sorry episode of which that proud character should be reminded.

This story was brought to mind when, in due course, the Scots group was ushered into the presence of a sitting of the Lords Appellant, in the Tower of London, and who should be in charge but the Earl Marshal himself. He did eye the Douglas distinctly askance. John hoped that this would not in any way prejudice their mission.

Archibald did not refer to the incident, however much he would have liked to do so; but he did not fail to emphasise the Scots present attitude of ascendancy after the northern victories and the rise to power of the new governor, the Earl of Fife. They had come, he declared, to usher in a new relationship with England, and an end to truces. He was not an eloquent man, save with sword and lance and biting tongue, and he turned to John to make their case to these lords, who in fact now more or less constituted the English Privy Council.

John adopted a more diplomatic tone, without being in any way diffident or over-careful. He announced that there ought to be an end to enmity between the two realms, age-old as this was, and a formal agreement to end warfare and the ridiculous claims to overlordship of the kingdom of Scotland by the monarchs of England. The Scots had recently demonstrated their power and ability in arms, in retaliation for English raids on their country; and now desired to make clear and evident their comparable effectiveness in the conduct of affairs of state and negotiation. It was the desire and intention of Robert, King of Scots and the Earl of Fife, Governor of the Realm, with the support of parliament and Holy Church, to enter into a formal treaty of peace and accord with England, in alliance with France, as established in the new Treaty of Boulogne, thus ending the series of truces so long signed and broken. To this end they had come as guarantors, and would hope that their lordships of England would, in the name of King Richard, likewise accept, agree and make guarantees.

Thomas Stewart added that, in the name of the Primate, Bishop of St Andrews, and Holy Church in Scotland, he, Archdeacon thereof, was entirely supportive.

There was silence round that table for long moments, as the English lords eyed each other. They had, of course, had some indication of the important reasons for this deputation when the safe-conducts were applied for, but the full scope and significance of it all had not been announced.

Nottingham murmured something to his colleagues, right and left, and at length nodded. "This must be considered, considered fully, my lords," he said. "It is . . . a large matter. We shall so consider. With care. We shall meet again on the morrow. For, for further discussion. Yes? Meanwhile, you will be His Majesty's guests here. Provided with all comforts. My Lord Chamberlain, here, will attend you." And he stood.

They all rose.

Archibald the Grim pointed a finger at the Earl Marshal. "Consider well," he jerked. "We can guarantee more than peace and goodwill . . . if required! I, Douglas, promise you!"

With that, the visitors were led from the chamber.

They had no complaints to make as to hospitality that evening and night, even though they were left fairly severely alone to enjoy it, only the Earl of Pembroke, son of the one who had defeated Bruce at Methven, coming to see that all was in order. Where King Richard was they were not informed. John and his brother-in-law Dalkeith shared a bedchamber. They wondered over the English reactions to their mission, both feeling reasonably hopeful. Would the other Douglas's interventions help, or otherwise?

Thereafter, in the forenoon, they found out. Led back to the tower chamber where they had met before, they saw that additional magnates were present, one no less than the Archbishop of Canterbury, Primate of England, with other clerics, which John saw as a favourable sign. This time it was not the Marshal, Nottingham, who presided, but Thomas, Earl of Gloucester, one of the king's uncles, a brother of John of Gaunt who was now aged and all but retired from affairs. He was haughty but not actually hostile, apparently. On the Scots' arrival he announced, without anything in the way of preamble, that he, and others, including the archbishop, had given full consideration to the proposals of "the Scotch commissioners" as he called them, and were prepared to agree to them in principle, for the sake of peace and welfare between the three realms. The details and wording of any treaty could be set forth hereafter, and if acceptable could be signed by His Majesty and witnessed and sealed by himself and others. Let it be seen to.

And that was that, brevity indeed. Gloucester got to his feet, and stalked from the room.

Although others rose, Archibald the Grim remained seated. "Was that a Plantagenet?" he asked. "Douglas could teach that one manners!"

There were raised eyebrows and frowns, John adding almost hurriedly to the effect that all, then, was well, and the wording of the treaty ought not to be over-difficult, with agreement indicated on both sides.

There followed some argument as to whom, on the English representation, should draw up the wording of the proposed compact; but in the end it was decided that Nottingham the Marshal, the archbishop, Pembroke and John of Gaunt's son, Henry, Lord Bolingbroke, were suitable representatives. After a further interval of talk and point-raising, and the summoning of clerks to write down the terms to be agreed, the others of the company left the chamber and the eight delegates sat again to their task.

Fife had urged John to seek to have the treaty terms kept as simple and short as possible, to avoid any unnecessary dispute over conditions thereafter; and he had roughed out a possible draft in his mind which could serve at least as a basis. His companions knew of this, and now eyed him.

Their opposite numbers waited for them, as the instigators of the project, to take the lead.

Nodding, John began by advising this of brevity, asserting that the more words the greater possibility of mis-interpretation and argument, the archbishop voicing agreement.

"Something to this effect," he went on, seeking to recollect the required sequence. "We, Robert the Second, King of Scots, and Richard the Second, King of England, bearing in mind the Treaty of Boulogne signed by Charles the Sixth, King of France, do hereby consider and agree that it is to the advantage of all three realms that an extension of that treaty should be established to include the kingdoms of Scotland and England, such as has not been so hitherto, to produce peace, harmony and accord henceforth, with an end to mere short-term truces and the prevailing cross-border raiding and warfare, and to ensure that all subjects do adhere to this accord under pain of treason against both crowns. This treaty, drawn up at London town on – date to be stated – to remain in force for the future, unless one or other of the undersigned monarchs or their successors, and their parliaments and councils, have full and just reasons to end it. This given under the Great Seals of Scotland and England." He had spoken very slowly, deliberately, aware of the scratching of the quills of the two clerks writing it all down on paper. He paused now, looking around him. "How say you?" he asked.

There was some stroking of beards, pursing of lips and throat-clearing but no actual protests.

"Let us have it again," the archibishop said, looking at the clerks.

The two of them, monks both, heads together now, compared notes, pointing quills here and there. Then one, coughing, began to read, with short pauses between phrases.

Listening, John found little fault with the rendering, save to correct the word truth to truces, after short-term, and London town as against London Tower. "It is . . . well enough," he said.

Nottingham spoke up. "Ought not the names of the monarchs be written in different order," he claimed. "England is the larger and greater kingdom. King Richard's name should come first."

Archibald Douglas snorted.

"It was King Robert of Scots who sought and proposed this treaty," John reminded. "Not King Richard."

"It is not important," the archbishop declared. "What is, surely, is that Holy Church's support and goodwill, in a matter of such concern over God's peace between the nations, should be set down. It *was* in the Treaty of Boulogne."

"I agree," Archdeacon Thomas put in.

"My regrets," John apologised. "Not being a churchman, I failed to think of that. It should go in. After London town, perhaps? With whatever words you may choose, my lord Archbishop."

Pembroke had his say. "This of truces. Were they so feeble that this treaty is necessary?"

Dalkeith answered that. "You know, as do we all, that the truces were broken time and again. Many, near the borderline in especial, judged that such did not apply to them! A full treaty, with the kings' signatures and seals, would be otherwise."

Again Nottingham made a point. "The age-old alliance of Scotland and France against this kingdom of England – it was not mentioned in the Treaty of Boulogne, I think. Does this new treaty end that ill pact?"

That was a poser for the Scots, John having to think fast, and getting no help from his colleagues, who only shook heads and frowned.

"The Auld Alliance is not a treaty," he declared. "It is but an understanding that if either realm is wrongously assailed in arms by England, each will seek to aid the other. With this new treaty of peace, that will not concern *us*, surely, or you. It also gives French and Scottish citizenship to folk of each realm, a matter of considerable moment, but which does not harm England.''

There was silence then, objections seemingly exhausted, at least in words. None of them, save that last, had greatly taxed John's wits. What was vital was that the notion of the treaty itself, as distinct from the wording, appeared to be accepted.

He caught the archbishop's eye, and that so important prelate nodded.

''I judge that, unless there are any other amendments, this wording is acceptable to put before His Majesty and his advisers,'' he said. ''They may have reservations, but in all that matters it appears to be satisfactory. Is that not so?''

''Save this of the French and Scotch alliance,'' Nottingham insisted.

Canterbury shrugged. ''That is not for us to decide.'' He rose, and with a sigh of relief John did likewise. So far, so good.

Archibald pointed at Nottingham again. ''Once you refused me satisfaction, Howard!'' he accused. ''Do not say that again you . . . draw back!''

The Earl Marshal turned away without answering.

''I will have two copies of the final treaty terms made out for you to take to your king,'' Canterbury added. ''If accepted. One signed by King Richard, and one to be sent back to us, signed by your Robert. In a day. Or two, perhaps. Yes?''

The Scots returned to their own quarters.

They did have to wait for two days, exploring London the while, until the archbishop himself brought two parchments to them, one all signatures and dangling seals and crosses, the other bearing only the agreed wording. Scanning these, John could see no obvious changes from what they had debated, and no inserted references to the Auld Alliance.

He thanked Canterbury for his help, and quite warmly, as did the other two, Archibald not being of a warm type, although he did observe that churchmen could have their uses.

So it was goodbyes, John with the precious documents, and to horse.

Four days later they dropped Archibald the Grim at Dumfries, he having no need to accompany the others northwards. John had to go on to Dundonald Castle, of course, with the treaty documents, for King Robert's acceptance and signature. After that it would be up to Fife to take the next steps.

He had scarcely hoped to find Marjory still with her father, for they had been away more than two weeks. He did not, but learned that she had taken the opportunity to go to Rothesay, on the Isle of Bute, where her brother Carrick was now making his home, his Annabella much liking the island and life there, yet readily accessible from the mainland, this visit largely to see her nephew, young David, whom she hardly knew, and who one day, presumably, would be David the Third of Scots. She had sailed there in one of the Renfrew small vessels.

The king, reading the parchments carefully, was well pleased with the wording and all it represented, and fervent in his praises of John and his companions, however feeble and halting his voice, and wondering how he could reward them. He signed, in shaky fashion, both documents there and then, and had the three guarantors witness it. As for John, his only desired reward was to get back to Marjory and the family at the soonest. But he recognised that the others could have their own priorities. He praised their assistance. He did not know about Dalkeith, but guessed that Thomas Stewart might well have ambitions for greater prominence in the Church.

The said Thomas offered John the use of one of the Renfrew boats to take him to Rothesay, if so he wished, since the one that had taken his half-brother had not yet returned, which looked as though Marjory was still there. This was accepted gladly. John took his farewells of his father-in-law and liege-lord, also of Dalkeith, and rode on with the archdeacon for the lower Clyde.

Thomas decided to accompany him to Bute, his duties at St Andrews appearing to be largely nominal. It made no very long sail, only some forty miles altogether, down the widening estuary, to swing off due westwards, to the south of the tip of the Cowal peninsula and across the mouth of Loch Striven. The Isle of Bute, almost twenty miles long but only a couple of miles across, lay in a sheltered position behind the long Kintyre, where it gained the advantages of the Hebrides without the general inaccessibility from the mainland, and the storms and navigational problems of that vast island lordship. Rothesay was its chief town, placed nearly midway up the east side of the island at the head of a bay, picturesquely situated below gentle, wooded hills.

The community centred round its tall and highly unusual castle, built not on any high ground or crag but amongst streets, although itself surrounded by a wide, water-filled moat. It was circular on plan, with four round towers at regular intervals, and an oblong gatehouse tower to the north, the enclosed courtyard some one hundred and forty feet in diameter, this holding many lesser buildings including a quite large chapel dedicated to St Michael. Oddly enough, there was no keep or central main tower, the gatehouse being itself large enough to house the main apartments, an all but unique feature. Just why it had been built thus was unknown, although there was a tradition that it had been so erected by King Magnus Barelegs of Norway, he who had had his dragon-ship dragged over the narrow neck of Kintyre to claim that lengthy peninsula as his own as part of the Hebrides although it was attached to mainland Scotland, this in 1098. At any rate, it had been greatly improved by Robert/John of Carrick, who chose it as his favoured home, suitable for a man of retiring disposition, however unsuitable in position for a monarch of Scotland. It had been in the hands of the High Stewards since the reign of Alexander the Third.

John was glad to find Marjory still with her brother and family, although concerned about getting back to Darnaway to her children. She got on very well with Annabella, who had pressed her to stay, and admittedly the Isle of Bute made a very pleasant place to spend time. She and Carrick had two children, David and a daughter Margaret, with Annabella pregnant with another. They made an extraordinarily unpretentious and quiet-living household to be the next to occupy the throne.

John had never met young David, although now in his later teens, a friendly unassuming youth, fond of boating, sea-fishing and archery, his sister a year younger, more lively and something of a tomboy. A family man himself, John felt at home here, but agreed with his wife that it was high time that they got back to Moray and their responsibilities there.

So they remained only the two days at Rothesay before re-embarking, with Thomas Stewart, to head back for Renfrew, to regain the horses for the long ride to the north, happy just to be alone together, Marjory eager to hear all about the events at London.

25

Only the one real problem awaited them at Darnaway, thankfully, family or otherwise. This was word of highly unsuitable activities near their Moray border, and by none other than another of Marjory's many brothers, Alexander, now Earl of Buchan, and made Lieutenant of the North, this excepting the earldom of Moray. He was making his principal seat at the castle of Lochindorb, near the Cromdale Hills, none so far off. From there he had been misbehaving himself, assaulting the local people, raping and ravishing, and much upsetting the Grants and Shaws and Macphersons, who were now appealing to their earl for protection. Marjory was much worried about this, that a brother of her own should be so damaging the name and reputation of the royal family, John likewise, needless to say, but uncertain as to how to deal with the situation, with this Alexader being not only a prince but having this new position and title as Lieutenant of the North. As Earl of Moray *he* was responsible for keeping the peace within his earldom; but its bounds were somewhat vague, especially in this Badenoch area. Something would have to be done, but what?

As it happened, the difficulty was not exactly solved, but dealing with it was delayed, postponed at least, by news reaching Darnaway soon after their return, dire if scarcely surprising news: the death of King Robert, at Dundonald. Apparently he had passed away quietly, in his bed, a man quite content so to go, whatever problems he left behind for the nation and his family. This meant, of course, a journey south again, for the funeral and the installation of the new monarch, Carrick. Marjory wept for her father, although admitting that he was almost certainly better off now than he had been for long. She worried about her brother, for undoubtedly he would not make a very effective king; and with the brothers *he* had, a hand, a strong hand, would be needed indeed. That hand would almost inevitably be Fife's; but he could hardly remain as governor or regent for a monarch of full age, his elder brother. Not that his style was important, but his attitude and behaviour would be. Scotland, like England, was going to be saddled with a weak liege-lord, with all that that implied. Trouble almost certainly loomed ahead.

Young Thomas, Master of Moray, was now old enough to go to see his uncle crowned, and the three of them set off, by ship, for the Tay and Scone, where both the interment and the coronation would take place, the youngster feeling excited rather than bereaved.

Perth town was packed with attenders for the two great events, an inordinate number of them appearing to be members of the Stewart family, of one sort or another, all therefore in some sort of relationship to Marjory. She was not a little embarrassed by this, in front of her son, who was completely bewildered by it all, for to have such innumerable uncles and aunts, cousins and kinsfolk, legitimate and otherwise, some calling themselves princes and princesses, was hard for a youth, brought up in remote Moray, to comprehend.

Amongst them all was Alexander of Buchan, not on this occasion accompanied by his countess but by his favourite mistress, Mariota de Athyn, by whom he had five sons. John felt that this was not the time to remonstrate with him on the depredations in the north.

At Scone Abbey the obsequies for the late Robert were elaborate, all but magnificent, however modest had been his lifestyle recently, Fife determined that the first Stewart king's memory should be revered, whatever might be the second's, the reflection upon himself being important. Carrick remained in the background as far as was possible, unlike most of his kinsmen.

The Primate, Bishop Walter Trail of St Andrews, conducted the service with dignity, aided by the Abbot of Scone, the prelate in the extraordinary position of having a rival for the primacy in the person of none other than FitzAlan, Archbishop of Canterbury, in London, who had been so helpful in the treaty negotiations; this because the two kingdoms acknowledged the two different Popes, at Avignon and Rome, the latter having appointed FitzAlan as a gesture of his disapproval of the Scottish attitude; not that Bishop Walter took the opposition very seriously. His oration on the virtues of the late monarch would scarcely have been recognised as referring to himself, as a paladin of puissance and virtue.

But once the royal body was lowered into the abbey crypt, and respects delivered piously by streams of princely mourners, the atmosphere changed almost abruptly from the funereal to celebration. The impression given was that, this necessary but sorrowful and lamenting overture now done with, all could properly engage in and enjoy what they had really come for, the festivities and opportunities of a new reign, and all that implied, for the ambitious, the power-hungry and the pleasure-loving. Marjory was much distressed at this.

The Morays did not attend the feasting that followed at Perth that evening.

The coronation next day must have been one of the strangest ever, with the new monarch anything but the principal figure thereat, all but reluctant, nervous and diffident, while his brothers, or most of them, were quite the reverse, Fife of course dominating all.

Back at Scone, for the service in the abbey, this for the administration of the Oath of Fathership, in which the new king swore to be the father of his people, to keep the peace of his realm so far as God allowed, and to show mercy and righteousness in all judgments, this said in little more than a whisper. Then the anointing with holy oil from the high altar.

All thereafter moved out and into procession, to chanting by choristers and the beat of drums and cymbals, to the nearby Moot Hill, a flat-topped mound, on the summit of which the throne was placed, this where the ancient Stone of Destiny had formerly been sited, it now somewhere in the Hebrides known best by Donald of the Isles, that man not present. Beside the chair, on this occasion, was placed another, almost as fine, and set only a pace rearwards, an innovation. The limping king-to-be had to be helped up the grassy hillock by Fife, symbolic in itself, there to be joined, flanked and backed, by all his legitimate brothers, all these now earls and lords, with the Primate, the Chancellor-Bishop of Dunkeld, the Lord Lyon King of Arms, the great officers-of-state, and the Keepers of the Great and Privy Seals.

Panting, Robert John, this the final time that he would be so called, at last seated himself on the throne, to ringing cheers from the great crowd thronging the hill, the Primate and Chancellor standing to bow before him as now the Lord's Anointed. Then the Lord Lyon, acting now as High Sennachie, a more ancient office, signed to a trumpeter, who blew a flourish, then, raising a hand, commenced to read from a parchment scroll.

"Hear me, all men high and low, behold the High King of Scots to be crowned, Ard Righ an Albannach, Robert, son of Robert, son of Marjory, daughter of Robert, son of Robert, son of Robert . . ." On and on he went, tracing the royal descent back through the Bruce, and all the generations to Kenneth MacAlpin who united Picts and Scots, and thence through all the misty Celtic names to Fergus MacErc, of the semi-sacred Fir-Bolg, who followed the missionaries from Ireland, but claimed descent from the pagan Eochaidh, the Horseman of Heaven, god-spirit of the early Celts. This took a considerable time, before he could finish, and bow, first to the throne and then to Robert of Fife.

That man stepped forward, to take the crown of Scotland from a cushion carried by the Abbot of Scone, and turning, hold it over the grey head of his brother.

"I, Robert, Earl of Fife and Menteith, Crowner of this realm of Scotland, as is my right and duty, do hereby, in the presence of all, crown you, descendant of all the fore-named, our anointed king." Stooping, he placed the circlet of gold on the head of their new liege-lord, and stepped back. "Hail, Robert, third of the name, High King of Scots!" he cried. "Hail the king! Hail the king!"

All on and around the Moot Hill took up the cry. "Hail the king! Hail the king! Hail the king!" On and on it resounded, while he whom they all hailed sat uneasily, head down, gazing at his clasped hands. If his Annabella could have been at his side she could have helped and guided him; but this was no day for the women; she would have her prominence on the morrow. Actually she stood with Marjory and John near the foot of the hill, watching her husband anxiously.

It was Fife who halted the shouting eventually by raising an arm and bringing a clenched fist down in a chopping gesture. Then, when he had gained silence, or approximately so, he made another and stranger gesture, this time with his foot, scraping the earth beneath him with the toe of his boot, to loosen the soil. Then he stooped low to pick up a handful of it, and turning to the newly crowned monarch offered him the earth.

"I, Robert of Fife and Menteith, give you the land of Scotland," he declared loudly. "I will aid you to hold it secure." And his hand gripped his brother's. With the other, he waved largely to the assembly. "On this Moot Hill of Scone," he called, "I, Robert, give you your crowned king!"

The emphasis on that "I give" was evident indeed, the lesson clear, to the new monarch, as to everyone else, who inclined his crowned head in acceptance rather than ac-knowledgment.

There was a pause, as the Lord Lyon beckoned. "David, son of Robert," he called, and from the hill-foot the slight figure of the new heir to the throne started to climb up, a deal more vigorously than had his sire, to go and stand at the other side of the said throne from his Uncle Robert. There were lesser cheers.

What followed was less dignified, at first, than the occasion demanded. The fealty-offering made an important part of the great day, and a lengthy part, when all the lords of the land queued up to make their oath of allegiance to their new liege-lord, each bringing a handful of earth from their earldoms, baronies and estates for the monarch to place his foot upon while they knelt and took the king's hand between their own two, and swore their fealty and support – this to emphasise that all the land was the king's, and that he, as superior thereof, should stand on it, every part of it, when receiving the fealty. To save the monarch having to travel round every corner of his realm so to do, this device had been long established, and soil brought from near and far; indeed there was a theory that the height of the Moot Hill was partly accounted for by all the handfuls of soil thus added at each coronation.

Now there was a distinctly unseemly jostling and pushing as sundry of the royal brothers sought priority in this gesture; and as it happened, the quickest and perhaps most agile was the only one who was not an earl, Walter, sixth son of the late monarch, Lord of Brechin, who managed to be the first to throw down earth and get on one knee before his eldest brother, and grabbing the monarchial hand muttered something approximating to the fealty-oath before rising and grinning at the others.

In theory, the kingdom's earls, as representatives of the ancient *ri* or lesser kings of the Albannach regime, should first make their oaths in order of seniority, which would have put Moray high on the list. But with all these princes to claim precedence, the other earls had to let them lead in this, and David, Earl Palatine of Strathearn, swore next, followed by Alexander of Buchan and the others; clearly Robert of Fife did not consider that it was necessary that *he* should have to make the obeisance.

Lyon, whose duty it was to arrange all in due order, was obviously concerned at the sort of competition evident, and when the last of the legitimate brothers rose, called loudly for the Earls of Angus, Lennox, Moray, Mar and Sutherland to come forward, these non-royal. So John actually went up ahead of his brother, the Dunbar and March earldom not being one of the original *ri*, however prestigious. He had his handful of earth ready, in a pouch, and went through the required procedure, the new king nodding to him, although still looking somewhat apprehensive.

Going down to rejoin Marjory and Annabella, they watched George go up in due course, no doubt reminding himself that if he had his right *he* should have been sitting on that throne, as the Cospatrick representative, rather than any Stewart. John did not mention this.

There followed the lengthy procession of officers-of-state and lesser lords and justiciars, prelates and mitred abbots, these last not having to swear, but only to bow and invoke God's blessing on the new monarch. The crowd, by now, had become less attentive and interested.

Eventually it was all over, and most, including Marjory and John, with George and Christian, returned to Perth, although the king, Annabella and their three children remained in the abbey for the night. There was more feasting that evening, presided over by Fife, and this the Morays did attend. And it was thereafter that Marjory learned from her brother that, since he no longer could be styled governor, he would have King Robert's first act as monarch the creation of himself as Scotland's first duke. Other realms had dukes as their highest titles, England now included, with John of Gaunt being made Duke of Lancaster. So he should be so created. And he would choose the style of Albany, indicating the ancient Celtic kingdom of Alba – Robert, Duke of Albany.

Marjory found this odd, but recognised that this brother, who would still largely rule the realm undoubtedly, was entitled to some distinctive style, and she supposed that duke would serve.

In the morning it was back to the abbey for the queen's

crowning, not all bothering to attend. This was to take place in the abbey-church not at the Moot Hill, and was basically a religious ceremony, although Fife, or Albany, again did the actual placing of the lesser golden circlet on Annabella's luxuriant head of hair, but without the hailing and flourish. She sat on a throne beside her husband, with her elder son David standing alongside; and when the fairly brief proceedings were over and the benediction pronounced, the new king made his first monarchial pronouncement as prompted by the other Robert. Somewhat falteringly he declared that he had decided to elevate his worthy brother to the status and position of duke, this in esteem and to celebrate the start of the new reign. So he was now Robert, Duke of Albany, the first such in Scotland. Then, glancing at Annabella, he added, almost in a rush, that he had also decided to create a second duke, in order that the succession to the throne should carry that style, now and in the future. His son and heir, David, would now be Duke of Rothesay and Earl of Carrick.

There were nods of approval at that – but not from Albany, who obviously had not been consulted, and who frowned darkly, especially when Annabella who did not like him, eyed him, brows raised beneath that golden circlet. John and Marjory smiled at each other. The new queen might prove to be a considerable asset, for this undeniably was of her doing.

So Scotland had two dukes, and a queen who knew her own mind, however uncertain a king in Robert the Third.

That signalled the end of these proceedings, and it was back to Perth, although Marjory paid a brief visit to the abbey crypt again where her father lay, the kingdom to embark on a new course, all wondering how fair a course that would be.

The Morays were not long in doing their own embarking. They had not spoken with Alexander, Earl of Buchan, but Marjory had had a word with Annabella on the subject and suggested that he should be given a warning by his eldest brother.

26

At Darnaway they returned to worrying news. Bishop Bur
or Barr, of Moray had become involved in serious trouble
with the Earl of Buchan, and that made for a dangerous
situation. That awkward and savage prince had, many
years before, married one of the many Euphemias, a
daughter of his sire's second wife, Euphemia, Countess
of Ross, by her previous marriage. This younger Euphemia had in due course succeeded to the earldom of Ross,
there being no male heir; and Buchan had married her
merely to gain some of the great Ross lands. He already
had, not a wife, but a favoured mistress named Mariota de
Athyn, of the Mackay line, by whom he had five children,
all sons. He had, in fact, never cohabited with the countess,
who usually lived in Forres. Now that lady was claiming
that that empty marriage should be annulled, as never
having been consummated, she presumably having found
someone else to her taste to wed. She had applied to the
Bishops of Moray and Ross to gain papal dispensation for
this, and they were agreeing to do so. But Buchan himself
was anything but agreeable, apparently, since it might well
mean the loss of those Ross lands he had gained; and he
was making dire threats against the prelates. Bishop Bur,
much worried, sought John's help and support.

Here indeed was a prickly thistle to grasp. What to do
about it? He could scarcely ignore the request from Holy
Church. And he had the responsibilities of his earldom.
Badenoch, part of the Comyn lands of which Buchan was
now the lord, bordered his own – and those borders were
very indistinct in some places, especially on Speyside
where some of his best tree-felling areas lay. He did not

want to have to get into actual hostilities with his wife's difficult brother.

Marjory said that Alexander was only making threats, so far, unspecified threats. Nothing serious might come of it. And there was no word that her brother had yet returned to Badenoch and Lochindorb.

There was a sufficiency of other, if lesser, matters for John to see to meantime.

But it was not long before they learned that Buchan had indeed come back to these parts, and this on another complaint, from Grant of Rothiemurchus, declaring that his people, or some of them, were being persecuted and afflicted by the Prince Alexander, and savagely indeed, for he was actually making a sport of hunting the forest-dwellers on horseback, like deer, and slaying them, a quite extraordinary accusation. Grant was one of John's vassals, and something would have to be done about it.

There was nothing for it, John reluctantly decided, but to go and see Buchan, and seek to have him reform his ways, at least where Moray was concerned. And he might be able to do something about Bishop Alexander's problem at the same time. He was grateful when Marjory announced that she would accompany him on this un-wanted errand.

Decision made, they did not delay. They set off south-wards up Findhorn, taking Brodie and Murray with them. It made no very lengthy ride, only some twenty-five miles. At Ferness, where they left Findhorn, they heard more of Buchan's depredations and ill-doings, learning that he was even being termed the Wolf of Badenoch. Marjory was ashamed to have to admit that he was her brother.

Threading the Cromdale Hills, no mountains these, they came to Lochindorb amongst heathery slopes. They noted the quite new township which had been constructed at the lochside, roughly built timber shacks with reed-thatched roofing, and occupied by some likewise rough-looking characters, caterans as Brodie called them, tartan-clad and hostile as to bearing, presumably Buchan's High-

281

land "tail". They also noted that the fess-chequey of the Stewart banner flew above the castle on its island, indicating that its lord was in residence.

There were boats moored near the cot-houses, and announcing that he was the Earl of Moray come to meet the Earl of Buchan, with the Princess-Countess their lord's sister, surly oarsmen did row them out to the island.

Their arrival had not gone unnoticed from the castle, and a party of four waited to meet them at the landing: Buchan himself, a very handsome lady who was presumably Mariota de Athyn, and two young men, sons no doubt. The woman at least greeted them, smilingly.

"So – Marjory!" Alexander exclaimed, hardly welcomingly, and searching their faces. "To what do I owe this . . . honour?"

"Neighbourly matters, Alex – since we *are* neighbours now," his sister answered coolly. "Of a sort."

The Lady Mariota spoke. "You are welcome to our house, Countess." And looking from one to the other of the men, "One of you will be my lord of Moray, I judge?"

"I am, Lady. And here is Brodie of that Ilk, and Duncan Murray, keeper of Darnaway. Are these your sons?"

"Aye. Andrew and another Duncan." She turned, to lead the way in. "Come, you."

Buchan, his quite good-looking features expressionless, followed them.

The Lady Mariota, whatever else, made an effective hostess, and the visitors were quite grateful for her behaviour, easing their difficult arrival somewhat, offering them refreshment and wine. She got little help from Buchan. Marjory chatted to her amiably enough, the men silent.

That silence could not continue, of course. Wine-glass in hand, John took the plunge. "Good-brother," he said, "we come because of complaints made to us by some of my Moray vassals, in particular Grants. It seems that you have been harassing them. Those on *my* land. Mistreating them. They appeal to me."

"Hielant scum!" the other answered briefly. "Getting no more than they deserve."

"I have never had any trouble with them, my lord Alexander. What have they done to offend you?"

"Sufficient. But I am not answerable to you, Moray, for my actions!"

"On *my* lands, you are."

"I am Lieutenant of the North, I would remind you!"

"That does not give you authority to override the Earl of Moray in Moray," Marjory intervened. "Unless he is acting against the king's interests. Which John certainly is not. Whereas you are, I think, Alex!"

"Your judgment, sister, does not greatly concern me."

"No? But our brother's, the king's, should do. And he is warning you."

"Warning me of what?"

"Penalties. Dire penalties if you continue to disturb the realm's peace. He made you lieutenant. He can unmake you, as easily. Even forfeit your earldom. The Buchan earldom has been forfeited before!"

"On your advising?"

"On more than ours. Others, many others. And including Holy Church!"

"Ah! The clerks! Those up-jumped nobodies! Think you that I care for their empty cursings and anathemas?"

"You ought to. They have the power to punish."

John took it up. "The Bishops of Moray and of Ross are already much troubled over this of the Countess of Ross, whom you have maltreated. Spurned. Married, and then abandoned. She would have the Vatican annul that empty marriage. And you reject her pleas, rightful pleas, since all you have wanted from her are her lands and moneys." He looked over at Mariota and her sons. "Then you could wed this lady."

"When I require your advice on my privy affairs, I will ask for it, Moray! Meantime, I advise you to hold your ill tongue! And I also advise that you leave this my house. And forthwith."

"Oh, we shall," Marjory assured him. "But we have given you the warning. Heed it, Alex. Or pay for your sins and cruelties." She turned to Mariota. "*You* will serve my brother best if you lead him to see where his weal, as well as his duty, lies!" She inclined her head. "We thank you for your hospitality, whatever his." And she signed towards the door.

John bowed, unspeaking, not looking at Buchan. Neither Brodie nor Murray had said a word, any more than had the two Stewart sons.

Mariota was looking unhappy.

Unescorted, the four went out, to head back for their boat.

"I fear that we have achieved nothing," John said. "That one will go his own wicked way. Was I mistaken in mentioning wedding the woman?"

"If he had considered it, he would have done it long since," Marjory told him. "They have been together for over a score of years. And he married Euphemia of Ross eighteen years ago."

"Will the king act?"

"I know not. He is as indolent as Alex is violent. Although Annabella might spur him on."

"What of the other? The Earl of Fife? Or Albany now?" Brodie wondered. "Would he have any control over this prince?"

John shrugged. "We can ask him. But he is no longer governor."

"He is offended over this of a dukedom for young David," Marjory said. "I do not see him hastening to help the king in this. He has never rebuked Alex so far. I have more hopes in Queen Annabella."

They had to leave it at that, as they entered the boat and were rowed over to their horses.

Had their journey been profitless?

The answer to that came even sooner than they could have anticipated. Two days later the word reached Darnaway that Buchan had descended upon Forres and set fire to his wife's house there, along with others nearby, and stormed through the town with his caterans, to the terror of the inhabitants. Fortunately the countess was over at her Ross seat at Cromarty meantime, or who knew what would have happened to her. Alexander was demonstrating his rejection of wise advice, and living up to his new style of Wolf of Badenoch.

Bishop Alexander arrived next day, in great agitation, after John had been to Forres to help calm and console the folk there, promising retribution. The prelate was also demanding action of some sort. This had happened in Moray, after all, and no great distance from Darnaway.

John had to act, yes, and swiftly. He supposed that he could raise a sufficiency of armed men to ensure defeat of Buchan's lawless horde. But was that the answer? Especially while the other was still Lieutenant of the North. It could be declared to be unlawful in itself. And end in bloodshed for his people. No, the first priority was to have that lieutenancy stripped from him, and then seek Albany's aid in taking the necessary steps to enforce law and authority on his errant brother, in the king's name. Marjory agreed with this. She would accompany her husband on his mission.

So it must be south again, and this most readily and swiftly by ship. But the new monarch was known to be living at his favourite home of Rothesay, however inconvenient this for the nation's affairs, Albany basing himself on Perth. So sailing to the Tay estuary was of little avail. It would have to be up and around the northern tip of Scotland, by the Pentland Firth, and then down southwards through Donald of the Isles' area and seaboard, a lengthy voyage. But better that than to see Albany first at Perth, they judged, and then have to ride across the country, to take ship again at the Clyde in order to reach Bute. Only the monarch could make or unmake a Lieutenant of the North.

Only one of the Moray Firth skippers knew the north-about waters, and the difficult passage of the Pentland Firth, and thereafter of the Sea of the Hebrides. So he had to be fetched from Burghead to take over their vessel, entailing some delay. But eventually they set off on their far from welcome journey, even though it was all to do with Marjory's peculiar brothers.

The sail northwards to reach that Pentland Firth, between mainland Scotland and the Orkney Isles, took longer than the one hundred and forty miles would normally have demanded, for Ewan the shipmaster was not going to risk facing the notoriously dangerous passage of that firth in darkness. They turned in therefore to Wick, to lie up overnight, the south-westerly breeze having aided them so far.

With dawn they sailed the further dozen miles northwards to round the great Duncansby Head, and so to turn westwards into very different conditions, where the Atlantic Ocean and the Norse Sea joined, and this in the comparatively narrow funnel between the Scots mainland and Orkney, a mere six miles across at the narrowest point. This forced the greater ocean swells, reaching the shallower eastern seas, into fierce tide-races and swirling currents, these made the more challenging by the different levels of the seabed. Moreover, islets littered the firth, round which the waters had to swirl, forming what were known as roosts, that is great whirlpools. Altogether a major navigational hazard for almost a score of miles, apt to be avoided by cautious sea-farers, especially as the prevailing winds tended to be south-westerly, demanding much tacking to and fro when heading as they were.

The dipping and rolling, lurching and swaying, left the passengers, indeed most of the present crewmen, in no doubts as to the hazards confronting them. But the man Ewan seemed alertly confident, and manoeuvred his vessel to good effect, sometimes seeming almost to backtrack and circle, more especially when passing the quite large island of Stroma in mid-firth. The Orkneys appeared closer on the right than did the cliff-girt Caithness coast on the left.

Marjory, clutching ropes and stays to keep herself upright, seemed exhilarated rather than frightened by it all,
to her husband's acclaim.

John himself had not realised quite how long a passage
was involved in this due westerly progress to Cape Wrath,
the corresponding headland to Duncansby at the other end
of the mainland, a full eighty miles, which in these conditions took them the entire day, although their progress
did improve the further west they went. Their skipper told
them that he was determined to get round and southwards
for a dozen miles or so beyond Cape Wrath, to be able to
shelter for the night in the inlet of Loch Inchard, behind
islets there – for the Sea of the Hebrides had to be treated
with almost as much respect as did the Pentland Firth.
John began to wonder whether they might have been
better to go all the infinitely longer way down and round
England and up the Irish Sea to gain their objective.

Once past the cape, the ship's motion changed markedly
from pitching and heaving to a steady sideways rolling,
back and forth, back and forth, in the long Atlantic flow.

They were not long in reaching, down a very rugged
coast, the ingoing of the looked-for Loch Inchard, where
they could draw in and lie up, in the dusk.

The next day's sailing southwards, with the great Outer
Hebridean Isle of Lewis on their right now, and in sight,
was less difficult, fairly open waters at this stage, that is for
some sixty miles, past many mainland headlands and deep
sea lochs but amongst no major isles. Then, with the
mighty mountains of Skye soaring ahead of them, their
skipper said that they had to choose their route. They
could continue on due southwards through the Inner
Sound, between Skye and the lesser isles of Rona and
Raasay and the Applecross peninsula, to pass long Skye
eastwards by the Kyles of Lochalsh and Rhea and the
Sound of Sleat; or, swinging westwards, by the Little
Minch, in more open waters, to pass it, and then on by
Rhum and Eigg, Coll and Tiree and so down onwards
round Mull, Jura and Islay, to reach Kintyre and even-

tually the Firth of Clyde. Which? The former was the shorter route, but the latter the less demanding as regards navigation, and the overfalls and down-draughts of these Hebridean waters.

John chose the outer, longer, but less complicated journey.

Whatever else, it made for dramatic vistas, of huge and jagged blue mountains, white cockle-shell sandy beaches and colourful seaweed-hung skerries and reefs such as they did not see on their eastern coasts, the Cuillins of Skye dominating the scene for many miles. But no major tacking or diversions were called for, and they sailed on at a good pace, however much they rolled, and Ewan from Burghead did not find it necessary to move inshore and lie up overnight in these circumstances. So they were able to keep sailing southwards without stopping.

That is, until two days later they were off the west coast of Jura, near the lesser isle of Colonsay, when three dragon-prowed longships came racing out to them, under sail and urgent oars, to hail them, and demand who dared to sail these waters without Donald, King of the Isles' consent? On John's reply that it was the Earl of Moray on his way to visit King Robert at Rothesay of Bute, there was a pause, and then a curt command that they must sail to Islay, where the Lord Donald was presently based, to obtain his permission to proceed. John shouted that certainly this would be forthcoming, that he had King Robert's sister aboard, and that he was friendly with Donald. He would be glad to see him at Islay.

So, escorted by the longships, they sailed on the further score of miles, to enter the Sound of Islay, between that isle and long Jura, where, halfway down, they were led into the haven of Askaig, and told to disembark.

Leaving their shipmen, John and Marjory were taken up a quite steep hill track for some distance by fierce-looking Islesmen, and into low grassy hills where, after perhaps a couple of miles, they came to a standing stone of Pictish days at the foot of a fair-sized loch in which there were two islets, one occupied by a small castle and the other by a little chapel. Boats were moored at a jetty, and in one of these they were rowed out to the castle-isle.

There they found Phemia, Donald's wife, who needless to say exclaimed in great surprise at the sight of her kinswoman and John, but with no lack of welcome. Hearing their account of it all, she apologised for their forced attendance, but declared herself glad it had brought them to Islay. She explained that she and Donald were here only temporarily, their normal homes being at the larger castles of Aros and Ardtornish in Mull and Morvern. This Finlaggan of Islay was, in fact, the caput or justiciary seat of the Lordship of the Isles, and here Donald had had to come to sit in judgment over a dispute between the islanders of Tiree and Coll over shell-fishing rights. He was presently at Bowmore, Islay's main township, but ought to be back shortly, and would be much pleased to see their visitors.

So they were kindly entertained, but did not have long to wait before Donald arrived, and expressed himself delighted to see them, however regrettable the manner of their coming. His people looked upon these seas as very much their own and tended to be suspicious of visiting vessels, as possibly Irish or Orkney raiders.

When they told Donald of the object of their voyage to Rothesay, he was understanding and approving of their mission to the king. He declared that he well knew of Alexander of Buchan's shameful activities, indeed was concerned over them, for some of his depredations had spilled over into the lands of clans that paid homage to himself; and he had wondered what he should do about it. So John and Marjory could add his voice to their own to King Robert and Albany in this matter.

Indeed, as talk progressed – for it was late afternoon, and the involuntary guests should spend the night at the castle – their host produced more positive proposals. He would accompany them to Rothesay, to back their cause with the king. And, since they could get there more swiftly in one of his longships, they could send their own vessel back to Inverness from here, the way they had come. After seeing the monarch, he, Donald, could take them across Clyde to Renfrew, where they could obtain horses to carry them on to Perth to see Albany, and from there ride back to Moray much more readily and speedily than returning by sea.

This seemed an excellent arrangement, and Phemia announced that she would also accompany them, to see her ageing mother and an unwed sister.

So it was agreed, and word sent back to Askaig for Ewan to return with the ship north-abouts, now escorted by a longship to ensure safe passage.

They spent a pleasant night at Finlaggan Castle. In the morning they enjoyed the experience, travelling in a dragon-prowed longship, Donald's own large craft, with its score of oarsmen, all bare-chested and chanting as they pulled on their sweeps to the beat of a gong, the great square sail hoisted and bearing the symbol of the Galley of the Isles. The two women did seem distinctly incongruous thereon.

The speed of the vessel was remarkable. Well might such be called the greyhounds of the seas. John reckoned that they were going fully twice as fast as one of his ships could sail even under the best of conditions. Donald estimated that they had some one hundred and twenty-five miles to cover, past the foot of Islay, then across and down the west coast of the long peninsula of Kintyre to round its mull, and then up the eastern side by the Kilbrannan Sound, to turn the north tip of Arran and enter the Firth of Clyde, and so up to Rothesay. They could cover it all in ten hours, he assessed – which seemed scarcely believable; so leaving at sun-up, they ought to be there well before dusk.

It made for exciting voyaging, the two women not complaining at the constant film of spray descending on them from the oar-strokes, nor the strong smell of male sweat from the grunting rowers. Donald pointed out to them sundry landmarks on the way, the smaller isles of

Gigha and Cara, two more of his castles at Kinlochkerran and Dunaverty, the great sandy bays of this Kintyre peninsula, the beetling cliffs of the mull thereof, which marked the southern limits of his lordship, and, once round that mighty headland, the high mountains of Arran far ahead, these well known to his guests but never before seen from the Kilbrannan Sound, called after St Brendan, one of Columba's brother-missionaries.

Bute reached in even better time than foretold, they sailed up to Rothesay, no doubt looked on askance by local fishermen who hastily pulled out of the way of the dreaded Islesmen.

Landing at Rothesay haven, to more alarmed staring, the four of them climbed up to the castle within its deep and wide circular moat. They had no difficulty in gaining access, the present King of Scots apparently little concerned with security.

Robert the Third – John had difficulty in thinking of him as other than Carrick – appeared to be quite pleased to see his sister, Annabella the Queen the more warm in her welcoming, although even she eyed Donald a little doubtfully, their five children excited by the visitors.

When it came to the object of the visit, and brother Alexander's behaviour, the king was not greatly exercised about it all, indicating that it was unfortunate, but that Robert of Albany ought to see to it all. John and Donald did persuade him, however, to cancel Buchan's appointment as Lieutenant of the North. Whether this would greatly concern the Wolf, or cause him to alter his ways in any degree, was doubtful; but at least it ought to make any action against him not contrary to law and privilege. Apart from that, the monarch left the said action to others. Scotland, it was to be feared, now had a distinctly feeble liege-lord.

They spent only two days at Rothesay, in the circumstances. They found the sons David and James taking after their mother rather than their sire and quite lively youths; and the three daughters, Margaret, Mary and Elizabeth, quietly pleasant girls.

Thereafter Donald took them up Clyde to Renfrew, and they saw the queen-mother and various of her many offspring. Archdeacon Thomas was there again, and he found John and Marjory suitable horses to take them on to Perth. Donald would not accompany them further; he did not like Albany, and doubted whether his presence would assist their mission.

Next day, then, they parted, on excellent terms, Donald promising to keep in touch with John over possible joint action against Alexander.

The ride to Perth, by Glasgow, Kirkintilloch, Cumbernauld, Stirling and Dunblane, eighty-odd miles, took them a day and a half, halting at Cambuskenneth Abbey overnight, where John had stayed more than once before. At St John's Town they found that Albany, who was apparently making Scone Abbey his base these days, was visiting the Thane of Glamis, up in Strathmore, but was expected back next day. So they repaired to Scone, where they were comfortably entertained. Being married to a king's daughter and sister could always help even the Earl of Moray.

When Albany duly returned, he did not actually express himself as glad to see his sister and her husband, but on learning of their objective, admitted that he was concerned over the reports of his brother Alexander's behaviour, and agreed that something would have to be done. This of the lieutenancy cancellation was good, as far as it went, but Alexander might well not let that restrain him, for it was doubtful whether he had ever put any great value on the appointment anyway. He, Albany, would send an envoy up to Badenoch to order an end to the savageries and ravishings; but something more would almost certainly have to be done.

When John mentioned that Donald of the Isles was angered by it and prepared to help in seeking to right matters, the duke was less than appreciative. They wanted no interference in mainland affairs by that one and his barbarous folk, he asserted. They could do without his aid.

John, and Marjory also, said that they considered this a mistaken attitude, that Donald was well disposed to the mainland regime, and could be a useful ally. But Albany dismissed that. Once let the Islesmen loose in the Highlands and they might well have difficulty in ejecting them again. No, it was up to Moray and Ross to deal with any breaches of the peace in their earldoms. *They* must see to this of Alexander.

How far was he to go in the matter, then? John demanded.

Take whatever steps were necessary, he was told briefly, this no great help, especially against one of the royal family. Marjory sought more explicit recommendations, but obtained none.

They did not linger in Albany's company, and fairly soon set out on their long ride home, John very unsure as to what was going to be required of him.

27

Arrival at Darnaway had them nowise relieved in their minds. The Wolf had been busy in their absence, and all the north buzzed with it. Angered by the Bishop of Moray's protestations and pronouncements against him, Buchan had descended on Elgin in force, and there actually burned the great cathedral, together with the church of St Giles, the Maison Dieu hospital, eighteen canons' manses, the houses of many chaplains and St Lazarus monks, and much else, terrorising the populace, sacking and ravishing. The renowned Lantern of the North had been lighted in terrible fashion indeed.

Appalled, John and his wife gazed at each other. What, in God's good name, was to be done about this?

They promptly went to the city to view the havoc, and seek to comfort the victims. And they found it all even worse than they had anticipated. The townsfolk were in dread and panic, fearing even further assault. Damaged buildings were everywhere. The cathedral, famed all over the land, was now a roofless, blackened ruin, its three tall towers damaged, its aisles wrecked, its windows all gone. The still more ancient St Giles, known as the Muckle Kirk, was all but demolished; hospices, manses and houses destroyed. Such ferocity against Holy Church had never before been seen in Scotland. It left the beholders all but speechless.

John did not know where to begin in seeking to commiserate and lament with the populace, not only with the churchmen, to express his horror, and to promise all possible help and succour, and what could be done to avenge it all. He and Marjory felt utterly inadequate.

"He ought to be excommunicated!" she declared. "This is beyond all, even for Alex. Excommunicated!"

"Think you that would greatly concern Alexander? He can care nothing for any religion, to do this."

"No. But excommunication, I am told, can direly hurt and wreck any man's life, whether he believes or not. Think of it, John. Excommunicated, he could not receive any of the Church's services, for himself or his family. Even Christian burial. He would become an outlaw, denied all rights, *dead* before the law. None permitted to deal with him. Could hold no office in any Christian land. His signature and seal made worthless. Oh, and much else. Even Alex could not face that!"

"Mmm. Perhaps, yes. Certainly it might aid me in any action I have to take against him . . ."

"We must go and see Bishop Bur at Spynie. Urge him to it."

"Could he do it himself? Or have to get it pronounced by the Vatican?"

"I know not, for sure. But we can find out . . ."

Having done all that they could at Elgin, which amounted to little indeed meantime, the couple rode the two miles northwards down Lossie, to the bishop's palace-castle. This they discovered to be shut and barred, but locals told them that the prelate was in fact within. He feared attack by the Earl of Buchan, and hoped to withstand siege.

Shaking his head, John went over to the moat's edge and blew on his horn. And when eventually he saw faces at a window, shouted that here were the Earl and Countess of Moray come to see Bishop Alexander. Open to them.

Possibly it was only the sight of a woman there that gained them entry, after some delay. They found the prelate in a great state of agitation and alarm, but thankful to see John, all but incoherent in his apprehension and anxiety, and convinced that the Wolf would come and treat him as he had treated his cathedral and shrine and subordinates. It took the visitors some time to calm him down.

When they came to the proposal for excommunication, Alexander threw up his hands in horror. No, no, he exclaimed, that would but bring down Buchan upon him in further fury forthwith, nothing more sure. It would be as much as his very life was worth!

They averred otherwise, saying that the threat of it might well achieve an end to these outrages and terrors, Marjory again recounting some of the drastic effects implicit in the pronouncement of the anathema and ban. Could the bishop himself announce it? Or had it to be issued by the Pope himself?

Alexander admitted that, yes, he could excommunicate. But he dreaded to contemplate it against this enemy of his, a prince of the royal line. Had he and his not suffered enough without risking further calamity and destruction?

John sought to assure him that he would provide strong guards to ensure protection in the event of Buchan continuing with his assaults and oppressions. He would arrange with his vassal lairds to be prepared to shelter and defend Spynie Castle with their utmost powers at all times. This he would see to forthwith. But it was surely to be hoped that the like would not be necessary, with excommunication impending.

Marjory added that, with the king and the Duke of Albany condemning her wayward brother and commanding obedience, Holy Church's malison should be sufficient to end the troubles. That, and hopefully pay compensation for the ill done.

Reluctantly and still very doubtfully, Bishop Alexander accepted these assurances. He would be prepared to declare excommunication if a promise to cease the outrages was not forthcoming.

So far, so good. But husband and wife were by no means so optimistic as they sounded.

They did not delay in paying another visit to Alexander, little as they relished the prospect. This time, they took a large company of mounted Moraymen with them, some two hundred, under Brodie, Ogstoun and some of the

Comyn landholders – these greatly resenting the transfer of the Comyn earldom of Buchan to the crown – to emphasise the message.

Leaving all these at Lochindorb's shore, under the very hostile regard of such of Alexander's caterans as were presently occupying the castleton there, John and Marjory were rowed out to the island.

Their reception there was typically mocking in its false brotherly welcome, although the Lady Mariota behaved more respectfully, even if her sons copied their father in manners.

The Morays well recognised that there was no point in beating about the bush. "We come, my lord Alexander, in pain, wrath and indeed shame, that you, a brother of the King's Grace, should have done what you have, in our absence, to our town of Elgin, and to Holy Church's shrines and properties there, the great cathedral itself destroyed and the people ravaged," John declared, without delay. "And we come not only with our own condemnation, and that of the churchmen, but that of the king and the Duke of Albany. It is almost beyond belief!"

"They called for the like!" Alexander declared. "I will not be afflicted by clerks!"

"The said clerks have their powers," Marjory observed.

"Words! Curses! Mouthings! To such I am deaf! But not to their insults and intrusions in my affairs."

"Your lawless acts have already cost you your Lieutenancy of the North," John added. "The king's, and your other brother the duke's, ire and condemnation. Now, there could be . . . worse!"

"You say so? What?"

"Excommunication!"

Even Buchan's snort of contempt was not quite loud enough to cover Mariota's gasp of alarm.

"More words! The haverings of little men!"

"But words of power and pain and punishment, my lord. Consider well before you dismiss what excommunication can do. You would become as good as dead, in law.

Dead — yet denied Christian burial! You and yours. Barred, not only by the Church but by the realm itself, from holding any office or position or title. Cease to be a prince or an earl. An outlaw. A leper indeed amongst men! Your family also. Are you prepared to face that? All that?"

Marjory took up the challenge. "All who would still choose to serve you to come under the ban. None must buy or sell with you. These sons and daughters of yours could not marry. And you are to be condemned in the hereafter, the next life. How say you to that, Alex?"

Her brother, lips tight, eyed her but did not speak.

Mariota de Athyn did so. She cried aloud, "No! No! No! Alex — no! Not that! You cannot . . . you *must* not. Not excommunicated! Never that."

Even the listening sons looked concerned.

"You, you should not believe all this," Alexander got out, less than assuredly. "They make the most of it. Seeking to affright us."

"We do not," his sister asserted. "We have been gaining sure word on this. It is as ill as we say. Worse. You become outcasts of mankind."

Mariota reached out to grasp Alexander's arm. "It must not be!" she declared, voice breaking.

He shrugged, and patted her hand. "As you will, woman! As you will." He looked at his sister, not John. "What must be done, then? To avoid all this?"

Marjory drew a deep breath. "Announce your . . . regrets, I would say. Swear that there will be no more of your villainies and savageries. Not only against the Church, but against all men. And pay some redress, some reparation. You will learn . . ."

"Some penance will have to be performed, I think," John added. "Some act of contrition."

"I will not bow and plead to clerks!" he was told. "Nothing will make me do that. I am Alexander Stewart!"

Marjory shook her head over him. "You agree, then, to end your wicked ways, your cruelties and assaults? Your attacks on the churchmen. And make payment in some measure. You swear it?"

He inclined his head, scowling.

"A nod is not enough, Alex. Swear it, I say."

"Do so," Mariota beseeched.

"Very well. I swear."

"So be it," John said. "We are all witnesses to that. We will inform Bishop Alexander. And request that he forbears in this of excommunication. And the Bishop of Ross likewise." He paused. "And, my lord, I advise that you disband most of your wild men, in token. And see that hereafter they keep the peace."

That produced no response.

Marjory turned to Mariota. "*You* see the rights of it all, whatever he does. Hold him to it, for all your sakes. And for the sake of others also, many others. And you will earn the thanks of that many, and of us all."

"It, it does not mean that he will have to go . . . to his countess, does it?"

"I think not, no. That was not spoken of." And she got a faint smile as they turned away, the only smile of the day.

John inclined his head to the woman, and followed his wife out. There was nothing to wait for, nothing more usefully to say, their unwanted and trying task accomplished, they must assume.

There were no goodbyes, other than Mariota's whispered ones.

Nevertheless, husband and wife did thankfully congratulate each other thereafter as they rode off homewards.

28

The relief of Bishop Bur when he was told that he did not have to pronounce excommunication on the Wolf was all but comic, he practically embracing Marjory when she told him so. John began to doubt, indeed, whether the prelate would have issued the dread anathema at all, so fearful had he been of the possible consequences. Even the matter of compensation, however vague, scarcely seemed to register with him at first, although later he began to assess and calculate. As for some suitable penance for the transgressor, he was prepared to leave that to others; indeed it was Marjory's suggestion that her brother should go to Albany at Scone to confirm his submission and promise of better behaviour, and there might be allotted some suitable act of contrition. Whether the Bishop of Ross, less close to Buchan's base, would be equally eased and content with it all, remained to be seen.

Since it was only themselves, and his own family, who had heard and witnessed Alexander's swearing to end his savageries, John and Marjory felt that they had to announce it officially, as it were; and while this ought to be done before the king himself, the present monarch being but little concerned, and Albany in effect ruling the land, it had better be to Scone that they went, both agreed. They would sail down to the Tay for this, to spare them more lengthy riding. They decided to take Thomas, Master of Moray, with them, he now old enough to be involving himself, in some measure, in the national affairs. One day he would be Earl of Moray, after all.

The late June weather ensured a pleasant voyage, and they had to spend only the one night aboard. At Scone, their arrival was greeted by Albany with rather more in the way of welcome than heretofore, he wishing to hear of the situation regarding his errant brother, and even somewhat interested to meet his nephew, whom he had never before set eyes on. What impression young Thomas made on him was not to be known; but that youth later told his parents that he thought his Uncle Robert would be a good man to avoid hereafter.

The information they were able to impart regarding the other uncle clearly relieved the duke. He expressed no gratitude for their efforts in the matter, but declared that this of the threat of excommunication had been useful in the circumstances, although not one to encourage the churchmen to make use of hereafter, since it might well give them over-much power in affairs of state, many of them being too much that way inclined already. But in this case its effectiveness made its use acceptable. This was as near to praise as that man was ever likely to get.

He agreed that some act of penance should be required of his brother, to emphasise the situation. He would have some suitable act performed, and here, at Scone, in his own presence, which ought to be effective in restraining Alexander from further indiscretions, and in making him aware where power lay in this kingdom, rather than at Rothesay Castle. He would invite some of his and Marjory's brothers and kin to witness it, but not others outwith the royal family, since it would not do to have any public humiliation of one of the monarch's brothers.

So worked the gubernatorial mind.

Albany informed them of a further decision of his own, to which he had apparently got the king's agreement, and which would help to keep Buchan, and indeed all Moray, in order. His own son Murdoch, Master of Albany, was to be made Justiciar of the North, not lieutenant, the which he would keep in his own hands meantime, but which would emphasise the royal authority and help to keep the Ross situation and those wretched Islesmen in their place. John did not like the sound of this, but he was not in a position to denounce it. He hoped that it would not affect his own powers and concerns in Moray, nor interfere with his friendship and all-but alliance with Donald of the Isles.

It was Marjory who intervened here, and declared that, since Moray was very much part of the north, it would be most unfortunate if her nephew Murdoch was to be put in a position to interfere, as justiciar, in matters of law in their earldom. Since, apparently, the next generation was now being allotted powers and status in affairs, she might approach the king to give some corresponding authority to her own and John's son, Thomas, here.

Albany, eyeing her almost warily, conceded that something such might well be suitable. Suppose that the Master was made Sheriff of Moray and Inverness? Would that serve?

Thomas blinked at this, his father looking bemused, but Marjory nodded agreeably. That would be convenient, she said, in this situation. So much for bringing their son south with them.

John, for one, was always glad when he was on his way back to Moray, his son now considerably doubtful about his mother's initiative and his new responsibilities as a sheriff.

They won home to learn of new problems arising to affect them, especially, as it happened, in regard to lawlessness and a sheriff's concerns.

Clan feuding was endemic in much of the Highlands, and not to be taken too seriously by the authorities of law and order, who preferred the unruly clans to be allowed to get on with their own affairs, bloody or otherwise, so long as these did not seriously affect their more law-abiding neighbours. But now, it seemed, fairly dire fighting had broken out between the Clan Chattan federation, which included Mackintoshes, Cattanachs, Shaws, Farquharsons and MacPhails, assailed by the large Mackay grouping and its various septs from the north, Raes, MacCullochs and Munroes. What this warfare was about was uncertain, but the scale of the hostilities was larger and more grievous than usual. And, unfortunately, the Mackays were reported to be aided and encouraged by Alastair Carrach, a younger brother of Donald of the Isles, who was basing himself on mainland Lochaber. Here was an embarrassing development. The Mackintosh was John's friend, and important in Moray's uplands. The situation could not be ignored. Young Thomas was quite alarmed, thinking that *he* might be called upon to act in the matter. However, he was not actually sheriff yet, only nominated, so . . .

Marjory remarked that perhaps they had been too hasty in bringing the Wolf into subjection? For if he had remained in his former aggressive and violent state, almost certainly he would have taken a hand in this, and shown who was master in these clan territories, and seen off the Mackays.

John was worried, especially over this of Donald's brother being involved. He did not delay in riding down to Moy to see the Mackintosh. He found that chief much concerned. There had been major raiding from across the Great Glen, with bloodshed, ravaging, women raped and abducted, cattle stolen and the like, greatly in excess of the normal feuding, the Shaws and Farquharsons the worst sufferers. This Alastair Carrach of the Isles seemed to be involved in much of it, with his MacDonalds, just why was not clear. The Mackays and their allies were mainly Easter Ross people, not Wester, and not normally under the influence of the Islesmen. He, Mackintosh, would have to muster all Clan Chattan, and probably the Grants' forces also, to deal with this if it continued. The Ross earldom appeared to be quite useless in maintaining order amongst its folk.

John promised to do all that he could to right matters. He supposed that his most effective course was to go and see Donald and urge him to deal with and restrain this brother of his.

Back at Darnaway, Marjory felt that a visit to Islay or wherever Donald might be at present would take John

303

away from his earldom for overlong. He had been absent from it a lot recently, with his many other activities. Why not send Thomas instead, with a message, as the new sheriff-to-be. It would be quite good for him to take on some responsible tasks; and Donald would heed him as his father's son.

That made good sense. Thomas expressed himself as quite interested to make the land and sea journey to the Hebrides, better than any sitting in judgment in some court at Inverness hearing boring details of petty law-breaking. He was instructed to ride down the Great Glen, with a small escort, to the foot of Loch Lochy and the Clunes and Arkaig area, where the Cameron chief at Achnacarry was friendly with both John and Donald, and would surely provide him with a boat and crew to sail down the firth of Loch Linnhe and so to Islay. He might have to go on elsewhere in the Isles seeking their lord, but no doubt a longship would take him on his quest – quite a notable errand for the young man. He departed hopefully.

The Mackintosh, whose Moy was none so far from Lochindorb, had told John that the Wolf had recently gone south, to the relief of all. His sons, not noted either for their good behaviour, were being somewhat subdued, this likewise appreciated.

John had a sufficiency of less dramatic matters awaiting his attention, to keep him occupied for the three weeks until Thomas arrived back from the west. That one was very pleased with himself. He had not found the Lord Donald at Islay, and had had to sail north to the castle of Aros on the Isle of Mull, and there had convinced him of the need for strong and speedy action to correct his brother Alastair. Donald had promised to see to it forthwith, and had been much angered by the information brought. Moreover, he would have orders sent to the Mackays and their friends to cease their raiding into Moray, or pay for it dearly. He sent his regrets to John.

So that was satisfactory.

John and Marjory paid a visit to Spynie, and there learned from the bishop that he had heard from his fellow-prelate that the Countess of Ross, much relieved over the Buchan situation, was asking her bishop now to go ahead with the petition to the Vatican for the annulment of her empty marriage, so that she might wed a chosen husband. Just who this was to be was not stated. She was most grateful to the Earl and Countess of Moray for their success with Buchan.

It occurred to John that those aggressive Mackays and their allies might be further dissuaded from southwards invasions by pressure from the north as well as Donald's from the west. These clans occupied much land up in Sutherland, even as far as the Reay country of Caithness, the two furthest north of all Scotland's earldoms, this as well as territory in Easter Ross. There was a young Earl of Sutherland who had recently succeeded a long-ailing father. If he could be persuaded to threaten the Mackays with retribution if they did not cease their depredations, that could be very effective. Indeed, with the Countess of Ross's gratitude, the three earldoms of Moray, Ross and Sutherland might form some sort of partnership, especially with Donald of the Isles' co-operation, so that all the north might be able to look forward to a highly unusual period of peace and prosperity.

John decided to go and see the new Sutherland.

The main Sutherland seat was Dunrobin Castle near Golspie, some forty-five miles north of Inverness as the crows flew, but more than twice that on horseback, with the firths of Beauly, Cromarty and Dornoch to be got round. So it was best to go by ship, a mere half-day's voyage from Inverness. He would take Thomas with him, and young Alexander, who would enjoy the jaunt.

They sailed up the so indented coastline in one of their small vessels, past the Black Isle of Cromarty, Tarbat Ness, Dornoch and Loch Fleet, to Golspie haven, from which they could see Dunrobin Castle on higher ground a mere mile or so to the north, a tall fortalice. Disembarking, and asking at the harbour as to whether the earl was at home presently, they were told that he was, but in fact that they had probably passed him on their way in, for he was this day engaged in one of his favourite pastimes of fishing for flounders offshore. Small boats out there were pointed out to them. So they re-embarked, and sailed out, with a fisherman, who had been mending his nets, to guide them, he presently pointing out his lord's little craft, with only two men in it.

It was a strange way for two earls to meet.

They found a couple of young men holding lines over a boat's sides, both quite roughly clad, with nothing to indicate which was the master and possibly the servant. But a shout from John had one gesturing, a slender, dark-haired individual in his early twenties, asking who they were to come thus close? When he was answered that it was John, Earl of Moray to see the Earl Robert of Sutherland, that produced astonishment and the hasty pulling in of fishing-lines and manning of oars.

The smaller boat was rowed alongside the larger, and a rope-ladder lowered to allow the fishers to climb aboard, with a rope holding their craft.

The two young men proved to be very much alike, fairly obviously kin. John held out a hand and introduced himself. The one taking his hand said that he was Robert, son of William son of William, and that this was his brother, Kenneth of Forse. He had heard much of his lordship of Moray, son of Black Agnes of Dunbar, and husband of the king's sister. He welcomed him to Sutherland, in however unsuitable fashion. He was told that they regretted spoiling his sport, but had come over matters of some import to both their earldoms. John introduced his two sons.

They sailed, with the boat in tow, not back to the haven but northwards some way to a jetty close to the castle's mound, to moor there.

Dunrobin proved to be a place strong rather than palatial, and conditions therein distinctly basic, with just

306

the two brothers residing, mother and father dead, with a minimum of servitors. But the visitors were made welcome enough, however unused their hosts might be to entertaining.

John did not delay in getting down to the subject of the unruly Mackays, and found this Robert quite agreeable to co-operate in restraining them. He declared that he knew that they were a wild lot, under their present chief's sons, especially the Caithness ones. He admitted that this of occupying lands in two earldoms complicated the problem, especially with the Caithness situation. John knew something of this, for the present Earl of Caithness was none other than David, Earl Palatine of Strathearn, another of Marjory's many brothers. The last of the ancient line of earls, linked to Orkney, had died leaving only two daughters; and the late King Robert had given the earldom to this David. But he, having lands all over the kingdom, over and above Strathearn, more or less ignored this northern territory, and apparently any authority in Caithness was exercised by the husband of the younger of the daughters, Sir William Sinclair of Roslin, this last in faraway Lothian. Sinclair was trying to keep some order in the north, but clearly not very successfully, hence the Mackays' ungoverned behaviour.

The Earl Robert said that he would speak with Sinclair and see what could be done to improve the situation. He imagined that that man would be glad to have help in keeping the peace in all the north. He would be heartened probably to hear of Donald of the Isles' involvement.

All this seemed satisfactory, as far as it went, and John saw no point in lingering. He suggested that Earl Robert should come and see him at Darnaway when he had something to report, especially over Caithness, and they would decide on joint action.

They parted, John content enough. He well liked these two brothers, however simple their style. They were back at Inverness just before darkness, Thomas and Alexander looking on it all as something of a holiday.

Robert of Sutherland proved as good as his word. Exactly a week later he arrived at Darnaway, with his brother, to announce that he had seen Sir William Sinclair at Dunbeath, and he had been well pleased to learn of the proposed compact between the earldoms, and would co-operate. Those Mackays, and others, well merited a lesson in behaviour, and he would act in concert with Sutherland and Moray in providing it. If Ross and the Islesmen also aided in the united effort, he could not see the errant clans continuing with their warfare.

John saw his concept of a partnership of earldoms coming to fruition, and thus greater than he had at first visualised. Probably never before had all north of Atholl, Mar and Argyll been known to act in concert.

Marjory congratulated her husband on his vision and initiative.

The two Sutherland brothers stayed for a few days at Darnaway, visiting Mackintosh at Moy and Grant at Rothiemurchus, to inform them and emphasise the improved situation. They were interested in seeing much of Moray, for, after all, their family name emanated from there, it being de Moravia, they being descendants of the famous Freskin thereof. They were interested in more than that indeed, daughter Mabella clearly appealing to them both, and she, now of seventeen years, not averse to their attentions. When they left for Dunrobin it was with suggestions that they would probably require to come back before long, in order to ensure co-operative action.

John and Marjory smiled to each other.

29

John, awaiting results from his efforts to pacify the north, received what amounted to a command from Albany to involve himself again in affairs further south. He was to attend a council at Scone, on important matters. Less than joyfully, he went again, by ship.

There, at the abbey, which had in fact become all but the seat of government of Scotland, displacing Edinburgh's Holyrood, he found himself to have been made a member of a small group, being called the Especial Council by Albany. This was not the official Privy or Secret Council of the realm, of which John indeed was a long-standing member, but a selection of Albany's own. It appeared that, with the king's inaction, all but sloth as the duke called it, Queen Annabella was taking a more active part in the nation's affairs, largely, it was said, to promote the position and influence of her eldest son, David, Duke of Rothesay, this against that of Albany his uncle. And she was being supported in this by the new Primate, Walter Trail, Bishop of St Andrews, and by Archibald the Grim, now Earl of Douglas, with not a few of the established councillors favouring her. So Albany was setting up this alternative and smaller council, it consisting of his brother, Walter, Lord of Brechin, an illegitimate half-brother Sir William Stewart of Jedburgh; Sir David Lindsay of Glenesk, a prominent magnate; and someone of whom John had never heard, a Sir John Ramorgny, from Fife, who must have some importance; and himself. He was distinctly concerned to find himself included in this grouping, which was apparently formed largely to counter the queen's party which, if he had to support either faction, he would have chosen, for he liked and admired Annabella considerably better than he did Albany. But the latter, ever well informed, had heard of his northern activities and the compact between the four earldoms there, and evidently decided that John would be a useful supporter.

This meeting was brought together basically to deal with the situation in England. Richard the Second had won the active support of the Earl of Hereford, the aged John of Gaunt's son and heir, a notable, effective and popular member of the Plantagenet line, who had returned from a crusade, and was much concerned with that realm's state. He was a great protagonist of the ideas of chivalry and knightly flourish. This was resulting in an access of strength for Richard and the declension of the Lords Appellant. Now this Hereford was advocating closer ties with Scotland, and emphasising the peace treaty as a permanency. Which was, of course, satisfactory. He, in Richard's name, was suggesting some demonstration of this bond of peace, and Albany was in agreement. So were Annabella and her friends, apparently, and in this matter they could co-operate. Albany proposed a joint embassage to London. The Earl of Moray, known to be friendly with the queen, and Sir David Lindsay, he being called the foremost knight in Scotland, were to go to Rothesay to see Annabella and seek to arrange this, and thereafter take part in the said embassage.

John was quite prepared to do this, seeing it as something of a help in uniting the two sides in the realm. He was also interested to meet and associate with Lindsay, of whom he had heard much.

While at Scone he learned that Alexander of Buchan, after making his penance at the Blackfriars Church in Perth, had, at Albany's direction, retired to Kinfauns Castle, none so far off in the Carse of Gowrie, where his brother could keep an eye on him. There he had been joined by Mariota de Athyn, but unfortunately their sons were still up at Lochindorb. John would have preferred them to be further from *his* territory.

So he and Lindsay, with whom he got on well, set off on horseback for Renfrew, where they would get a vessel to take them to the inconveniently placed Rothesay of Bute, John telling his own shipmaster to sail to the Forth and up the firth to Airth, the nearest fair-sized haven to Stirling, there to wait for him.

Meantime he and Lindsay rode by Dunblane, Stirling, Cumbernauld and Glasgow to Renfrew where, to their surprise, they found that they did not have to go on to Rothesay, for the queen was in residence at Renfrew Castle at present, the old Stewart home, and her sons David and James with her. On the way, Lindsay had told him that, although he was known as of Glenesk, up in Angus, his family originated in Lothian, at Luffness, where they still owned the castle, although it was left in the keepership of the Bickerton family, which had John raising his eyebrows – for it was a Bickerton from Luffness who had stabbed the Earl of Douglas in the back at the Battle of Otterburn, the battle won by a dead man.

Annabella was glad to see John and, despite her enmity and suspicions towards Albany, well enough pleased that some sort of co-operation should be established for the sake of her husband's kingdom, and this of the English gesture could signify that. She had heard of John's recent activities in the north, and his success in making the four earldoms act in concert, and much approved. She saw why Albany desired his support.

It was agreed that Hereford and old John of Gaunt should be informed that a Scottish party, representing both King Robert and the governor, would visit England in due course to represent a sealing of a permanent peace pact, it was hoped with France partaking also, this symbolising a state of amity between the three nations not hitherto known. She would ensure a worthy delegation from her side, possibly even including her son David, Duke of Rothesay, heir to the throne. She was anxious for him to assume a greater role in the realm's affairs, young as he was – and he was proving to be a strong character and with much promise. One day he would be more than a match for his uncle Albany.

All amicably settled at Renfrew, the two visitors took their leave of the queen and her sons, and rode back to Airth, where they parted, Lindsay to continue on to Scone to render his report, John to set sail for Inverness. The latter felt that it had been a worthwhile mission.

At home he learned that Marjory had had another visit from the Sutherland brothers, who came to inform that the Mackays had duly seen where their interests now lay. Sinclair and themselves had been promised due obedience and respect. They had stayed for a couple of days, Mabella the obvious attraction. So John's Moray clans could look forward to an end to raiding and savagery from across the Great Glen. Also Donald of the Isles had sent word that his brother Alastair Carrach was now removed from the mainland and sent to cool his heels in the Outer Hebrides.

The Morays, relieved, hoped that an era of comparative tranquillity lay ahead of them, deserved they trusted. The only cloud still on the horizon was the continued presence of the sons of the Wolf at Lochindorb. It was to be hoped that their father's fate would act as a restriction on their inherited impulses.

For the remainder of that year peace did prevail in the north, although the proposed embassage to England had to be postponed owing to troubles in the southern kingdom, this led by the Gloucester faction. John and Marjory enjoyed a fairly peaceful autumn and winter, although Thomas found no lack of petty crime to keep him busy at Inverness. The Sutherlands found reason for visits to assure that all went well further north, and Mabella did not hide her pleasure at their company, her preference being for Earl Robert quite evidently. It looked as though they would be having a son-in-law to add to the family before long. It was not often that daughters of earls and countesses and the like could wed for love rather than lands and position.

It was late March when the blessed period of peace and order at Darnaway was suddenly ended, and not by clan warfare, Moray involved only indirectly. It was in Mar and Angus, to the south-east, that trouble broke out. Duncan Stewart, one of the Wolf's sons, led his brothers on a wild assault on the Braes of Angus, with a host of caterans from the Monadhliath area, slaughtering, harrying and burning a wide swathe of that upland country. Why there was not known. Sir Walter Ogilvy, Sheriff of Angus, had summoned all lairds and landholders to arms to assail these invaders, these including Sir David Lindsay of Glenesk, Sir Patrick Gray of Broughty, Guthrie of that Ilk and many another, and they had marched, to meet the Highlanders at Glasclune in the Stormont. There had followed a fierce battle and, extraordinarily as it turned out, considering the quality of the Angusmen, they were soundly beaten by the caterans. These presumably used the narrows of Glen Brierachan to aid them, Ogilvy and his brother, with Guthrie and Ochterlony being slain, and even Lindsay and Gray wounded, with scores of their people, a situation scarcely to be credited. That these mountain-men should have overwhelmed a large force of knights and Lowland men-at-arms taxed the imagination. John judged that they must have made the land fight for them, as Wallace and Bruce had done almost a century before, using the narrow passes for ambushing, marshes to bog down horses, woodland to hide their numbers. It all made dire news.

John was much concerned, and not only for his wounded friend Lindsay. These aggressors were, after all, from his Moray, and he could be held, in some measure, responsible for keeping them in order.

So much for the four earldoms compact! Something must be done. The fact that the leaders were nephews of the king, however illegitimate, added to the enormity of it all.

What, then? He would send to the Mackintosh to assemble a host of Clan Chattan and Badenoch Grants, in his name, who ought to be able to fight fellow-Highlanders on their own ground, as it were. He would gather a force of his own people, Brodies, Ogstouns, Comyns and the like, to join them. And he would go and see Robert of Sutherland, to enroll his aid if possible. Surely that would be sufficient to deal with these barbarians, however fierce fighters they were?

Marjory agreed that he could do no less. Presumably the wretches had now returned to Lochindorb.

The Mackintosh sent word that he would do as directed; and that, yes, the Wolf's sons were back at their base. John asked himself why they had made this raid on Angus? It was a long way from Lochindorb. If bent on aggression and spoil they could have attacked nearer home. Was it that, aware of the Moray, Ross, Sutherland and Caithness alliance, they were being careful not to bring down such great force upon themselves, and so chose more distant prey? John could think of no other reason for it.

He visited Dunrobin Castle, and the brothers there agreed to co-operate. They could raise, say, five hundred men at short notice, and could join Moray's people whenever called upon. Was there any point in seeking Caithness help, so far north?

John thought probably not. How many men could these Stewarts muster? They had defeated quite a large force of Angusmen. When their father had burned Elgin, it was claimed that he had descended on the city with thousands; but that was probably an exaggeration. Could the sons raise as many, and more? Did they, the earldoms, have to assemble thousands also? It seemed all but inconceivable that such numbers would be needed to put down these young scoundrels. But better over-many than too few. It was left that John would send word for a hasty forgathering.

Considering it all, he decided that, as far as was possible, secrecy was desirable, this so that the Stewarts did not get to realise that they were going to be assailed in strength. It was to be presumed that they kept only a modest number

314

settled at their castleton by the lochside. That loch was the problem – but possibly also the answer. If an unexpected descent could be made on the location, and the castleton people dealt with, then the Stewart sons themselves could be isolated on their island castle. The loch itself was not so large that it could not be more or less surrounded, to prevent the besieged from sending messengers out to summon their large numbers from the upland fastnesses. But no lengthy siege was to be envisaged, for the word would get out somehow to the cateran supporters, and it might come to bloody battle.

An attack on the castle? There were only a few boats there, not enough to ferry out a sufficiency of fighters for an assault. Rafts! Was that the answer? After all, timber was in great supply none so far off, cut timber from the felling operations, this waiting to be floated down the rivers to the firth ports, down Findhorn, Spey, Divie and Lossie. If, secretly, his log-men could move timber, dragged by garrons, to hidden spots near Lochindorb without arousing suspicion, then, bound by ropes into rafts, many rafts, many men could be floated out to the island, to take it. The castle was not a large one, and there would be no sizeable garrison. Capture the Wolf's sons on it, and this without any large-scale fighting. That should be the aim. It ought to be possible.

In consultation with Brodie and Duncan Murray, the strategy was worked out. Messengers were sent to the foresters. And Mackintosh was told quietly to assemble his clansfolk at the forested area of Ferness, on Findhorn, a mere six or seven miles north of Lochindorb, with the hills of Aitnoch in between, where the Sutherland contingent could join them without much difficulty, the Moray force to approach the loch from the east. That ought to serve for a united but surprise assault. John was no seasoned warrior, but he saw this as practical tactics.

Six days thereafter, then, assemblies at Ferness and at Braemoray on the Dorback Water.

*   *   *

On St Serf's Eve, 19th April, John led a mounted company of no fewer than seven hundred down Findhorn, and then up the tributary of the Dorback, southwards the dozen miles or so to Braemoray, under the isolated peak of the Knock thereof. There they halted to await messengers from Mackintosh and Sutherland at Ferness, four miles westwards across high moorland. The word arrived fairly promptly. Their allies were assembled, and would move southwards at noon, some to take up positions on the far side of Lochindorb, some to be able to come to the assistance of the Moray force attacking the castleton, if this was necessary, all as had been arranged.

So John could order his people to advance the further six miles, at the trot, southwards – and hope and pray that the two assemblies had not been observed and reported to the castleton.

Thankfully, about an hour later, his horsemen, emerging from the Dorback valley, could see no sign of alarm or reaction amongst the cot-houses and sheds half a mile ahead. Swords drawn and lances at the ready, their trot was changed into a canter, and the seven hundred thundered down on the castleton. Even as he led the way, John could see men in large numbers, not mounted, appearing along the far side of the loch.

No battle was forthcoming. Men, and women and children also, as they heard the beat of hundreds of hooves, emerged from houses to stare, and then, wisely, to flee for woodland nearby, cattle bolting also, all clearly in no state to face a charging host. Without having to strike a blow, John went riding amongst the cottages, shacks and barns, complete surprise effected. Indeed, he felt almost foolish in bringing down his hundreds on this homestead, amongst barking dogs and scattering poultry. But their objective was gained, a large armed force able to face the castle-island in mid-loch, unopposed.

The loch was about half a mile wide, and numbers of men were now to be seen strung along the further shore. Those on the island would be well aware of this also, and perceive that no escape nor summoning of help would be possible in that direction.

John spread his men out along this shore also. Now for the rafts.

Couriers went off to hasten the foresters with their timber and ropes. There might well be no great urgency now; with this assault surprising the Lochindorb people, they could not have alerted the cateran numbers in the hills to south and west. However, that could not be taken for granted, and the sooner the attack was made on the castle the better.

There were only five boats moored beside the castleton. The raft-building would take some time. It was just conceivable that the Stewarts might see their position as hopeless and yield without a fight, even if not very likely. So, with Robert of Sutherland come riding along to them, John suggested that they, and some others, might pull out in a couple of the boats, to challenge the castle's occupants to surrender, emphasising the situation, hopefully. And as soon as the first rafts were ready, these to put out from the shore, laden with men, to demonstrate the potential for attack. He sent the remaining three boats to tow the rafts out.

Their own boats had only some three hundred yards to go before John could blow on his horn for due attention – although no doubt their approach was being watched keenly. He recognised that there was the danger of arrows being discharged at them, so they stopped some distance from the castle. It occupied most of the roughly square islet of some two hundred yards in each direction, the building consisting of thick walls some score of feet in height, crowned by a parapet and wall-walk, with large round towers at each angle but no central keep. The entrance was by an arched gateway on the eastern side, this apparently the only access. There was a lesser outer courtyard to the south.

No response, by voice nor arrows, came to the horn-blowing, although they could see the heads of watching men above the parapet. John waited, to give time for the first rafts to appear. When he saw these, he blew again, and then shouted.

"Duncan Stewart and brothers, I, Moray, with my lord of Sutherland here, command that you surrender this hold, this in the king's name. For shameless and treasonable conduct. This loch is surrounded. And by a sufficiency of men from three earldoms. Yield, I say, or suffer!"

Silence greeted that.

John called again. "There is no least hope for you, no escape. None can aid you. Yield. We can bring many hundreds against you, on these rafts."

Still no reply.

They waited, to allow more rafts to appear, towed slowly behind the boats, in strings of three or four, perhaps a dozen men crouching on each. At least no arrows came from the castle.

The first rafts had almost reached the leaders' two boats when there was reaction at last. A voice sounded hoarsely, above the creak of oars.

"We have many men. None so far off. They will come to deal with you. As we dealt with those of Angus!"

"We are ready for any such," John answered. "And have many more than you see. And mounted. Many hundreds. It must take time for your caterans to assemble, when they hear. We are *here*! We can land our folk on your island. And take it, long before you could gain any help. And hang you from your own walls!" John added that a little self-consciously.

There was another pause. Then a jerky return. "If we yield, we require promise of freedom. To go where we will. Not assailed. Otherwise, we bide and fight you off. And our people will come on you."

John and Earl Robert conferred briefly. This possibility had not been overlooked. Their main objective was to get rid of these brothers from Moray. They did not, in fact, wish to be faced with hanging nephews of the monarch, however scoundrelly, nephews of Marjory also. Let Albany see to the like. Better to agree it, let them go.

"You will leave this Moray," John called, then. "Depart, and not to Ross nor Sutherland where you would be hunted down. Nor to the west and the Isles. Go south. Is it agreed?"

No lengthy pause. "Agreed." That one word was abruptly announced.

"Very well. You will have boats. We await you. And more of our men are coming to surround you. And all your shores are guarded." Additional rafts were appearing, all the time. "Haste you. We will not wait overlong."

They did have to wait for a while, with the rafts ever coming up to make a ring round the islet. But John recognised that the Stewarts could not just jump into boats and leave without some delay, arranging even a hasty departure, and deciding who left and who stayed.

When eventually two boats were rowed out to them, three brothers could be seen in one, Duncan, Alexander, Andrew, and Walter in the other with James, some of their men rowing, but no women therein. Duncan was not the oldest, Alexander that, but he was very much the leader, and no doubt it had been he who had done the shouting. They all stared expressionlessly at John and his companions as they came up.

"Your father is, I understand, at Kinfauns near to Perth," John called, as his own oarsmen pulled his boat round. "I advise that you see the Duke of Albany at Scone before joining him."

That received no reply.

The four boats were rowed to land together, where the massed ranks of Moraymen awaited them. Disembarking, John, with Sutherland, again addressed the brothers.

"Your people here will have horses? They departed into yonder woodland when we appeared. Can you gain mounts there? Or must we find you garrons from our woodmen?"

Duncan Stewart looked sour. "We will find our own."

"So be it. Go you. If you have left others in the castle,

319

they can follow you. Some of our people will follow you also, now, to ensure that you do not attempt to join your caterans in the hills. Perth and Scone for you. Is it understood?"

Curt nods greeted that.

"Off with you, then. And be thankful that we did not hang you!"

That served for leave-taking. The brothers scowled at all around them, and strode off southwards for those wooded slopes, John telling Brodie to take a couple of hundred of their mounted men to ride after them, and not to leave them until they were well on their way. It was only early afternoon still, and once the miscreants found their horses, they ought to be able to get as far south as almost to the Drumochter Pass and over into Atholl, this largely through Grant and Macpherson country where they would find no friends. No large numbers of their castleton supporters to be allowed to go with them. There must be no turning back for the brothers.

Seeing the last of them, and bidding Brodie and his men farewell, John and Sutherland thankfully turned to ride northwards, task accomplished. They would leave Lochindorb Castle to whoever the Stewarts had left behind, meantime, and hope that it would spare them any further trouble.

It was three days later before Brodie returned to Darnaway, to report that the brothers were through Drumochter and still heading south through Atholl. There had been no real difficulties, although no love lost between the two groups. What Albany would do about his nephews remained to be seen.

30

All was well in Moray for the rest of that summer, this gratefully acknowledged. They heard nothing from Albany, nor the king, and made no complaints about that. Marjory and John saw quite a lot of the Sutherland brothers, who could sail down from Dunrobin in half a day. They were not surprised when, in late July, Robert formally asked for the hand of Mabella in marriage, and were happy to grant it, their daughter nowise the reluctant party. The wedding would be celebrated at the commencement of September, on the Nativity of the Blessed Virgin, this also to coincide with the harvest festival.

But before that looked-forward-to occasion, a summons arrived from Albany for John to go south. It seemed that the Gloucester trouble had been settled in England, and Hereford was now in full command there, acting for his weak monarch as Albany did for King Robert. And the proposed chivalric meeting was to be held in mid-September at London, French representatives also agreeing to attend. An illustrious Scots team was to be present, the Earl of Moray amongst them, along with two of his brothers-in-law and other notable characters. This would inevitably occupy some considerable time; so rather than miss his daughter's nuptials that event was brought forward so that John could give her away, neither she nor the groom making any complaint as to that.

So the bishop married them in Elgin Cathedral, this being rebuilt after the burning, to much rejoicing, John mock-seriously warning the bride to beware of her new brother-in-law Kenneth, who seemed almost as much attracted to her as was Robert.

So, soon thereafter, John took his leave of Marjory. She would have liked to have accompanied him, but felt that they could not both be away from Moray and the family for a fairly lengthy period. She urged her husband to remain in England for no longer than was absolutely necessary, to which he acceded heartily. They were both still very much in love with each other, despite now having a grown-up family, and felt unfulfilled when they were apart for any length of time; indeed their young people were apt to smile and remark on this. When John did set off for Leith, Marjory accompanied him to Inverness just to wave him farewell, with renewed urgings to haste him back at the final clinging to each other.

He had assumed that he would travel to London by sea but, although it turned out that George was one of the Scots party also, and could provide shipping for all, it had been decided that the journey should be made by land, this to emphasise the coming together of the realms, to all on the way down through England, safe-conducts and offers of hospitality sent by King Richard especially for that purpose.

John was glad to see, as well as his brother, Sir David Lindsay, recovered from his wounding on the Braes of Angus, amongst the representativees. Albany saw them off from Edinburgh but did not accompany them, sending his son, now Earl of Fife, along with the two princes, the Earls of Strathearn and Atholl. The Earl of Angus represented the Douglases.

They made a pleasant enough and unhurried parade down through the English shires, being well received overnight at abbeys and castles, although not a few of the owners of the latter had already preceded them to London for the occasion. It took them a full week to reach the Thames.

The Earl of Hereford himself came out to meet them at their last halting-place at St Albans' great monastic establishment, a heartily authoritative individual, now the power behind the throne.

They were received at the Tower of London by King Richard, handsome but weak about mouth and chin, backed by sundry notables including, John noted, Howard, Earl of Nottingham, Earl Marshal of England, with whom he had disputed years before over Berwick, friend of Hotspur Percy, he who had refused a duel with Archibald the Grim. He eyed the Scots, especially John, with no favour, whatever the present circumstances.

The French representatives had already arrived, and with all the English lords and prelates come for the celebrations, the Tower was full to overflowing and there was no room for the Scots therein. So John, with his brother, Lindsay and others, found himself housed in York Place, the London palace of the Archbishop of York, scarcely the most suitable lodging, since that dignitary, like his predecessors, claimed to be the most northerly metropolitan, and therefore supreme over Holy Church in Scotland. It lay close to the Thames, which was to feature prominently in the present proceedings.

Various celebrating activities were laid on for the next two days, Hereford very much in charge, although King Richard was present at most: mock combats between teams from the three nations, and also between different English earldoms and lordships; archery contests; horse-racing; processions through the streets with the banners of the great ones; barge-sailings on the wide river with bands of musicians; even bear baiting, the chivalric aspect emphasised wherever possible, this being Hereford's especial concern.

But the principal demonstrations of chivalry were to take place on the third day after the Scots arrival, tournaments on a grand scale, massed and individual, the massed ones to be held in the park of Westminster Palace, the individual, of all places, on the famous bridge over the Thames.

This last was an astonishing structure, built over a century before to replace the former wooden crossings. It was enormous, consisting of no fewer than nineteen piers with pointed stone arches, towers at both ends and even houses bordering its sides, with booths and stalls. It was sufficiently wide for that. The central portion was free of buildings, and it was here that the knightly tourneys and joustings were to take place, there being ample space, the entire bridge being very long as well as wide, one of the prides of London. High stands had been erected on each side for privileged spectators.

Challenges and gauntlet–throwing, it appeared, were the order of the day, knightly champions offering to prove their prowess in the lists.

The forenoon, in the park, was devoted to mass conflicts, starting with the three nations' arrays, Hereford himself leading the English array, Strathearn the Scots. It was understood that there were to be no evident winners or losers in these contests, however successful some might seem in comparison with others, this to ensure that there should be no national offence produced, however many casualties there might be amongst the participants. John had no part in this, but watched from the sidelines.

But, as it turned out, he was not to be merely a spectator. His turn was to come. Amongst the challenges to individual combat issued from the Tower, came two for the Scots: one from Lord Welles, apparently accepted, as the supreme English knight-at-arms, crusading companion of Hereford, this to Sir David Lindsay, recognised as a most notable chevalier and gallant duellist; the other from the Earl Marshal Nottingham to John Earl of Moray.

No reasons were given for the latter. John was not renowned as a combatant, the reverse rather as a negotiator and diplomat. Why this? Presumably Nottingham was remembering old controversy and wishful to redeem his reputation with the Scots over refusing the contest with Archibald Douglas.

John was less than happy over this totally unexpected summons. He had attended tourneys, to be sure, but had never actually taken part in one; and his military activities had been fairly modest and had not involved hand-to-hand fighting. He had ridden at set targets with a lance, in competition with George, as a young man, but never with any great enthusiasm, and that a long time ago. But he could scarcely refuse this announced summons from so highly placed a personage as the Earl Marshal. George was much amused by it, declaring that here was his brother's opportunity to show that he could do more than talk for Scotland and act the courtier – that is, unless he wanted himself, George, to act for him? So it had to be.

A suit of armour and helmet to fit him had to be selected. His own horse would serve well enough. A reluctant knight-errant, he hoped that by watching Lindsay's joust, which was to take place first, he might gain some guidance as to the best tactics to employ.

A French duke and the Earl of Somerset led off, on that London Bridge, charging down on each other in fine style, lances couched, these with blunted points, indeed specially crowned tops, to ensure no serious injury to the combatants, shields at the ready. No swords, axes nor maces were used in such chivalrous duels. At the first clash, the duke and earl both managed to strike glancing blows, but these insufficient to do more than deflect off shield and armoured shoulder. A second charge, from alternate ends, each having about seventy-five yards to gain impetus, resulted in both managing to avoid each other's lance by inches, with their mounts all but colliding, the earl's stumbling but not unseating its rider. The third attempt was more effective, Somerset's shield actually warding off a lance stroke with such protective force as to wrench the duke's lance right out of his grip, it falling to the ground. To cheers the earl was declared the winner, and after bowing to the loser, he went to receive a scented glove from Queen Anne of Bohemia.

Then it was Lindsay's and Welles's turn, much expected from these experts, although they were less lofty in status than the first two. Their initial charge did not disappoint, as they met with a resounding clash, with so great an impact as to break Welles's lance against Lindsay's helmet with a force that caused the latter to reel in his saddle but to keep his seat somehow as they plunged past each other. There were shouts from the onlookers that here was cheating, the Scot must be tied to his saddle. Hearing this, Lindsay, drawing rein, jumped down to the bridge-flooring, to prove them wrong. At the other end of the lists, Welles was provided with another lance, and a second dash was made. On this occasion they collided, with horses and men too close to wield their spears with any effect, and they hurtled on past without any decision. But in the third gallop, Lindsay's lance struck squarely on the other's shield, with enough force to knock him right out of his saddle to crash to the bridge, with the clatter of steel, and there to lie. To cheers, the Scot wheeled round and back to his foe, there to jump down, to stoop and help the half-stunned Welles to his feet, and, leaving the horses, assisted the shaken man back to his esquires, who came running out to their lord. There was no doubt as to who was the winner of this bout either, as Lindsay went for his glove from the royal hand, amidst resounding applause.

And now it was for John to face Nottingham, distinctly apprehensive but seeking not to show it, George offering him good advice. At the horn-blowing signal to start, he lowered his lance and dug in his spurs. His mount, although never before involved in a tourney, at least knew its master, and plunged forward in good style.

John had noted the lessons to be learned from the two previous contests, and realised what he must try to achieve and what to avoid, these long lances awkward to balance, and if making a strike, apt to prove a danger to their own wielders. So he gripped his most firmly against himself under his right elbow, and kept his eye steadily on his advancing target, Nottingham's shield which was held across the other's breastplate.

At the last moment, as they reached each other, the Marshal jerked his horse violently aside, swinging his spear round in a half circle, not pointing it, so that it struck John's shoulder armour with a clang, but not sufficiently hard to unseat him, his own lance missing his turned-away opponent by inches. They plunged on past each other, little achieved.

John, panting, reined round at the other end of the lists, warned by this of last-moment twisting aside in the saddle. He must be prepared to do the like. But that was, in fact, no way to make a telling stroke. Full headlong impact was obviously necessary, dangerous as that must be.

Seeing Nottingham ready at the other end, he spurred forward once again, this time prepared for both head-on clash and sideways swipe. These helmets that they wore, while protecting head and face, did restrict view, and so little chance was offered to discern last-moment decisions – although this of course applied to both of them.

John did see his foe's forward-bending, all but crouching in the saddle, which looked as though this time he would aim at a direct thrust. Should *he* dodge? Why, when what was aimed at was the unseating or disarming of his opponent, not repeated avoiding of blows? He headed his mount straight for the other, lance level and firm.

Nottingham did the like, and the two horses struck each other, rearing in fright, which threw both lances upwards and somewhat askew. John was jarred in the saddle as the other's crown-headed spear jerked up from striking the edge of his shield, struck first his shoulder, and then, the round protective head of it wrenched right off by the impact, the spear-tip beneath slid on over the armour and into the narrow gap between breastplate and helmet-neck. Deep into the throat the point drove, with all the weight of the charge behind it, drove and remained, as the lance was dragged out of the wielder's grip and the two horses plunged on in opposite directions.

The Earl of Moray knew much in those timeless seconds before he crashed to the ground. He saw Marjory, eyes full of love, holding out warm arms to him. He saw his children looking at him. He saw his mother, Black Agnes, smiling and beckoning him on. And back to Marjory. He saw her lips moving, but saying he knew not what, save that it was kind, kind. And then he knew no more.

John Dunbar lay on London Bridge and stirred not, gone to a better kingdom than England, or even Scotland, as George ran out to him.

HISTORICAL NOTE

Thomas Dunbar duly became Earl of Moray, serving the realm well, and dying at the Battle of Homildon in 1412, leaving a son, another Thomas, who became a hostage for James the First's release from English captivity. Eventually the earldom became vested in the crown.

Alexander, Earl of Buchan, the Wolf, died of natural causes three years later, and was buried with full religious ceremony behind the high altar of Dunkeld Cathedral, where his fine monument still stands. His sons made no major mark on history, save for Alexander, the eldest, who stormed the castle of Kildrummy to capture the Countess of Mar in her own right, and so married her, to become Earl of Mar, she apparently coming to accept him, although the earldom of Mar descended to his illegitimate son Thomas. The father commanded the royal army at the famous Battle of Harlaw against Donald of the Isles in 1411.

Robert the Third died in 1406, an ineffective monarch to the end, when he was succeeded not by David, Duke of Rothesay, who was captured and starved to death at Falkland by his uncle Albany, seeking the throne for himself. He would have slain the younger son, James, also, had he not escaped to England, where he remained a prisoner for eighteen years before finally returning to Scotland and occupying the throne as James the First. Albany, acting as regent, died, aged over eighty, in 1419, and was succeeded by his son Murdoch as second duke, whom James executed along with his two sons in 1425, paying for the sins of the late regent.

Sir David Lindsay married Catherine, a legitimate daughter of Robert the Second, and was created first Earl of Crawford. His descendant, the twenty-ninth Earl of Crawford, is premier earl of Scotland today.